D-SHIFT

Matthew L. Marlott

D-Shift
Copyright © 3rd ed. 2025

This book is dedicated to Tammy, who never had a problem seeing the real person inside.
The events in this story are set in the year 2017. It wasn't a good year, and it certainly wasn't a great year, but it was a year all the same.

Table of Contents

Prologue

Nancy Clark did not like her name. It was not her last name that perplexed her—Clark was a common name for certain—but rather her first name that bothered her. That was her beef with her parents, particularly her mother, who had named her after a fictional character that the older woman had grown up reading about.

Nancy was a very old-fashioned name, and kids her age simply did not possess such a name anymore. It reminded her of faded, black-and-white, old-timey photographs, fishing holes and summer dresses and such, and that was simply *not* her.

She thought about this as she pedaled down Bitter Creek Road, the winding asphalt lane that led toward town, or away from town, as it happened at the moment. She preferred to bike down this winding stretch on Saturday mornings when the weather was nice, and she would bike past the Breckenridge Institute of Discovery upon her scenic left, scenic due to the surrounding stretch of trees broken only by patches of green grass.

She would pedal down Bitter Creek Road, turn at the T-crossing that led to the Institute or back to the interstate, and then pedal back home. She did so for the exercise—that was always good—but mostly because she enjoyed it. It got her blood pumping and gave her that high that athletes sometimes got, and it brightened the rest of her day.

Nancy had just turned seventeen; she was older than the other girls in her junior class, but that was because her parents had not enrolled her in kindergarten until she was seven. However, this did give her a certain advantage when it came to grades, but then again, the age difference wasn't so great as to make that much of a testing difference, so this was yet another quirk about her life she puzzled over while biking.

She was thin and athletic, she had light-brown hair that curled near her shoulders, and her eyes were a pleasant hazel that reminded her of the time of year just before summer turned to autumn. Today, she was dressed in a spotless white T-shirt with red shorts lined with white stripes along the sides, a type of dress that one would see in an old movie that her parents would have watched in their day. Her bike was a bright red with a grey metal basket on the front, that basket serving a purpose now by holding her smartphone, as her outfit gave her no pockets in which the thin slab could reside.

She briefly gave this overall appearance a quick thought, the appearance of the matching colors of her outfit with her bike, and though she was not so concerned with that while biking, she did wonder if the various scientists and other nerdy types nearby could see her from whatever labs they were working in within the Breckenridge Institute of Discovery. That musing led to whether or not said scientists were currently thinking strange and experimental thoughts about such a sight as a pretty teenage girl on a bike might instigate.

"Why are mad scientists always on my mind whenever I pass this place?" she thought in slight amusement. *"I can just picture them peering out the window while guessing my weight and blood type…Makes sense for a bunch of science-types cooped up in a lab all day…Of course, there's no telling what they actually do in there…Wait…What do they do in there all day?…I really have no idea…"*

She pondered this, but she did not have the opportunity to ponder it for long. She was in the midst of passing the Institute, halfway past it in fact, when the unimaginable occurred. Something happened that could not be categorized in simple terms within her simple view of life. It happened at the worst possible moment, that moment being the moment when she was actually passing the large building complex, and it happened without one whit of warning…The Institute exploded.

It first came upon her as an uncomfortable heat, a rise in temperature that rippled the visual air around her. She then felt the hair stand up on the back of her neck, on her arms, and even on her head for that matter, and then there was a flash of light to her scenic left. The light was a bright blue, it expanded in a giant ball of luminescence that one only saw in movies, she was then hit with a wave of great force, and Nancy found herself flying off of her bike to the dark-grey asphalt below. The sound came a hair of a second later, a blasting "BOOM!" that nearly crushed her eardrums, and she could not even hear herself scream as the shock of it all set in.

The pavement before her wavered and blurred in the sun as she felt her eyes move back and forth and up and down at top speed. She could feel them moving all over the place within her orbital sockets, and it made her very dizzy. The violent lack of control of her eyes gave her vertigo, and she felt like throwing up, but it stopped after only a few seconds, though it took her a bit to force her sudden nausea to go away.

She sat up, and the first things she noticed were her skinned knees and a throbbing pain in her right wrist, but the second thing she noticed took her mind away from her own injuries, and that was the large smoking crater where the Breckenridge Institute of Discovery had once stood. It was completely gone, vanished, or vaporized as the case may be, and this shut down her thought process for a second.

"Oh my God, oh my God, oh my God…" she babbled, but her ears were still ringing, and she was, for all intents and purposes, deaf, so she was not at all sure if "Oh my God" was what she was actually saying.

She pulled her smartphone from the grey basket affixed to the front of her royal-red bike, and she was lucky that she had latched the lid to the basket, because her bike was currently on its side. She hit the power button of her smartphone, and the screen turned on for a brief moment, but there was a spark and a flash, and then the screen went black. Her hand stung from the sudden shock it emitted, and she tossed the phone away as she shrieked in sudden surprise.

She began to cry, not so much from the pain of her skinned knees and her right wrist, but mainly because she had just gotten that phone for her birthday, and its sudden death upset her greatly. She gingerly picked up her phone and placed it back in her bike's basket, picked up her bike with great care due to her injured wrist, and took to the long and torturous task of biking back home.

Her whole body shook as she slowly recovered from the shock of the ordeal, and though biking helped her think under normal circumstances, at the moment it was helping her come down from the massive amount of adrenaline coursing through her.

"What happened, what happened, what happened…" she babbled to herself, but this time she could actually hear herself, and that was good.

She wiped tears from her cheeks as she took in a deep breath in order to calm down. She sounded like a crazy idiot to herself, so she took a swallow of her own saliva and breathed in slowly, and though this helped, it did not prevent her from shaking, and that proved difficult on her already injured body.

It took her a bit longer than usual to get to the edge of Schiffman, the quaint little rural town she resided in, and by the time she got to her house, she was feeling a little more like her old self. Still, her ordeal had not just shaken her physically, but emotionally as well, and she burst into tears as she entered her house through the front door.

"I'm dying!" she screeched out, and though this statement was by far an exaggeration, it was how she felt at the moment, and it perfectly summed up her shock and horror over what had just happened.

"What?" was all her father could ask.

Roger Clark stood up from the forest-green couch he sat upon while simultaneously hitting the mute button upon the small black remote in his right hand. He was a fairly tall man with thick brown hair and a block for a face, but he was caring, and he loved his wife and kids, so that was all that mattered to Nancy at the moment.

The man that was her father took one look at her and changed his confused tone to one of immediate concern.

"What happened!" he asked as he rushed to her side.

Nancy noticed for the first time that her spotless white T-shirt was stained red at the top of her left shoulder, and this was yet another unhappy realization for her already addled brain to process. The day had started off so well, and now it was a horror show of merciless pain and unwanted tears.

She wiped her eyes clear of tears and tried to breathe normally, but it was proving difficult.

"It…It blew up!" she choked out. "It blew up and knocked me off my bike!"

"What?" asked her father with a confused gaze. "What blew up?...Nancy! Calm down and tell me what happened!"

This loud and rather excited conversation attracted others, and Nancy's mother and younger brother entered the room a moment later. Her mother took one look at her and panicked, immediately hijacking the conversation in a not-so-helpful way.

"Oh, my God, Nancy!" cried her mother. "You're hurt! What happened to you!"

Many people had told Nancy that she was a younger image of her mother, but she did not care for that comparison, regardless of how accurate the comparison was. Deirdre Clark was a practical woman with a daydreamer side, a conflict of adjoining philosophies that somehow worked in harmony with whatever task she had at hand, and Nancy loved her as any daughter would love her mother, but she frequently disagreed with her on many things, so she had to purposefully set aside her angst toward the older woman because she needed to. She needed to explain herself, and by explaining herself, relieve her own shock.

"It blew up!" said Nancy shakily. "The Institute…It blew up!"

"Institute?" asked Jason. "What institute?"

Jason was the typical younger brother, annoying and constantly doing stupid things, but Nancy put up with him because he was her only brother, even though there were many times when she wished that he wasn't. Jason was fifteen and had the same facial features as Nancy, those features belonging to their mother, but he was rather stupid at times, so she did not like to claim him as a brother when in public, though such a ploy rarely worked for obvious reasons. Nevertheless, Nancy was still in shock and definitely still in pain, so she immediately corrected his stupidity, though she rarely did so at any other time. Most of the time, she simply ignored him.

"The Breckenridge Institute of Discovery!" she cried. "I was biking past it when it blew up!"

"The Brecka what?" asked her father. "What are you talking about, Nancy?"

It was one thing for Jason to not know what she was talking about, because he was clueless most of the time, but for her father to not know?…That was odd.

"The Breckenridge Institute of Discovery!" repeated Nancy. "The Institute on Bitter Creek Road!"

"She's delirious!" panicked her mother in overwhelming concern. "We have to get her to the emergency room, Roger!"

"What!" asked Nancy in clear disbelief. "I'm not delirious! The Institute blew up! Didn't you hear it? It sounded like a nuclear bomb went off!"

"There is no institute on Bitter Creek Road, Nance," said Jason in confusion. "There's nothing out there but fields and trees."

"What are you talking about?" asked Nancy in equal confusion. "You went there on your class trip last year! How can you not remember that!"

"We went to the zoo!" said Jason in loud frustration. "What are *you* talking about? Did you hit your head when you fell off your bike?"

Her mother interceded within this obvious delusion, the delusion that Nancy's younger idiot of a brother was having about the Institute's non-existence, but the older woman's interceding statement did not give Nancy any confidence in the situation at hand.

"We have to get her to a doctor right now!" cried her mother. "She must have hit her head!"

"She's just addled," frowned her father. "She needs to sit down."

"She can do that on the way to the emergency room," said her mother quickly. "I'm getting my purse. If she thinks there's a building that blew up on Bitter Creek Road, then she must have a concussion. We are leaving *now*, Roger."

Nancy stared in openmouthed surprise at her mother's confirmation of the same notion that her father and younger brother had just served her, that notion being that there *had never been* a Breckenridge Institute of Discovery on Bitter Creek Road, and this was the moment Nancy realized that something wasn't just wrong, but very, *very* wrong.

Chapter 1…The First Shift

Nancy laid down on her bed and stared up at the ceiling.

She had been driven to the E.R. earlier in the day, driven to Schiffman Medical to have her bones X-rayed and her wounds attended to, but the whole experience had left her somewhat frazzled.

It turned out that she had abrasions on her legs and on her left shoulder, right along with a fractured right wrist. Her wrist was in a small cast that left her fingers free for manipulation, but this was not what bothered her at the moment. What bothered her was that she did indeed have a small concussion on the upper back-left portion of her head, and it was this small injury that everyone had decided to focus upon.

This focus was largely due to her insistence on the explosion and complete vaporization of the Breckenridge Institute of Discovery, an entire building complex and an entire government-funded scientific research center that everyone had tried to convince her had never existed.

"How can everyone forget an entire building complex?" she thought as she stared up at the white plaster roof above her. *"How is that possible? I've biked past that complex every Saturday morning for the last three years! I've been inside the show building there! How is any of this possible?"*

"I hate this…" she said quietly to herself. "Everyone thinks this stupid concussion has given me brain damage…like I'm crazy or something. I know what I saw…I know what I felt! I got blasted off my bike, for crying out loud!"

Nancy wanted to call her best friend, Rain, but that was currently impossible due to her now defunct phone.

Rain Fischer was a bit of an eccentric; she had bright streaks of purple in her short black hair accented by the colorful cat ears she liked to show off at all hours, cat ears on a plastic band that she had ordered off the Net. The girl also wore a long black show tail on the back of her blue jeans, and coupled with the large gold star earrings Rain sported for all to see, Nancy had always come off looking as "the normal one" whenever they hung out together.

Nevertheless, Rain understood Nancy better than anyone else in Schiffman, but this was neither here nor there, because Nancy could not reach the girl at the present time.

Her distress over this, however, was quickly countered when her mother knocked upon her bedroom door and entered, that knock meant only for courtesy, because the older woman was going to enter whether Nancy wanted her to or not. It was clear that her mother had no concern for her privacy, and this was one more thing that Nancy did not agree with when it came to interacting with the older woman.

"Mom!" she protested. "You can't just barge in!"

"Nancy, don't be such a brat," clucked the older woman. "You have a visitor. Your friend, Rain, is here. I told her to wait downstairs, because I didn't know if you were feeling up to seeing her at the moment. I didn't know if your pain medication was working or not. I thought you might be asleep."

"It's not as bad as it was," frowned Nancy. "And anyway, even if I had been asleep, knocking on the door would have woken me up."

"Look, Nance," frowned her mother, "I know you're in pain, but that doesn't give you the right to be rude."

"Fine, whatever," sulked Nancy. "Tell Rain she can come up."

Her mother gave her a disapproving stare, and Nancy quickly recanted her previous tone.

"*Please*…tell Rain that she can come up," she sighed.

"That's better," said her mother.

Nancy shook her head in displeasure as the older woman shut the door. She really needed a lock on her door, but her mother would not have it. It bothered Nancy that she could not have privacy within her own home, within her own *room,* for that matter, but this nuisance was an old one, and not something to dwell upon now. No, she needed to talk to Rain, someone who understood her, and someone who had an open mind when it came to the weird and mysterious.

"And weird and mysterious is exactly what this is, if not utterly horrific," thought Nancy unhappily. *"All of those people at the Institute…just gone in a flash…and no one remembers that they ever existed…but I do. I know what happened. I was there. I saw it happen…I have GOT to tell Rain. Someone has got to know that I'm not crazy or brain damaged because of this stupid concussion. Rain will believe me. She has to!"*

Rain, of course, entered a moment later.

Today, the young woman was dressed in a camo tank top and baggy black cargo pants held up by a thick black leather belt with a shiny silver skull buckle, but this was nothing unusual. She normally dressed in such a fashion, but what was not normal was the black biker's cap topped lazily upon her head, the wide brim cast at a curious upward angle, and Nancy could not help but stare at it. The big yellow cursive words *Brat Cat Confessions* were splayed out across the top of it, but Nancy had no idea what that referred to.

"Hey, Fancy," said Rain.

Rain had been calling her "Fancy" ever since they had first met. It was a reference to the clothes that Nancy wore, those clothes being dead average for a girl her age, but for some reason or another, Rain considered that fashion "above her own normal style in class," and so the girl had dubbed her "Fancy," and the name had stuck.

Nancy wanted to say hello, but she could not shake her attention from Rain's curious-looking hat.

"You've started wearing hats now?" she asked. "What happened to your ears?"

Rain gave her an odd look, that look consisting of tilting her head to one side while raising one eyebrow, and in this case, she tilted her head to her own right and raised her left eyebrow.

"My ears are fine," she said in slight confusion. "You know I don't wear earrings…and I've worn this hat every day for the last two years, Fance."

It was then that Nancy noticed something she probably should have noticed before, but the attention of Rain's hat had drawn her vision away from it. Rain was not wearing her gold star earrings, the same earrings that she had worn for as long as Nancy had known her. For that matter, Rain had clearly misunderstood what Nancy had meant by "ears," as the ears in question were the banded cat ears that the strange girl always wore, not her actual ears.

"I was talking about your cat ears," said Nancy as she sat up on her bed.

Rain looked at her with an even deeper confusion set within her dark-brown eyes.

"Cat ears?" she asked. "What are you talking about, Nance?"

It was unusual for Rain to use Nancy's actual nickname; that usually meant she was weirded out by something, but Nancy did not care about that at the moment. She spotted something about her best friend that was *impossible*; it had to be, so she hopped off of her bed to make sure that she wasn't going crazy.

"What the…?" asked Nancy in slight horror. "You…You don't have any holes in your ears! You've been wearing those gold stars for as long as I've known you, and now it's like you've never had your ears pierced at all!"

Rain backed away from her, a look of fearful concern upon her round face.

"Uhhh…" said the girl hesitantly. "That's because I've never *had* my ears pierced, Nance. I…uhhh…Are you all right? I think, maybe, I should get your mom…"

"No!" snapped Nancy, but her forceful tone made her friend jump a little.

Nancy held her face in her right hand and shook her head.

"I…I'm sorry," she said quickly. "I'm really sorry. I didn't mean to scare you."

She lowered her hand and watched as her friend nodded in slow reply, but Nancy could tell that the girl was somewhat frightened for some reason, but not because of the outburst from a moment before. It occurred to her that her parents must have told Rain that she was "addled" because of a concussion, and that little error had to be her mother's doing; Nancy was sure of it.

"What's going on then?" asked Rain. "Are you sure you're all right?"

"Yes," said Nancy in quick reply. "It's just…nobody believes me about what happened, and…you're the only person who has an open enough mind to believe my story."

She watched as Rain's face visibly relaxed into the ease of confidence that Nancy was so familiar with when concerning her friend. The eccentric young woman sat down upon Nancy's bed, gave her a quirky half-smile, and then shrugged.

"Okay," said her friend in her typical laissez-faire manner. "Then tell me your story. It can't really be all that strange…"

"It is," sighed Nancy.

She did not know how she was going to explain this one, but she had to try. As weird as Rain could be, Nancy wasn't even sure if her eccentric and open-minded friend would believe her, but there was no one else to relate her story to, so it was Rain or no one.

"It's like this…" said Nancy shakily.

She paced back and forth as she told her story, that pacing a nervous habit that she'd always had, but Rain didn't seem to mind.

"I was biking down Bitter Creek Road like I always do on Saturday mornings," explained Nancy, "but as I passed the Breckenridge Institute of Discovery, it exploded…and it didn't just explode, Rain…It freaking vaporized. There is nothing left of it but a huge smoking crater, and that building complex was huge. You could see it from the highway…"

"The what now?" asked Rain in severe confusion. "The Breckelridge what?"

Nancy closed her eyes, leaned her head back, and sighed. She threw up her hands in frustration, and she had to mentally strain herself in order to avoid getting upset.

"The Breckenridge Institute of Discovery," she said with a false calm. "It was a government funded laboratory complex right off of Bitter Creek Road. It blew up; it…it just vaporized, and now nobody remembers it ever existed."

"*Oookaaaay*," said Rain with wide eyes.

"I'm telling the truth!" hissed Nancy.

Rain raised her hands palms out as her eyes widened even further, so Nancy apologized once more.

"I'm sorry," she said quickly. "I'm just…I'm upset over the whole thing. No one believes me about what happened."

"What exactly happened then?" asked her friend. "How did this building…err…*vaporize*?"

"It just blew up in a blazing big ball of blue light," said Nancy, but her own explanation caused her to balk in strange humor. "Sorry…there were a lot of b's in that sentence."

They both gave a short chuckle, and it was a necessary break of levity, but Nancy continued on with her story after that little humor session. She did not want to get sidetracked.

"The air rippled around me at first," she explained, "and all of the hair on my body stood up…"

"*All* of it?" asked Rain.

Nancy frowned and rolled her eyes at that comment.

"Rain, please," she said unhappily.

Rain gave her a half-smile and shrugged.

"Fine," she said in a flat tone. "What happened next?"

"All of my hair stood on end," continued Nancy, "and it was like that feeling of static electricity when you, like…uhhh…rub a balloon on your head, and then your hair sticks to it? It was like that."

Rain nodded in agreement, but then her expression turned to careful thought and then worry. Nancy did not know what to make of it.

"Go on," said her eccentric friend.

"Well," breathed Nancy, "after that, I was hit with the shockwave. It felt like I got hit by a semi…I got blasted right off my bike...and then the boom hit, and it was so loud, I couldn't hear for a couple of minutes afterwards. I tried to call home after that, but my phone just shorted out. It sparked, and I had to drop it because it stung…Oh, and that's why I didn't call you earlier, by the way. My phone is toast."

"That sucks," said Rain, but her voice sounded weird.

Nancy studied her friend's face for a moment, but the expression upon Rain's face was…disconcerting. Rain looked as if she had just seen aliens abduct her neighbor, and this odd expression bothered Nancy a lot.

"What?" she asked. "What is it?"

Rain's eyes widened as she shook her head once.

"I believe you," she replied a moment later. "That's what."

"Really?" asked Nancy in complete surprise.

She really hadn't expected Rain to believe her, even as open-minded as the girl was, and Nancy could tell that Rain wasn't lying about that belief, either.

"Well, maybe," replied Rain in a shaky voice. "You may be a lot of things, Nance, but imaginative is not one of them."

"Hey, now!" protested Nancy. "I am too imagina…Wait…*That's* why you believe me?"

"Yeah," shrugged Rain. "You like what you like, and you don't embellish, so that story is about as believable as it gets to me. There's no reason for you to lie…At least, I can't think of one…and there's enough detail in your story to make it plausible, as impossible as it sounds…so yeah…I believe you. At least, I believe that *you* believe it happened."

"Thank God!" breathed Nancy in relief. "Everyone else thinks this concussion I have has made me crazy."

"A concussion normally causes memory loss around a traumatic event," replied Rain. "It normally doesn't create an elaborate scenario that's so detailed…plus, you're not the kind of person who actively looks for attention. You tend to do your own thing like me, and you don't really give a crap about what other people think…which is probably why I like you so much, but that's beside the point…

"Point is...Point is, I don't think you're lying or making anything up to get attention, and I don't think this concussion could cause a hallucination that cohesive…but then again, anything is possible, and there have been cases where a concussion has caused vivid hallucinations—"

"You're using your sciencey voice again, Rain," frowned Nancy. "Keep it simple so I can understand you, please."

Rain smiled and waved her left hand toward her.

"Exactly," she grinned. "Right there! You just described in detail phenomena that actually check out according to the laws of physics, the hair raising and the sonic boom part, and science is not your strong point…and neither is telling a decent lie."

"Thanks…I think," said Nancy slowly, but then she thought better about it. "Hey, wait a minute! Are you calling me stupid!"

Rain snorted out a sharp laugh and shook her head.

"No," she chuckled. "I was just saying that you're not good at those particular things. You're good at other things, and science and lying aren't those things."

"Yeah, yeah," frowned Nancy. "Nobody believes me, though."

Her eccentric friend looked thoughtful for a moment. She tilted her head to her own right and held her chin in her right hand. This was her "Sherlock" pose, as Nancy liked to call it, and this usually indicated to Nancy that Rain was onto something important.

"What is it?" she asked. "Do you know something, Rain?"

"I'm assuming that what you're telling me is the truth," said her eccentric friend, "and therefore I need more information. Now…I can tell you right now that I have *never* heard of any 'Breckenridge Institute of Discovery,' but you're saying that it *did* exist, and that everybody knew about it…until it blew up…or 'vaporized,' as you put it."

"Yes!" said Nancy in excitement. "I wasn't lying! Nobody seems to remember anything about it. That building complex was there, right off of Bitter Creek Road. Now there's nothing but a smoking hole there, and nobody remembers it ever existed."

"Okay," nodded Rain. "I got that part. So…you got caught in the shockwave from the blast, but you didn't get caught in that 'big blue ball of light', as you put it, so you seem to be the only one who remembers it ever existed. Okay…so let's assume that your proximity to the blast is why you remember it…Have you noticed anything else unusual? I have a theory, and I need you to think hard on this, because I don't know if I'm correct or not."

"Yes," said Nancy quickly. "I have noticed something else that's different…You. You're different."

"I'm different?" asked Rain in surprise. "How so?"

"You're mostly the same," replied Nancy, "but there are some little changes. You never wore hats, for one thing, and you wore a pair of gold star earrings every day for as long as I can remember."

"*Really*?" asked Rain in yet more surprise. "Are you sure?"

She took off her black biker's cap and studied it for a second.

"I've worn this hat for the last two years," said Rain matter-of-factly. "I've had it ever since you helped me sneak out and catch that Brat Cat Confessions concert."

"I don't even know who that is!" said Nancy in exasperation. "Not to mention that your ears don't even have holes in them! That's what *really* freaked me out. You've worn those gold star earrings for as long as I've known you, and now you don't even have any evidence that you ever wore earrings in the first place…It's weirding me out."

Rain's dark eyes widened yet again as she processed this while putting her hat back on.

"Well," she said thoughtfully, "if that's the case…then my theory makes sense. I think you've travelled into a parallel universe, Fance. If that's true, then there are other things that are probably different, too."

"Another dimension?" asked Nancy in surprise.

She had never even thought of this, but now that she *was* thinking about it, it all made sense.

"I'm in a different dimension?" she reiterated. "How is that even possible?"

"Well," said Rain in her "thoughtful" voice, "a dimension is actually a means of locomotion, or movement, as it were. We live in three dimensions, forward and back, side to side, and up and down, but other means of travel are possible—we know that—so you obviously moved along one of these lines of travel and dimensionally shifted to another universe.

"There's a theory that an untold number of universes exist all at once, but they exist upon different frequencies, so they all kind of overlap one another like…like one painting painted over another…and another…and another and so on."

Nancy was shocked at this revelation. She was no science-fiction geek, but she understood the gist of what her eccentric friend was saying, and this disturbed her to no end.

"But how do I get back to mine!" she whined.

"You don't," said Rain in a matter-of-fact tone. "If this Institute you described vaporized, then it's a good chance it erased itself from existence, which means it doesn't exist in *any* universe, and considering they were the ones who caused it…that means that they would be the only ones to have an answer for you…and since they're gone…you're out of luck."

Nancy did not want to cry in front of her friend, but she ended up doing it anyway. She let forth a slight whine as her tears came, and she did her best to wipe them away, but it was difficult to hold in the surge of helplessness she felt at that moment.

Rain gave her a sympathetic look and then frowned.

"This is all just hearsay, Nance," replied the young genius, "but even if it isn't…it's great that you didn't get vaporized right along with all those scientists…I would have lost my best friend, and the worst part is…is that I would have never even remembered you had ever existed."

Nancy wiped her eyes and nodded her head. She didn't want to cry anymore, but she also didn't feel like talking anymore. Nevertheless, she thought of something that even Rain's super-scientific mind hadn't thought of, so she voiced that question without hesitation, because it was important that she knew the answer.

"Wait a minute," she sniffed. "If I traveled here, then what happened to this universe's Nancy?"

Rain's eyes widened again as she thought about this.

"Oh…" she said in sudden revelation. "I hadn't thought of that. I…I have no idea. Maybe you merged into one person? I don't know. You kept your memories from the other you? I really don't know. This is all way out of my league, Nance. I don't know."

Nancy sat down upon her bed next to her best friend and wiped her eyes clear of the last of her remaining tears. She resolved herself to look on the positive side of things; Rain was just guessing about everything anyway, and without further evidence, Nancy didn't know if what had happened to herself was real or just a concussion-based fever dream. She really didn't know.

"I guess things aren't that bad," she breathed. "They could be a lot worse. I still have my family, and I still have you, and it would suck so badly if any of you had disappeared, so I guess it's okay…Yeah, I'm okay. I'm glad you believe me, too. I do understand that all of this could be in my head anyway."

"It's a possibility," shrugged Rain. "Honestly, though…it would be so cool if you really had traveled along another dimension to a parallel world…You would be the first human being to ever do that, for all we know…You would be a…a uhhh…a…dimensionaut. Yeah…I like the sound of that. A dimensionaut, like an astronaut, only instead of space—"

"I get the picture," replied Nancy. "I guess that *is* cool…Well, it would be if anybody actually knew about it, but since the Institute erased itself, and that's *if* I'm not crazy, mind you, then it's kind of a moot point."

"Well," smiled Rain, "as long as nobody knows, then you're safe. We don't want Overlord Karg of our dictatorship to find out, or you'll get dissected."

Nancy's heart jumped in her chest at this news.

"We live in a dictatorship!" she gasped.

Rain broke into raucous laughter and playfully bumped shoulders with her.

"No, you dork!" she laughed. "We live in a constitutional republic!...Ha, ha, ha! Oh, you should have seen your face! It's hilarious!"

"I freaking hate you," scowled Nancy.

"Oh, come on," smiled Rain. "You can't tell me you actually believed that?...Oh…I really think you did…That's…Oh…uhhh…"

The look on Rain's face was one of quiet and rather unconcealed concern. It bothered Nancy to the point where she had to ask what the eccentric girl was thinking.

"What?" she asked. "What is it?"

"Oh…" stalled Rain. "It's just…well…"

"What, then?" asked Nancy. "You're making me nervous."

"I was just humoring you," said Rain in a surprised tone. "I…I really…I don't know what to think."

"You think I'm crazy," frowned Nancy. "You think I'm making this up, don't you?"

Rain sighed as her shoulders slumped in apparent defeat.

"I don't know what to think," she said unhappily. "You're my best friend. I'm supposed to trust you, but what you're saying is…well…it's…"

"Unbelievable," sighed Nancy in return.

Rain shrugged and laid one consoling hand upon Nancy's right shoulder.

"Look, Fance," she said sheepishly, "it's not that I don't believe you; it's just that…you *do* have a concussion, and I may not be an expert in neuroscience, but I *can* say that a brain injury, even a minor one, can cause magical thinking or delusional thoughts."

"You're saying I'm brain damaged," frowned Nancy. "That's what you're saying."

"I'm saying that maybe you should get an MRI," said Rain with a tight-lipped frown. "I think we should just make sure that there isn't something more serious going on…just in case."

"More serious than travelling across dimensions?" asked Nancy. "Really? I know what happened to me, Rain! I saw the Breckenridge Institute of Discovery disappear in a great big ball of blue light!...Ugh…That *wasn't* my imagination. My broken wrist, my concussion, and my skinned shoulder can attest to that."

"You crashed your bike," shrugged Rain. "It happens. That's why they tell us to wear safety gear."

"No," said Nancy with a shake of her head. "No, that's not it. I was blown off my bike by an explosion, and that's all there is to it. Whether you were humoring me or not, your theory on being in a parallel dimension is the best answer I've got, because nothing else makes sense."

Rain shrugged and gave her a worried frown.

"Nance," she said unhappily, "my cousin Ben got messed up in a motorcycle accident. For a couple of weeks, he thought he was a Dawn Elf from World of Battlecry. You know that game, right? He'd been playing it right before he was in his accident, and…and somehow that got jumbled up with his reality because of the TBI he had—that's a 'traumatic brain injury,' in case you didn't know—and *he* was wearing a helmet. You *weren't* wearing a helmet, so it doesn't surprise me in the least that you're a little confused."

"I'm not talking about some stupid game!" said Nancy a little angrier than she had wanted to.

Rain flinched at the tone of her voice, but Nancy quickly recanted. The last thing she wanted to do was chase off her friend.

"I'm sorry," said Nancy quickly. "I'm sorry…I…I wasn't talking about anything like that. Not like 'World of Battlecry.' Jason plays that stupid game all the time. He's constantly drawing those 'elves' or whatever.

"Anyway…Anyway, that's not important. Your cousin was on a motorcycle, and to be fair, I'm surprised he wasn't confetti after his accident. I was only on a bicycle, and I wasn't even peddling fast.

"Not to mention that I *hate* fantasy and science fiction…You *know* that. Why would I make this up? Just use some of your famous 'logic' you like to use so much…Think about it. I don't have anything to gain from this. I'm not failing at school, I'm not in trouble at home, and *yes*…my mom *can* be annoying…but that's no reason for me to pull a fast one or…or go looking for attention I don't want. I *hate* it when all eyes are on me. You know that!"

Rain looked thoughtful for a moment, and when she finally spoke a second later, she spoke in her 'sciencey' voice. Normally, this tended to annoy Nancy, but right now, it was a positive sign, a positive sign that perhaps she was finally getting through to the stubborn girl.

"Well…you *do* make a compelling argument," shrugged Rain. "You certainly don't sound or act like you're lying or looking for attention. You seem genuinely upset about what you *think* happened."

"I don't *think* it happened," scoffed Nancy. "I know it did."

"That may be," frowned Rain, "but that just worries me more. That tells me that there are only two possibilities…three if I want to stretch it. The first two hinge upon you telling the truth. If that's the case, then you either crossed into a parallel universe, or you suffered a TBI that has you thinking you crossed over. The third one is a bit of a stretch…and that is…that is you're lying so that you can gain something…but I'd sooner believe that you dimensionally shifted than believe that. You really are a terrible liar, Nance."

"So you believe me?" asked Nancy.

"I believe that you *are* telling the truth," frowned Rain, "and that scares me. That scares me, because according to Occam's Razor, the simplest explanation is usually the correct one. I think you may have a TBI, Nance, and you need an MRI in order to confirm it. A CAT scan…something."

Nancy groaned both physically and mentally, but then she thought better about it.

"Fine," she shrugged. "It's not going to find anything…but okay. I don't have magical thinking, Rain. I don't believe I'm an elf or an orc or a…a pirate…ballerina…astronaut."

Rain guffawed at that image, and Nancy had to chuckle due to the infectious nature of the unintentional joke. Her super-intelligent friend simply smiled and gave her a quick shoulder bump.

"I think we'll figure this out with a little use of the scientific method," said Rain with a confident tone. "What you need is reason, logic, and facts to work with…even if you won't admit it. There's a bit of a scientist in you, Fance, methinks, methinks."

"The heck, you say!" laughed Nancy.

"We'll just study this logically and take notes," smiled Rain. "Will that convince you?...No matter what the result is?"

"Yes," agreed Nancy. "If I have a…a TBI…then I'll just have to deal with that…but if I don't…"

"Then you're a dimensionaut," shrugged Rain. "You're a dimensionaut, the very first one, as far as I know, and that will be…*interesting*...to say the least. So we're agreed?"

"Agreed," nodded Nancy.

She did not believe for a second that she had a "TBI," but she was confident now she could get her best friend onboard about what had really happened at Bitter Creek Road.

Rain was a lot of things, but a fool she was not, and Nancy knew this. She knew with a million degrees of certainty that if Rain had any evidence, any at all, then the young genius would dive into this "dimensionaut" business feet first and with bells on. Rain was good like that; she was different, true, but more importantly, she was true to her word.

Once the eccentric girl had a little more information to work with, then she would help Nancy figure this whole thing out. Nancy just had to trust in herself and her ability to convince Rain that she was telling the absolute truth.

✳✳✳✳✳

Nancy yawned and stretched as the soft light of morning blanketed her in its warmth. She immediately regretted that action, as her skinned shoulder and broken wrist gave her a surge of pain, so she withdrew into herself for a moment. She needed her pain pills, but she took a few seconds to collect her wits before going to the bathroom to get them.

Rain had helped her get it together in more ways than one the night before, and Nancy was eternally grateful for that, because if the theory that her very-intelligent friend had come up with was true, then she had to get used to this new universe, and quickly. She did not know how many things had changed in her life, and she didn't want any nasty surprises popping up in her face.

She reached up and rubbed her eyes, but she noticed something very strange. Her eyes felt bigger and bulgier, but she chalked that up to being a little addled from the day before…until she reached up to brush her hair from her face. The palms of her hands ran over her ears and felt *tips*…actual *pointed* ends at the tops of her ears. She felt her ears with her fingers; they felt long and slender and pointed, and this caused her to panic.

"No, no, no, no, no, no, no…" she said as she quickly bolted from her bed.

She ran to the bathroom and flicked on the light, and what she saw in the mirror nearly caused her heart to stop.

Her face was narrow and slender, she had an elegantly pointed chin now, her nose was smaller and perfectly shaped in its own unique elegance, but her eyes were *huge*, at least twice the size they normally were, and of course her ears were long and slender and pointed exactly as she had felt them to be.

Her lips were slender lines, and her mouth was smaller, but she had not noticed these details before. Her hair was no longer the soft brown that she was used to; it was now a subtle auburn instead, but her huge eyes were still the same hazel that she had always had, so that hadn't changed.

She leaned against her bathroom sink and took in a deep breath. She looked down at her long and narrow fingers and held them up for inspection. Her arms were slenderer now, and her hands were smaller, but her fingers were narrower and definitely longer.

Her light-blue nightgown hadn't changed at all…but her body certainly had. She was the same height but skinnier, or slenderer, as the case may be, and her breasts were much smaller. She was beautiful in a very elegant but strange way, but her new look reminded her of a character from one of those anime shows, or maybe one of those fantasy characters that her brother sometimes played on his online game.

She wondered if she were simply dreaming, but the very real pain in her shoulder and wrist told her that she was not.

"It…It *is* true!" she gasped out, but her voice was not her own.

Her voice was melodic, beautiful in that strange way as before, and it took her a moment to process this new development.

"It happened again…" she said to herself, and it took her another moment to get used to her new voice. "That means Rain was right! I've crossed again…but this time…"

This time wasn't just some minor change in the people around her, and it wasn't the fact that everyone had forgotten the existence of the Breckenridge Institute of Discovery. This time was a lot more drastic, and this disturbed her on a deep level.

"What if it's only me?" she asked herself, and this bothered her even more.

Normally, she would have taken a shower after waking up, but she decided to forego this particular activity for the day due to this new and very unwanted extenuating circumstance.

She exited the bathroom, went to her dresser, and quickly changed into the clothes that she would be wearing for the rest of the day. Her clothes had not changed at all, and this caused her even more concern, because she had a deep fear that only she had changed and no one else had, and that she would be ostracized as a freak, some strange science experiment gone wrong.

"Which is kind of what happened," she thought nervously. *"In fact, that IS what happened…Oh…I'm scared now…What if Mom and Dad see me and then attack me?…Wait…They wouldn't do that; they love me…Yes. I'll just check first. I'll see if they've changed, too. If that's the case, then I'll just have to act like nothing's wrong…and learn to live like whatever it is we've all become, but…I'll worry about that later. For now, I'll sneak a peek and then figure out what to do."*

She put on a pair of jean shorts and a royal-blue T-shirt, slipped on a pair of white sneakers over her matching white socks, and then walked to her bedroom door. She noticed that even though her clothes were the same, they were all smaller to fit her new form, and that was actually a good sign.

"If my clothes are smaller than normal," she thought in hopeful contemplation, *"then that must mean this version of me has always been this small, and that might mean that everyone is like me. I never thought I'd hope that everyone out there looks like me, but this has been weird from the very beginning, so I just have to hope for the best now."*

Nancy opened her bedroom door a crack and heard voices from downstairs. She crept out a bit into the hall and made her way to the edge of the stairs, slinking along as quietly as she could. She got just to the edge of the stairs when a stern voice ambushed her from behind, causing her to let loose a high-pitched shriek.

"What are you doing?" asked her brother.

Chapter 2…The Second Shift

Nancy clutched her chest as she turned to view her thoroughly-irritating younger brother. She nearly had another frightening start as she looked upon him, momentarily forgetting what she, herself, looked like.

He had a slender face, a small mouth, an elegant nose, and huge eyes just like her, although he was not quite as slender in the body as she was, but that was more than likely due to the fact that he was a guy and not a girl.

Nancy had to catch her breath and calm herself just to look at him…His huge eyes were especially unnerving.

"You scared me!" she hissed. "Don't do that!"

"Then don't act like a ninja sneaking around the house," frowned Jason. "What are you doing anyway? Are you eavesdropping on Mom and Dad? Why? All they're doing is getting breakfast like usual."

Nancy had to bite her lower lip to keep from screaming. She wanted to yell in his face, yell at him that *nothing* about this was usual, but she held in her anxiety and ignored his questioning.

"It's none of your business," she frowned. "Never mind, dork. It doesn't matter."

"Whatever," frowned her brother. "And don't call me a dork, dork."

Nancy did not have the time to entertain her own irritation at her annoying little brother. Jason was a nuisance at the best of times, but now was not the time to concern herself with his presence, so his ability to be a nuisance was at the low end of her attention.

She deliberately ignored him and walked downstairs into the living room, determined to see what else had changed.

Her father was sitting on the couch as he normally did every morning, remote in hand while watching whatever it was that passed for news anymore, and he briefly looked up to give her a warm smile.

"Good morning, sweetheart," he said in a lazy fashion. "Your mother is making breakfast."

Nancy gave the older man a once-over before responding. Though his name was Roger, she had never thought of him as such, but staring at his thinner face, huge eyes, and long pointed ears, she could not help but think of him as someone other than her father. His first name came to mind because he looked like a stranger, a really *weird* stranger at that, but she fought her own defensive instincts and forced herself to reply in a pseudo-polite manner.

"Good morning," she said quickly.

Her reply was more of a blurt than anything else, and this caused her father to scrunch his eyebrows inward and question her further.

"Are you all right?" he asked in deep concern.

Nancy had to mentally force herself to remain calm. Now that she had shifted across universes again, shifting along yet another dimensional line, it was imperative that she blended in, or she would surely be locked up somewhere for being crazy.

"I'm fine," she said more calmly. "I just need to sit down and eat."

"Okay, sweetie," said her father. "You go ahead and get some breakfast."

"I will," she said, but she realized that she did not sound certain about this.

It occurred to her at that moment that she had forgotten to take her pain medication, but it also occurred to her that she was not really in that much pain today, and that was good. Her left shoulder was still bandaged with that nasty skin wound, and she needed to change that bandage, but she figured that necessity could wait until after she had eaten. She was hungry, and that hunger was keeping her from thinking in a productive manner.

She walked into the kitchen and sat down at the kitchen table, and her mother turned to see who had intruded upon her own precious cooking area.

The woman's face was an older version of Nancy's own, slender with huge eyes and pointed ears and auburn hair, and this bothered Nancy for some reason, probably due to the fact, she surmised, that if she were going to change skins, at the very least she could look different than her mother.

"You're up late," said the older woman.

"I know that, Deirdre!" snapped Nancy.

Nancy had indeed snapped out that abrasive reply, and it had most likely been caused by stress and the simple presence of her mother, but she immediately regretted this action, as she knew it would only draw to her some very unwanted and unhappy attention.

Her mother frowned and gave her the staredown, and even though her face was different in many ways, Nancy could still recognize that look anywhere and in any form.

"*What* did you call me?" asked her mother in a slightly-threatening tone.

"I…I'm sorry, Mom," replied Nancy in quick apology.

She found herself blurting out a defense as quickly as possible, and that defense barely made sense, even to her.

"I…I couldn't find my pain medication," stammered Nancy, "and I was hurting but I was too hungry to think and my bandage needs to be changed and I—"

Her mother shook her head in confusion and raised one hand in protest, that hand holding the spatula she was currently using to flip the pancakes she was frying in a pan on the stove behind her.

"Slow down!" ordered the older woman. "Just calm down and take a deep breath."

Nancy took her mother's advice and tried to look calm, but it was difficult.

"That's better," said her mother. "You're obviously still shaken up from your accident, so I'm going to get you some pancakes, and then we'll find your pain medication and change your bandage, okay?"

"Okay," replied Nancy.

There was a nervous tension in her voice, an anxiety that was no longer beneath the surface but had bubbled up to haunt her, and the realization of this bothered her almost as much as the anxiety itself.

Her mother eyed her one more time and gave her a slight frown, that frown looking so much odder by the fact that the older woman's lips were thinner and smaller than they should have been.

"And don't call me by my name, Nance," said the older woman. "That's disrespectful. You know better than that."

Nancy stared down at her empty plate and thought about this.

"So really nothing's changed except the way we look," she thought. *"Everybody's still the same as they always were...At least, it appears that way, so that's good. As much as Mom rubs me the wrong way, I don't think I could handle it if her personality was any different.*

"Still...just the physical part of this is going to take some getting used to. I'm a lot thinner than I used to be, and I'm probably not as physically strong anymore because of it...Not that I was that strong to begin with...but I was athletic, and...Oh, no...my bike...Is it going to be harder to ride my bike?...I...I guess I'll have to test that out once I'm done here.

"I could bike over to Rain's...I need to call her, anyway. I wonder if she remembers our conversation yesterday? If what she said is true, then she might remember the conversation we had, but she won't know

that I've shifted again. Although, knowing Rain, she'll certainly ask if anything's different…Boy, is she in for a surprise."

It occurred to Nancy that if her physical mass had changed, and if that change could affect how much weight she could lift or push against, then the size of her eyes and ears mattered as well. She blinked a couple of times as she looked around the kitchen, but her eyesight didn't seem to be any different.

"Well, that's a disappointment," she thought unhappily. *"You would think that I would at least get better vision with such huge eyes, but I guess that was too much to ask for."*

Nancy's line of thought was interrupted as her mother took her plate and served her a couple of large pancakes. The older woman opened the fridge, pulled out a block of butter and a bottle of syrup, and handed the items to her.

"Thank you," said Nancy without thinking.

Her mother stared at her for a moment with those huge eyes, her expression one of strange concern.

"Are you sure you're feeling all right?" asked the woman in obvious worry.

It occurred to Nancy that the thanking of her mother was highly unusual for her, and this confused her, so she simply nodded a "yes" in reply to her mother's question.

"All right," sighed her mother with a shrug, "but I think we'll keep an eye on you for a couple of days. You have me a little worried, Nance."

Nancy did not like the sound of that, but there was nothing she could do about it. Her mother was simply *that* kind of person, the controlling type that wanted to…*control* everything. It bothered her that her mother interfered in her life so often, but then it occurred to her that at present her mother was simply worried about her over the "accident" and the concussion, and this somewhat eased her anxiety over the matter.

Nancy cast aside those thoughts in order to eat. She took to fixing her pancakes the way she wanted them, but her breakfast activity was interrupted by the entrance of her younger brother.

Jason had his drawing pad in his hand along with a couple of art pencils, but that was not what held Nancy's attention. It was the drawing upon his pad that had caught her eye.

"What's that?" she asked as she pointed at the picture he had drawn.

Jason stared down at his pad before sitting down to the right of her. He flipped up the pad and gave her a sheepish grin.

"It's my OC for something I'm working on on Quirk Art," he replied.

Nancy stared in fascination at the drawing.

Jason was actually a talented artist, but his particular skill at drawing was not what had attracted her to his current work. He had drawn an actual *human*, what everyone *used* to look like, although the man in the picture was dressed in studded leather armor and was wielding a pair of knives.

"You drew a human?" she asked in surprise.

"No," snorted her brother. "It's an elf, dummy. You know I don't draw real people. Real people are boring."

Nancy realized that everyone still considered themselves to be human, and that a real human was now considered something out of fantasy, an "elf," as it were, and that was almost too odd for her to process.

"Oh," was all she could say.

An idea came to her, and it was useful for the time being. She needed to give Rain some idea of what kind of change had occurred, and even though she really didn't want to deal with Jason right now, she decided that asking him for this favor was the best plan she had in light of her predicament.

"Could you draw me something?" she asked quietly.

"What?" asked Jason in surprise. "You actually want me to draw something for you?"

"Could you draw me a human…uhhh…an 'elf'?" she asked. "Like a girl elf? Just put her in normal clothes, though."

Jason gave her an odd look but then shrugged in compliance.

"Okay," he said nonchalantly. "That's a weird request, but whatever."

He didn't even reply after that but instead took to drawing on the next page of his pad. It took Nancy a moment to realize that he had actually complied with her request.

"Wow," she thought in unexpected surprise. *"That was easy. I honestly thought I was going to have to pull teeth for that one."*

She thought no more on the matter and took to eating her pancakes, and by the time she was done eating, Jason had already finished his drawing. He held up the pad and showed her his work.

"How's this?" he asked.

The drawing was of a young woman in a miniskirt with a large black belt around her waist. She had feathered curly hair, something that one would have seen out of the 1970s in style, but she looked fairly normal as far as attractive young women went.

"That's great," said Nancy. "Could I have it? I want to show it to Rain."

Jason gave her the evil eye, those eyes accented and completed by a deep frown. The look was even more pronounced because of his huge visual orbs, and this frightened Nancy a little. She was not sure if she was ever going to get used to the new "look" the human race now sported.

Jason lowered his pad to the table and snorted once in obvious derision.

"Do your own art," he said unhappily. "Don't take credit for mine."

"I wasn't going to!" protested Nancy. "I was just going to…uhhh…show her how good your art is. That's all."

"Oh?" he asked in surprise. "Really? 'Cause I could always use…Wait…Are you lying to me?"

"No," argued Nancy. "You can put your name on it…Actually, you should put your name on it…Besides, Rain knows all I can draw is a stick figure, so she wouldn't believe me if I said it was mine anyway."

"Okay," shrugged Jason. "As long as that's what you want it for, then I don't have a problem with it."

He took a moment to write his name on it, then tore the drawing from the pad and handed it to her.

"There you go," he said matter-of-factly. "It's an original Jason Clark. It'll be worth a fortune someday."

Nancy rolled her eyes as she accepted the drawing. It was indeed worth a fortune, but only to her, and only because of the context in which she needed it.

She got up from the table and started to leave, momentarily forgetting where she was and what she had been doing.

"And where do you think you're going?" asked her mother.

"I was going over to Rain's…" started Nancy, but her voice trailed off as her mother shook her head no.

"We have to find your pain medication," said her mother in a stern voice, "and then we have to change your bandage. After that, you may *ask* to go over to Rain's."

Nancy frowned as she realized that this little part of her life, this little part of her life that bothered her in a big way all day, every day—her controlling mother—really hadn't changed at all.

*****

Nancy biked over to her best friend's house. The strain on the pedals wasn't as bad as she had first estimated, so there really wasn't anything to worry about in that respect. No, it was her arrival that upset her, or rather, that Rain was talking to someone whom Nancy did not favor…*not at all*.

She pulled up to Rain's backyard after she got off her bike and moved it back around to where she normally put it while visiting her friend. That was when she noticed the young man who Rain was talking to, the eccentric girl's normally invisible neighbor, a young man by the name of Danny Princeton. She recognized him immediately, even with his screwed up slender face and huge eyes, and this caused her no end of concern.

She hated Danny, and with good reason…He had spread a particularly nasty rumor about her involving another young man whom, once upon a time, Nancy had been interested in, but that rumor had prevented her from ever dating that particular young man, and she had never forgotten that transgression.

Danny was gangly and awkward looking, though in his current form with the huge eyes and slender face, he almost looked attractive, but that did not lessen her anger toward him. No, she did not like Danny Princeton, and aside from the fact that this young man was a gigantic nerd and a social pariah, it irked her every time Rain talked to him, because it was like a stab in the back from her best friend, and she had no stomach for that.

Rain immediately acknowledged her presence and gave her a nod. The eccentric girl's features were altered, of course; she had the same big eyes and small mouth that everyone else had, and that was a little disconcerting, but Nancy went with it.

Rain had on a tie-dye shirt and blue jeans that were torn at the knees, but this was not all that surprising. What was surprising, however, was that Rain was no longer wearing the hat from yesterday but had a large green ribbon in her hair instead, and this made Nancy stop and stare at it for a moment.

She temporarily forgot about the intruding presence of Danny Princeton, but that moment of forgetfulness passed as soon as he opened his mouth.

"We'll talk about this later," said the young man to Rain. "I think that's an interesting concept, but I don't know how viable it is. I'll look online and see if anyone's posted anything about it…but I seriously doubt they have."

"Well, let me know," said Rain matter-of-factly. "I'll tell you what I find."

"Okay," said Danny in a flat tone.

He looked over to Nancy and gave her a nod.

"Nancy," he said in acknowledgement of her presence.

"*Danny*," frowned Nancy in return while putting a strong and resentful emphasis upon his name.

The young man merely frowned, shook his head, and walked off. He rounded the back fence separating Rain's yard from his own and disappeared from sight.

Rain turned toward Nancy and gave her a half-frown.

"You should be nicer to him," she said unhappily. "He doesn't have any friends as it is."

Nancy swore under her breath and shook her head.

"I don't have to do *anything* for that dork," she replied. "Plus, I didn't come here to see *him*. I came here to talk to you. I have some important news."

Rain's thin and dark eyebrows raised, making her already big brown eyes look even bigger. It really was off-putting, and Nancy had to catch herself from saying anything about it.

Rain, however, did not realize anything was wrong. She spoke to Nancy as she always had, straightforward and without deception, and this gave Nancy some comfort for the moment, a little jewel of normalcy in her otherwise very strange day.

"Oh?" asked Rain. "News? Is this related to yesterday?"

"Yes," breathed Nancy. "You could definitely say that."

She took a moment to park her bike at the side of Rain's house, flipped open the grey metal basket affixed to the front of her royal-red vehicular device, and pulled out the drawing her little brother had given her.

"Take a look at this," she said as she handed the drawing to her best friend.

Rain took a look at it and nodded as her face scrunched up in obvious praise.

"That's not bad," she said. "Jason must be getting better. Although, I don't know why he has to draw the boobs so big."

Nancy snatched the paper away from her and stared at the drawing for a moment.

"They're not big," she said in confusion. "They look normal-sized to me."

"*Riiiight*," said Rain with a roll of her eyes. "If that's normal, then ninety-nine percent of all women have small breasts. Are you sure that concussion didn't do more damage than you thought?"

It occurred to Nancy that more about the world had changed than just their outward appearance, and this bothered her, because she did not know what else had changed in the wake of this revelation.

"I'm fine," she frowned. "I just wanted to ask: Do you remember what we talked about yesterday?"

Rain gave her a strange look. It was a look that screamed, "Are you okay?," and it was mildly insulting at that.

"Of course," replied the eccentric girl. "You claimed that a building complex called 'The Breckenridge Institute of Discovery' vaporized and knocked you off your bike, and we came up with a theory that you changed universes by travelling along a dimensional line that didn't previously exist before.

"However, we also discussed the very real possibility that your concussion has caused your belief in that…ahem…*theory*, and…unfortunately…that's probably the real answer…but you didn't listen to me on that…I did, however, promise to help you with this by thinking logically and using the scientific method…Now…is that what you mean by 'what we talked about yesterday'?"

Nancy felt a huge wave of relief wash over her. She was suddenly glad that she did *not* have to explain everything again, or for that matter, try to convince Rain that she was not lying or crazy. The eccentric young woman did not really believe her as it was. Still, Rain had remembered what had transpired during their discussion yesterday, so that was a good thing, and Nancy went with that good fortune in the hopes that she could convince her best friend of the truth of the matter in its entirety.

"Oh, good," replied Nancy. "You had me worried that the memory of our discussion got erased or something."

Rain raised one eyebrow in open curiosity. This was her "What do you mean?" look, and though it didn't come out to play that often, it was coming around a lot more often as of late due to extenuating circumstances.

"It happened again," explained Nancy. "I shifted again."

"What?" asked Rain in disbelief. "Really? How can you tell?"

"Oh, I can tell," said Nancy with wide eyes. "I can definitely tell."

"Explain," said Rain. "This should be good. I want to hear this."

Nancy frowned at the girl's tone. It was clear that Rain did not believe her this time.

"I'm telling the truth," frowned Nancy. "Everything's different again. Only this time…"

She handed Jason's picture back to her friend, and Rain took it and looked down at it in confusion at first, but that confusion changed to a wry smirk.

"Let me guess…" she said in mild humor. "Everyone's boobs were this big, right?"

"Yes," said Nancy, but then she thought better about it and shook her head no. "I mean, yes, but that's not how I know. This picture of…of a—"

"An elf," finished Rain. "She's wearing normal clothes, but she looks like a Dawn Elf from World of Battlecry. It doesn't surprise me that Jason would draw one. He's always playing one online."

"Whatever," said Nancy with a wave of her hand. "That doesn't matter. That's what we all were yesterday. We were…*elves*…but we called ourselves human. In fact, the way we look *now* is what we would have said was an elf…I think. I'm not really into fantasy like you and Jason, so I don't really know."

Rain was obviously surprised at this bit of news. Both of her eyebrows raised, and this made her eyes look absolutely *huge*…Its effect was unnerving.

"*Really*?" she asked in disbelief. "Are you sure you're all right, Nance? We have to go to school tomorrow, and I was hoping you'd be there."

"*Yes*!" hissed Nancy. "We all changed from human to elf, or whatever you want to call us now, and everything's different!"

"*We're* human, Nance," said Rain in concern. "Furthermore, if what you're saying is true, then you shifted again, but this time the shift was a lot more drastic. I mean, shoot, if this really happened like you said, then my boobs got smaller. That's depressing in and of itself."

Nancy could not help but chuckle at that remark. Rain always had a way of lightening the mood.

"I…I really am telling the truth," said Nancy. "I'm not crazy or anything. Yes, I have a concussion that's slowly going away…"

She reached up to the back of her head to feel the small lump, but she could no longer feel it.

"Actually, it's not really there anymore," she frowned. "Come to think of it, I wasn't in as much pain this morning as I was yesterday, and my mom said the abrasion on my shoulder was looking much better."

"I know your legs certainly do," said Rain thoughtfully. "Wait a minute…"

Her intelligent friend knelt down and inspected Nancy's bare legs.

"Your skinned knees look *much* better," said Rain in confusion. "That is really weird…Actually, it's more than weird. You shouldn't be able to heal that fast."

"What do you mean?" asked Nancy in sudden concern.

She was not sure what this new development meant.

"I mean it's like you're regenerating," said Rain as she stood up. "There are a number of animal species that can regenerate…The axolotl comes to mind…That's a kind of salamander that's native to Mexico, if you didn't know."

"No, Rain," sighed Nancy. "I didn't know that. I'm not a nerd like you."

Rain gave her a mild frown before continuing on.

"It's a salamander that can regenerate," she continued. "There are species of lizards that can regenerate, but humans…humans can't do that, Fance. They don't have that ability."

"What are you saying?" asked Nancy.

"I'm saying that you might be telling the truth," frowned Rain, "that you might have actually crossed universes…like a…a uhhh—"

"Dimensionaut?" finished Nancy.

"Exactly," said Rain. "Wait…How did you know what I was thinking?"

"You said the exact same thing yesterday!" replied Nancy in frustration.

"I did?" asked Rain. "I have no memory of that. Are you sure? I just came up with that term in my head a second ago, and I was about to say it, but you beat me to it."

Nancy stared at her as if she were stupid.

"How in the heck would I know a term like that?" she asked in disbelief. "It's not even a real word! You just came up with it yesterday!"

Rain gave her a concerned look and shook her head.

"Nancy, I don't remember saying that at all," she said in adamant denial. "I just came up with that term a few seconds ago."

"But…" said Nancy, but her voice trailed off as she realized something.

"If she honestly can't remember that," she thought in sudden fear, *"then this 'shifting' must be the cause of that. That is…It's…not good."*

"Are you all right?" asked Rain. "You look sick all of the sudden."

This was too much for Nancy, and she felt tears reach her huge eyes.

"You did say it yesterday!" she choked out. "If you can't remember it, then that means your memory is changing along with the world! That means the only person who I can talk to about it won't remember anything I say about it!"

"It's just a word, Nance," said Rain in concern. "You don't have to cry over it…and I still remember our conversation by the way. I remember the story you told me, how your hair stood up and you got hit by a shockwave first and then you heard the boom after that. That's what got me interested in your story in the first place. I didn't think you could make something up like that off the fly."

"I didn't," said Nancy as she wiped away her tears, "…but you did make up the word 'dimensionaut' yesterday."

"Obviously," shrugged Rain. "I must have, or you wouldn't have known it…Still…this whole thing is really weird. I mean, if you really *are* telling the truth…"

"I am," sniffed Nancy.

She tried to calm herself as she wiped her eyes clear. She nodded in acknowledgement of Rain's logic, and this made her feel a little better.

"For the record, I think you *may* be telling the truth," said Rain in a serious tone. "I think this dimensional shifting has hastened the healing process in your body, but that's localized to just *you*. Everyone else just changes with no memory of the previous life because they're not actually changing at all.

"You're the only one shifting, so you're in an entirely new universe, which means this is a different version of me than the one yesterday. Because of that, little differences can change how a conversation goes, and that's probably why…in *my* memories anyway…I have no recollection of coming up with that term. Do you see what I'm saying?"

"But if I shifted, then why would yesterday's version of me have the same conversation with you?" asked Nancy. "Wouldn't that be a whole different version of me?"

"We went over that yesterday," said Rain thoughtfully. "Remember? And I have a theory about it, but you're not going to like it."

"What's that?" asked Nancy.

"The scientists in that building complex got erased from existence along with the actual buildings," said Rain thoughtfully, "but you weren't close enough to the blast radius for that to happen to you specifically. No, something else happened to you. It obviously did, or you wouldn't be here talking to me.

"I think there *should* be many different versions of you, but there's actually only *one* now, and you exist in *all* universes at once. That's why you're healing faster. This version of you is the only *real* version, and it's connected to every universe possible, and that ambience, that…that *connection*, is speeding up your healing, allowing you to regenerate in days what takes weeks or months for other people."

Unfortunately, this made no sense whatsoever to Nancy.

"Either you're the smartest person in the world," she frowned, "or I'm just naturally stupid, because I have no idea what you just said."

"I'm saying you're like a god now," frowned Rain. "I'm saying that you, just *you*, not any other version of you, is the only version that exists, but that version exists in every single universe possible, all at the same time."

"But what does that *mean*?" asked Nancy in growing frustration.

"It means that you remain the same in every universe," explained Rain, "but the human consciousness is too limited to sense every universe at the same time, so when you sleep, your mind shifts to another universe. You aren't physically shifting, Nance, but your consciousness is…I really don't know how else to explain it."

"So there's a universe where we all look like elves," asked Nancy, "and my mind just popped in here to visit? Is that what you're saying?"

"Yes…" replied Rain uncertainly. "Sort of. I believe the original you was the one who existed when the explosion happened, and now your mind is shifting from one universe to the next. So I guess you're technically not travelling along a dimensional line, but your waking consciousness is. Does that make sense?"

"Yes," frowned Nancy, "but if that's true, then that makes things so much worse!"

"How so?" asked Rain.

"That means I'm going to shift *every day* for the rest of my life!" exclaimed Nancy.

"It's not that bad," said Rain in a hopeful tone. "Personally, I'm a little jealous. Actually, I'm *a lot* jealous."

"What?" asked Nancy in solid disbelief. "Why?"

"You get to experience something no one else has ever experienced!" said Rain in excitement. "You're the first human dimensionaut! Do you know how incredible that is? Do you have any idea what I'd do to experience what you're experiencing right now?"

"I'd give it to you if I could," pouted Nancy. "I just want to live a normal life. I don't want to wake up in a new body every day, and even then, it's not just my body that changes. There are other changes, too."

"Like what?" asked Rain.

"Like that green ribbon in your hair," frowned Nancy.

"My *Remember the Irish* ribbon?" asked Rain. "What about it?"

"You've never worn it before," said Nancy. "This is the first time I've seen it."

"What?" asked Rain in confusion. "I've worn this for the last two years…ever since you helped me sneak out and see that *Remember the Irish* concert."

Nancy threw up her hands and let out a small cry of frustration.

"Are you kidding me!" she cried. "You said the same thing yesterday about some other stupid band! Only you weren't wearing a ribbon but a hat, and it had something about cats and confessions on it…"

"Do you mean *Brat Cat Confessions*?" asked Rain.

"Yeah," frowned Nancy. "That's the one."

Rain looked truly stunned for a moment. Her huge eyes flitted back and forth at rapid speed, and Nancy could tell she was processing something that didn't make sense to her.

"What's that look for?" asked Nancy. "Why do you look more freaked out than me?"

"It's…It's just that…" stammered Rain.

"It's what?" asked Nancy. "What are you thinking about? What did I say that's got you so freaked out?"

Rain shook her head as if to clear her thoughts, and when she spoke again, it was in a near whisper.

"*Brat Cat Confessions* is a hard-core punk band," said Rain quietly. "Nobody's supposed to know I like that band, Nance…not since a kid got killed at one of their concerts three years ago. Their concerts always bring in the police…People get really violent during their performances.

"I talked with a girl online who had her nose broken right after she showed up. Some guy said 'hello' and straight up punched her in the face…Yeah, don't mention that name around here. My dad would kill me if he knew I listened to that band."

"Well, you were wearing their hat yesterday," frowned Nancy, "…at least when we were all human…I'm sorry…when we were all 'elves.'"

Rain's eyes peered off into nowhere for a moment as if she were making a decision in her mind, and then she turned her attention back upon Nancy.

"Okay," she said with a strange firmness in her voice. "I believe you now. I wasn't really sure before; I was *kind* of humoring you, but now I believe you…Oh, don't give me that look…I have to have some solid evidence before I can trust anything people tell me…You know that…It doesn't matter. I believe you.

"There's no possible way you could have known the things you know without having shifted, so here's what we're going to do. I'm going to give you a notebook, and you're going to describe each day to me, and I'll write the differences down in the notebook. I'm not as good an artist as Jason, but I can draw your face each day, make some notes about the changes, and then give you back the notebook. You'll keep the notebook."

"How will that help?" asked Nancy. "My consciousness shifts…not some notebook. That won't shift with me."

"*Oooooh*," said Rain as she smacked her own forehead. "I can't believe I missed that…Wait, no…No, wait. If you *are* connected to every universe, then what you say and write down in this notebook might keep…I really don't know. We'll just have to make an experiment of it, okay?"

"Okay," frowned Nancy. "I guess it beats going from day to day all willy-nilly with no one to talk to. At least you'll have a reference…Maybe if I keep the notebook on me when I sleep, it'll transfer over. I don't know what's going to happen, either."

"Good," smiled Rain. "Then let's do this. Let's get started…Ummm…Oh, yeah. First, there's something I want to show you."

"Oh?" asked Nancy. "What is it?"

"It's a little pick-me-up," said Rain.

She motioned Nancy over to one of the rear windows of her house.

"Do you see that web in the window?" she asked.

"Yeah," said Nancy in uncomfortable pause.

She did not like spiders…not one bit. They had too many legs and those big fangs, and seeing a web was just as bad for her as seeing an actual spider…That meant there *was* a spider, and she just hadn't located it yet.

"Don't give me that face," smiled Rain. "Look at this. Look at this little web."

"What about it?" asked Nancy.

"Do you see how small it is?" asked her eccentric friend.

"Yeah," shrugged Nancy. "It looks like a little umbrella."

"Yes, but that's not the important part," explained Rain. "Look at that little dot underneath the web."

"I don't…I…" stammered Nancy. "I don't want to see some dead bug, Rain."

"That's not a dead bug," smiled Rain. "That's the spider. It's a filmy dome spider, to be exact."

"They're that small!" said Nancy in horror. "That means they could be on me, and I wouldn't even know it!"

"Don't freak out," sighed Rain. "Just take a moment to look. You see, the filmy dome spider is my favorite spider. It's so small that most of the time its fangs can't even puncture human skin."

"*Most* of the time?" asked Nancy in slight fear. "What about the rest of the time!"

Her huge-eyed friend waved her off.

"You're overreacting," said Rain. "The filmy dome spider is harmless. More importantly, though, it serves a very important role in the ecosystem. It eats the nasty little bugs that we all hate…like gnats and mosquitos."

"I guess," breathed Nancy.

She really did not like looking at it, small as it was.

"My point is…" sighed Rain. "My point is that *you* are like the filmy dome spider."

"What?" asked Nancy in confusion. "What do you mean?"

Rain smiled and gave a double-handed motion toward the tiny creature underneath the umbrella-shaped web.

"Most people don't even realize the filmy dome spider exists," explained Rain, "but they're all over our state. They serve an important role that helps everyone. *You*—yes, *you*, Nance—You are doing that right now."

Nancy was a little more than confused. She could not see how her role in the grand scheme of things coordinated with that of a tiny spider.

"What do you mean?" she asked out of frustration. "You're not making sense."

"Don't you see?" asked Rain. "*You* are the very first dimensionaut!…Well, technically those scientists were, but since they were erased from existence, I'm going to give that award to you."

"How does that compare to a…a…*spider*?" asked Nancy.

She shuddered as she mentioned the offensive word. She really did not like spiders.

Rain laid one slender hand upon Nancy's non-injured shoulder and gave it a small squeeze.

"No one knows that you can travel across dimensional lines," said Rain. "Only you and I know that. But doing so makes you important, Fance. Probably the most important person on Earth right now."

"How so?" asked Nancy.

"Think about it!" said Rain in excitement. "You can travel to parallel universes! You can see all of the accomplishments that other universes have made! Why, you could travel to a universe that has the cure for cancer…or has interstellar space travel, or…or has discovered a lost play of Shakespeare, or…or anything else that's fantastic. All you have to do is write down how those scientific or artistic achievements were made…and you could change the world!…Well, the world you're currently in anyway."

Nancy thought about this for a moment, and her conclusion was…better than it had been.

"I guess that's good," she said hopefully.

"Of course, it's good!" said Rain in excitement. "You can travel the multiverse!…No…You *get* to travel the multiverse! I would kill for that opportunity…Not that I would actually kill someone for that—it's just a figure of speech—but you see what I'm saying."

"I guess so," sighed Nancy.

She did not really feel "special." She felt more like "cursed."

"Cheer up, Fancy," smiled Rain. "Things aren't nearly as bad as you think they are. We're going to study this from this day forth. Isn't this exciting!"

Nancy shrugged. Her life had taken a swift and sudden tumble downwards; she did not like this new development at all, but she now knew that Rain was fully onboard, and that gave her a small glimmer of hope she had not had before.

Chapter 3...The Third Shift

Nancy awoke a little before six-thirty in the morning. She always did on school days; it was just a natural quirk she had, and shifting between universes hadn't changed that.

She stretched out all six arms and yawned, her lips splitting into four different directions as she opened her mouth to release that yawn, and the sensation of this action was so strange, so invasively *weird*, that it temporarily stunned her.

She held up her two upper hands and stared at them in wide-eyed amazement, because they were nothing even remotely resembling human hands. Each hand had two long and slender fingers with a long and slender thumb, and the skin upon them was a tough, leathery-looking mottled brown bedecked by darker brown spots.

She scrambled out of bed, and she was distinctly aware of all six of her arms moving in sync with each other to help her with that task. Her strange new two-toed feet landed with a thump upon the light-blue carpet of her bedroom, and she raced to the bathroom in order to look in the mirror.

What she saw horrified her.

Her face was much rounder than it had been yesterday, but her skin held the same brown and mottled leathery quality as her arms, and she had no hair. Her eyes were closer to a normal size this time, but they were jet black, like ebony pits sunk into a leather briefcase. She had two smaller eyes above that, two more above that, and yet two more above that, all the way up her forehead, each pair closer together and smaller than the last, all the same sable color as her primary eyes. Her mouth was the most disturbing, however, as it was in four pieces that split outward when she opened her lips, like the mandibles of an insect, and this disturbed her a lot.

She studied her six arms in the mirror, moved each of them separately, and just that action, that simple action of willing her brain to move each one independently of the others, was tough for her to process. Each arm had its own sleeve within her nightgown, so it was clear to her that everyone in this new universe had already accommodated for this, but it was still weird.

She felt something twitch in the back of her panties, and she turned to view the large abdominal structure bulging from the back of her underwear, much like the abdomen of a spider.

This oval construction of weird biology was covered by a huge section of cloth sewn into her panties, so it was clear that showing it off was obviously taboo, but she pulled down the back of her panties to take a look at it anyway. It looked like the abdomen of a spider, its width a little less than that of her bottom, and its length a little more than half the length of her back. It was narrow and oval shaped, not a bulb like that of a house spider, but more like the arrowhead-backend of a hunting spider, and she mentally checked that information for later use.

She pulled the cloth down a little farther to view the two, small, finger-like organs on the very tip of it, and she dimly remembered reading something about "spinnerets" on spiders, so she simply assumed that this was what they were. She found that she could wriggle them if she concentrated on doing that, but the action felt really weird, so she pulled up the cotton cloth of her panties until her new "abdomen" was covered as it had been before.

"Wonderful," she said, but her voice sounded all garbled and hissy.

She studied herself in the mirror and tried to frown, but her new quad-lips didn't do that very well. She reached up with her top right hand to move it near one of the smaller eyes above her normal ones, but all she got was the strong sensation of something moving toward her head. She waved her top two hands around her head, and that sensation of movement was so strong that she could sense where her hands were without actually looking at them.

"These new eyes don't really see like my actual eyes," she thought, *"but they pick up movement like crazy. My actual eyes look black as night, but I can still see well enough, and I can still see in color, so that's good...Ugh...I guess I'm going to have to get used to my new self each day, or the rest of the day is going to be...difficult. This is waaaaay different than yesterday; that's all I can say."*

It occurred to her that her fear of spiders had waned for the moment, mainly because she *was* one...or at least, she felt like one. Still, she did not know how she was going to react when looking upon someone else in the same state, and this worried her.

"I don't want to freak out every time I see someone else," she thought. *"It's bad enough that I look like this...but other people? They're going to give me a heart attack if I don't toughen up right now.*

"I don't really know how evolution works, but something tremendously different must have happened for the human race to end up looking like this...

"Ugh...I can feel those 'spinnerets' wriggling about. Oh, this is so gross...Wait...I wonder if I can make webs?...Wait...That means it would come out of my butt...Ewww...I'm going to stuff that thought way down deep and lock it away. That's just more mental trauma I can't afford to suffer...Wait...How do I go to the bathroom? Oh, this day is going to drag on...I can tell."

Nancy shook her head as she stuffed/tucked away those disturbing thoughts. Even that simple motion of shaking her head took some getting used to, as her new "eyes" made the turning of her head an amusement-park-ride experience. The smaller eyes on her head were really good at detecting both motion and light, and her brain hadn't quite gotten used to that yet. Still, she was determined to get ready for school; it was Monday after all, and she did not want to be late.

She went to her bedroom dresser and pulled out a pair of jeans and her dark-blue school pride shirt, and both articles of clothing had been altered for her new form. Her school pride shirt had six sleeves, and her jeans had a large denim cover for her new abdomen. The back pockets of her jeans were on the "abdominal sleeve" instead of centered over her bottom like a normal pair of jeans, so that was different.

She quickly took off her nightgown and changed into her new clothes. Her body was way different concerning her face, her new limbs, and the strange spider-like abdomen she had, but all of her girl parts were still there, so she breathed out a sigh of relief at that.

"I guess it's not that bad," she thought. *"It's only going to last for today…I hope. Oh, God, I really hope this only lasts for one day. I really hope I'm not stuck this way for the rest of my life…Oh…Oh, no…I shouldn't scare myself like that. That's too terrible to think about…And here I was worried about 'shifting' every day. Now I can't wait to shift again. Even being an 'elf' is preferable to this."*

She thought about this as she looked around for her sneakers. She could not find her shoes anywhere, so she opened her sock drawer to at least grab a pair of crew socks, but her sock drawer was full of her underwear, so she took a moment to think about this new development as well.

"We must not wear shoes," she thought nervously. *"That means the very concept of shoes doesn't even exist here…That's so w…Wait a moment…My notebook!"*

She rushed to her bed, picked up her pillow, and breathed out a sigh of relief at the sight of the green notebook Rain had given her. She flipped it open and felt her heart leap in excitement as she looked at the first two pages. Rain's drawings and notes were still there, still the same ones the eccentric young woman had drawn yesterday, and Nancy tried to smile, but her new quad-lips just kind of opened a little in response to her happiness.

"This is great!" she said in excitement, but her voice sounded just as garbled and hissy as it had before.

She tried to frown again at the sound of her own voice, but her new lips just couldn't quite do it.

"Okay, maybe this isn't so great," she said, wincing at the sound of her own voice. "Doesn't matter. This will only last for one day, so it's not like I have to get used to it or anything. I just need to keep positive."

She nodded to herself in acceptance of this fact, sucked in her breath, stuffed her special notebook into her backpack, and headed downstairs.

School awaited; she was still a junior in high school, and though she wanted to just up and stop functioning in the real world because of all of this…*insanity*…in her life, she knew the real world would not allow her to. The real world went on with or without her regardless of what universe she was in, and the real world had consequences for the actions she might take, so dropping out of society was not something she could actually do.

She had to go to school, she had to interact with her family, she had to do her homework and her chores and everything else, so the only real thing this shifting did was make everything more *complicated*, and Nancy did not like that one bit. It stuck in her, but she knew, at the very least, she had Rain, so there was that, and *that* would have to do.

*****

Nancy sat down next to Rain at their designated lab table within their biology class.

Her "abdomen" poked out through the back of her seat, and that was something she was going to have to get used to, as well as simply walking around barefoot all day long. The skin on her feet was thicker and tougher than elsewhere on her body, so she did not feel the ground as much beneath her bare feet as she would have in her normal body, but it was still weird.

Nancy looked over to her best friend, and Rain looked just as freaky as she did. The eccentric girl had a darker-colored skin, almost black, but it still held the same leathery quality as Nancy's, so nothing had changed there. Still, everyone looked so different that Nancy didn't even know if who she was looking at *was* Rain, and that bothered her.

"Whoever is sitting next to me is obviously a girl," she thought. *"I can tell that pretty well, but I don't know if it's actually Rain or not…"*

"Rain?" she asked in a meek voice, albeit a garbled and hissy meek voice.

"Yes?" asked Rain as she turned her head. "What's up, Fance?"

Nancy breathed out a sigh of relief at this development. Her friend was still her friend, regardless of what form they all took on. However, Rain's freaky, spider-like appearance, along with the girl's split mouth, made it look as if Nancy were watching a B-horror movie every single second of the day, but she pushed that thought down just so she could function in any kind of a productive manner. It was simple necessity.

"I have the notebook," said Nancy quietly. "It hasn't changed."

"Give it to me," said Rain quickly and with a motion of her top right hand.

Nancy opened her backpack and handed her the green notebook from yesterday. Rain flipped through the two pages, but what she was thinking or what kind of expression she had…Nancy had no idea.

"This can't be right," said Rain quietly. "Did you mess with it?"

"No!" hissed Nancy. "I didn't do anything to it!"

"But this isn't what I wrote yesterday," said Rain in confusion. "It's my handwriting, though…and these drawings…those are mine too, but…I don't remember drawing these…I drew you as you are now."

"You don't remember because of…" started Nancy.

She looked around to make sure no one was eavesdropping, but Mr. Wagner had not come in yet, so everyone was busy blathering away to each other without issuing so much as a speck of attention toward their little table.

"You don't remember, because everything's changed," whispered Nancy.

"So why didn't this change?" asked Rain, a small note of identifiable confusion in her hissy voice.

"I don't know," shrugged Nancy. "I kept it under my pillow, though, and I slept on it."

"Why would that matter?" asked Rain.

"How would I know?" asked Nancy. "You're the genius, not me."

"Fine," sighed Rain. "The truth is, Nance…I have no idea what's happening to you. I've just been guessing."

"Well, your guess is as good as mine," said Nancy firmly. "It was your idea to keep the notebook, and it looks like it's working…"

Rain raised her top left hand to scratch her cheek, and Nancy noticed the jangling gold bracelet on her dark wrist for the first time.

"Wait," said Nancy. "What's that?"

"My bracelet?" asked Rain. "You know what it is, Fance. I've only worn it since I've known you."

Nancy would have rolled her eyes if she could have. She probably did, but she couldn't really tell.

"Why are *you* different in every single universe?" she asked. "First it was gold star earrings, then a hat, then a green ribbon, and now it's this bracelet. Why is that? What about *you* makes you change each time, because for the most part, my family has stayed exactly the same as they are no matter what."

Rain shrugged, and Nancy realized there were no answers forthcoming there.

"Never mind," she said unhappily.

Rain stared at the notebook in front of her for a few seconds longer and then slid it back over to Nancy.

"Keep that away from prying eyes," she said quietly. "I have to make another drawing of you at lunch, anyway. When we're at lunch, that is."

"Okay," replied Nancy, and she slipped the notebook back into her backpack.

Mr. Wagner walked into the classroom, effectively signaling the end of everyone's gossip and other social talk. The man looked strange in a dress shirt and tie, a dress shirt with six long sleeves, but Nancy did not let this bother her. She figured this kind of weirdness was par for the course after yesterday.

"All right, class!" said Mr. Wagner as he clapped all six of his hands together. "You should all be ready for the test today! I don't want to see any down faces or hear any complaints! You had the weekend to study, so it's time to put all books and papers away for the exam. Come on, come on, hop to it!"

Nancy felt her heart leap into her throat. With everything that had happened to her, she had completely forgotten about her biology exam. She shook in anxiety as Mr. Wagner handed out the test to each student, but her anxiety rocketed through the roof once he placed that test in front of her.

"What is this?" she thought in a mental panic.

In front of her were questions and diagrams that she honestly did not know the answer to. On one page was the female reproductive system, but it was the reproductive system of whatever it was she happened to be now, and though the page said the *human* female reproductive system, it was most certainly *not* human, or at least not the type of human she was used to.

Nancy shook as she realized there was no *possible* way for her to pass this class. It occurred to her in horrible awareness that if she changed bodies every single day, there would never be a test in Biology that she could actually pass. She shook not just in anxiety, but in the terrible knowledge that she had *never*, not *once* in her entire educational life, *ever* failed a test.

It was too much for her to bear. She felt a heavy liquid leak from her two main eyes, but they were not tears but thicker, like syrup or sap. She was crying, she knew that, and that knowledge was due to the fact that she was really, *really* upset. She let forth a little whine, though that whine was garbled and hissy, and Rain acknowledged it even though the eccentric girl was not supposed to talk during the test.

"Nance?" asked her best friend in concern. "Are you all right?"

This was all it took for Nancy to truly break. She grabbed her backpack and ran from the room, deliberately ignoring the protests of Mr. Wagner, but she was beyond all reason at the moment, so there was no other option for her but to run. She took off down the hall toward the nurse's office; she wanted to go home, and that's all there was to that.

She made her way to the nurse's office and sat down upon the bench outside of it. She wasn't ready to go in just yet; she just wanted to sit and stew in her own misery—she needed to—but someone else came up and sat down on the other end of the bench, and this intrusion broke her momentary fit to see whom it was that had sat down beside her.

It was a boy from her school, but who he was or even what grade he was in, she did not know. This boy's skin was a mottled grey with black spots, he wore a black T-shirt and black jeans, and that was about all of the information she could get just by looking at him. He was a boy from her school, and that was it.

He took a look at her and shook his head. He said something under his breath, but she had no idea what it was that he had said; she just couldn't make it out. Nevertheless, she did not like the implications of this action, so she reached up and tried to wipe her eyes clean of the sticky goo they were currently excreting…At the very least, she needed to look presentable to this stranger.

"Why are you crying?" asked the boy.

His voice sounded vaguely familiar, but she still couldn't place it. However, his garbled and hissy voice had a note of genuine concern in it, so she answered him in kind.

"I just found out I'm going to fail a class," she sniffed.

She tried unsuccessfully to shake off the sticky goop on her fingers, but this proved to be difficult. The sap from her eyes was clear in color, but it stuck to her fingers like snot, and it was just gross in general.

"Here," said the boy.

Nancy looked over to the boy as he pulled a large blue handkerchief from his right pocket. He handed it to her, and she proceeded to wipe her fingers and eyes with it.

"Thank you," she sniffed.

She offered it back to him, but he simply shook his head no.

"Uhhh…Just keep it," he said hesitantly. "It's yours now."

She couldn't blame him for not wanting it back, so she folded it up and set it next to herself on the nurse's bench. She did not really feel like talking, but this boy was unusually nice, so Nancy decided to open up a little.

"If you want to know why I was crying," she said unhappily, "I'm going to fail a class, and there's nothing I can do about it. I've never failed a class in my life. I hate this."

"What class is it?" he asked.

"Biology," replied Nancy. "I've never gotten a bad grade in my life, but now I'm going to fail, and there's nothing I can do about it."

"Why is that?" asked the boy.

"Because I can't pass the tests," said Nancy.

She did not know why she was talking to this stranger, but she felt like she needed to; she needed the relief that only an impartial listener could give.

"That sucks," replied the boy. "I don't know what that's like. I pretty much ace my classes."

"Good for you," sniffed Nancy. "That's what it used to be like for me, but not anymore. There's no possible way I can pass Biology, and I can't explain why. I could easily have aced Biology in the past, but there's no way I can do it now. No way at all."

She stared down at her multiple hands and clasped all three pair with their matching counterparts. She was not really used to this new body, but that didn't matter at the moment. Nancy wanted this shifting to stop; she didn't care if she was stuck in this body or any other, but she wanted the shifting to stop so she could just have some normalcy in her life, or at least a facsimile of it.

She decided to talk to this stranger like she would any other stranger in polite company, because that was the normal thing to do, and she needed that normalcy more than anything at the moment…She just did.

"Why are you here?" she asked. "At the nurse's office, I mean."

"I have a migraine," said the boy. "I was going to the nurse, but I saw you crying, so I stopped here to see what was wrong."

"Oh," replied Nancy. "You should see the nurse then. I left class without permission, so I'm sure I'll be called to the principal's office. Not like it matters. I got injured on Saturday, and that's what this cast on my arm…uhhh…this top one…that's why I'm in a cast…so I'll just say I was in so much pain that I had to come here. We were in the middle of a test, but I think Mr. Wagner will excuse me and let me take a makeup test. The problem is…is that it won't do any good…I'll still fail it."

"Why will you fail it?" asked the boy.

"I told you," replied Nancy in frustration. "I can't answer the questions."

"Yeah, I know you said that," said the boy, "but you never explained why."

"You wouldn't believe me if I told you," said Nancy as she waved him off.

"It's Biology," replied the boy. "It's not that difficult. There has to be some reason why you would *always* fail it. You're not stupid, so I don't see why that would be a problem."

"For you or anyone else, it wouldn't be," said Nancy, "but my case is special. Let's just say I have a condition where I can't remember anything from one day to the next, but it's only the biology class that I have that problem with. It has to do with my accident on Saturday. I…I wish I could explain it, but I just can't."

"I could help you with that," said the boy.

"What can *you* do?" snorted Nancy. "I don't know you, and you don't know anything about me. I don't see how you can help."

"I can give you a study sheet before every test," shrugged the boy. "You're a junior like me, and I'm in Mr. Wagner's eight o'clock class, so you'll have three hours to study before eleven. I know that's not a lot of time to study, but…it's better than nothing."

Nancy looked upon this stranger with a glimmer of hope. She did not know who he was, but if he was willing to share his study sheet…that meant she had a chance of passing the tests.

"You would do that for me?" she asked in honest surprise. "Why would you do that? I don't even know you."

The boy shook his head and snorted once. He stood up and brushed off his black jeans before turning his attention back upon her.

"I've got to see the nurse," he said bluntly. "If you want my help, Nancy, just tell Rain when you need it, and she'll give you the study sheet."

He walked into the nurse's office, but his parting comment left Nancy thoroughly stunned. She now knew who he was, and she felt like a complete fool for talking to him at all.

"That was Danny Princeton," she thought in a mental stupor.

*****

Nancy shut her bedroom door and walked to her bed to sit down next to her best friend.

"So you ran into Danny, did you?" snorted Rain.

"Very funny," replied Nancy. "You've been waiting all this time to say that, haven't you?"

"Pretty much," shrugged Rain. "He told me he talked to you outside of the nurse's office. He said he'd give me his study sheet when you needed it. I'd make one for you, but I pretty much remember everything in my head, and I don't really take notes…Plus, you know what my handwriting is like."

"Yeah," sighed Nancy. "Your notebook is proof of that."

Rain elbowed her with two of her left arms and nodded once. Nancy looked upon her in alarm, but she could not read the expression on her friend's face in the girl's current form anyway, so she simply waited for whatever the eccentric girl was going to say.

"Are you going to tell me the real reason you went to the nurse's office?" she asked. "I have to go home in an hour, so you'd better spill it."

Nancy looked down at all three pairs of her hands and sighed again.

"You know why," she said.

"I know," replied Rain, "but I want to hear it from you."

"I got upset because I couldn't answer any of the questions," she said. "I don't have the same parts from day to day, so how could I possibly answer any questions in Biology? There's no way I could fill out the diagrams or answer anything but multiple choice, and then I'd have to guess on those. It was just…impossible for me to handle. I've never gotten a bad grade in my life."

"That *is* upsetting," said Rain. "I do understand what that would be like. I don't know how *I'd* react to it, but…I know it would be upsetting."

A thought occurred to Nancy, and she had to say it; it had been digging at the back of her mind for a very long time now. She stared at her friend and tried to frown, but her quad-lips still couldn't quite make the motion.

"Why are you so smart, Rain?" she asked. "Why can't I be like you?"

Rain looked away and stared at the bedroom door for a second.

"Oh, boy," she breathed. "That's a tough one. Ummm…First of all, I am *not* smarter than you. That's not how intelligence works. I'm good at some things, I'm *excellent* at some things, and then there are other things…like mechanics, for instance…that I'm…well…not so much."

"But you're super intelligent," said Nancy unhappily. "You're a genius. It's not fair."

"It *is* fair," said Rain firmly. "I told you, there are some things that I'm just not good at…and…well…you *are*."

"Like what?" asked Nancy.

She really wanted to know, and she was curious as to what Rain's complete answer would be. This was a topic she had often thought about but had never brought up before, mainly because she had not wanted to put herself out there and look like an idiot in comparison to her best friend, but now that she was stuck in this impossible situation, such a question did not seem all that unreasonable.

Rain raised her top right hand up to her quad-lips, and Nancy could only assume that the way the two long and slender fingers of Rain's right hand…the way they rested across her chin and lips was an indication of Rain's "thinking expression" for this particular biological form. She was right, of course, because Rain sighed and answered Nancy's own earnest question a moment later.

"You can tell when a guy likes you," shrugged Rain, "and you're better in social settings than I am. You're definitely more athletic. I wouldn't want to get into a fight with you, that's for sure. I'm sure you'd kick my butt."

"But those won't help me later in life," replied Nancy, "…even if they were true."

"They *are* true," corrected Rain. "You really *are* better at those things than me…and for that matter, social skills will take you a long way in life. You can also spot when someone is lying to you…and you don't fall for scams. Remember that time I almost ended up giving that phishing site my World of Battlecry password? You spotted it immediately. I would have lost my account if you hadn't said something…not to mention I would have had to tell my dad to cancel his credit card."

"I guess," said Nancy in hesitant acceptance. "I think I'd rather be like you, though."

"Why?" asked Rain. "You're great just as you are. There are a lot of times I'd rather be like you."

"Liar," replied Nancy. "You're just saying that."

"No, I'm not," said Rain. "It's true. Plus, I told you this before, but I'm jealous that you get to be the first dimensionaut. I'd kill for that."

"I'd give it to you if I could," said Nancy. "I know I've said that before, but I mean it. You can have it…but that has nothing to do with intelligence."

"It kind of does," said Rain. "If I were athletic like you, then I would have been biking right beside you, and then we could have both been dimensionauts."

"I wish you had," sighed Nancy. "That means you'd be shifting with me…Ugh…I can't believe I'm wishing that on my best friend. Does that make me selfish?"

"Not really," replied Rain. "I guess you would be if I didn't want it, but I want it, and I know I'll never have it, so that makes me sad. You've…kind of bummed me out now."

"Well, then you really are a good friend," snorted Nancy.

"Huh?" asked Rain. "Why's that?"

"Because now we get to be bummed out together," finished Nancy.

Rain sighed as her shoulders slumped. This was a physical indication that she was frustrated, but once again, Nancy could not tell if she were *actually* frustrated. Their spider-like faces prevented her from reading even simple emotions, so Nancy could definitely relate to her well-meaning friend's supposed frustration, if not for the same reasons.

"Look," said Rain thoughtfully. "I've been thinking…I think…I think this is not nearly as bad as you make it out to be. Personally, I think this whole thing sounds crazy to me, but *you* believe it to be true, and the evidence you've given me is so well-crafted that my logical mind just can't pass it off as an elaborate hoax.

"For one thing, your injuries are real. You were clearly hurt on Saturday, and…well…you're not as hurt today. Your injuries are healing at a phenomenal rate, and nobody seems to have noticed *but* me. Now…that either means you're telling the truth and I'm somehow in the loop—don't ask me how, because I don't know how—or you're lying and everyone…and I do mean *everyone*…is in on the joke.

"Personally, I would rather have been the one to cross dimensional lines, but that didn't happen, so…I have to deal with that disappointment."

"*That's* a disappointment!" gasped Nancy in disbelief. "You've got to be kidding me!"

She wanted nothing more than for things to return to normal. Apparently, Rain did not feel the same way.

Her eccentric friend turned and looked her right in the eye…or eyes, as it were…Nancy was not really sure if Rain was staring at her in the eyes or not, but she got that gist from her all the same.

"Of course, it's a disappointment," sighed Rain, and this time she did sound crestfallen. "I should have been the one to have this. I mean, you clearly don't want it…"

"I don't," said Nancy adamantly. "On that we can agree."

"That's what I'm talking about," said Rain in obvious frustration. "I want this. Why can't I have it?"

"I don't know," snorted Nancy. "None of this makes any sense to me. You can thank those jerks at the Breckenridge Institute of Discovery for that. They did this to me…and they didn't even have the courtesy to *not* get blown up…"

Rain guffawed at that rather dark statement, and Nancy snickered a little at her own ill-meaning joke. They had a good laugh over it until her eccentric friend waved her top two hands at Nancy to stop.

"Seriously, though," said Rain, "I feel bad for those people. That fate sounds…*horrible*…to me."

"I know," sighed Nancy. "The truth is that…that they probably never even felt it or knew that it happened. Maybe it was just like…'poof'…and they were gone. I guess…I guess the best we can wish for on that front is that they didn't feel any pain."

Rain's quad-lips turned upward in what Nancy could only assume was a smile.

"See?" smiled Rain. "*That's* what I'm talking about!"

"What?" asked Nancy. "Did I miss something?"

"No," said Rain with a shake of her black, leathery head. "You…Your intelligence. You found something positive in that horrible situation. I mean, the situation is still awful for those people, but you made me feel better about it with just one sentence."

Nancy thought about this, but she didn't really see it.

"I guess," she said in mild confusion.

"There's no 'guess,' Nance," said Rain firmly. "You're just as smart as me, but in your own way. I mean, look at Danny…"

"No," said Nancy quickly.

Danny Princeton was a sore subject that she did not want to talk about.

"What do you mean 'no'?" asked Rain. "You talked to him today about your 'problem' with Biology. I thought that meant…"

"That meant *nothing*," frowned Nancy. "The simple fact is that I didn't recognize him, Rain. This stupid 'spider' form prevented me from figuring out who he was until it was too late."

"Spider form?" asked Rain in confusion.

"Never mind," said Nancy with a wave of her top right hand. "The point is…is that he lied about me. He spread that dirty rumor, and there is no reason to forgive him for it. It was mean and awful…"

"I could talk to him," coaxed Rain. "I could just explain…"

"No!" hissed Nancy in swift anger.

Rain jumped a little at the tone of her voice, but Nancy quickly recanted. She was being too short with her friend as of late, and though it was due to frustration and fear, it was still unacceptable. At this point, Rain was definitely the only person on Earth who still understood her, what she was really like on the inside, and that made Rain more valuable to Nancy than any other person alive, even her own family.

"I'm sorry, I'm sorry," said Nancy quickly. "I didn't mean to snap at you."

"Nance…" said Rain slowly, "I know I promised to keep quiet about you around Danny, but don't you think it's time that you…"

Nancy shook her head no, and Rain's quad-lips frowned as her shoulders slumped. Nancy knew that Rain was trying to be the best friend she could be, but Danny…he was someone who was truly deserving of contempt.

"He slandered me," frowned Nancy. "He spread that lie, and now I couldn't get a date if I wanted one…and no boys have asked me out since then, either, so you know I'm right."

"Join the club," sighed Rain. "You don't see boys knocking down my door…that's if I felt like dating anyone, mind you…and right now I don't. I've got other things I want to do with my time."

"Let's just drop it," frowned Nancy. "I'm depressed enough as it is."

Rain sighed and propped up her dark leathery head with her two upper hands, leaning her knobby elbows upon her knees. Her gold bracelet jangled against itself as she took that position, but even the sight of that made Nancy unhappy. It was a reminder of how much things had changed.

"Fine," said Rain unhappily. "I just wish you'd cheer up, though. I still think this is the discovery of a lifetime. I mean, I would so love to shift with you. That would be awesome. I'd like to take account of all the major and minor differences between each universe…"

"Be my guest," said Nancy dryly.

As far as she was concerned, Rain was more than welcome to it.

"Not that that's possible," she thought unhappily.

"I'd love to," said Rain. "I keep wondering if there are any major changes to the Earth itself, but then I start thinking about all of the changes that may have happened to *me*, and my thoughts get hijacked by that frustrating little notion."

Nancy pondered this. Rain was mostly the same, and there were only minor differences that Nancy, herself, had noticed, like the little trinkets Rain wore, for instance.

"I really don't know, Rain," shrugged Nancy. "You've changed your favorite thing to wear during both shifts…wait…I think the first time I shifted must have been during the accident itself, so that means I've shifted three times, not two. You were wearing a hat that day…Saturday, that is…and that was the first time I knew something was wrong…In fact, now that I think about it, I'm wondering if your memories of me have changed."

Rain stared at her in what looked like her "thoughtful" expression; it was hard to tell.

"That *is* a good question," said Rain with sudden interest. "You've been my best friend for…*forever*. I know all of the likes and dislikes of *this* universe's Nance…For instance, I know that your favorite color is green, but you don't like to wear green clothes."

This surprised Nancy. Rain's statement about her favorite color was true, and she couldn't help but wonder what else had remained the same.

"Go on," urged Nancy. "That's actually true. What else can you tell about me?"

Rain cocked her head to one side in what Nancy would normally call her "thinking" face.

"You…like birds," said Rain, "but you don't like bird watching."

"Yes!" said Nancy in excitement. "That's right!"

It occurred to her that some of the most important things in her life had remained the same, and this made Nancy happy for a moment…but only for a moment. The whole situation still weighed upon her, but at least she had *some* things to hold onto.

"Your favorite bird is the cardinal," said Rain in growing enthusiasm. "You like the male cardinal's red feathers, and you like the orange color of its top two eyes."

"Yes, that's ri…!" began Nancy.

But then her brain made sense of what Rain had said, and *that* didn't make sense at all.

"Wait…what?" she asked in confusion. "*Top* two eyes? Cardinals only *have* two eyes, Rain, and their eyes aren't orange; they're black."

"Really?" asked Rain in strange wonder.

"Yeah, *really*," snorted Nancy.

"They don't have two eyes *here*, Nance," said Rain matter-of-factly. "They have eight, just like us. The bottom six are black, but the top two are larger than the rest, and they're orange…on the males, anyway. They're orange for the purpose of attracting a female, and they're also for the purpose of luring predators toward them and away from the females."

Nancy thought about this and felt herself sinking into a mire of anguish. For some reason, it had never occurred to her that even the animals changed when she shifted. Looking at the vast sea of information she was lacking every time she shifted weighed upon her like a battleship anchor, sixty thousand pounds of pure anxiety, and this was a little too much for her. She held her head with her top two hands and tried not to panic, but it was difficult.

"This is too much," she breathed out in audible anxiety. "It's just too much. I don't know if I can handle this anymore. Even the birds change when I shift. It's too much."

"It's fine," said Rain confidently. "It's going to be fine. You'll get used to it. I know I would…"

Nancy stared at her friend and frowned in defiance of that positive statement, but then an idea came to her, and she felt a glimmer of hope for coming up with it.

"You…" she said slowly, "*You* can help me! You seem to remember most of what we talked about over the last three days, and my notebook hasn't changed, so you can help me…You can help me, right?"

Rain cocked her dark leathery head to one side and gave her a slight upward turn of her quad-lips. Nancy was pretty sure that this was Rain's "smile," and the sight of it plus the realization of its recognition gave her even more hope.

"Of course," said Rain matter-of-factly. "You wouldn't be able to keep me *from* helping you, Fance. You're my best friend, and you always will be. Why would…*this*…this shifting…make that any different?"

Nancy gave her own smile in return. Rain was a lot of things, but she wasn't a liar…at least, never to Nancy. The eccentric girl lied to her parents quite often, but never to Nancy.

"Thank you," she said in stark relief, and she meant it. "Thank you, Rain. If this is my life now…thank you for helping me. I really need it. You're the only one I can trust with this."

"I know," smiled Rain. "We'll figure this out. We'll take it day to day and see how it goes…*however*…"

"However what?" asked Nancy in nervous reply.

She did not really like, want, or need any conditions to their friendship.

"I get to catalogue your changes," finished Rain. "I want to study this as much as possible. This is too much of a discovery to pass up, and I want to study it in detail…Okay? Do we have a deal?"

The answer to that question was so simple and so automatic that Nancy did not have to think about it.

"Deal," she said quickly, and that was that.

Chapter 4…The Fourth Shift

Nancy woke up around six-thirty in the morning again. She was grateful that this little ability of hers, the ability to wake up without an alarm, was still with her. At the very least, she had some common denominators to hold onto.

She reached up to rub her eyes but thought better about it. She studied her hands instead, because they were the first indicator of what she could expect. Her hands were normal for the most part, and she only had two arms and two legs this time, but her skin was covered with a fine, speckled-white down, little feathers that were each the size of a pencil head. Her new feathers were speckled with dots of brown, and when she used her fingers to push back some of the down, her skin felt rough and bumpy, and it was a dark-orange color.

She reached up and felt her face, and it felt normal save for the down upon it, but her hair was gone, replaced by long and elegant feathers that swept backwards in a V, and she took a moment to run her fingers through them.

"This is better than yesterday," she said to herself, and her voice sounded a little more normal today.

She hopped out of bed and walked to the bathroom, flipped on the light, and inspected herself in the mirror. She looked human for the most part, but she was covered all over by the speckled down that was prominent upon her arms, except for the plumage on top of her head, which sported long purple and green feathers that glinted a little in the light.

"I like it," she smiled, and her reflection smiled back at her. "This is so much better than yesterday…and my voice sounds better, too. This might be a good day."

She left the bathroom after finishing her morning business and dressed for school. She sifted through her clothes within her dresser and felt elated at the fact that they were all normal again. She chose her red T-shirt matched with her stone-washed jeans, located her socks and sneakers, and prepared for another day at school.

She nearly forgot her green notebook, but she went back to her bedroom, took it out from beneath her pillow, and flipped it open just to check if the information was still there. It was indeed still there, though the picture Rain had drawn the previous day was hideous in nature, and Nancy thanked the powers that be that she was not stuck in *that* form for the rest of her life.

"I guess this shifting isn't all that bad," she thought to herself. *"It's good if I look like I do today. The feathers on my head are really pretty, and it certainly beats yesterday…I did NOT like yesterday…Ugh…But that's neither here nor there. No, I'm going to do better today…You know…I can't wait to see what Rain looks like. I wonder what colors her feathers will be?"*

She pondered this little development as she practically skipped down the stairs to get ready for the bus.

*****

Nancy sat down next to Rain at their favorite table. Today's food was unusual for the norm in the cafeteria; it consisted of a huge mound of corn with some glistening bits in the center, and that was it.

She had gone home yesterday before lunch, so whatever had been served in the cafeteria had not been sampled, not by her, at least, and she was glad for that. It sickened her to think that a giant fly might have been on the lunch menu the day before, so a big mound of corn today wasn't so bad…

Plus, she was starving. She hadn't eaten at all yesterday because she'd been afraid to, and though she'd had some cornflakes for breakfast, it didn't quite make up for not eating anything the day before. Still, she was wary of the plate of food set before her. This shifting business had made her wary of pretty much everything.

"What is this stuff?" asked Nancy. "I'm having such a good day, and I don't want to spoil it…but this corn is all they gave us, and it looks weird."

"Are you kidding me?" asked Rain.

Nancy looked to her friend, and she couldn't help but give herself a mental smile over Rain's appearance. The eccentric girl was dressed in a green tee with a white "Remember the Irish" logo emblazoned across it, and she was wearing a pair of her black cargo pants, but that was not what gave Nancy a smile.

Rain's downy feathers were a dull and speckled gray, and the feathers on her head were jet black, like crow's feathers, and this gave Nancy a selfish inner smile, a happiness that she had to kick herself for. She finally shone a little brighter than her genius friend, and though that thought was terribly selfish, she couldn't help but revel in it.

Rain, on the other hand, did not seem to notice Nancy's ogling of her appearance. The eccentric genius was too busy chastising her over their food, or rather the lack of Nancy's knowledge upon the subject.

"Tuesdays are the best," continued Rain. "We get mimizu corn today. It certainly beats the crap we normally have to eat."

Nancy watched as her eccentric friend took a large forkful of corn, stuck it in her mouth, and made the "Mmmm" face. Rain caught Nancy's unusual attention toward her and commented upon it.

"What?" asked the girl. "What's that look for? I like mimizu corn. Is that so strange?"

"No," shrugged Nancy. "I guess not."

She picked up her fork and dipped it into the giant corn mound, took up a scoop of it, and popped it in her mouth. It was strangely delicious, though there was something mixed in with the buttery corn that she could not identify.

"This *is* really good," she said in strange wonder. "Though I don't know what these little chunks of meat are. What is this, anyway? It has a strange flavor. It's a…a strange 'earthy' flavor…kind of like raw carrots, but not so much the carrot taste. I mean, it's not bad, but I can't identify it."

Rain gave her an odd look as Nancy took to eating her lunch in earnest.

"Seriously?" asked her friend in disbelief. "You don't know?"

Nancy chewed and swallowed another mouthful of "mimizu corn" and then replied to her unbelieving friend.

"No, seriously," she said in response. "I…I *shifted* again, remember?"

She whispered the word *shifted* and looked around for a second to make sure no one was listening, but everyone else was busy carrying on with their own conversations, so their little discussion was safe.

Rain rolled her eyes and shook her head.

"Stupid me," she said in self-deprecating awareness. "I forgot about that."

She picked up a little chunk of meat, popped it in her mouth, chewed, and then swallowed.

"It's earthworms," she said matter-of-factly.

Nancy was in the middle of swallowing when she heard this fact, and she nearly choked upon the lump of corn that was currently moving down her throat.

"Excuse me?" she asked in disbelief. "Ha, ha. Very funny…Seriously, what is it?"

Rain raised both of her eyebrows, those eyebrows consisting of slightly larger black downy feathers set within the grey around them. She gave Nancy a serious look, and that look caused Nancy no small amount of concern.

"It's earthworms," she said once more. "I wasn't making a joke."

Nancy felt her stomach heave as she dropped her fork into the pile of corn beneath her. She held her hand to her mouth and tried not to vomit, but the thought of earthworms in her stomach made this denial of sickness particularly difficult to ignore.

"Are you all right?" asked Rain.

Nancy held up her right palm and nodded as she waited for her stomach to settle. She put her hands down upon the table and took in a deep breath; she needed to calm down a bit.

"And this day was going so well," she said unhappily, but Rain simply laughed.

"I guess you're not used to mimizu corn," said her eccentric friend.

Nancy turned to say something, but she was sidetracked by the presence of someone walking past their table. It was a boy dressed in a collared red shirt, a style that had died out a long time ago, and this particular color did not go well with the off-brown slacks he was wearing. His downy feathers were a dull red, but his head feathers were black, and this gave him the overall appearance of a cardinal in ill-matched clothing.

"Hey, Danny," said Rain quickly. "Why don't you sit with us?"

Nancy released a mental groan at this information, for even though Danny had offered to help her yesterday, she had not forgiven him for spreading rumors about her last year. He was still on her hate list, but she did not want to argue with Rain over this development, so she decided to stay quiet.

He sat down across from them at their small table and looked upon Nancy with wary eyes. She wanted to ignore him, so she dipped her fork into her pile of corn and popped that bit into her mouth, temporarily forgetting that she was disgusted by what she was eating in the first place. It did not occur to her that she was eating what she was eating until she was halfway done swallowing it, and the look on her face must have been priceless, because Danny released a short chuckle and gave her a keen smile.

Nancy did not like this at all. She gave him an angry scowl, but Rain intervened before she could say anything.

"Nance," said her eccentric friend, "you should thank Danny for the notes he gave you today. You were able to pass your makeup test because of them."

Nancy held her downy face in her downy right hand and took in a deep breath. She did not want to thank him, but he had pulled her fat out of the fire, so she reluctantly did so.

"Thanks…I guess," she said in a low voice.

"You're welcome," said Danny.

Rain took control of the conversation and steered them all away from the awkward road they were headed down. She had told Nancy that she was poor in a social sense, but Nancy had not really believed her then, and she certainly did not believe her now.

"So, Danny," asked Rain, "did you do any research on what we talked about?"

"Yeah," said Danny, "but I didn't find anything outside of science fiction. There really isn't any kind of consistent theory on multiple universes."

Nancy immediately shot her friend a look of shock mixed with hurt, because those were the two emotions she was feeling over this betrayal. It was one thing to involve someone else that could be trusted, but considering that Rain was the only person she *did* trust, the thought of telling anyone else was unacceptable, and the thought of telling Danny Princeton, the boy who was nothing more than a rumor-spreading liar…was horrendous.

"What?" asked Rain in a defensive tone. "I had to tell someone about our 'hobby.' I can't do all of the legwork on my own. You think I'm a genius, but I have my limits, Nance."

Nancy looked toward Danny, and even though she hated him, she knew he wasn't stupid. He had to know something was up, and she was right. He looked between the two of them with slightly narrowed eyes, and even though his face was covered in downy red, that expression of distrust was easy to make out.

"What is this about?" he asked.

"It's none of your business," blurted Nancy.

"Nancy!" scolded Rain in an unhappy tone. "Don't act that way."

Nancy did not want to get into an argument with her. She dipped her fork into her food and munched away on it, forgetting once more what that food was made of. It took her three more forkfuls to figure it out, and once she did, she dropped her fork into her corn and held her face in her right hand again.

Rain intervened again, and that consistent intervention was grating upon Nancy's last nerve. Danny was not someone she wanted to interact with *at all*, and even if he hadn't spread that dirty rumor last year, even if he was just Rain's invisible neighbor, he was still a giant dork, and hanging out with him was a death knell for anyone with a social life.

Nancy looked between her fingers upon Danny and saw the anger on his downy, scarlet face. It stunned her for a second, and Rain intervened yet again, but she was not that helpful.

"Just give her some time," said Rain.

"Forget it," said Danny in an angry tone. "I'll eat somewhere else."

His look and tone sparked an immediate fire within Nancy. This rumor-spreading cockroach had no right to be angry with her as far as she was concerned; he was a dirty liar, a social pariah at best, and she wanted him gone. She let him know as much; she could not help herself.

"Good," she said from behind her right hand. "Leave then. Get lost."

She heard him curse under his breath, so she lowered her hand and stared him down. He glared back at her, stood up, and picked up his plate, but he did not walk off before chastising her.

"You can't treat people like that," he said angrily. "I've never done anything to you, and you treat me like crap. You can fail Biology for all I care. Good riddance."

Nancy was stunned at his audacity. Her mouth dropped open in absolute disbelief at his attitude; *he* had wronged *her*, not the other way around.

"You've never done anything to me!" she hissed. "You know what you did!"

Danny looked upon her with definite confusion in his eyes. He sat back down and set his plate back upon the table, and that look of confusion on his face gave Nancy a shot of doubt in her heart. It was unsettling to her that he might not know what it was that he had done, the spreading of the rumor that had started this hatred in the first place.

"What are you talking about?" he asked. "I've never done *anything* to you."

The tone of his voice sounded honest, the look on his face backed this up, and Rain was right when she had said that Nancy could tell if someone was lying, and it did not look like he was trying to slip one past her.

Nancy felt sick inside; she began to wonder if she had made a terrible mistake, and though she did not want to remind him of his transgression, she needed to know if he was telling the truth.

"You…You said that I had…" she stammered. "You told everyone that…You spread that rumor about me last year about…about me and…and *Bobby Schmidt*."

She whispered Bobby's name…She did not like to be reminded of him. Bobby was one of the most popular boys in her junior class; he was on the football team, a running back, and Nancy had drooled over him from day one. Now she purposefully avoided him…She could not stand to be reminded of the rumor any more than necessary.

Danny shot her a look of pure indignation, and Nancy did not like that look. He was acting as if he did not know what she was talking about, and that simply could not be possible. *He* was the one that had spread that rumor…or so she had been told.

"What are you talking about?" he asked. "What rumor?"

"You know what!" hissed Nancy.

"No, I *don't*," frowned Danny.

Nancy pointed her fork at him in an accusatory manner. She was tired of this act already…At least, she thought it was an act, and she called him out on it.

"Don't lie to me!" she said angrily. "Brinn Clevenger told me you were spreading that rumor, and then everyone started treating me like a…a…You know what happened!"

"Brinn Clevenger?" asked Danny. "Do you mean Bobby's girlfriend?"

Nancy heard the very distinct sound of an old record on a record player scratching to a sharp halt within her mind, and at first, she could not respond in any meaningful way to this new development, as it sabotaged her ability to think straight.

"Say what now?" asked Nancy.

This was indeed news to her. In fact, it was incredibly shocking news that gave rise to a swift and burning rage as she put all of the pieces together.

"That dirty little…!" she thought in a mental heat. *"She told me Danny had spread that rumor, and I believed her like an idiot just because nobody likes*

Danny…That…That pernicious, lying, backstabbing, little…"

"Nance?" asked Rain. "Are you okay? You look like you're going to murder someone."

"I just might," replied Nancy through gritted teeth. "That dirty little liar told me that Danny spread that rumor, but she's the one that did it, because she knew I liked Bobby!"

Danny leaned back as he shook his downy scarlet head once in surprise.

"You've hated me all this time because of *that*?" asked Danny in disbelief. "Why would I spread a nasty rumor about you? I don't even know you."

Nancy dipped her fork into her mound of corn, popped the utensil into her mouth, and chewed away in angry temper. She swallowed her food, realized that she was eating earthworms again, and then realized that she was too angry to even care about it.

It came upon her that she had to apologize to Danny, to *Danny Princeton*, the biggest loser in school, and this ate at her a bit, set her on edge, but she knew she had to do it…It was the right thing to do.

"I…I'm sorry, Danny," she winced.

She had said it, it had come straight from her own lips, but it was still a *vastly* uncomfortable thing to say.

Danny did not reply to her apology. He looked down at his own mound of "mimizu" corn, but his eyes were distant, as if his mind were far and away from the cafeteria that they were currently in.

No one said anything for a few seconds, but Danny finally replied before things got truly awkward.

"I can't believe you thought I spread a rumor about you," he said unhappily. "Why would you believe that?"

Nancy truly felt like slime at that moment. Her own predicament of shifting along dimensional lines seemed trivial in light of her treatment of Danny, because though she changed bodies every day, the damage she had done with her own behavior had remained in *every* universe, and that was a bitter pill to swallow. There was nothing she could say to him in response to his question that would make things better, so she decided to lie, because that was the only option she had left.

"I don't know why," she replied. "I wasn't thinking straight. I said I was sorry."

Danny did not say anything in return. He picked up his plate and left the table without another word. Nancy watched him go with a feeling of pure liquid guilt eating away at the pit of her stomach. This was terrible, and she knew it, and she knew that there was nothing she could do about it at the moment, and that made it so much worse.

Rain looked upon her and frowned.

"Now you've done it," said Rain unhappily.

*****

Nancy picked up a tennis ball and tossed it across Rain's backyard. Rain's dog, Weirdo, chased after the small green orb only to snatch it up between his small jaws.

Weirdo was a Dachshund, a wiener dog, and his long body and gangly trot always caused Nancy to stare at him like a sideshow freak, but thanks to her shifting, Weirdo was even weirder than usual. Instead of having fur like a normal dog, Weirdo had thick brown feathers all over his body; he was like a mutated cross between a chicken and a hot dog, but Nancy thought he looked better this way. He wasn't quite as ugly and strange with feathers instead of fur.

"Weirdo looks better with feathers," she said without thinking.

"What's that?" asked Rain. "What do you mean?"

The eccentric young woman eyed her own dog in an obvious attempt to mentally visualize the small canine without feathers, and this was accented by the tilting of her head to her own right. With her downy face and long, sweeping black feathers on the top of her head, the effect of Rain's tilting head caused Nancy to think of a cockatiel, and she burst into laughter without meaning to.

"What's so funny?" asked her friend.

Unfortunately, Rain tilted her head in the other direction, this time to her own left, and Nancy completely lost it; she laughed so hard that she had to hold her stomach. Rain tilted her head back to its normal position and frowned, and Nancy could tell she was not amused.

"Stop laughing at me," said Rain unhappily. "I know you're laughing at me. That's not cool."

"I'm sorry, I'm sorry," laughed Nancy. "Oh, but I wish I could take a picture and show it to you tomorrow! Oh, you look so funny when you tilt your head!"

"Do you mean like this?" asked Rain.

She tilted her head to the right again, and Nancy laughed so hard that she found herself begging her best friend to stop.

"Stop!" she laughed as she wiped away a tear. "Oh my God, stop…Oh, that's so funny…I would probably die if you said 'I want a cracker!'…Oh, I wish I had my phone…I would so show you what I'm talking about…Wait…Wait a minute…That gives me an idea."

Rain moved her head upright again and scrunched down her eyebrows in confusion.

"What's that?" she asked.

Nancy took a moment to settle herself down. She wiped away a couple of tears and then took a deep breath before replying.

"Does your dad still have that old instant camera?" she asked.

"Yeah," shrugged Rain, "but why do you…?"

Rain's own sentence trailed off as her dark eyes widened in comprehension.

"I'll go get it," she said quickly.

She trotted off to the backdoor of her domicile and disappeared within. Nancy waited patiently for a few minutes, and during that time she played fetch with Weirdo. However, she did not have to wait for long. Rain came back out with the ancient device, a real relic from the eighties…It looked like a block with a camera lens on it.

"Got it," said her eccentric friend. "I had to find it and put some batteries in it, but it's still got film, so we're good."

"Great!" said Nancy in excitement. "We can tape the picture to the notebook! Maybe it'll keep like the notes and the drawings."

"Well, I already drew you today," replied Rain, "so we're in no danger of losing what you look like in case this picture doesn't hold."

Rain held up her dad's historical throwback and looked through its window. She lined it up with Nancy's profile, her finger hovering over the snap button.

"Say peanut!" she said, but Nancy held up her hands in protest.

"Wait, wait!" she said in a frantic rush.

Rain lowered the camera and tilted her head again in confusion. Nancy had to will herself not to laugh at that amusing expression.

"What?" asked her friend. "I was just going to take your picture."

"I know," smiled Nancy, "but don't you think you should be in it, too?"

Rain's eyes widened for a brief moment as this idea processed within her genius brain, and Nancy gave herself a mental smile for actually coming up with a good idea, an idea that Rain had not thought of.

"Right," said Rain quickly.

The eccentric girl huddled in close to Nancy and held up the camera in front of the both of them.

"*Saaaay* peanut!" said Rain.

They both smiled, and she snapped the picture.

The camera flashed and spit out the undeveloped film, and they patiently waited for the picture to appear. Rain gave the small picture a quick shake, and the grainy photo appeared a few seconds later.

"Ugh," grunted her eccentric friend. "The quality of these pictures…"

"It's good enough," breathed Nancy.

And indeed, it was. They now had a good solid photo of the two of them in their "cockatiel form," and hopefully it would stay in the notebook as it was.

"This was a good idea, Fance," said Rain. "I'm proud of you."

"What!" asked Nancy in false umbrage. "I may not be a genius like you, but I'm not stupid."

They both had a good laugh, but Rain's smile turned into a frown a second later.

"What is it?" asked Nancy.

"It's…It's just…" stammered Rain. "Well, it's just…About Danny…"

Nancy groaned and shook her head.

"Will you drop it?" she asked in frustration. "I already apologized to him!"

"Yeah," frowned Rain, "but that's not the point. I think he's upset because you automatically blamed him for something he had no reason to do. How would that make you feel if someone did that to you?"

"I know that," frowned Nancy. "I made a mistake. I already apologized to him."

"Yeah, but…" started Rain, but she didn't have a chance to finish her chastisement.

Danny Princeton appeared at the very edge of Rain's backyard, and Nancy likened his sudden arrival as one would to some dark creature that suddenly appeared when you said its name three times in a row. It was a little unnerving, completely unexpected, and not exactly wanted.

"Hey, Danny," said Rain nonchalantly. "We were just talking about you."

Nancy gave herself a mental groan. Rain was good in certain social contexts, but in others, she was not. The young genius had been accurate about her social fumbling in some respects.

Danny walked toward Rain, and he held a sheet of paper in his hands, but he didn't say anything. He didn't look at Nancy as he focused his attention upon Rain.

"I found something interesting you might want to look at," he said. "I found it online from the Frankfurt Scientific Community in Germany."

He handed the paper to Rain, and she gave the sheet a brief once-over.

"This *is* interesting," she said. "This reaffirms my theory that every universe vibrates on a different frequency…Thanks, Danny. This is a big help."

"Hopefully, it helps with your project," said Danny in reply.

"Oh, this isn't for me," said Rain matter-of-factly. "This is for Nancy."

Danny frowned, and this caused Nancy to wince before he actually said anything. She knew something unhappy was coming her way, but there was nothing she could do about it but grit her teeth and bear it.

"Never mind," he said in a gruff voice.

He turned to leave, and he got a few steps away before Nancy decided to react.

Danny was a giant social outcast, he was kind of creepy with his morose behavior, and being anywhere near him was like being near a plague carrier, but Nancy knew she had honestly wronged him, and she couldn't let things go on this way without trying to repair that damage.

Still…he was *such* a dork. His clothes were way out of style, his hair was always a little greasy like he hadn't washed it, and he sometimes talked to himself…and all of that was when he was human. Nancy had no idea how being such an outcast could carry over multiple universes, but the thought of that gave her a sudden stab of sympathy for him, so she had to say *something*…It was the right thing to do.

"Danny, wait!" she said unhappily.

He stiffened at the sound of her voice, but he turned to look at her anyway.

"I'm sorry," she said unhappily, and Nancy felt her own pride slither down her throat.

He didn't say anything as he looked down at the grass beneath his feet, but his dark eyes seemed to stare at nothing, as if he were deep in thought. Nancy did not know what she could possibly say to make things right, but she gave it her best shot anyway.

"I was wrong," she said. "Please, don't hate me. I made a mistake."

It took him a few seconds, but when he replied, he did not look at her, and she could not blame him for that.

"Okay," he said in a quiet voice. "I guess…Whatever."

He turned around and walked back to his own yard, and Nancy felt a little better over his response, as short as it happened to be. She watched him go, but he stopped before he reached his yard, mumbled something to himself, turned around, and came trudging back up to them. He stared at her for a moment without saying anything, but this only made Nancy nervous. Danny was weird enough, and she did not know what he was going to do.

After what seemed like an eternity, he finally spoke.

"Why did you think I spread a rumor?" he asked.

Nancy was not sure how she was going to answer that question. It occurred to her that maybe Danny was dangerous; maybe he was one of those weird silent types that just up and slaughters their family without so much as a hint of warning, and this thought made her even more nervous, so she decided to lie.

"I…I told you," she stammered. "Brinn Clevenger told me you spread it."

Danny frowned and shook his head, and Nancy felt a little spike of fear stab through her.

"So?" he replied. "She was lying. Why did you believe her? You never even checked out her story to see if it was true."

Nancy looked over to Rain for help, but the eccentric young woman was looking upon both of them with wide eyes, and those were her "panic" eyes, so there was no help forthcoming there…Nancy was on her own.

"I don't…I don't know!" stammered Nancy.

She was lying, of course, but that was due to fear…Plus, she didn't want to make the situation worse by acknowledging the fact that Danny was a social pariah.

"I thought Brinn was my friend," said Nancy quickly. "There wasn't any reason for me to…to *not* believe her."

Danny lowered his head as if in thought and whispered something to himself.

It was the way he dressed, how he kept to himself, and how he *talked* to himself that freaked her out, and that was why she had immediately placed the blame upon him. However, the truth was that he was innocent in the matter; she knew that, but that didn't make dealing with him any easier.

Danny was one of those people that had to be *dealt* with, not interacted with, and Nancy had a firm grasp of who belonged on each of those two lists. In the past, she had simply avoided people she had to *deal* with, but at this moment, she did not have that option. She *had* to deal with him.

He looked up at her and frowned at first, but then he nodded his head once to himself as if in agreement with…whatever voices he was talking to.

"Well…" he said slowly, "if anyone says anything else about me…then you should come to me first. I don't do…I didn't do anything."

"I know that," said Nancy quickly, but inside she was feeling some relief.

It looked like Danny was coming around…or at the very least, being less weird.

"I'm sorry," continued Nancy. "I should have known better anyway, so…so it's not your fault."

"Good," said Danny brusquely.

He took a moment to look at Weirdo run across Rain's backyard before turning his attention back upon the both of them. He stared up and into the distance for a moment as if he were thinking, but what he said immediately set Nancy on edge.

"Why do you want to know all this stuff on multiple universes?" he asked.

That was the one question Nancy did *not* want to hear. Rain was the only person she could really trust with that information, and even if Danny had not spread the dirty rumor that was floating around about her, he was still too…too *weird* for her to trust with that.

"I can't really tell anybody what happened anyway," she thought in sudden anxiety. *"They'll either think I'm crazy and I'll get locked up, or they'll notify the authorities and I'll get taken away to some secret government lab. As it stands, my family thinks that what I said about Breckenridge was a result of my concussion, so I'll just let them believe that. They don't need to know the truth. Nobody but Rain needs to know the truth."*

She decided to lie again.

"It's a hobby of mine," she said after a moment of silent thought. "I…I just think it's fascinating. I'm not really into science fiction, but I…like the idea of multiple universes, and I was…was thinking of writing a book about it."

"Oh…" replied Danny. "Wait…You like to write?"

Nancy was not sure how to answer that question. The truth was that she most definitely did *not* like to write; she did not think she had any talent for it, but she could not recant on her lie now. He would know something was up.

"Oh…uhhh…yeah," she said in stupid reply.

"What do you write?" he asked her.

Nancy realized that she was now laying down a long track of lies, and she was going to get hit by that train eventually, but she couldn't think of anything else to do in light of the situation…so she simply laid down more tracks.

"R…Romance mostly," she stammered, "but I think the idea of multiple universes is cool, so I was…I was going to write a romance about two people from different universes falling in love."

"Oh," said Danny with a shrug. "I like to write science fiction and fantasy. I'm writing a fantasy novel right now. I'm about halfway done with it. I think it's going to be four or five hundred pages long, but…I haven't decided."

His choice of genres were the two subsections of media and literature that Nancy could not stand, and this only reaffirmed the awkwardness of having to talk to him, but she had gotten herself into this mess via her own clueless stupidity, so she decided to humor him.

"I…I'm not really into science fiction and fantasy," she replied, "but I do think the multiple universes thing is something that hasn't been done a lot, and it's actually interesting to me, so I was going to…I mean…I *have* been doing research on it to give me ideas. Rain's been helping me with that."

Rain looked between the two of them and finally decided to step in.

"Yeah," agreed Rain. "I also think the idea of multiple universes is fascinating, so Nancy and I agree on this one. I don't really like romances, but this gives me an opportunity to study the multiverse theories that are floating around out there…In fact, you could benefit from this research too, Danny. You write science fiction."

"Yeah," shrugged Danny. "I can help out, I guess. I guess we can all write different stories about it."

"Well," said Rain in sheepish honesty, "my interest is purely academic, but it's still genuine."

"That's fine," said Danny.

He looked back over his shoulder and then turned to address them both. His mannerisms were weird to Nancy, just as weird as everything else about him. He just came off as…*weird.*

"I think this was easier when I hated him," she thought in unhappy retrospect.

"I gotta go," said Danny in blunt reply. "My mom is coming home with takeout from Dragon Heart of China."

"Oh, I love that place!" said Rain in excitement.

She frowned a second later, but Nancy already knew why.

"*Luuckkyy,*" pouted Rain. "My parents might go there once a year."

Danny gave her a weak smile and shook his head.

"Anyway," he said, "I'll see you."

He then turned and walked off without another word, and this time he did go. He disappeared around the edge of Rain's backyard fence, and Rain turned to Nancy as soon as he had left.

"That went well," she said dryly.

"I guess," replied Nancy. "Still…I don't think you should have asked for his help."

"Why?" asked Rain in audible confusion. "We need all the help we can get. Besides…he doesn't know the real reason you're studying multiple universes…and that was a good lie, by the way."

"There's no such thing as a good lie," frowned Nancy. "A lie is a lie."

She felt bummed out all of the sudden, and that was not because she had lied. It was a combination of everything…her shifting, her controlling mother, that rumor…

Rain noticed something was up.

"What's that look for?" asked Rain. "You looked like you were about to cry there for a second."

Nancy frowned and shook her head.

"I just…I have so much stress," she said unhappily. "There's just too much going on, and this…this shifting's at the top of it, but…every time I see Danny, I get reminded of that rumor. It bothers me."

"Well," said Rain thoughtfully, "*I* know what the rumor was…but do you?"

Nancy could not help but look at her genius friend as if she had suddenly become stupid.

"Of course, I do!" she hissed.

Rain backed off a little, but Nancy quickly recanted her hostile attitude.

"I'm sorry," she frowned. "I really am. This whole mess has me wired…Anyway, you know what the rumor is, Rain. Why would you even ask that?"

"Because you shifted to an entirely new universe, Nance," explained Rain. "Maybe the rumor changed from your original universe. It might be different."

"Oh," replied Nancy in surprise.

She had not thought of that little contingency. She really did not want to repeat the nasty little rumor that had been spread around school, but she needed to know if it had changed.

"The rumor is…" hesitated Nancy. "The rumor is that I…I posted a very nasty encounter with Bobby

Schmidt on 'my' Friends and More Space page. I don't even *have* an F and M page. Not that it would matter. I would never do what it said in that rumor anyway!"

Rain gave her a sheepish look and nodded her head yes a couple of times.

"Yep," she confirmed. "That's it. I guess that *hasn't* changed."

"That's what I was afraid of," sighed Nancy. "That hasn't changed at all."

"I have the address," shrugged Rain. "We could always go look it up and see what's on it."

Nancy could not help but look upon her best friend with a twinge of horror.

"What!" she said in disbelief. "I don't want to see that!"

Rain cocked her head to one side again, and that motion was inherently funny due to the fact that it reminded Nancy of a cockatiel, but she did not feel like laughing this time.

"Why?" asked Rain. "It can't possibly be your page, Nance!...err...can it?"

"No!" protested Nancy. "I've never done anything like that! I'm not an idiot."

"I know," said Rain. "I was just making sure. Even so, you don't have an F and M page, so we might as well check it out and see exactly what the heck is even on there."

"I...I don't know," stammered Nancy.

Part of her wanted to see it, but another part of her was afraid to see it, and yet another part of her knew that this fear was irrational, because she had *never* done anything like that or had even *thought* about doing something like that. Only a fool would post something like that on an F and M page anyway; it was social suicide.

"We need to know, Nance," frowned Rain. "I've never looked at it myself, so I can't just tell you. If I could,

I would. Right now, we need to go check it out, or it's just going to eat at you…like it's been doing this whole time."

Nancy felt strange inside over the matter, but she knew deep down that Rain was right.

"Fine," she said in a defeated tone. "Let's go do this real fast…You're right…I need to know. I don't want to see it, but you're right."

They walked inside Rain's house and made their way down the wooden steps of her basement.

Rain's parents let her make a little hidey-hole in the basement where her PC was parked; it was where Rain did most of her thinking. Rain called it her "man cave minus the man." Nancy never really did understand the humor in that description, though, but that was Rain for you. Rain had an odd sense of humor.

Rain sat down in her swivel chair, grabbed her mouse, clicked onto the net and waited patiently as her browser popped up on the screen. She typed in the address, and both of them waited in breathless silence for the supposed "page" to pop up…and it did.

"Oh, my…" said Rain in a strange tone.

Nancy's picture was on the page, and there was an account in her name, but that was just the tip of the iceberg. It was the long and incredibly painful post about Bobby Schmidt that immediately caught Nancy's attention, as well as Rain's attention.

Her eccentric friend read off a tiny part of the post in a flat and monotone way, but her vocalization did not displace the agonizing embarrassment of its content. It was horrifying to listen to, so it was a definite mercy to hear Rain's voice trail off as the post went on.

"Guess what, ladies," she droned, "Bobby Schmidt is hotter than we all thought. He took me up on my offer. We met up behind the bleachers behind the track, and we…uhhh…oh..."

Rain shook her head in stupefied amazement.

"Oh, wow," she said in a strange voice. "That is…graphic."

"I know!" hissed Nancy.

Rain jumped a little at more of Nancy's hostility, but this time Nancy did not recant on that tone of voice. No, this time tears reached her eyes, and unlike the day before, those tears were not a sticky sap but real tears, so she let them flow.

Rain looked up at her with an expression of real sympathy.

"Hey," said the eccentric girl in a quiet voice. "Hey now, it's not you. Anyone who takes two seconds to look at it can tell that it's not you."

Nancy nodded her head in understanding, but that didn't make her feel any better. She swallowed hard and wiped away at her tears.

"Anyone could have seen this," choked Nancy. "Bobby must have seen it! He had to have heard about it. He must have seen it."

"Does he even know how to use the net?" chuckled Rain.

Rain's off-color humor was infectious, and Nancy couldn't help but laugh a little, even though she was still crying somewhat. Nevertheless, it angered her, the whole of it, and she could not let it go.

"Brinn must have posted this," said Nancy in a wavering voice.

"She clearly wanted Bobby for herself," said Rain sympathetically. "She must have known you don't have a Friends and More Space page. All she had to do was get a picture of you from your mom's page."

"Why does my mom do such stupid things!" hissed Nancy. "Doesn't she know not to post anything about me!"

"You never told her," shrugged Rain. "Plus, she's proud of her kids."

"That doesn't help me now," frowned Nancy.

Rain shook her head and laid a sympathetic hand on her shoulder.

"It doesn't matter," said Rain softly. "It's not you. You know it's not you, Nance, so it doesn't matter."

Nancy wanted to listen, but she felt a terrible darkness tug at her heart.

"It matters to me," she scowled.

Her tears came again, and she wiped them away, but it was futile.

"I hate Brinn!" she choked out in angry response. "I hate her! I'd like to rip the feathers off her head and glue them to her back!"

Rain's eyes widened at this angry statement.

"Wow," she replied in a surprised tone. "I'd pay money to see that."

Nancy chuckled a little at that statement, and they both shared a quiet little laugh over the image. Rain somehow always made her feel better about herself and about life in general, and Nancy was suddenly glad that Rain was her friend.

Rain was her lifeline now. In the past, Nancy had never thought she had ever needed one, a friend that you desperately needed to help you get through the hard times, a real and honest lifeline, so she decided to vocalize that realization; she felt she needed to.

"I'm glad you're my friend, Rain," she sniffed.

"What?" asked Rain in confusion.

"I'm glad you're my friend," repeated Nancy, albeit in a shaky voice. "I don't know what I'd do if you weren't around. I just…I just couldn't deal with this at all without you."

"And I'm glad you're my friend, Fancy," said Rain with a soft smile. "I really am. You help me all the time too, so…I'm glad too."

Nancy just had to accept that their friendship was a good enough armor against the trials she was sure to face, because her shifting had not stopped, and she did not know if it ever would.

Chapter 5...The Fifth Shift

Nancy woke up on time again, sat up, and stretched. She looked down at her hands, but today they looked absolutely normal, like normal human hands, and she only had two arms and two legs, so things were already off to a good start. She rubbed her eyes, yawned, and then smacked her lips, but everything felt normal.

"This is starting out good," she said to herself, and her voice sounded perfectly normal this time. "Maybe things are back to normal now."

She hopped out of bed and walked to the bathroom, flipped on the light, and smiled as she looked in the mirror. Her smile faded as she stared at her reflection, for though she looked perfectly normal in almost every aspect, the one glaring difference in her appearance was a truly startling one.

Though her long brown hair flowed down from both sides of her head, there was a giant bald spot that streaked right down the center of her pate. She reached up to the back of her head and realized that it looped all the way down to the back of her neck, like a giant shiny bald track she could run a toy car across.

"*Ewwww!*" she said unhappily. "I'd rather be a spider again than have this...It's...This is...eww."

She took off her clothes in order to take a quick morning shower, and that's when she noticed the rest of the disturbing change that the new day had brought. She caught sight of it in the mirror when she turned around, the thick streak of hair that ran down the center of her back, the same color and texture as the hair on her head, and this caused her even more distress.

"*Really?*" she asked herself in disbelief. "It's like the hair on my head went to my back!...Oh, I can't wait for this day to end. I would rather be a lizard or a fly or anything else but *this*. This is just…*wrong*."

She took her shower and then spent five minutes attempting to blow-dry the hair on her back. It struck a surreal chord in her, and she realized that each shift was probably going to be just as disturbing, so she was just going to have to get used to it.

She went to her dresser, put on her undergarments, pulled out a blue T-shirt with a large white #1 symbol upon it, slipped into her T-shirt, pulled out a pair of her favorite blue jeans, and then slipped into them as well.

There was a knock at her door, and her mother poked her head in a second later.

"Good morning, sunshine," said her mom.

The woman's head was identical to Nancy's in terms of baldness, so Nancy could only assume that her mother had a long mane of hair on her back as well. Still, that did not excuse the older woman's intrusions upon her privacy. It was an old, *very* old umbrage that Nancy held against her mother, and that had not gone away, even with the advent of her dimensional shifting. It was infuriating.

"Mom!" she said in exasperation. "Why do you do this to me? Please, don't just barge in. I could have been naked or something."

"I've seen you naked," frowned her mother. "I gave birth to you, young lady."

Nancy rolled her eyes and shook her head. She had expected the older woman to say something like that, but she had still hoped that her mother would do something unexpected, like remain silent for the rest of the year.

"Don't give me that look," said her mother. "I came up here to ask if you wanted eggs or pancakes for breakfast."

"What?" asked Nancy in disbelief. "I don't have time for that! I have to catch the bus!"

"Catch the bus?" asked her mother in strange surprise. "There's no school today. It's Awareness Day. Did you forget already?"

"Awareness Day?" asked Nancy. "What in the heck is Awareness Day?"

Her mother looked upon her as if Nancy were bleeding out of her eyes. It was both concerning and a little insulting, but Nancy was only interested in the answer she was sure to receive for asking that question.

"Did you hit your head?" asked her mother. "Never mind. Do you want eggs or pancakes?"

The older woman had not answered her question, but Nancy did not want to push it. She did not want her parents to notice anything unusual about her, and forgetting an entire holiday qualified as "unusual." It was a moot point, however, as Rain would fill her in on the details of said "Awareness Day" anyway.

"Eggs, I guess," said Nancy hesitantly.

"Come down when you're ready," said her mother.

The older woman walked off to go downstairs, but Nancy was left feeling slightly confused.

"There's no school today?" she thought. *"Did I miss something?...No...I couldn't have missed anything. This must be because I shifted...but I didn't think holidays changed with each shift...Wait...Maybe they don't. Maybe this is just a one-time deal. Still, I have no idea what this 'Awareness Day' is. I'll definitely have to find out from Rain."*

Nancy sat down on her bed and slipped on her socks, but that was the moment that something else caught her eye. It was something that she had gotten used to, so used to, in fact, that it took her this long to realize that it was missing. She had not even caught this little but very obvious change when she had been taking her shower.

"Where is my cast?" she thought as she stared at her right arm.

Her cast was indeed missing. She felt her right wrist with her left hand, but there was no pain and no indication that her wrist had ever been broken. It was weird, but once again, she had no choice but to assign blame to the fact that she was shifting, so she wrote it off as good fortune, because she really didn't want to wear the itchy thing anymore.

"I need to talk to Rain about this," she thought. *"Maybe she has a theory about why things are so wonky today…Wait a minute, my notebook!"*

Nancy quickly pulled up her pillow and breathed a sigh of relief at the sight of her green notebook. She opened it, flipped through the pages, and felt her breath catch in her throat as she looked upon the previous day's entry.

"It's still there!" she thought in excitement. *"Rain is going to flip!"*

She looked down at the instant photo glued to the page before her. It showed in distinct detail Nancy and her eccentric friend's downy feathers and long glistening head plumage, and Nancy realized that this was all the evidence she would ever need to fully convince Rain that Nancy, herself, was indeed shifting.

"Yes, yes, yes!" she said happily. "This is going to be a good day!"

She looked up from her notebook toward the bathroom and spied the bathroom mirror through the open door, and this reminded her of her current look.

"Well, maybe not that great," she frowned.

✶✶✶✶✶

Nancy biked to her best friend's house. Even though there was no school, today was turning out to be a crappy day. Her dad and her brother looked perfectly *fine*; they each had a good full head of hair, and this bothered Nancy in its cosmic unfairness.

She moved her bike around to the backyard as always, and naturally her friend was in the backyard with her dog, waiting as if she had known that Nancy was going to show up, even though Rain had had no warning beforehand.

"How do you always know when I'm going to show up?" asked Nancy as she walked her bike to the side of the house.

"I don't," replied Rain matter-of-factly. "I just figured because it's Awareness Day, you'd show up soon. Besides, Weirdo had to do his business out here, and I just decided to play fetch with him for a bit."

Nancy gave her friend a once-over. Rain was wearing an old black T-shirt with some band called "Black Death Doornail" on the front in red letters, and she had on a pair of worn-out black cargos, not her usual pair, but Nancy's attention was naturally drawn toward her best friend's hair. Rain had purple streaks in her short dark hair as before, but there was a definite bald track on her head, and Nancy was selfishly glad that the women in her own family were not the only ones to display this genetic error.

Rain noticed her attention and commented upon it.

"What are you looking at?" she asked. "My earrings? You're always pointing them out for some reason."

Rain was indeed wearing a pair of large, brass, crescent-moon earrings, but Nancy had not even noticed those. No, it was the big bald track on the eccentric genius's head that held her attention.

"It's like having your vision drawn to a big ugly wart on someone's nose," she thought in hideous fascination. *"I wonder if that's how others see me? It's so nasty…I hate it…Ugh…Can't WAIT to shift again. I certainly wouldn't want to be stuck in this universe."*

"No, that's not it," said Nancy. "It's your hair…Actually, it's *our* hair to be exact."

"Oh?" asked Rain. "What about our hair?"

"I'm not used to having a big bald streak in it," snorted Nancy. "Not to mention the…ugh…*mane* on my back."

"What do you mean?" asked Rain. "Are you telling me we look like guys in your universe?"

"What?" asked Nancy. "No…unless…well…we have a full head of hair, if that's what you mean."

"Oh," blinked Rain as she processed this.

Nancy could tell that her genius friend was indeed processing this bit of information, as the expression on her face was one of both surprise and disbelief.

"That *is* odd," said Rain after a moment of intense thought. "I can't really imagine that. I just can't seem to picture it. Having hair on my head and not my back?…That *is* weird."

Nancy did not try to argue with her. It occurred to her that, for Rain, her hair had always been this way because she had never shifted; Rain's consciousness was always stable within *this* particular universe, so she could not see the differences between them.

"Never mind," said Nancy with a wave. "Let me get my notebook. You *have* to see this."

"Oh?" asked Rain in open curiosity. "Did the picture hold?"

"It did," smiled Nancy.

She opened up the grey metal basket on her bike and pulled out her notebook. Technically, it was Rain's notebook, but since Nancy had it twenty-four-seven, she thought of it as hers anyway.

"Are you lying to me?" asked Rain. "Don't get me wrong, I would *love* it if you were a dimensionaut, but part of me still thinks you're full of it. I mean, like I said…I *want* to believe you, but…"

Nancy opened up her notebook, looked down at the glued-on photograph, and handed the open page to her.

Rain took one look at it, and her dark eyes goggled outward in surprise as her mouth opened up in a gasp.

"But that's not the picture we took yesterday!" she exclaimed. "How is this possible!"

Nancy felt a little annoyed at this response. She had honestly thought that her best friend was past any disbelief, that she believed Nancy wholeheartedly, but apparently Nancy herself had been wrong on this little fact, and that kind of hurt her a little.

"I thought you believed me," she said, and she couldn't help but sound a little hurt.

"Well…" said Rain in sheepish reply, "I kind of did, but I also didn't. I work with evidence, Nance. Scientific data."

Nancy motioned toward the notebook in Rain's hands.

"And?" asked Nancy. "What do you call this?"

Rain closed her eyes, took in a deep breath through her nose, and exhaled slowly. Nancy was familiar with this little nuance of her eccentric friend…It meant Rain was about to explain an epiphany.

"Considering it would be impossible for you to fake this with what limited knowledge and facilities you have to work with in such a short time," replied Rain, "that time being the amount of time it took for you to leave my house, go to your house, interact with your family, and then go to bed…I have no choice but to assume that you were telling the truth…and if that *is* the case…then that means…Good Lord! That means there really was a Breckenridge Institute…"

"Of Discovery," finished Nancy. "It did explode, and now I'm shifting every day. I wasn't making it up."

"Well, then," said Rain as her eyes widened for a brief second. "Let's keep documenting everything…and more importantly…let's keep this to ourselves."

"Agreed," said Nancy. "You don't have to tell me twice on that."

"Okay, then," nodded Rain.

Nancy studied her best friend for a moment. She could tell by the slight tremor in Rain's hands and by the girl's jitteriness in general that Rain actually believed her this time, truly *believed* her, and that gave Nancy some well-deserved satisfaction.

She motioned toward the notebook again and smiled.

"So what do you think of the picture?" she asked.

"It's adorable," said Rain with a grin. "You look so precious…like a…a…human parrot…or a…a cockatiel."

Nancy laughed at that apt description and stood next to her friend so they could both inspect the picture together.

"That's you," she said as she pointed at Rain's image.

"Huh," replied Rain thoughtfully. "I'm all grey with black feathers…It's not flashy like your plumage, but it suits me, methinks, methinks."

"I guess it does," said Nancy. "But anyway…what do you think about all this? Now that you know it's all real, what do you think about it?"

Rain tilted her head to her right and gave her a quizzical look. This was the normal look that Nancy was so familiar with, and it was only marginally marred by the bald streak on the young woman's head.

"What's there to think?" asked Rain in disbelief. "You're shifting along dimensional lines to whole new universes…*if* my theory is correct, and that's still a big if. The truth is, Nance, that I don't really know *what's* happing to you…I mean, I suppose *everything* could be shifting along a dimensional line and you're the only one that remembers, but according to Occam's Razor, the simplest explanation is usually the correct one, and my original theory is the simpler and more plausible one, so I'm going with it."

It occurred to Nancy that she had forgotten something important that she had wanted to ask.

"That reminds me," she said quickly. "I need to ask this before I forget…What is 'Awareness Day'? I have no idea what that is. I've never heard of it before."

"*Really*?" asked Rain. "It's a special day set aside for everyone to appreciate what others do for you in your life. Everything closes down on Awareness Day, like school, for instance, and you're supposed to do something nice for someone you care about...or do something nice for someone you like, if you're not close with anyone."

"*Oooooh*," said Nancy as comprehension set in. "That's why Mom made us breakfast on a weekday…I guess that's why she came to my room this morning."

"Exactly," said Rain. "That's how it works."

Nancy frowned as she thought about this. She'd had no way of knowing what Awareness Day was, so she had not done anything nice for Rain, and this bothered her. Rain had been her best friend for…well…*forever*…and she had the feeling that *this* universe's Nancy would have done something for her every year.

"I'm sorry, Rain," she said unhappily. "I didn't know about Awareness Day…I…I didn't know…or I would have done something for you."

Rain elbowed her and grinned.

"You already did," she said happily. "You showed me this! This evidence made my day, Fance…Heck, it made my entire year! This is possibly the greatest scientific discovery ever made in the *entire* history of mankind…It's phenomenal!...Thanks for that, by the way."

"I guess," shrugged Nancy.

She did not think that simply proving she wasn't lying was an action she had actively done to appreciate her friend, but Rain seemed okay with it, so she was just going to have to accept that…but it still didn't seem like it was enough.

"Maybe I can do something for her tomorrow," she thought. *"I'll just explain about today if there's no 'Awareness Day' in the next universe."*

Her thoughts were interrupted by the familiar presence of Danny Princeton as he rounded Rain's fence and entered her backyard. Rain looked up from their precious green notebook and gave him a courtesy greeting.

"Hey, Danny," she smiled. "Happy Awareness Day."

Danny looked exactly like he had in Nancy's original universe, although he was wearing a plain black T-shirt and black pants like he had on Monday. He had short black hair with long bangs that hung down the sides of his face, and his expression was so gloomy that Nancy suddenly remembered why nobody liked him.

Aside from the fact that he was so awkward looking, everything about him was dark; he was just so emo…or goth…or whatever it was that everybody else called those outdated fads that worked like people repellent. Plus, his hair was always slightly greasy like he hadn't washed it, and he was always mumbling to himself and…

Nancy caught herself before she could be sucked down into that derogatory spiral; she had been down that troubling mental road already. As it stood, she really did not know him very well, but she could not help but feel sorry for him because of these very noticeable social flaws…though the fact that she had hated him just yesterday was not lost on her.

He walked up to them and gave them a nod, but his slouching shoulders and gloomy expression were obvious indicators that his day was off to a bad start; at least, it looked that way to Nancy.

"What's wrong?" she asked without thinking. "You look down."

Danny's profile straightened as he lifted his downcast gaze and looked at her in confusion.

"I…I didn't realize we were talking now…" he stammered.

"What do you mean?" asked Nancy in equal confusion. "I told you yesterday that I was sorry for treating you badly. I'm not going to do that anymore…although I may take Brinn Clevenger's head off…that lying pig."

Danny gave a short chuckle, and his demeanor improved somewhat. He did not comment upon Nancy's personal vendetta against Miss Clevenger, but instead changed the direction of the conversation to something that had caught his attention, something that Nancy had forgotten to hide.

"What are you two looking at?" he asked.

"The project we're working on," said Rain matter-of-factly. "Take a look."

Nancy wanted to stop her from handing over the notebook; she did not want anyone else to know what was going on with her, but Rain handed it over before she could even say anything. Nancy simply watched in horror as Danny flipped through the few pages they had so far.

"This is a neat idea," said Danny with an impressed look. "You've put a lot of work into it. The makeup in this picture is first rate. I like the detail you put into the feathers…although having a picture of the bug drawing on this page would be better."

"That's supposed to be a spider hybrid," said Rain nonchalantly. "And before you ask, I didn't come up with any of this. This was all Nance."

Nancy had no idea what Rain had told Danny in confidence, but it was clear he had no idea everything in the notebook was…well…*real*, so she was not going to rock that boat. Nevertheless, Danny looked up at her as if seeing her for the first time, and this bothered Nancy a little bit, though she did not know why.

"This was your idea?" he asked.

"Y…yes," stammered Nancy. "It's a project I…I've wanted to do for a long time. It goes hand-in-hand with the book I want to write…that…that Rain is helping me with."

"That's why she was upset yesterday when she heard I was talking to you about it," explained Rain. "This is *her* project, and she doesn't want anyone stealing her ideas, but she doesn't know you like I do. I know you wouldn't give anything away to anyone."

"No," said Danny with a slight frown. "No, I wouldn't."

Nancy winced at his tone. It was a clear indication that he was taking this a little more personally than it actually was…not to mention that she flat out hated him yesterday, so there was that.

"It's okay," said Nancy unhappily.

She winced at the very thought of explaining anything to him, but she did it anyway. It was the right thing to do.

"I blamed you for something you didn't do," she continued, "so you can understand why I acted the way I did."

"Yeah," replied Danny slowly. "I guess…It's cool…Yeah."

"Good," frowned Nancy, "because I haven't been having a good day."

Rain tilted her head to her right as she looked up at her in surprise. Her left eyebrow raised as she did this, and this simple action made Nancy feel a little better, if only because it was something "normal" that Rain did quite often, and normalcy was on short supply for Nancy as of late. She grabbed onto "normalcy" wherever she could find it.

"Oh?" asked Rain. "You didn't tell me that. What's wrong?"

"I look hideous; that's what," replied Nancy. "You know what I'm talking about. I look so bad that I'm just counting down the minutes until tomorrow."

"You don't look hideous," said Danny in flat reply. "You still look pretty to me…"

Nancy looked over to him in surprise. Danny's eyes widened as realization of what he had just said dawned upon him, and his cheeks turned a mild red. Rain simply laughed at his awkward expression.

"Stop laughing," said Nancy as she elbowed her eccentric friend in the side. "If someone thinks I'm pretty, then I'm pretty. You don't have to laugh about it. That just reinforces the belief that I'm ugly."

Rain looked up at her in surprise, but that surprise quickly turned into a smirk.

"Mrowrrr!" she said as she made a clawing motion in the air. "Phhht! Phhht!"

"Very funny," frowned Nancy.

It occurred to Nancy that perhaps Danny was throwing out an olive branch to her, and compliments were in some way expected upon this "Awareness Day," so she decided to thank him for it.

"Thank you, Danny," she said as she turned toward him.

Danny didn't say anything but looked down at the ground and scratched the back of his neck with his right hand.

She had realized this before, but Nancy reaffirmed it within her own mind a second time…She did not really know him very well. He was invisible at school for the most part, and he had only appeared on her radar because of the Brinn Clevenger incident, so trying to discern his personality and his personal reactions was somewhat difficult.

She figured he had been honest about his statement; it was an honest observation he had made, and now he was a little embarrassed by it.

Nancy figured him to be like a crab that carried around a shell. When things were too much for him, he hid inside his shell and waited until he could function again. This shell was his reticence, his inability to cope with reality coupled with his ability to push others away by not saying anything, so seeing the real him outside of this shell was a difficult task.

"I guess that was your Awareness Day gift," said Nancy. "I'll take it. I need to feel good about myself sometimes."

"Yeah, okay," shrugged Danny.

"We're not doing anything today, Danny," said Rain. "Do you want to hang out? We were just killing time anyway."

"I don't know," said Danny. "I'm supposed to join a raid on World of Battlecry."

"Well, then," replied Rain. "Well, then, you'd better go. You can't miss a raid. You'll miss out on the loot."

"That's what Jason's doing today," said Nancy. "He's always online…like every spare second. I never get a chance to use the computer."

"You only have one?" asked Danny.

"*Yeah,*" said Nancy warily. "My family's not made of money. PCs are expensive anymore. I had a smartphone with Wi-Fi, but it died on me. It actually shocked my hand when it self-destructed."

"That sucks," said Danny. "Was it old?"

"No," said Rain in flat reply. "She just got it for her birthday."

"Oh," frowned Danny. "That *really* sucks, then."

"Tell me something I don't know," sighed Nancy.

Rain took that as a cue to change the subject, so she gingerly took the green notebook back from Danny. She flipped open their precious research data and took one last look at her own picture.

"So, Danny…" she said while still looking at the grainy photo. "What do you think about multiple universes? Do you think we'll cross dimensional lines one day?"

"I don't know," shrugged Danny. "Maybe…but the way I figure, humans won't be able to do that until thousands of years from now, and that's only if it's possible. Maybe there aren't multiple universes…It's all hearsay anyway."

"Oh, I wish that were true," thought Nancy in a sudden strike of bitterness.

Rain looked up from their notebook and gave Danny a wry grin.

"Why do you think that?" she asked coyly.

"Because…" explained Danny, "we don't have the technology to do anything like that. You're talking about punching a hole in our reality, about going somewhere outside the known laws of our universe…what little we know of our universe anyway."

"You don't think there are multiple universes overlapping one another?" asked Rain. "Like set on a different frequency?"

"Maybe…I don't know," said Danny. "I mean, our universe is set to Pi, it has to be."

"Agreed," said Rain thoughtfully. "That does seem to be the most logical number. The more random things appear, the more they come closer and closer to Pi, so our best guess would be 3.14159…something…something…infinity."

"Gee, that was accurate," snickered Nancy.

"Geez, give me a break," smiled Rain. "It's an infinite number…At least, we think it's infinite. If it has an end, we haven't found it yet."

"Even so," replied Danny, "it's just an off-hand theory. The whole multiple universes thing is just conjecture. I mean, the people that believe there are multiple universes are probably the same ones that believe lizard people secretly rule the world."

"The heck you say!" smiled Rain. "You mean they don't?"

Danny smiled a little at that. It occurred to Nancy that she had not seen Danny smile very often, and this got her to thinking about what he was like around his friends, but then she had the sudden realization that Danny probably didn't *have* many friends, and Rain was probably the closest thing he had in that respect.

"That's probably why he just walks into her backyard without calling or anything," she thought. *"Normally, that would be a rude intrusion of privacy, but Rain seems to encourage it…I wonder if he likes Rain?…I don't know if I want to follow that little wonder…It's a disturbing thought…Ugh…Danny is just…He's so weird…"*

She was snapped from her wayward musing by a gentle push from her best friend. Nancy looked down at Rain in startled surprise, but the eccentric genius simply smiled back at her.

"You back with us?" asked Rain. "I asked you a question, but you were just staring off into space."

"Oh," said Nancy sheepishly. "I was thinking…Never mind. What was your question?"

"Do you think there are lizard people who secretly rule the world?" asked Rain.

"What?" asked Nancy in complete confusion. "I…What are you talking about? Lizard people? I just thought Danny was making a joke…"

"It's an actual conspiracy theory," smirked Rain. "It's been a popular one for some time now."

"*Really?*" asked Nancy in no small wonder. "I've never heard of that."

Rain chuckled and Danny gave a short laugh. Nancy's cheeks burned as she realized they were making fun of her over her lack of knowledge on the subject.

"Stop laughing at me," she frowned. "How was I supposed to know anything about a stupid lizard conspiracy?"

This only made Rain laugh harder, but Danny simply smiled and stared down at the grass.

Nancy did not want to feel embarrassed over something so stupid, but her cheeks burned a bright red anyway. She felt helpless when it came to comparing her own intellect with Rain's, and her eccentric friend's laughter was only driving forth more embarrassment, embarrassment that Nancy did not want nor need, because she was already sensitive about her "average" IQ.

"Stop it," she said unhappily.

"Your face!" laughed Rain. "It's so red! You look like a strawberry!"

Nancy did not want to get angry, especially not at Rain, but her temper got the best of her. She did not like being made fun of, especially in front of a stranger, and Danny was, at best, a stranger.

"Yeah, and why don't I take a marker to that bald streak on your stupid head," she frowned. "I'll draw a dirty picture on it while you're asleep."

Rain's smile wilted as she took a step back due to the look, tone, and content of Nancy's retort.

"Hey!" she said uncertainly. "What are you…Are you mad at me?"

This situation was stupid, it was juvenile and irrelevant, but the pressure Nancy felt in general, that stress she had over this whole shifting business…it made her crack, and her eyes welled up with tears. She wiped some tears away as Rain's face fell at the sight of it.

"Hey, now," replied her friend. "I wasn't trying to be mean. It's nothing to cry about…"

Nancy suddenly realized that Danny was still in her presence, and to cry in front of him…She did not like that at all. She had already shed tears once before in front of him, but she had thought him a stranger at the time, but this time was different. This time she knew who it was who was standing in front of her, and…she did not like it.

"I…I'd better get back to playing World of Battlecry," said Danny in a nervous tone.

"No, wait," said Rain quickly. "I want to take a picture with you."

"What?" asked both Nancy and Danny at the same time.

"Yeah…for the notebook," explained Rain.

This was a phenomenally bad idea. It occurred to Nancy that if Danny saw himself in his own photo, then he would know something strange was going on…She wasn't sure if tampering with an instant camera photo was even possible once it was taken. Whatever they were all going to look like tomorrow, or the day after that, or the day after that…it was going to change, and the photo would not. Danny was going to ask how they had altered the photo, and that was not good.

Rain, however, had an entirely different opinion upon the subject.

"Wait right here!" she said in excitement. "I'll go get my dad's camera!"

Rain took off toward her house and disappeared within without so much as another word, leaving Nancy stranded with Danny, and this was bad, because Nancy was still wiping tears from her eyes.

They both stood there in awkward silence for what felt like an eternity. Nancy had nothing to say to him, and even if she had wanted to say something, she had no idea *what* to say. Danny was a nerd, a dork…a…a social punching bag, and his interests were so far apart from hers that it was like making contact with an alien from outer space. She wouldn't even know where to begin.

Danny rocked backwards upon his heels and shoved his hands into his pockets. He looked truly uncomfortable, but what he did next surprised her…He made a clever joke.

"So," he said sheepishly. "So, uhhh…how about this weather, huh?"

Nancy gave a mild laugh without meaning to, and Danny followed suit.

Asking about the weather was one of the oldest tropes on any kind of media. It was an incredibly stupid thing to ask, because no one ever cared about the weather unless a hurricane was on top of them. It was a joke made in reference to people who had nothing to talk about, and this…*this* made Nancy laugh. It was stupid, but it made her laugh *because* it was stupid, so she gave Danny a few positive points in her own mind, a few notches up the ladder in respectability.

"Gee," she replied, "that there weather, huh? It's just all around us, am I right?"

They both laughed as Nancy wiped away her remaining tears. She felt a little better; that little tangent had worked at calming her down. It was the anxiety and stress, really, all of the pressure from the last few days that was wearing upon her, but at the very least, she knew this already, so that was an advantage for her.

"At least I know I'm stressed out," she thought as she dried her remaining tears. *"That makes things a little easier. Now I can work toward a solution…or at least get used to how things are each day…One day at a time. I've just got to take it one day at a time."*

Rain returned with her father's ancient camera. She held it up to show to Danny as she walked toward the both of them.

"My dad bought this camera thousands of years ago," she grinned, "in the ancient year of 1985. Cool, huh?"

"Yeah," replied Danny. "How does it work?"

"I'll show you," said Rain.

She sandwiched herself between Nancy and Danny and held up the camera at just the right angle. Nancy didn't even have a chance to protest against the action before Rain completely dominated the situation.

"Everyone, say cheese!" said Rain.

She hit the button and took the picture, but Nancy did not like this. She did not want Danny in the pictures, not because he was weird, that was only part of it, but because he was absolutely *not* to know the truth. He was a stranger, really, and Nancy did not trust anyone other than Rain with her secret, a secret that was too important for anyone else to find out, a secret that could possibly get Nancy dragged away by the government, because that was what always happened in the movies, and movies were the only reference point Nancy had on this situation. She was in uncharted territory, and that scared her in a deep psychological way.

*****

Nancy sat down on the living room couch next to her dad. He was currently watching a documentary on World War II, but as far as she could tell, history had not changed in that respect. That war was still considered America's greatest war, Hitler was still the bad guy in it, and a lot of people died because of it.

Nancy was comforted by this fact in a strange way; it was one thing to change bodies every day, but it was entirely another to live in a completely different historical timeline.

Her line of thought was interrupted by the entrance of her mother. The older woman came in through the front door carrying a paper bag full of groceries, but instead of looking happy or focused as she normally did, she looked irritated, and that irritation was directed solely at Nancy. Nancy had no idea what she had done to garner such a look, but whatever this was about, she did not want to deal with it.

"This can't be good," she thought in growing anxiety.

Her mother marched through the living room and into the kitchen where she set down her bag of groceries upon the kitchen table. She immediately marched back into the living room and gave Nancy an unforgiving accusatory stare.

"You need to answer your phone when I call you, young lady," she said unhappily.

"What are you talking about?" asked Nancy in more than slight confusion. "My phone is toast. You know that."

"Excuse me?" asked her mother in growing anger. "Your phone is *toast*? What does *that* mean?"

"It shorted out on Saturday," said Nancy in nervous confusion. "It shocked my hand…You saw it…It's fried…"

"No, no, no," said her mother with an angry shake of her head. "That phone had better not be 'fried'! Do you know how much it cost your father and I?"

"It happened when I had my accident!" protested Nancy. "You saw it after you took me to the emergency room!"

Her father turned and gave her a concerned stare, but her mother was definitely not in a "concerned" mood. She glared at Nancy as if her eyes were about to spontaneously combust.

"Excuse me?" asked her mother. "Are you mocking me? After everything I've done for you today!"

"What are you talking about!" asked Nancy in a panic. "You saw it! Dad opened it up, and it was fried! It was after we came home from the E.R.!"

"Nancy?" asked her father. "I don't remember you having any kind of an accident, and we certainly never went to the hospital on Saturday. Did you hit your head or something? Are you all right?"

Nancy looked in horror upon her father and then her mother. Apparently, there *was* a reason she was no longer in a cast, and that reason was currently hanging her out to dry. Her "accident," the very reason she was in this B-horror movie that was her life, had apparently never happened in this universe, and now she was suffering for it.

"Y…You don't remember?" she asked in a daze.

"Don't entertain her fantasies, Roger!" snapped her mother. "She's broken her brand-new phone, and now she's making up stories like she used to when she was little!"

"I'm not making up anything!" cried Nancy. "I did have an accident on Saturday! I broke my wrist…"

Her voice trailed off as she looked upon her parents' faces. It was clear by the confused and concerned look upon her father's face and the look of sheer disgust upon her mother's face that she was not getting out of this one by telling the truth, and there was no lie that she could think of that would save her, either.

"You're grounded," hissed her mother. "Up to your room…now!"

The older woman pointed toward the stairs, but Nancy knew this was not fair.

"But I didn't do anything!" she whined.

"Now!" shouted her mother.

The older woman's voice was so loud that it caused Nancy and her father to jump a little in their seats. This cut it for Nancy; she felt her emotions boil over, and she was crying even though she didn't want to.

She got up from the couch and bolted up the stairs, more for the sake of getting away from her mother than actually following the older woman's orders, but in truth, she did not want anyone to see her cry, because her life was already complicated and embarrassing enough without a show of tears.

She ran into her bedroom, slammed the door shut, and laid down on her stomach upon her bed. She wept into her hands, but her fingers touched her bald pate, and this caused her to cry even harder. Her bald streak and the hair on her back were nothing more than added insult to injury, and she had officially had enough.

"I hate this!" she thought in mental anguish. *"Why can't everything just go back to normal? Why did this have to happen to me? I'm not like Rain...I don't want to travel to other universes! I don't want to be a 'dimensionaut.' I just want to be normal..."*

She laid there until she ended up falling asleep on her stomach, but sleep did little to ease the depression in her spirit and a longing for the past in her heart.

Chapter 6...The Sixth Shift

Nancy woke up in the clothes she had worn the day before. She pushed up a little from the bed and rolled over, noticed the first of the sun's light entering through her bedroom window, and groaned as she stretched a little.

To her credit, it was the crack of dawn, so she was right on schedule school-wise, but her voice sounded normal, and this worried her a little bit. She did not want to be permanently stuck in a world where women had bald streaks running down the middle of their heads and large tracts of hair on their backs, so her "normal" voice made her heart jump a little, because she still held a silent fear that one day she would just stop shifting and be stuck in a world that was terrible for her.

One quick inspection of her arms and hands, however, changed her mind in a hurry. Her arms were a dark forest-green, and they were covered with very small, kite-shaped scales.

She held her right hand in front of her face and studied it. She had four fingers and an opposable thumb, so that had not changed, but she had large yellowish-white and hooked nails that angled like claws, and the palms of her hands were the same yellowish-white color but soft, not like the scaly hide that resided everywhere else on her skin.

"What...What is this?" she asked herself, but her voice sounded perfectly normal, so there was no change there.

She reached up and felt the top of her head, but she was completely bald, no hair at all, and she felt strange bony ridges that started just above her eyes and traveled over her bald scaly head down to the back of her neck.

She groaned as she got out of bed and walked to her bathroom. Sleeping on her stomach was something she did not normally do, and it had taken its toll in terms of rest, but that did not matter at the moment, because what she really wanted was to inspect herself within the bathroom mirror.

She flipped on the light and looked in the mirror. Her reflection was very reptilian; it reminded her of a human-snake hybrid, but her eyes were still very human, still the same color she was born with, that pleasant hazel she loved to compare to early Autumn, so at least that hadn't changed.

The ridges on her head were of the same hard substance her nails were made from; they were an off-white and somewhat-yellowish color, but they looked like tiny little horns, or perhaps claws or fangs sticking out of her skin. They were weird-looking.

She took off her clothes to prepare for a shower, but she gave herself a once-over before stepping into the tub. Her abdomen, her entire torso, for that matter, was soft and yellowish-white like the palms of her hands, but her back, buttocks, and legs were covered in the dark forest-green scales that she sported upon her face and arms. She had a very small nub of a tail where her actual tailbone was, but she couldn't move it or anything; it was more like a big lump than anything else.

"Oh, well," she said to herself as she stepped into the tub. "This is better than yesterday. What was it that they used to tell us in kindergarten?...I guess you get what you get and you don't throw a fit...It's better than yesterday, so I won't complain."

She thought about this and realized that her situation was all about perspective. Her life was only as bad as she made it out to be. She wanted to be hopeful for the new day, she *needed* to be hopeful for the new day, but then she remembered what had occurred the evening before, and she realized that there were some things that were simply *out* of her control. Her mother was one of those things.

"I just need to…to reason with her," she thought unhappily. *"I'll just lie and say I had an accident…I hit my head and…and I thought I'd gone to the E.R., but it was only a dream. Maybe the phone broke when I fell and hit my head…or something like that…Whatever the case, I can't be grounded. I have to be able to document everything with Rain or…or I'll lose track of how many changes have occurred…plus Rain will have a fit if she can't record anything."*

She turned on the shower and was relieved to feel hot water pour over her.

"I'm always afraid that some kind of weird sludge will come out of the nozzle," she thought in mild humor. *"I don't know why that scares me…"*

She'd had that fear ever since she was little, and now that she was shifting every day, that fear was actually a viable one and not some small child's ridiculous fantasy.

She finished her shower, toweled off, and traveled to her dresser to get ready for school. She was shaking from the chill of just getting out of a hot shower, so her mind was only on the task of grabbing something, anything, to wear.

This was the reason, of course, why she just stupidly stood there naked in front of her dresser as Jason opened the door to her bedroom. He looked exactly like her in terms of green scales and little off-white horns on his head, but she immediately knew it was him the moment she laid her surprised eyes upon him.

"Mom said to come down for…" he started, but then his eyes went wide as his mouth dropped open. "Oh my God!"

Nancy freaked. She was used to her mother barging in on her; she had warned the older woman about a million times not to do that, but Jason was another story. There was never…*ever*…*ANY* reason why he should simply walk right into her room…There just wasn't.

"GET OUT!" she screeched, and her younger brother immediately stepped back and shut the door.

She yanked a pair of panties and a bra out of her open drawer, grabbed a pair of blue jeans and a faded charcoal shirt, and slammed her dresser drawers shut. She was shaking now, but not just from the cold. She was both furious and humiliated, and the only comforting thought that came to her was that at least they all looked like snakes now and Jason hadn't caught her as she had originally looked when she was human. That would have been too much to bear, but as it stood, this was bad enough.

She quickly dressed, but it was somewhat difficult simply because of the inordinate amount of rage she felt.

"Can't *believe* he did that!" she breathed as she put on a pair of white socks for her matching white sneakers. "Now I'm mad! Now *I am mad*!...This is *her* fault! This is all her fault!...I...I'm going to do it...I'm going to tell her off this time...Thinks she can ground me for something that wasn't even my fault...Not this time, no..."

Her phone rang, and she picked it up off the top of her dresser without thinking. She pushed the receive button, put the phone up to her ear, and practically shouted into it.

"What!" she said angrily.

"Don't yell at me, young lady," came the voice of her mother. "Get down here and get ready for the bus."

"I know that!" hissed Nancy. "You don't have to call me from downstairs..."

"You had better change that attitude right now," said her mother. "I was thinking about ungrounding you, but your attitude has to change..."

Nancy immediately recanted her well-deserved anger in light of this information. It was a teen survival instinct to switch gears with parents at a moment's notice, and she'd had plenty of practice with this due to her overbearing mother.

"Okay, okay," huffed Nancy. "I…I'm sorry. I'm just…It's just…Jason…"

"I know," said her mother, and there was a hint of amusement in her voice.

Nancy did not find her mother's "humor" funny at all, but she did not have a chance to complain. Her mother dominated the conversation because she *always* dominated the conversation, and shifting hadn't changed that.

"I'll consider ungrounding you," continued her mother, "but you are *not* to lie to me again. Am I clear? You're lucky I found your phone on the kitchen counter last night after you went to bed. Don't lie about losing it again."

"Oh…" said Nancy in surprise.

She had the sudden and stark realization that she was talking into her now fully functional smartphone, and this confused her for a bit. This was certainly a strange occurrence, but it was also a good one, so she went with it without argument.

"I…I won't," stammered Nancy.

She felt her anger evaporate in a "poof" of strange relief.

"That's better," said her mother. "And I'll be sure to notify you myself next time and *not* send Jason…"

"I need therapy!" came Jason's stressed and horrified voice from the background.

Nancy couldn't help but chuckle a little over her brother's backseat statement. She heard her mother give a short laugh before speaking again.

"Now come down here and grab a strudel," said her mother. "You have to eat something, and you can't miss the bus."

"Oh…okay," said Nancy uncertainly. "I…I'll be down in a second."

This was an amazing turn of events for her. Aside from Jason's horrendous intrusion upon her privacy, Nancy decided that her day was already improving, and she wondered what the rest of it would bring.

"I hope it keeps getting better," she thought in nervous temper. *"It's all about perspective. I have to remember that…Keep positive, Nance. Just keep positive."*

✳✳✳✳✳

Nancy walked side by side with Rain down the sidewalk of Nancy's little cul-de-sac. Her house was one of the three that graced the big asphalt circle at the end of her street, but they had left the boredom of that residence to go walk in the late-day sun for a bit. When they did this, they usually walked down the street to the gas station at the corner, bought cold drinks and some candy, and then walked back to Nancy's before the sun went down. It was a weird little ritual they did whenever Rain was able to come over to Nancy's side of the neighborhood.

Today, Rain was dressed in a black and white T-shirt with a skull and crossbones on the front, and this somehow matched well with the faded and ripped black jeans she wore over her khaki boots.

The eccentric young lady's scales were an off-tan color, and she had dark-brown lines that crossed back and forth across her arms and down the top of her bald head. She reminded Nancy of a desert rattler, a description Rain might actually be offended to hear, yet that description was so apt and fitting for Rain, considering her personality.

"I don't get it," shrugged Rain. "It doesn't make sense."

"I know," frowned Nancy. "I'm not sure what went wrong."

"I don't think anything went wrong per say," said Rain. "We're just missing some variables."

The "variables" in question had to do with yesterday's photo in the notebook. The photo had kept, but not everyone within it had…and that was disturbing to Nancy. She and Rain looked human within the picture save for the bald streaks on their heads, but Danny's image looked like they did *today*; he looked like a human-snake hybrid with red scales and white and black lines on his arms.

It was strange that the photo had changed in such a way…It made no sense.

"I don't get it, either," replied Nancy. "I could understand if *I* didn't change in the photo, but the simple fact is that *you* haven't changed in either photo, too…but Danny did. Why would that happen? I don't understand."

"I don't understand, either," shrugged Rain. "For one thing, if only your consciousness is shifting, then why is the photo not changing with every new universe you shift to? Even the drawings don't make sense…They should change, too. I could eventually figure out why that is; I might be able to come up with *some* theory anyway, but then this goes and happens. Danny changed with the new universe shift, so…it feels like I'm back to square one."

Nancy thought about this.

"Maybe that's a good sign," she said hopefully. "Maybe the shifting is petering out, and soon I'll just end up in one universe, and that'll be that."

Rain looked at her in quizzical wonder. This expression was done by tilting her head to one side and raising an eyebrow, but in "snake form," it consisted of tilting her head to one side and raising the little claw/bone/horn ridges above her eyes. Rain had these small "horns" like Nancy did, only hers were jet black in color, but whatever color they were, there was a small line of them above each eye that took the place of where their eyebrows should have been. Nancy couldn't help but study them as she waited for her genius friend to reply.

"How so?" asked Rain. "How do you mean, I mean…You know what I meant."

"Err…not really," replied Nancy.

"I meant…" sighed Rain. "I meant that I thought you wanted to go back to your 'original' universe. You've told me that…that in your original universe you looked like you did in yesterday's photo, only with your head covered entirely with those weird tufts. You said that none of the…the…what was it?…Oh, yeah…None of the 'hair' was missing."

"Yeah, I did say that," replied Nancy, "but at this point I don't even care anymore. I just want to *stop shifting*. If I end up in a world where everyone's a…a big purple blob…then so be it. This has got to stop. It's stressing me out so badly that…that I can't really function."

"How so?" asked Rain. "I find it fascinating. I would *love* to shift like you do."

"I know, Rain," frowned Nancy. "You've only said that since it started."

"Well, it's true," shrugged Rain. "I want so badly to study it. I would *love* to see whole new patterns of evolution and historical changes and…and…different kinds of pudding."

They both burst out laughing at that remark.

"What!" chuckled Nancy. "*That's* why you want to shift?"

Rain looked up at her and smiled.

"Hey, now," she warned. "There's never a scientific mystery that *doesn't* involve pudding."

"Whatever," smiled Nancy as she waved off her friend.

"Seriously, though," frowned Rain. "Why do *you* get to shift? Why couldn't it be me? I'm the one who really wants it. You don't want it at all…It's not fair."

Nancy had a sudden hit of déjà vu. She was certain that she had said something along those lines in comparison with her intelligence to Rain's.

"Huh…" she thought in strange retrospection. *"And here I thought I was the only one who felt cheated. I guess Rain feels the same way…I should have known that…I…I should have seen it."*

"I'm sorry," she said without thinking.

"Why?" asked Rain.

Nancy studied her best friend's face and realized that she could easily read the puzzled expression upon her in spite of the fact that she now looked like a human-snake hybrid. It was the eyes, really; Rain's eyes were human, and as far as Nancy was concerned, the eyes did not lie.

"What do you mean 'why'?" asked Nancy.

"Nancy, this isn't your fault," sighed Rain. "Sure, I think it'd be great if I could shift, but you had nothing to do with that. You were just biking down Bitter Creek like you always do on every Saturday morning. It wasn't you who blew up the…the Breckenridge?…The Breckenridge Institute of Discovery."

"No," agreed Nancy. "No, I didn't. It's just…I feel…*selfish* about the whole thing."

"Don't," smiled Rain with a shake of her scaled head. "I may not get to shift, but I *do* get to study someone who does…and that's still something great."

"I guess," shrugged Nancy.

She did not feel that her shifting was "something great." She felt it was a serious burden, a nightmare warning to all those who might plunge headlong into the darker depths of science, and she just wanted it to stop.

"Don't guess," said Rain. "There's no 'guess.' You're shifting along dimensional lines. I didn't believe you at first, but now that I know it's a one-million-percent fact, it…excites me."

It was Nancy's turn to cock her head to one side and raise one of her bony eyebrow ridges. Rain laughed at that look, and this made Nancy smile.

"Not like that," said Rain with a wave of her hand. "I mean, of course it's exciting to document all of the major and minor changes that occur between shifts. For example, what did you first notice when you woke up this morning? How did looking different make you feel? In fact, how different *are* you? What was it like being in the other forms—"

"Whoa, whoa!" said Nancy quickly. "I don't...I mean...You're asking me too many things at once."

"Okay, okay," breathed Rain. "Just...take your time...Explain some of this to me."

Nancy thought about how to best explain this.

"I always check my hands and arms first," she said thoughtfully. "I take a shower in the morning, so that gives me a...ahem...'full' view of everything...Of course, *that* got sidetracked when Jason barged in on me while I was still naked..."

"What!" exclaimed Rain in swift reply.

Rain's outburst startled Nancy, and it took her a moment to respond.

"My stupid brother barged into my bedroom before I could get dressed," she said matter-of-factly. "In fact...I think I may have scarred him for life."

Rain laughed, and her earnest laughing caused Nancy to follow suit, instantly brightening both of their moods.

"Oh..." said Nancy as she remembered something important. "Yeah, and...apparently my phone is back from the dead and works just fine."

"Really?" asked Rain in sudden interest. "You told me it was fried."

"It was," frowned Nancy, "and now it's not...Come to think of it, I don't even have my cast anymore, or the abrasion on my shoulder...Let's see...It's Thursday, and the accident was on Saturday, but my cast disappeared yesterday, so..."

"That means you healed a broken wrist in four days," finished Rain. "Wow. That's…That's actually pretty cool."

"I guess," said Nancy, but then she realized something. "Hey, wait…What if this is all connected?"

"How so?" asked Rain.

"You explained to me a while ago that shifting between universes kind of…of healed me a little each day," said Nancy. "The phone shorted out because it was caught in the blast, so maybe it healed a little each day with each shift because it was also caught in the blast…Uhhh…'repaired' a little each day."

"Yeah, I can see that," replied Rain, "but that doesn't explain the notebook, the photos, or yesterday's photo."

"I know," said Nancy. "But I just have this…this *feeling* that it's all connected somehow. I don't know how to explain it."

"Huh," replied Rain. "That is weird."

They stopped talking for a bit as they crossed a side street and entered the local Busy-All. They each took a can of soda from one of the glass fridges within the store and looked around for some candy that they liked, but they were sidetracked by someone they knew from school.

"Hi, Allen," said Rain politely.

The young man turned around and smiled. Allen Smith was one of the few African Americans in their junior class, Nancy lived in a predominately white middle-class neighborhood, after all, but looking at him now, there was no way she could tell what his ethnicity would have been in her world…He looked almost like her.

His skin was bedecked with a lighter color of green scales than hers, but his "head ridges" were exactly the same color as Nancy's, and this was a little odd to her. Nancy had been raised to avoid racism in all its forms, but some part of her mind figured that different-looking people looked…*different*…in every universe. It had never occurred to her that they would not.

"Hey, guys," said Allen. "What's up?"

"Nothing much," shrugged Rain. "Just hanging out at the local Busy-All…well, for about as long as it takes for us to pay for our stuff."

Allen adjusted his glasses and took a moment to give a puzzling stare toward Nancy. She found the look to be invasive, but she didn't want to say anything mean or combative. Nevertheless, she couldn't help but question him about it.

"What?" she asked. "Why are you looking at me like that?"

"Oh," said Allen in sheepish reply. "Uhhh…I just heard from Danny that…that you two were getting along now."

Nancy gave herself a mental smack on the head. Danny did indeed have a couple of friends *other* than Rain, and Allen was one of them. Still, the mention of her name to someone else via Danny Princeton's lips…it bothered her. It bothered her a lot.

"Yeah," frowned Nancy. "I already apologized to him. I don't want him saying anything mean about me behind my back."

"Oh, no," said Allen with a shake of his head. "It wasn't like that. He just said he liked talking to you."

But Nancy did not know how to feel about that.

"Liked talking to me?" she thought in growing alarm. *"We've barely talked at all. What the heck?"*

"He said he was helping you with some project," continued Allen, "but he wouldn't say what it was. I couldn't get it out of him, so he must like you, because he was locked tighter than Fort Knox on that."

"Oh," blinked Nancy.

"At least he didn't say anything about my 'project,'" she thought. *"That's good, I guess."*

"Yeah," said Allen thoughtfully. "He's got me curious now. What exactly *are* you working on?"

She thought about the best lie for the occasion, but she decided to simply expound upon the lie she had already told Danny. Nevertheless, it was so slick that she momentarily impressed herself with her ability to deceive, and this was in spite of the fact that Rain had said she was a 'terrible liar.'

"A book," lied Nancy. "It's a romance, but it's got a heavy science-fiction theme, and I needed a guy's perspective…and Rain can't help me with that, or I would just consult her."

Rain gave her the evil eye, but Nancy ignored her.

"*Ooooooh*," nodded Allen in understanding. "No wonder he didn't want to say anything."

"Don't tell anyone, please," frowned Rain. "It's supposed to be a secret."

Allen shook his head no in response and raised both hands, palms out.

"Oh, I won't," he said quickly. "Your secret is safe with me…uhhh…as safe as standing around in the Busy-All and blurting it out in front of random strangers can be anyway."

Rain guffawed at Allen's accurate little statement, and they all had a good shared laugh.

Allen had already paid for his goods, so they said their goodbyes as he left. They paid for their own goods and started the walk back to Nancy's house shortly thereafter.

They crossed the street without much in the way of conversation and headed back to the sidewalk.

"Huh," said Rain a moment later.

"Huh, what?" asked Nancy.

"Danny said he liked talking to you," said Rain matter-of-factly.

"So?" asked Nancy.

"I think he's warming up to you, is all," said Rain.

Nancy shook her head in response to that observation. She had a slew of problems involving her "shifting," and the last thing she needed was any kind of drama involving Rain's neighbor.

It had been easy to hate Danny, but it was much more difficult to get to know him. For one thing, she actually needed to *want* to get to know him, and considering everything that was going on in her life, there wasn't much *want* there.

"I don't want to hurt his feelings," she thought in sudden anxiety, *"but I don't really want to hang out with him...Plus...he must 'like' me? What did Allen mean by that? Did he mean 'like me' like me? Or was he just being polite in a general, you know, 'like me' kind of way? I mean, Danny can't be attracted to me in a romantic way...I pretty much treated him like trash for what I 'thought' he did, so that can't be right...Oh...What if he's one of those guys that just latches onto a girl that shows him any little bit of attention?...*

"No, that can't be it. He'd have actively gone after Rain if that were the case. Rain's attractive in her own way, and if it's one thing I know about guys, it doesn't matter how weird or ugly a guy is, he will pursue the most attractive girls even though he doesn't have a snowball's chance in...

"Doesn't matter. The problem here is...The problem is that Danny is...he's just plain weird. Weirder than Rain, and that's hard to pull off. To hang around him, like, on a regular basis and be active friends with him...I don't know if I can do that...Is that selfish? I just...After everything that's happened...I don't know if I want to be seen with him.

"The entire school already thinks I'm indecent...Brinn is soooooo dead when I get ahold of

her...Shame I don't have any classes with her this year...Ugh...

"But anyway, back to Danny. I don't really know what to do about him. He's like that awkward cousin that your parents want you to hang out with when all you want to do is talk to your friends...He's not my friend...Not really. I don't know what he is...

"I really hope Allen didn't mean anything by 'like me,' because I can't handle a crush from Danny Princeton. My social standing is bad enough, but hanging out with Danny will plummet me to the very depths of—"

"Nance!" exclaimed Rain.

Rain's sudden and sharp tone popped Nancy out of her train of thought.

"What!" she replied in alarm.

"I've only asked you the same question three times," frowned Rain, "and you've been staring off into space like a zombie...You had me believing you'd shifted again, and I was talking to a mindless husk."

"What?" asked Nancy in irritated confusion. "No!...I was just thinking…"

"And what were you thinking?" asked Rain.

Nancy waved her off. It was one thing to talk about her major problems, but something like Danny…wasn't worth mentioning.

"Never mind," she said unhappily.

It occurred to her that she would not be able to dissuade Rain's pestering with a simple "never mind," so she strained to think of a believable lie to tell the eccentric young woman. The young genius was no fool, but she could straight up be fooled if the lie was convincing enough.

"If you must know," said Nancy in slow reply, "I was thinking about…about the whole shifting business. I was thinking…err…I was wondering why you can remember me talking about all of this stuff yesterday when…when my consciousness wasn't even in this form yesterday…"

She stopped talking as she realized that she had just pointed out a very significant hole in Rain's theory of "consciousness shifting," and she had come up with that problem by sheer serendipity.

"Oh," blinked Rain in surprise. "I never thought of that. I…I have no idea."

Nancy had to study her friend's expression for a moment. Rain was truly surprised, and she looked upon Nancy as if her best friend had suddenly exploded.

"What's that look for?" asked Nancy in sudden hurt.

She did not like the implications behind it.

"I'm not stupid," she said unhappily.

Rain shook her head and held up her hands in defense.

"I don't think you're stupid," she protested. "Not at all. I told you that you have a more…*practical* intelligence than I do. I'm surprised, because I honestly should have spotted that huge flaw. It doesn't surprise me *at all* that you saw it. You're good like that."

Nancy accepted this, but inside, she knew better.

"I came up with that off the fly," she mentally frowned. *"That was not intentional, and I don't believe that I'm 'good like that.'"*

"Perhaps time and space are liquid for you," shrugged Rain. "Perhaps every version of you is traveling across dimensional lines at different points in time, and you don't know it, because there's only one conscious version of you from your world. That…That makes sense, actually. It's kind of like the single electron theory."

"Single electron theory?" asked Nancy. "What's that?"

"Professor John Wheeler proposed to theoretical physicist Richard Feynman that all electrons in the universe are identical because they are all actually the same electron," explained Rain. "He proposed that one single electron is simply moving back and forth through time and space, and because it's everywhere at once, it only appears that there are many of them, but in reality, it's just the same one. Maybe something like that is going on with you."

"How so?" asked Nancy.

She really only understood part of what Rain had said, but she asked the question anyway.

"Every single version of you was present at the Breckenridge explosion," explained Rain, "and so every single version of you is swapping out with another version of you. I mean, personally, I don't think the single electron theory is true, but maybe something like that happened to you. Maybe the world where you came from isn't 'universe number one,' because there is no 'universe number one.' I mean, if every universe exists at the same time on an infinite number of frequencies, then…"

Nancy suddenly felt dizzy as her genius friend continued to drone on about something that was way, *way* over her head. They were almost back to Nancy's house, but she slowed to a stop as the world began to wobble in her vision. She suddenly felt sick, like seasick, and she was keenly aware of the growing feeling to vomit as her stomach roiled.

"Nance?" asked Rain in concern.

Nancy's vision blurred as if something were rapidly vibrating her eyeballs. The sensation was terrible, truly awful, and she stumbled as she lost balance. She fell to her hands and knees as her eyes moved back and forth and up and down at top speed.

The impact of hard concrete upon her knees hurt with a fierce throbbing, but that was nothing compared to the nausea that swept over her. She felt like vomiting, but she held it in, because throwing up was one of the things in life that she avoided at all costs, mainly because she considered it truly vile.

As her vision blurred, she stared down at her green-scaled hands, and for a fraction of a second, she thought she could see her *real* hands, her human ones with the healthy peach of skin that she was so used to, but a calling of her name distracted her from this.

She heard her name called, but it was not Rain's voice that called her but someone else, someone she did not recognize as being either male or female, and it sounded far off and muffled, as if heard through the water-filled space of an aquarium.

And then it was over. She held in her breath as the sensation to vomit passed and her vision returned to normal.

"Nance!" came Rain's concerned cry. "Nancy! Are you okay? Talk to me!"

Nancy nodded a couple of times and stood up on wobbly legs. She looked over to her best friend's tan scaly face and saw the real concern in the eccentric girl's eyes.

"Yeah," replied Nancy. "Yeah, I think…I think I'm good."

Rain grabbed her by the shoulders and studied her.

"What happened!" she asked.

"I don't know," replied Nancy. "Everything just went weird for a moment, and I got dizzy…I don't…I don't know what happened."

"Oh, boy," said Rain in audible concern. "Let's get you inside. I hope this doesn't have to do with your shifting…That would be terrible, considering we don't even know what's really happening with you. Hopefully, this is just a normal sickness…err…something that isn't that bad and can be treated in a normal way, mind you. I'm not wishing for something serious to happen to you…Oh, no…Can't lose my best friend. That would suck."

"You think?" asked Nancy as she held her own head in her right hand.

Rain gave a brief chuckle, but she grabbed onto Nancy's right arm with her left hand and didn't let go.

"Come on," said her friend. "You need to sit down."

"O…kay," said Nancy slowly.

Rain's behavior was a little "smothering" as far as Nancy was concerned. The young genius was acting a little funny over the matter, so Nancy decided to corner her on it.

"I can walk by myself," she said quietly. "I'll be fine. You don't have to baby me."

"I know you can walk," said Rain quickly, "but you didn't see what I saw."

"What?" asked Nancy.

"Your eyes were moving all over the place," said Rain anxiously. "It was like you were dreaming and in REM sleep, but your eyelids were open. It was freaky. It freaked me out. Not only that, but they were moving so fast that there's no *way* you could have been doing it on purpose. Not that you would do that on purpose, but still…"

Nancy tried to picture this in her head, but doing so made her a little dizzy, so she quickly decided not to try that image again.

A cold memory occurred, one she had buried, and that was the violent motion of her eyes just after the Breckenridge explosion. She had forgotten about it, but Rain's description of what just happened brought it back to the surface of her mind, so she shoved it back down again.

She did not want to believe that the whole "moving eyes" thing was something serious; it was safer to believe it was just a weird fluke, so she buried it once more. She had no idea what had just happened, but she sincerely hoped it would not happen again. The first time had been bad enough.

Her knees hurt, as did the palms of her hands, but that was because she had dropped to the sidewalk like dead weight. This pain, however, did not bother her as much as the memory of the calling voice did…That voice had not sounded like Rain in any way, shape, or form.

"Can you tell me what happened?" asked Rain as the eccentric teen guided her to the front door of Nancy's house.

"I told you…" breathed Nancy, "I don't know."

"Try your best," said Rain.

Her insistence was irritating, but Nancy couldn't blame her. If Rain's eyes had been moving around in a weird way, Nancy would have called her out on it, too.

"I got dizzy," said Nancy. "I got nauseous, and it felt like I was going to throw up, but I think I felt that way because everything in my vision started wobbling."

"Like seasickness?" asked Rain.

"Yeah," breathed Nancy. "I guess. Then I heard someone calling my name…"

"That was me," said Rain.

"No…it wasn't," said Nancy. "It didn't sound like you at all. It sounded like…like if someone pasted a man and a woman's voice together. It was…weird."

"I'll bet," said Rain. "I think maybe you should lie down. Take a load off."

They walked into Nancy's house, said a brief hello to Nancy's father, and made their way upstairs. Nancy did her best to look inconspicuous as they traveled past her dad, but he was fully immersed in whatever history show he was watching, so she didn't have to try very hard.

Jason walked out of his room when they reached the top of the stairs, but he stopped as he stared in open curiosity at the pair. Nancy realized that Rain was still guiding her by the arm, so they had to look funny in a suspicious way, but Rain put an end to Jason's gawking with one well-timed word. She looked him dead in the eye and gave him a mock frown.

"Pervert," she said.

Jason covered his scaly face with one scaly hand and walked back into his room without a single spoken word. Both Nancy and her eccentric friend gave out a giggle as they made it into the safety of Nancy's bedroom.

"That was entertaining," said Rain as she shut the bedroom door.

Nancy laid down upon her own bed and took in a deep breath. She was not sure what had happened with the moving eyes and the dizziness, but whatever it was, it had seriously alarmed her, and now she was worried.

"What if this is serious?" she thought in anxious tremor. *"What if I can't see a doctor because it's shifting related? Will it kill me?...I...I don't know what to do..."*

"Are you okay now?" asked Rain.

Nancy looked up to her best friend and gave her a weak nod.

"I think so," she said. "It's just...now I'm worried."

Rain sat down at the end of the bed and patted her on the leg.

"Do tell," she said.

"It's not funny," frowned Nancy. "I was thinking...I was thinking that if this incident was shifting related, then I can't see a doctor about it. I don't even think I would be able to get a CAT scan or an MRI, because they might find something really weird, and then...then they might take me away."

"I think that only happens in the movies," said Rain.

"Even so," explained Nancy, "it bothers me. I feel so helpless right now. I feel like I have no spine...like a...a uhhh..."

"A jellyfish," replied Rain.

"Exactly," said Nancy. "I feel like a jellyfish that's baking in the sun…You know that feeling? Like you're just totally helpless."

"Nance," sighed Rain, "if you feel like this is serious, then we need to tell your parents right away. If you have to get a CAT scan or an MRI, then so be it. You can't ignore it if it's serious…Even so, it may have just been a one-time deal…We don't know. If it happens again, then we will *definitely* tell your parents. *I'll* definitely tell them, and you won't be able to stop me."

Nancy thought about this for a moment.

"That has to be the most endearing yet creepiest thing you have ever said to me, Rain," she replied after that moment of thought.

"Thanks!" smiled Rain.

"I'm not sure if that was a compliment," replied Nancy.

"Close enough for me," shrugged Rain. "But seriously, Nance, you can't think like that."

Nancy sat up and studied her friend's face. It was clear Rain was still worried about her, and it was easy to tell that in spite of the girl's snake-like appearance.

"You're not spineless," said Rain. "And for that matter, Jellyfish have no bones, because they don't need them. We humans use muscle attached to bone in order to move, but jellyfish contract their bodies in water in order to create hydro-propulsion."

Nancy had no idea what the eccentric genius was on about now.

"What does that have to do with anything?" she asked. "I know jellyfish can move in water…What I was saying was I felt like a jellyfish *outside* of water."

"I know," said Rain with a sheepish smile. "It's the same as if a human gets swept away into the middle of the ocean. It's not our environment, so we're not equipped to handle it."

"*Yeaaaaah…?*" asked Nancy. "And…?"

"And nothing," explained Rain. "You think you're spineless because you feel like a jellyfish on land, but that feeling is something *anyone* would feel, because *none* of us are equipped to travel along dimensional lines to whole new worlds any more than a jellyfish is equipped to live on land…I mean, heck, *I* would feel overwhelmed if I were shifting, and *I* want it…Do you see what I'm saying?"

"I think so," replied Nancy, but in truth, she was still a little confused.

"You're scared and you're stressed," said Rain, "but that's normal. The whole dizzy spell with the crazy eyes thing isn't normal, but like I said, if that happens again, then we'll definitely have it checked out, but…in general, what you're feeling is normal…

"You're not spineless; I know that…In fact, you're handling this a lot better than most people would…You really are. I think a lot of other people would think they had gone stark raving mad if this had happened to them, and they'd end up in a mental ward somewhere. You've kept yourself together and even kept positive most of the time. How can you possibly call that spineless?"

Nancy thought about this and realized her eccentric genius of a friend was right.

"I…I guess you're right," she said thoughtfully. "I guess it really is all about perspective."

"*Rain is right,*" she thought in a sudden uplifting of spirit. "*If I have any hope of seeing this through to its end, no matter what that end may be, I just need to keep positive.*"

Still, part of her…a rather dark part of her…wondered what that "end" would be.

Chapter 7…The Seventh Shift

Nancy awoke right on time again. The first rays of dawn were streaming in through her window once more, so she yawned and blinked a couple of times to get with it and get moving.

The first thing she did every morning since the shifting began was inspect her hands; it was always the first indicator of what was to come. *This* time, however…This time was different. This time she really did freak.

Her hands were completely see-through. Her skin was transparent, as were her muscles, and she could actually see her translucent finger bones through her hands. She could see clear liquid pumping through her like thick water, and even her bones, though translucent, did not look completely solid.

"What is this!" she cried out in horror.

Her voice sounded completely normal, but that did nothing to calm the panic she now felt. It was then that she saw for the first time the odd and soft glow emanate from her now transparent skin; it was a deep-blue color, almost black, and it became brighter as her fear reached a steep pinnacle of terror.

She had to force herself to calm down. Considering that she was *not* melting and/or turning into an amorphous blob, Nancy took in some deep breaths to keep from completely losing it. As she did so, the most amazing thing happened…She stopped glowing.

"What is this?" she mentally asked herself. *"I…I'm afraid to look in the mirror now. Will I be able to see my own organs and brain and whatnot? And what was with that glow?…What is going on today?"*

She reached up and touched her hair, although it felt odd to her, as if the strands were thicker and made of rubber. She brushed her fingers along her skin, but her skin felt...*squishier*...It was incredibly strange.

Nancy held up her hand to the dawn light and watched in amazement as the sun's rays passed through it. She could feel the mild heat of the sun upon her palm, but even more amazing was the sensation of feeling it *pass* through her.

"This is the strangest day yet," she thought anxiously, *"but it's Friday, so I need to hustle. I may have shifted, but as far as the world is concerned, it's just another Friday. I still can't miss the bus."*

She walked into the bathroom and flipped on the light. The figure in the mirror caused her to cringe, mainly because it was nearly indescribable. She could see through the skin on her face and see her translucent skull, but her eyes had not changed at all. They were white orbs with hazel irises and black pupils, and when she closed her left eye to wink at her reflection, her eyelid was a solid pasty light blue that was so light in color that it was almost white.

"Why are my eyes different?" she wondered. *"I don't know...Wait...What would Rain think? How would she explain it?...I...I don't really know...Wait...They must be different so I can actually see. Maybe if they were see-through, I wouldn't have proper vision...So why are my eyelids?...Oh, wait...I have to be able to sleep...Duhhhh. Can't sleep if I can stare through my own eyelids...Yeah, that makes sense. I think...I think I'm beginning to catch on now..."*

She ran her fingers through her hair in order to inspect it. Her hair was a little thicker than she was used to, but it looked like her normal hair, only translucent, like her bones.

"At least I have hair again," she thought.

She undressed in order to get into the shower, but the sight of seeing her own translucent skeleton, along with the outlines of her own transparent organs…that was a little much. Nancy stared at her own pumping heart for a second before tearing her eyes away from the mirror, and she was suddenly glad for the invention of clothes.

"I can see everything!" she thought in slight disgust. *"It's so gross…It's so…It's so…Wait…What the…!"*

Her train of thought was interrupted as her skin began to glow again. This time she shone a dark-yellow light, and she was distracted by this for a little bit, but the glow died down and eventually died out a few seconds later.

"Why am I glowing different colors?" she thought in confusion. *"This world…This…This universe is so…so weird!"*

She took her shower, and the hot water eased her fears somewhat. She toweled off when she was done, but she kept a towel wrapped around her just in case her brother was stupid enough to barge in again, plus the towel kept her from gawking at her own now very visible internal organs.

She picked out a simple red shirt with short sleeves and decided to wear a pair of regular blue jeans, and this surprised her a little, because there had not been one universe where her clothes had differed from her original universe, save for the day when she'd been a spider-hybrid, but even then, her clothes had only been altered to fit her new form…Otherwise, they had not changed at all in color or type.

She slipped into her clothes for the day as she thought about this balance in universal regularity.

"At least some things stay the same," she thought. *"I don't have any clothes I don't like…"*

The door to her room pushed open as her mother entered unannounced. The older woman looked just like Nancy in terms of transparent skin and thick, translucent hair, but Nancy knew by her domineering attitude that it was one-thousand percent definitely…her mother.

"What is taking you so long?" demanded the older woman. "Get a move on! The bus will be here any minute!"

Nancy's ire was evoked in the fraction of a second. She was ultimately tired of this intrusion, and it had ultimately frayed her last nerve.

"Mom!" she said angrily. "Don't barge in on me!"

Her skin began to glow red, and then it shone like a beacon in the night, a bright and raging crimson, so bright that it temporarily blinded her. Her mother's demeanor, however, switched from irritation to pure rage at the sight of this vermilion aura.

"Nancy Amelia Clark!" hissed her mother. "Don't you dare threaten me!"

Her mother, the woman named Deirdre Clark, was on her in a second. The older woman grabbed her by the left arm and pushed her up against her own dresser. Nancy had never seen her mother so angry before; she did not know what this was all about, but it caused her to momentarily cower in fear. She was certain that the older woman was going to strike her, and repeatedly.

The red glow of Nancy's skin changed to a deep-blue color, almost black, but it shone brightly as if stuck in some paradox of darkness and light, and it pulsed for a moment as if it were a warning to anyone who could see it.

"I didn't do anything!" she screeched.

The strangeness of her own situation coupled with her mother's swift and murderous attitude caused her to break down, and she felt tears come to her eyes. The light of her skin flickered between dark blue and purple until it settled upon a color that resided somewhere in-between.

Whatever was going on, her mother released her grip on Nancy's arm and backed away. The look on the older woman's face may have been surprise…It was hard to tell, considering what she looked like now.

"Nancy!" breathed the older woman. "What is going on with you!"

"I didn't do anything!" wept Nancy. "I didn't…I didn't do anything…"

She broke down into sobs as the light emanating from her skin changed to a pale violet. Her mother simply stared at her in bewilderment, but Nancy didn't care. She was breaking down now, because the day had definitely *not* started out well, and the start of her day was usually an indication as to how the rest of it would go.

✳✳✳✳✳

Nancy got into her mother's sedan, sat in the front passenger's seat, shut the door, and then buckled herself in. Her mother sat in the driver's seat and shut her own door.

"I called in for you," said the older woman in a matter-of-fact tone.

"But I don't feel sick," said Nancy quietly.

Her mother buckled in and then started the car.

"You heard the doctor," said her mother, only this time her voice was laced with obvious concern. "We don't know what's going on until we get the results back on your bloodwork. We just want to make sure that nothing serious is happening."

"There's nothing going on——" started Nancy, but her mother would not have it.

"Don't argue with me," scolded the older woman. "You're flashing so often that you look like a Christmas display. That's not normal. If you flash red in school, they'll call the police on you. It's a good thing I came up to your room this morning, or things could have been a lot worse. As it is, I had to call into work, and at least I have an excuse other than 'I had to pick up my daughter from jail.' You certainly can't go out in public like this."

Nancy had been thinking about this all morning. Apparently, her "glow" had to do with her mood, and apparently everyone in *this* universe already knew how to control that little feature, but Nancy was not *from* this universe, so she did not have that obviously learned skill.

"Flashing means something ENTIRELY different where I come from," she thought unhappily. *"It's just one more stressor to add to a long list of stress. I'm built differently in every new world, so there are biological features that can get me into trouble, and I don't even know it until I'm actually IN trouble…and apparently 'flashing' red is considered a big-time threat here…but it's not like I wanted to KILL anyone…I was just a little angry, is all…"*

"I'm sorry if you thought…" said Nancy slowly, "if you thought I was going to attack you or something. I wasn't…I was just a little upset because you barged in on me again…"

Her mother sighed and nodded her head in response.

"I know you get frustrated sometimes," said the older woman, "but you have to remember that your father and I do the things we do because we love you. I just wanted to make sure you didn't miss the bus…I guess it doesn't matter now, though…"

Nancy gave a soft laugh at that apt remark, and her mother smiled back at her.

"Don't think this is a day off, young lady," said the older woman. "We just can't have you going all wild and whatnot at school. You're seventeen now, and next year you'll graduate high school…We have to make sure you can get into a good college. You can't be missing too many days…"

"I know, Mom," sighed Nancy. "I'm doing my best."

"Good," said her mother. "Keep it up and stick to your guns. You don't want to be left behind in life. There are too many people out there who can't find a career, and it's because they don't have higher education."

"No, it's because there are no careers left to find, just part-time jobs," thought Nancy in irritation, but she did not voice her opinion.

Unfortunately, her skin did that for her. She began to glow in a pale-green light, and this was not lost on her mother. The older woman frowned and shook her head.

"At least I know what you're thinking," she said unhappily. "You may not want to listen to me, Nance, but once you're out in the real world, you'll wish you had."

"How can I?" thought Nancy in frustration. *"The 'real' world changes every single day, and I can't keep up with it."*

She glowed a little brighter for a moment as she thought about this.

*****

Nancy walked around Rain's house and into her best friend's backyard. She held her precious green notebook in her hands, and that was a good thing, because convincing her mother to let her visit her genius friend was like throwing an egg through a brick wall. Nevertheless, the older woman had relented, but Nancy suspected it was because her mother felt sorry for her.

Rain was standing there next to Danny, but they both looked as equally disturbing as everyone else. Nancy simply could not get used to the transparent skin and muscle or the illusion of floating eyes within a semi-liquid skull. Thankfully, she only had to put up with the visible head and not any other part of the body where she could see working internal organs.

Still, in spite of all of the oddness of their appearance, Rain's attitude upon seeing her was not normal for the eccentric young woman. Danny was his same quiet and somewhat morose self, but Rain was a little *too* happy.

"Fancy!" said Rain in excitement.

Today, the young woman was wearing a grey T-shirt over a white undershirt to go with her traditional black cargo pants, and on her transparent ears hung a pair of small gold earrings with pink pearls on the bottoms of them.

Danny, on the other hand, was dressed in black jeans with a matching black T-shirt, the same thing he always seemed to dress in, and this just lent more justification to the fact that Nancy thought of him as weird.

Aside from that quick inspection of their clothing (something Nancy did automatically and without any focused thought), she decided to address Rain's oddly chipper attitude.

"You're excited to see me," said Nancy in slight confusion.

"Of course!" said Rain. "Your mom said that you were sick today…I really had to try hard to convince her that you could come over…Wait…Where's your bike?"

"My mom drove me over here," said Nancy with a slight frown. "I have to call her when it's time for her to pick me up."

"I don't understand," frowned Rain. "You look fine to me. Why did you miss school, and why wouldn't she let you ride your bike?"

Nancy's frustration struck again, and she began to glow a pale-green light. Rain's reaction was immediate; the girl's face fell into a distinct puddle of unhappiness, and her shoulders sank in disappointment.

"Excuse me for asking," she said unhappily.

"No, you don't understand," said Nancy in frustration, but this only caused her pale-green "aura" to glow brighter.

Rain took a step back at the strength of the glow.

"No, wait," said Nancy in desperation. "I'm not irritated at you. I'm frustrated with my situation because I…I can't control this stupid glow of mine."

Both Rain and Danny looked at each other and then looked at her in strange surprise.

"Really?" asked Rain in complete surprise. "You're flashing out of control?"

This was kind of a stupid question, but Nancy responded to it anyhow.

"Yes, Rain," she sighed. "It's been happening all day long. I thought my mom was going to kill me this morning when I…ugh…'flashed' red at her."

"Whoa," said Danny suddenly.

"Oh, Nance," said Rain in open concern. "Why didn't you call me?"

"I couldn't," frowned Nancy. "My mom dragged me to the doctor and they took a blood test and…ugh…It's a good thing it's the weekend, because there's no way I can go to school like this."

"Do tell," replied Rain. "You can get arrested for going red…Wait…Is this out-of-control thing because of…"

"Yes, Rain," frowned Nancy. "That's exactly why."

"*Oooohhhh*," said Rain with wide eyes.

"I don't understand," said Danny in audible confusion. "Why are you flashing out of control? I've never heard of anything like this before…"

"I have," said Rain. "It's usually the result of a TBI, but in Nancy's case…never mind. Point is, it's not good, that's for sure."

"No kidding," replied Danny. "My parents would kill me if I flashed red at them."

"I figured that out pretty quickly," frowned Nancy. "But…ugh…that doesn't matter, because I managed to get here anyway. My mom wasn't going to let me come over, but I grabbed our notebook and convinced her that you were going to give me today's homework."

"*That's* why she gave in," said Rain in sudden comprehension. "I guess I'm not as persuasive as I thought."

Danny reached over and grabbed the notebook from Nancy's hands without asking.

Nancy felt a jolt of fear strike her; she did not want Danny to see the picture from two days ago. He looked like he did right now within the photo, but Nancy and Rain looked completely alien, or at least they would to Danny, and there was no feasible lie she could come up with to explain this anomaly.

"Wait, Danny…" started Nancy, but her "aura" spoke louder than her voice.

The glow of her skin turned a dark blue, and it was so strong that Danny dropped the green notebook to the grass below. He backed away from her, but the expression on his face was unreadable.

"Why are you afraid of me?" he asked in a slightly-hurt voice.

"I…I'm not…" said Nancy as she stooped and picked up her notebook. "I was just…It's just…"

"It's our project," explained Rain quickly. "She's afraid someone is going to steal our idea."

"What?" frowned Danny. "I'm not a thief."

"It's not that," said Nancy. "I just…"

She tried to think of something to say, anything at all to explain this, but nothing came to mind, and she just kept drawing a blank. She just stood there as her voice trailed off, and to make it worse, it was clear that Danny was expecting a justifiable reason as to why he couldn't see the notebook, but none came.

After a long and awkward moment, he threw up his hands and walked off in what Nancy could only assume was disgust.

"I have to go anyway," he said in a curt voice, but he did not look at them as he walked away.

Neither Nancy nor Rain said anything as he disappeared around the side fence of Rain's backyard. It was an awkward silence that stifled them, or at least it did for Nancy, but the only thing she could think of was a hope that tomorrow she could repair the damage done because of her current "condition."

Nancy's glow changed from a dark blue to a pale green once more, only this time it was very bright.

"That's not what I wanted," she said unhappily. "I didn't mean to chase him off."

"He'll be all right," said Rain. "Just give him a little time. You can just explain it to him tomorrow. It's not like he or I ever go anywhere."

"Yeah," said Nancy. "I guess."

But this time she actually felt bad. In the past when it came to Danny, she would not have shed a single tear for him, she had hated him that much, but that was all because of a dirty lie told by a pernicious young woman who clearly hated Nancy, so insulting him or driving him away now was…wrong.

Nancy's glow changed to a rich burgundy color as her frustration changed to guilt mixed with depression. She reached up and wiped some tears from her eyes, but she didn't voice her unhappiness; there was no need to.

Rain reached down and picked up their precious notebook. She then laid one transparent hand upon Nancy's shoulder and gave her a sympathetic look…at least, that's what it looked like, but it was hard to tell.

"This is getting out of hand," said Rain. "You can't blame yourself for something that isn't your fault, Nance. I know we've had this discussion before, but it's important that you understand that. There are going to be times when your shifting is going to put you in a bad situation…but I'm still here. I know what you're going through, so I'll help you."

Nancy nodded as she wiped away her tears. Her aura of depression slowly waned as she pulled herself back together.

"I'm trying," she sniffed. "I really am. I hate this shifting. You have no idea how much I hate it."

"I have a pretty good idea," said Rain.

"No, you don't," frowned Nancy. "This is all their fault! Those scientists at Breckenridge…They did this to me! And I can't even hate them for it, because they don't even exist anymore. It's terrible."

"Well…that's why we should look on the bright side of things," said Rain.

"Like what?" pouted Nancy.

"Like this notebook," said Rain. "We are both still part of the greatest scientific research ever done in human history. That has to count for something."

"I guess," frowned Nancy.

"Open it up," said Rain. "I want to see yesterday's picture…You have to understand, Fance, that to me…uhhh…from my point of view, anyway…we took the picture yesterday at your house, but you still looked like you do now. You've never actually changed to resemble anything in any of these pictures…"

Something odd struck Nancy all at once. It occurred to her that what Rain had just said made no sense.

"What do you mean?" she asked. "I looked like what?"

"You…You look like you do now," stammered Rain.

"But that means…" said Nancy slowly. "Do you know what that means?"

"What?" asked Rain in slight confusion. "No…What does that mean?"

"It means that I and I *alone* am the *only* one shifting," said Nancy firmly. "There can't be multiple versions of me all shifting at once."

"What?" asked Rain. "How do you figure?"

"Because I can't control this…ugh…'flashing,'" finished Nancy.

Rain smacked her own transparent forehead with her own transparent right hand.

"*Ooooohhh*…of course!" said Rain excitedly. "You can't control your flashing, so that means any version of you from any other universe wouldn't be able to control it, either…But you didn't *have* this problem until today…That means that…that you must be the original!...But that still doesn't explain how you still know you're shifting from one day to the next. I don't get it."

"Do I?" asked Nancy. "What was I like yesterday?"

"The same as today, except without your flashing problem," explained Rain. "We talk like this, we take a picture, and then the picture changes the next day. That's how it looks from my side anyway."

Nancy had a sudden lightning bolt of inspiration.

"Wait! What if…What if *I'm* not the only one who's shifting?" she asked.

"What?" asked Rain. "We just established that you were."

"No, no," said Nancy. "Something weird is going on here…Weirder than normal, I mean…What were you doing last Saturday morning?"

Rain paused for a moment as she stared off into the distance, and she held her chin within the fingers of her translucent right hand. This was her "thinking" pose, or her "Sherlock" pose, as Nancy sometimes liked to call it.

"Hmmm, let me think," said Rain. "What was I doing?...Oh, yeah!...I was on Dad's radio. I picked up a strange broadcast."

Nancy thought about this and realized that she was definitely on the right track. She had a theory, her very first real scientific theory, and she needed to know if she was right.

"What was the broadcast?" asked Nancy.

"I don't know," shrugged Rain. "I was listening to police radio, but then I started playing with the dials to pick up anything else, because after a while, police radio gets boring. It was all static until I got on one frequency that just blasted out a high-pitched squeal. It hurt my ears."

"What time?" asked Nancy.

"I don't know," shrugged Rain. "I don't remember. I have a good memory, Fance, but it's not *that* good."

Nancy nodded once in understanding, but inside she was brimming with excitement. She began to glow a bright-blue light, and Rain's eye's widened at the sight of it.

"Whoa," said the eccentric young woman. "What's up with that?"

"Don't you see?" said Nancy in audible excitement. "You must have picked up the Breckenridge explosion!"

"It's possible..." shrugged Rain, "but I don't see how..."

"You picked it up!" said Nancy excitedly. "Whatever they did must have...have 'touched' you. You weren't bathed in it like me, but it touched you! That's why your picture's been changing, and that's why you remember talking to me about these things!"

"What?" asked Rain in surprise.

"My guess is that our conversations would be like they always are," said Nancy, "but they can't be, because *I'm* the only one shifting. If you weren't affected, then I would be explaining this to you *every single day*, and nothing in this notebook would ever change. The pictures would always show you as you are in the current universe I'm in, but they haven't. So even though you're not shifting, you still remember what *I*, the me from the *original* universe, has told you!"

"What does the notebook have to do…" started Rain, but then her eyes widened as she visibly realized something.

"I was using that notebook when I heard the broadcast," said Rain slowly. "I was going to write down anything interesting…but then that squeal hit, and I was afraid I'd broken Dad's radio…so I never took note of it…I didn't want any incriminating evidence pointing towards me. That radio's my dad's baby."

"So the notebook *was* with you," breathed Nancy. "Then that just lends more credence to what I was saying!"

"Credence?" smiled Rain. "Look at you using big words all of the sudden! I'm proud of you, Fancy. I knew I could make a scientist out of you."

Nancy waved her off.

"Very funny," she snorted. "But anyway, you know I'm right."

Rain shrugged and gave her a half-smile.

"The truth is, Nance," she said half-heartedly, "we don't have enough information to back up any of our theories. What you're saying *could* be true, but the fact of the matter is that we…we just don't know, so I take these pictures in order to keep track of what little I can keep track of.

"Furthermore, because the notebook is with you, I don't have positive confirmation that you're not altering it in some way. I'm not saying I doubt you in your shifting, but anyone else would look at this situation and just shake their heads. They'd scream 'little girls with pictures of fairies' all over again. It's just not enough."

Nancy was crestfallen at this revelation from her best friend, and her light dimmed to a pale yellow, but then it brightened to a royal blue as she realized something.

"You keep the notebook!" blurted out Nancy.

"What?" asked Rain.

"You keep it!" repeated Nancy. "If I'm right, and you and the notebook have been slightly altered by the Breckenridge experiment, then the picture we take today will hold even though I won't have the notebook. Then you'll see…"

"It's a good idea," shrugged Rain. "Unless you creep across town in the middle of the night to steal the notebook so you can alter it, it's about the best plan of action we have. *However*…I'm going to *hide* the notebook…just in case."

Nancy did not like the implications of that statement, and her aura dimmed to a pale yellow once more.

"Hey, I'm not a liar," she said with very noticeable unhappiness. "Not with you anyway. I wouldn't do that."

"Don't take it personally, Nance," frowned Rain. "I have to know with one-thousand-percent certainty that you're telling the truth…I…I have to. It's what being a scientist is all about…I can't just take your word for it.

"For one thing, if what you say is true, then we really *have* made the greatest scientific discovery in all of human history, and that's better than winning the lottery for me. It's what I've always dreamed of since I was little. You have to understand where I'm coming from…I'm not trying to be mean."

Nancy's pale-yellow aura slowly dimmed as she thought about this.

"All right," she said with growing confidence. "But you're going to see that I'm right! You'll know it tomorrow."

"We'll see," said Rain in sheepish reply. "Now…let's take a look at this notebook."

She opened up the notebook and flipped through it. She shook her head at the photo from the day before and grinned.

"It never ceases to amaze me how realistic these photos are," she said in earnest. "I really, really, really, *really* want to believe you, Nance. For one thing, if you really are this good at doctoring photos in such a short time, then you are wasting your time pulling a prank on me, methinks, methinks. Not to mention that you have my chicken scratch down to a literal T. I'd recognize my handwriting anywhere."

Nancy crowded in on her to view the notebook page and the photo from yesterday.

"We were snake-people yesterday," she said confidently. "You got worried about me because my eyes…"

"Were moving all over the place," finished Rain. "I remember…but we didn't look like this."

"I know," said Nancy, "but at least you remember. That lends more…credence…to my theory. I think you *were* affected, just indirectly."

"Are you getting smarter?" asked Rain in slight surprise.

"Hey!" said Nancy in distinct unhappiness.

Her aura changed to a pale green, but Rain simply busted up into abject laughter. Nancy's irritation died down as she realized that she was the butt of a joke.

"Har, har," she half-smiled. "Very funny."

"Ah, Fancy Nancy," smiled Rain. "You still fall for the obvious."

Nancy shook her head and patted the photo on the notebook.

"We're getting sidetracked," she said impatiently. "What do you think of the photo?"

Rain's eyes widened a bit as she studied it.

"I *think* if this is one of my multiple selves," she said slowly, "…then I feel sorry for her. She doesn't even have hair."

Nancy twirled a thick and slightly rubbery strand of her own hair.

"If you can call *this* hair," she said. "I guess it's better than Bald Streak Nancy. Still, I miss my real hair."

Rain looked at her and frowned. Her lips were transparent and her teeth were translucent, so her expression looked very Halloween in origin, something that would scare a small child from Nancy's world, but that was neither here nor there. Nancy simply wanted to know what that expression was even for.

"What is it?" she asked. "What's wrong? You're not offended about the hair thing…are you?"

"No," sighed Rain. "It's just that…if you're telling the truth, then…then the Nancy I'm talking to right now isn't *my* Nancy. You come from a different universe…You're a visitor here, and that thought makes me kind of sad."

"Why?" asked Nancy.

And she really wanted to know. For the most part and aside from some very small details, Rain was the same in *every* universe, and from what the eccentric young genius had told her, Nancy was pretty much the same as well.

"You and I are pretty much the same in every single universe, Rain," explained Nancy. "I'm not sad, because I know you'll always be waiting for me when I wake up in the morning. It's one of the things that's kept me from falling apart."

Rain gave her a slight punch on the arm and grinned.

"Aww!" she smiled. "That's so sweet!...But I'm still keeping this notebook."

"Fine," sighed Nancy. "That's what I want anyway. You'll see soon enough that I'm not lying."

"I…hope so," said Rain hesitantly.

Nancy was about to say something, but her train of thought was sidetracked by the sudden notice that something was missing…or rather *someone*…in the loosest definition of the term.

"Rain?" she asked. "Where's Weirdo?"

"Oh…My mom took him to the vet," replied Rain. "He wasn't feeling too well last night. He's been moving really slowly and whimpering a lot."

"Oh," said Nancy. "I hope it's nothing serious. My parents won't let me have a pet, so Weirdo's the closest thing I have to one."

"A surrogate pet," said Rain with a sheepish smile. "That's kind of sad, Fance."

"I know," said Nancy. "Still, I just…I don't know, I've always wanted a pet…maybe not a *dog*…"

"Oh, I see!" smiled Rain. "So you're too good for Weirdo, huh?"

"What?" asked Nancy, but she shook her head as she realized that Rain was only joking. "No, it's not that. I was just hoping for a cat."

"What's wrong with dogs?" asked Rain.

"Nothing," shrugged Nancy. "I like little dogs like Weirdo…but big dogs scare me."

"I can see that," said Rain. "I'm not fond of big dogs, either. I'm afraid they'll go crazy and rip me to pieces…like in that one movie that was based on that book by that famous author…What was his name?"

"I know what you're talking about," replied Nancy. "I don't like those kinds of stories, though. I like the funny ones where the dog is playing a sport or something."

"Those are ridiculous," smirked Rain. "If dogs were that smart, I'd have taught Weirdo how to fold clothes by now."

They both gave out a short chuckle at the thought of the wiener dog folding laundry.

"It does make you wonder what goes on in their heads," said Nancy. "Can you imagine running around all day long chasing after things in the yard and waiting for some human to fill up your bowl or give you some good leftovers?

"You can't think a dog ever gets bored, or we'd see a lot of depressed ones. It would be really convenient if simple activities like that could keep me interested in life. It's not like they're smart enough to know what they're doing is boring to us. It's not like there's a downside to being a dog…"

"Other than sniffing another dog's butt," chuckled Rain, "or eating your own poop…"

"All right, all right!" laughed Nancy. "I didn't think that one through."

"And here I thought you were getting smarter," smirked Rain.

"Hey now!" said Nancy in mock offense. "I've just been thinking about things more often as of late…mainly because I'm forced to, but that's beside the point."

"So you're using your brain," shrugged Rain. "That's a good thing. I mean, I've never thought you were *stupid*, but in the past, you had your likes and your dislikes, and you never really ventured…"

"Outside the box," finished Nancy. "I know. But now it's different. I want to know what's happening to me, and…what's potentially happening to you…I want to understand this. It's all one big mystery to me."

"It's a mystery, because that's what science is," said Rain. "Science isn't magic. Do you think, for instance, that if someone came back in time from the year…*oooooh*…3000…and they had technology that you didn't understand, but they dressed up like a stage magician and used that technology to pull off the impossible…Would you think that what they were doing was real magic?"

"Yeah," shrugged Nancy. "I guess so…but if they're dressed like a stage magician…"

"Okay, okay," nodded Rain. "Let's just say he's dressed in normal clothes…"

"Why does it have to be a guy?" asked Nancy.

In truth, she had no idea why she had asked that, but now that she was thinking about it, there was no real reason why "future guy" couldn't be a "future girl." Rain, however, did not seem interested in that little difference.

"It doesn't matter," said the eccentric genius. "The point is…is that…it's all just science. If some guy…or *girl*…traveled back in time and told you they knew magic, but all they were really doing was using future technology…"

"Then I'd believe it was magic," shrugged Nancy. "So?"

"So that's what's so fascinating about science!" said Rain in excitement. "What looks like magic to us now…teleportation, telepathy, regeneration, time travel…all of that is possible…well, *theoretically* possible…if we just understand the science behind it.

"What's happening to you is a mystery, and I want to know what's going on with you just as much as you do. Now that I know you're interested in the science behind it, and now that I know you're actively coming up with your own theories on it…we can work together to find out what actually happened."

"I thought that's what we were doing," said Nancy in confusion.

"I was putting down information, sure," explained Rain, "but that's about it. Now it's time to start formulating those theories and methodically studying this thing. You see what I'm saying?"

Nancy did indeed understand what her best friend was saying. They were on the same page for once.

"Yeah," she shrugged, "but I don't know how far we'll get. Whatever those scientists did, I can't possibly fix it…at least…I don't think I can within my lifetime. I'm like that dog looking up at a human and wanting that tasty treat, but I don't know how the treat is made or where it comes from…I just know the human has it. That's what it feels like with those Breckenridge scientists. *They* had the technology that did this, and now *they're* gone…erased."

"But you've got me," smiled Rain. "I'm on the case now."

Nancy sighed, and her aura began to glow a pale yellow again.

"Great," she breathed. "That's like asking a smarter dog to help me figure out where the treats come from."

"Hey!" said Rain in clear disappointment. "I'm smarter than that!"

Nancy's aura died as her laughter picked up. She realized at that moment that Rain's reactions to such statements were equal to her own when the young genius's intelligence was on the line. The eccentric young woman was being a hypocrite, and for some reason, this struck Nancy as funny.

"Now you know how I feel when you dismiss *my* intelligence," she said with a shake of her head.

Chapter 8...The Eighth Shift

Nancy awoke to a plethora of smells. It was the scent of soap mixed with sweat mixed with laundry detergent mixed with old wood mixed with toast mixed with...Nancy had to shake her head just to concentrate. The waft of literally everything within the area of the entire house seeped into her, and it was overwhelming.

She sat up within the dawn's light and rubbed some crust from her eyes. This gave her the opportunity to study her hands, but they were not human, and even though she knew they wouldn't be, she was still somewhat crushed over this fact.

Her hands and arms were covered with a thick brown fur that held a reddish tint, and her fingernails were thicker and more sloped, not quite claws, but close enough. Her nails were a mix of white with black striations, as if she had dirt under them, though she instinctively knew they were clean.

"What now?" she asked herself in irritation.

But she had to pause a moment at the sound of her own voice. Her voice was an octave lower than she was used to, not quite a boy's voice, but still somewhat disturbing to her own sensibilities.

"Wonderful," she sighed, but her voice still grated on her nerves.

She lifted her arms to stretch and yawn, but one sniff of her armpits caused her to retch. She quickly lowered them and silently pouted while still in bed.

"My pits don't stink," she thought unhappily. *"It's this stupid sense of smell..."*

She reached up in a reflexive motion to touch her nose with the fingers of her right hand, but it felt rough and somewhat bumpy, yet moist like it was wet with snot. She rubbed at her nose for a moment to dry it, but she could tell that nothing was leaking from her nostrils, and that in itself was strange.

"What is going on today?" she asked, but the sound of her own voice made her cringe.

"That doesn't even sound like me," she thought in growing unhappiness. *"It sounds like a stranger is talking with MY mouth. It's so weird...Oh, well...I'd better get moving and get ready for school. I'd better see what's waiting for me in the mirror anyway. It's going to be a horror show; I just know it."*

She got out of bed and made her way to the bathroom, but in truth, she was not surprised by what she saw in the mirror.

Her face looked human, but it was covered with reddish-brown fur like the rest of her body. Her eyes were still the same, but the rest of her head certainly wasn't. The tip of her nose was black and glistened with a visible moisture in the florescence of the bathroom lights, her scalp was covered with a thick mohawk of upraised fur that was the same color as the rest of her, and her ears were slightly pointed.

She opened her mouth to say something to herself out of reflex, but then she noticed her teeth were sharper than a normal human's, and she felt the sudden urge to run her tongue over them just to make sure what she was seeing was real.

"This is crazy," she thought in mild anxiety. *"Totally nuts...Of course, it's still better than yesterday...or the time I was a spider...or that time I...ugh...had the bald streak down the middle of my head. That was the worst by far...So close and yet so far away...Sigh."*

She undressed for the shower and took a moment to notice that her entire body was covered with thick fur. She did not think about this until the hot water from the shower hit her, and by the time she was done with her daily bathing, she felt like she was wrapped in a wet rug.

"Oh, come on!" she whined as she grabbed a white bath towel off of the nearby rack.

Incidentally, the towel was twice the size it should have been and a lot thicker, almost like a winter blanket. She thought about this for a moment as she dried off, but the answer as to why was pretty obvious.

"So some things do change by necessity," she thought. *"The towels are bigger and thicker because this stupid fur absorbs so much water. I wonder if my clothes are any different? They must be in order to accommodate this fur."*

She walked to her dresser and pulled out her underwear, a pair of faded blue jeans, and a white T-shirt with green stripes across the front. Each and every article of her clothing felt thinner except for the jeans, but the jeans felt somewhat stretchy, as if less cloth had been used to make them or some other material had been added in to replace whatever material made up "jeans." She had no idea how jeans were made, but she was certain that her current pair were definitely *not* what she was used to.

"What the heck?" she asked herself.

She forced herself to ignore the weird sound of her voice. She'd only had to put up with an equally-irritating voice once before, and that was when she'd been a spider. She knew she had to speak eventually, so she decided then and there to just ignore it. However, she could not ignore the cheap and thin feel of her clothes.

"Why do all of my clothes feel napkin thin?" she asked herself.

She carefully put on her clothes, but despite the thin feeling of the material, they were still quite durable, and this puzzled her a bit.

"I bet I couldn't wear these if I were human," thought Nancy. *"People would be able to see right through*

them. I guess this thick fur prevents that now, but…I don't understand why they're so thin in the first pla…"

It hit her all at once, and she smiled as she realized that she had just figured out an important scientific fact all on her own.

"It must be heat," she said out loud. "It must be too hot to wear normal clothes, too hot with all this fur, so we wear these to keep us from sweating to death…I figured something out!…Rain would be so proud."

She opened up her sock drawer but discovered more underwear and jeans. Clearly, no one in this world wore socks, but she looked down to her right and saw her sneakers next to the dresser where she always put them.

Nancy felt more confident about herself today thanks to her scientific epiphany a moment ago, so she continued on with her inquisitive mood and puzzled over the meaning of shoes without socks.

"No socks," she thought in sudden interest. *"Shoes without socks. I guess we don't need them since we have fur…Makes sense."*

She gathered up her backpack and books and opened her bedroom door, but she was immediately assaulted by a horrible smell. She sniffed once and immediately recoiled at the scent of raw sewage. She heard the flush of a toilet from her brother's room, and her mind practically shut down at the implications generated by that sound.

"I can smell *everything,*" she whispered in sudden horror. *"Ewwwwww!"*

Jason exited his bedroom door a moment later but stopped as he caught sight of her.

He looked exactly like he had always looked, only now he was covered in thick reddish-brown fur just like she was, he had a black and somewhat moist nose just like she did, and his ears were slightly pointed like hers, though the mohawk of fur on his head was a lot shorter than hers.

He looked at her in confusion for a moment before speaking.

"Why do you look like someone just died?" he asked. "And why are you carrying your backpack?"

"What?" she asked in equal confusion. "What do you mean?...It's for school, dummy! Why else would I be carrying my backpack?"

Jason frowned and then gave her an ugly look.

"It's *Saturday*, dummy!" he said in obvious irritation. "Did that fever you had yesterday fry your brain?"

Nancy gave herself a mental smack for forgetting what day it was, but it was Jason's mention of a "fever" that actually confounded her.

"Fever?" she asked. "What fever?"

Jason stared at her as if she were an alien that had just stepped out of a UFO.

"The raging death fever you had that made Mom take you to the doctor!" he said in exasperation. "Are you with it at all?"

"That's right!" thought Nancy in surprise. *"I missed school yesterday, so in this universe, it wasn't because of 'flashing,' because that's impossible, so it had to be for something else. Apparently, I had a fever instead."*

"Yeah, yeah," replied Nancy. "I'm just a little confused, is all. I remember now. I wasn't exactly with it yesterday."

"No kidding," snorted Jason. "I don't think you're with it now, either."

"I'm fine," frowned Nancy. "Don't be a little jerkface."

"Whatever," said Jason. "I'm not the one who thought it was still Friday."

Nancy ignored him by waving him off and going back into her room. She shut the door and slung off her backpack, setting it beside her bedroom dresser.

This turn of events was actually a good thing, because "fever" meant her school absence was excused.

"I wonder if it's a fever in every universe?" she thought for a moment. *"I'll have to ask Rain...She might know or have a theory on it...Ugh...That means I'll have to get Mom's permission to leave. That's going to be tough."*

She was, however, confident in her ability to coax her mother into letting her go to Rain's. The older woman had let her go yesterday, after all.

*****

Nancy walked her bike into Rain's backyard, but the eccentric young woman was not waiting for her.

"It's Saturday," she thought, *"so Rain may think I've gone biking down Bitter Creek...but there's no way I'm going down that road again...Not anytime soon anyway."*

She knocked on Rain's backdoor, but no one answered.

"Rain!" she called. "It's Nancy!"

She knocked again, but still no one came to the door.

She was about to call out again when she heard the distinct sound of footsteps behind her, and her nose was assaulted with an unfamiliar scent. It smelled like a musty attic mixed with bacon, and it caused her to spin around to see what the source of such a mix of odors could be.

It was Danny. He walked into the backyard and stopped as he saw her. The young man had light-brown fur with a short dark-brown mohawk upon his head, but other than that, he looked basically the same as he always did. He still wore the same dark and depressing getup he always wore, though Nancy suspected his clothes were just as thinly made as hers.

"She's not here," he called from his safe distance of thirty feet.

"What?" asked Nancy in confusion.

"She's not here!" he repeated, only louder.

"I know," replied Nancy. "I heard you…Do you know where she went?"

"She and her parents went to the vet," called Danny. "They got a call—"

"Wait!" said Nancy.

She was already tired of shouting across the lawn. She marched forward to talk to him face to face, but he backed away as she approached him.

"What's wrong with you?" she asked in confusion. "I'm not going to bite."

He frowned and stood his ground, but Nancy did not like the meaning of whatever it was he was thinking. As it stood, his "scent" got stronger the closer she got, and she commented upon it against her better judgement.

"Why are you backing away?" she asked unhappily. "I'm the one who should be backing away. You smell like a musty attic mixed with bacon."

Danny's frown only deepened, and Nancy immediately regretted her tactless, if wholly accurate, statement.

"And you smell like pancakes and old lady perfume," replied the young man.

Nancy shook her head in irritation, but she was the one who had said something nasty first, so she ignored his retort.

She walked up to him within talking distance, but she could already tell he was uncomfortable. It was clear that some things held together in a strange continuity between universes, like her "flashing" changing to a "fever," so it was obvious to her that her "flashing" insult from yesterday had translated into something else here, something that was probably worse.

"Great," she thought in unhappy silence. *"I don't even know what it was I did, either."*

"Let's just stop this," she frowned. "I'm not mad at you, Danny…I just want to know where Rain went."

"I told you," said Danny. "She went to the vet with her parents. They got a call because her dog is really sick."

"Oh," said Nancy in surprise. "I hope he's all right."

"I guess," shrugged Danny.

"There's no 'guess,'" said Nancy in audible irritation. "Rain's had Weirdo since she was three. She loves that dog. He's a part of their family…Heck, *I* love that dog. I feel like he's a part of *my* family."

"Wait," said Danny in confusion. "Since she was *three*? You're telling me that dog is thirteen years old?"

"Yeah…" said Nancy hesitantly. "Why?"

"Dogs don't normally live that long," explained Danny. "Not any that I've seen, anyway."

This news hit Nancy like a freight train. It was clear she was visibly distressed over the matter, because Danny immediately picked up on her mood.

"I…don't know how sick he is, though," he finished in awkward reply.

Nancy let this sink in. She had a terrible feeling she would not see Weirdo again. No one she knew had ever died before, except for the Breckenridge scientists, but she had not actually *known* them, so their passing was a shock but not much else.

She felt tears reach her eyes, but she quickly wiped them away. She really did not want to cry in front of Danny again.

"I…I don't…know what really happened," said Danny in yet another awkward reply.

"It's fine," sniffed Nancy. "You didn't know that dog like I did."

"I've known him for a few years," said Danny. "We moved in four years ago. I mean, I don't have any pets, but I just always thought of him as a dog, so…"

Nancy nodded in understanding. It was hard for people without pets to understand what it was like to lose one, but she understood what it was like because she felt like Weirdo was her surrogate pet, so she did feel upset at the thought of losing him.

"He's not my dog," sniffed Nancy, "but that doesn't mean I won't miss him if something happens to him."

"I don't understand," shrugged Danny. "He's just a dog."

She did not expect him to understand, but his callous statement made her a little angry. Still, she was not going to chase him off this time. That would be wrong, and she knew that, so she tried to think of a way to explain it to him without sounding angry or upset, but it was difficult.

"He's someone who's been around for as long as I've been friends with Rain," replied Nancy. "Rain grew up with him. He was just a little puppy back then, so you should understand how—"

"I get it," finished Danny. "You don't have to explain it…I…I'm going to go now. I just walked over here because I heard you at the door."

He lowered his head and turned to walk away, but Nancy stopped him. She felt the need to apologize for yesterday, though she did not know what she had done within *this* universe to anger him.

"Wait, Danny," she said quickly.

He stopped and turned around, though the look on his face was that of surprise.

"What?" he asked.

"I just wanted to say…" stammered Nancy. "I…I just wanted to say that I'm sorry about yesterday."

She did not know what she was sorry for, but it was the best improvisation of an apology that she could come up with off the fly, so it would have to do.

Danny lowered his furry head and then nodded a couple times. He turned to walk away, and he got maybe five steps, but then he turned and looked upon her with a strange expression.

"Why do you hate me?" he asked.

This surprised Nancy. She thought she had already explained to him that she didn't hate him anymore. It was one thing to be angry with someone over something nasty that they had done, but it was entirely another to be angry with someone over something that they had *not* done, and Nancy knew this.

Still, Danny was weird, and there were times when Nancy wondered if he were dangerous, dangerous in the way that quiet outcasts were in their unassuming manner until they appeared on school grounds with a loaded shotgun. Danny often struck her as this type of person, but she knew it was wrong to treat him poorly because of this unfounded fear.

"I don't…*hate* you, Danny," she said in awkward reply. "I thought I told you I was sorry about the Brinn Clevenger incident."

"That's not what I'm talking about," said Danny.

He sounded morose, though the light-brown fur on his face gave him a "safer" quality than his voice suggested. Nancy did not know what to think of his continually downcast mood, but she did her best to answer him. She kind of wanted the conversation to end so she could go home, but she did not want to be rude about it.

"What are you talking about, then?" she asked cautiously.

He was hesitant to tell her; she could sense it somehow, but this emboldened her a bit, so she patiently waited for his reply.

"I…I don't understand why you always…" he stammered. "You…You always look at me funny, like…like I'm a criminal or something. You barely talk to me at all when I'm over here with Rain."

This bothered Nancy, because it was actually accurate. Still, she knew what to say in this situation, and that in itself was surprising.

"Danny, I don't talk to you because I don't *know* you," she replied. "It's hard to talk to someone you don't know. I mean, I know who you *are*, but I don't really *know* you. I don't know your likes or dislikes, I don't know if what I'm going to say is going to offend you or not…Do you understand?…I don't…I don't *know* you…and that's why I hardly talk to you sometimes. Don't you have trouble talking to new people?"

He looked down at the grass beneath their feet and shrugged.

"People don't talk to me," he said, but this time there was a distinct unhappiness in his voice.

"Don't you have any friends?" asked Nancy. "Isn't Allen your friend?"

"Yeah, Allen's my friend," said Danny. "I mean, he's not my only friend…I have other friends, too. We hang out and play games online, but…I don't really have any friends who are girls."

"Rain is your friend, right?" asked Nancy.

"I guess," said Danny. "She's the only girl who will talk to me, but I think that's just because we're neighbors."

Nancy had a strange feeling hit her. It was clear to her now that Danny was lonely. He had friends, but what he wanted…what he *needed*…was not something she was sure she could help him with. She knew at that moment that what he needed was a special someone, a girl who liked him for who he was, and that was a tall order.

"So you want to know more girls?" asked Nancy. "Is that it?"

He shrugged and didn't say anything for a moment.

"I want to know what's wrong with me," he said unhappily. "I want to know why everybody hates me."

"When you say 'everybody,' do you mean girls?" asked Nancy. "Is that what you mean?"

He shrugged again, but Nancy was pretty sure that was what he meant.

"When we came here, I thought things were going to be better," said Danny. "I thought I was finally going to be normal."

Nancy realized right then that the things that were difficult in her life did not mean that she was the only one with problems, and it was clear that Danny's problems ran much deeper and were much more prevalent than hers.

"Aside from my shifting," she thought in growing pity, *"I've never really had problems in my life. Yeah, Mom is an old problem, but she's still my mom, and I think most girls my age have that problem…and of course, there's Brinn Clevenger…but I'll deal with her later…Danny, though…I think I know why Rain is so nice to him…It's because no one else is."*

"Danny…" sighed Nancy. "You have to be confident in who you are before you can expect anyone else to be. Look at Rain…She does whatever she wants and doesn't care what anyone else thinks…and she's perfectly happy about it. I like who I am…for the most part anyway."

"But everybody likes you," said Danny.

He frowned, but frowning was not a strong enough word for the look on his face. He looked truly defeated, and this actually hurt Nancy. She had not expected to ever feel *sorry* for Danny Princeton, but looking upon him now, she could not see him in any other light. She knew what he needed, though she did not know how to help him with that.

"You just need to be more open," said Nancy. "If you want to meet girls and feel…a part of everything…then you just…you have to be more confident and…and have a voice. I'm not saying you have to change the things you like to do…I mean, I don't particularly like video games, or fantasy, or anything like that, but there are a lot of people who do…but even if they don't, that doesn't mean you can't be friends with them. I know Rain likes that stuff and I don't, but we're still the best of friends."

"I guess," said Danny, but he didn't sound convinced.

"Danny…" said Nancy in frustration, "you're like a snail in a shell. You're never going to meet anyone if you're always in the safety of that shell. You actually have to *talk* to girls in order to get to know them."

"I don't understand them," frowned Danny. "I want to talk to them, but everybody treats me like I'm a criminal…or like I have some kind of plague. Even if they didn't treat me like that, I wouldn't know what to say."

"Girls are easy to understand," said Nancy. "You just have to talk to them normally. There's no 'special' way to talk to girls. They're people, too. They want to be treated equally…not like…like something alien or…or someone you'd put on a pedestal…Well, maybe Brinn Clevenger would like to be up there…"

Danny gave a slight chuckle at that name drop, and this gave Nancy a smile.

"The point is…is that you just have to open up," said Nancy.

"I don't know how to do that," said Danny.

"You just did," replied Nancy. "You just talked to me like a human being. You have to be more like that…I don't mean asking people why they hate you, but…just be…*friendlier*."

"It's not that easy," he said. "If it were that easy, I'd have done it by now...I...I just want...I want to meet a girl who finally likes me."

Nancy smiled at that remark, though that smile was not intended to be offensive.

"You...You'll meet someone," she said after a moment. "I think the problem you're having is that you're so...so wishing for it to happen that it's not going to happen. The more desperate you are, the less likely you'll find anyone. Trust me, you'll find her when you're not looking. It's how these things work out.

"You know those books that always give advice on how to pick up women? They make you think that reading that book is going to magically allow you to have a girl on each arm...but that's not how it works. It's a lot harder to get a girl to like you in that way than what they make you believe. It's because they're actual *people* and not some object with a switch you can flip. There's no magical formula for it...

"You just have to be yourself, but more importantly, you have to be *confident* in yourself. That's why you just have to...to open up. I mean, don't think just because you haven't met that right person doesn't mean you'll never meet her."

"I guess," he said after a moment. "I never thought of it that way...You know...you're really smart."

Nancy was a little offended at first by that comment, but she inherently knew it was not intended to be an insult.

"I try," she said. "Look...you must have had girls who you liked in the past. Did you ever try and talk to them?"

He looked back down at the lawn and shrugged.

"Yeah," he said anxiously. "There have been girls I've liked, but...they didn't like me...I thought when I'd first met Rain that she might like me, but..."

"She's a little *too* into what she does," smiled Nancy. "Yeah, I know Rain. The only thing she's interested in is—"

"Science," smirked Danny. "She's always talking about some new theory she learned about online."

Nancy rolled her eyes over that one.

"Tell me about it," she snorted. "Yeah, Rain is different, that's for sure. Even so, you and her just aren't…uhhh…"

"Compatible," finished Danny.

"In that way," clarified Nancy. "You strike me as more of a dreamer, Danny."

He looked up and gave her a quizzical look.

"How so?" he asked.

"You like fantasy and science fiction," shrugged Nancy.

"So does Rain," he said.

"Yeah, but as a way to pass the time," said Nancy. "It doesn't speak to her like it does to you…I'm just guessing, though. Am I right? Does…Does that kind of thing define you?"

"Yeah," said Danny, but he sounded confused. "Actually, I don't know. I don't really know what *defines* me. I don't know what that means."

Nancy gave a motion with her right hand to describe his current clothing.

"I can tell by the way you dress…the color of your clothes and whatnot…and just your general attitude that you…you seem…" she hesitated.

It occurred to her that if she finished that statement, it might offend him, but it was too late to back out now. Danny would not let her.

"Seem what?" he asked in confusion.

Nancy sighed and just finished her observation. There was no point in lying about it.

"You seem morose…grim…*depressed*," she finished. "I can tell by your attitude that you've drawn into yourself…like that snail in a shell I was talking about. Did you ever think that you might like science fiction and fantasy because it's…like…an escape, you know? You said you were writing a fantasy book. Does it feel like…you're…more at home in a different world than here?"

Danny shrugged, but his frown spoke volumes.

"Yeah," he said unhappily, "but I don't want to change that. I like science fiction and fantasy. What's wrong with that?"

"Nothing," said Nancy with a shake of her head. "It's just…do you really *like* it…or are you just using it as a crutch?"

"What do you mean?" asked Danny.

"Is it something you really like," asked Nancy, "or is it something you're using to identify with?…In other words, are you using it as an escape to a different world because you don't like the way you are in this one?"

"No…I don't think so," he said. "I might be sometimes, but…I think it would be cool to visit other worlds…like alien planets or places where magic is real. Haven't you ever thought about that before? Wouldn't you like to see whole new worlds?"

The answer to that question was so ironically simple that Nancy burst out in a short fit of laughter.

"I've had my *fill* of that," she chuckled.

He gave her an odd look; it was the exact same look Rain often gave her, a raising of his left eyebrow as he cocked his head to the right, and this made Nancy laugh a little more.

"You look exactly like Rain when you do that!" she chuckled.

He frowned and then looked back down at the grass beneath his shoes. Nancy finished her short fit of amusement and then shook her head in recognition of his mood.

"Okay, okay," she said quickly. "I'm willing to believe that you really like fantasy and science fiction…but this whole depressing goth slash emo thing is definitely a cry for help."

She made a motion with her right hand to address his clothing, but Danny just frowned.

"Goth and Emo are two different things," he said.

"What?" asked Nancy.

"Goth and Emo are two different things," repeated Danny. "Emo began in the late nineties and is still popular today. It's a movement that began with alternative rock and punk that centered around emotional lyrics designed to provoke or invoke an emotional response to the person listening to it. Emo borrowed some of the dark dress and habits from the Goth movement, but they're not the same thing."

"Really?" asked Nancy.

She realized at that moment that Danny was actually very intelligent. In a lot of respects, he was just like Rain.

"Then what is Goth?" she asked.

"The Goth movement started in the late eighties," explained Danny. "It started with the advent of popularity in vampire roleplaying games, although it increased the popularity of alternative rock and punk, so Goth and Emo have that in common.

"A lot of people would say it started with post British Punk back in the early eighties, but I think my definition is the one for over here. I think it really picked up over *here* with the advent of vampire RPGs. Here, the Goth crowd was two generations ago, and that generation was one of the most violent and unforgiving generations of our time. It had one of the highest murder rates in our country's history…They were crazy, if you ask me."

"Really?" asked Nancy. "That's kind of scary. They acted like vampires?"

"No, no," corrected Danny. "They just increased the popularity of the whole vampires and werewolves genre."

"Like those popular books that got made into movies?" asked Nancy.

"Yeah…" said Danny slowly, "but those are way watered down compared to what the Goth crowd was into. I mean, the generation before us were the ones that made Emo popular, but they definitely diluted the meaning behind the black clothes and makeup and everything that the Goths were into."

"So why do *you* wear black clothes?" asked Nancy. "You don't wear any makeup."

Danny looked truly uncomfortable for a moment, but Nancy was not sure what to make of that look.

"I don't…I just…" stammered Danny. "I don't feel like I fit in."

"I knew it," thought Nancy. *"He's made himself an outcast, even if he doesn't realize it. He's made himself a perpetual loner, and now he doesn't know what to do. No wonder he's the way he is. Little social failures set him back, and they stacked and stacked until they became one giant one…Sad."*

"Look, Danny…" she said. "You're never going to meet someone with that attitude. You have to leave the safety of your shell if you want to get a girl."

"I don't know how," frowned Danny. "I told you that."

"Really?" scoffed Nancy. "You've already come out of your shell just by talking with me. I lumped Goth and Emo together, and you corrected me, and then when I asked what Goth was, you gave me a detailed answer. You were interesting at that moment…You just have to come out of that shell, and eventually you'll meet that special someone. That's how it works. Trust me…I know how girls think. I am one, and it's clear you don't know any…"

"I know Rain," said Danny.

Nancy laughed in spite of herself. It was not good to make fun of her best friend…at least, not behind her back.

"Rain is *not* a typical girl," said Nancy, "and she is *definitely* not a good example for how most girls think. Rain's a little special in that category…"

They were sidetracked by the sound of a vehicle pulling into Rain's driveway.

"Speak of the Devil," said Nancy.

They heard people exiting a car, the shutting of car doors, and then people entering the house.

"I…I probably ought to go," said Danny quickly. "It's not good for me to just be hanging around in her backyard while she's gone…"

"I'm here," said Nancy quickly. "I don't think she's going to care…"

Her voice trailed off as the backdoor opened and Rain stepped out.

The young woman had thick grey fur covering her body with a thick shock of black fur upon her head, and today she was dressed in faded black jeans and a thin black cover shirt over a white undershirt. She had multiple gold studs in her pointed ears ranging from the bottom to the top along the outer edges, and Nancy identified that little feature as "the difference" between this Rain and all the others. Every Rain seemed to have some little feature that was altered in some way, and this just gave Nancy more confidence that her theory on Rain being "touched" by the Breckenridge explosion was not so much a theory as it was a fact.

Rain took one look upon them and nodded once.

"I was hoping you were here," said the eccentric young woman.

"Rain...uhhh...I heard from Danny..." started Nancy.

"Yeah," said Rain as she walked up to them. "Weirdo was really sick...He had multiple organ failure...so...we had to put him down."

That was exactly what Nancy had *not* wanted to hear. Her eyes watered a little as she looked upon her best friend for some kind of reaction, but there was none. Rain's eyes were...*dead*...and Nancy did not know what to make of it, but it worried her, nonetheless.

"Oh, Rain," she said in growing sympathy. "You should have called me...I would have gone with you..."

"No, it's okay," shrugged the young genius. "He was old and sick, and I knew he was going to die someday...I made peace with it a long time ago."

Nancy looked over to Danny, but the young man's eyes were downcast as usual. She really did not know how to address this matter, for one thing...not to Rain, and not with Danny standing right there.

She turned back toward her best friend in order to offer some consolation.

"Even so," she said, "it couldn't have been easy. What did your parents think?"

Rain shrugged and sighed.

"My mom cried her eyes out," she said flatly, "and then she got onto me on the way home."

"What?" asked Nancy. "Wait...Why?"

"Because I didn't show any emotion," frowned Rain. "She thinks I have Asperger's Syndrome."

"Azpurgers?" asked Nancy. "What's that?"

"It's a form of autism," explained Danny, "though I don't think they call it Asperger's anymore. It's called something else, but I don't know what."

"Yeah," sighed Rain. "They called it 'higher functioning autism' back in the day. I tried to tell her I don't have that, but she wouldn't hear it…It doesn't matter. She'll probably forget about it in a day or two."

Rain looked over to Danny and frowned.

"I'm sorry, Danny," said Rain unhappily. "I don't feel like hanging out today…Maybe tomorrow, okay? I just want to talk to Nancy for a bit…"

Rain's subject of conversation changed so quickly that Nancy had to stop and process what was going on just to make sense of it. It occurred to her that even though Rain's mother may not have seen a change in behavior with her daughter over the death of their beloved pet, Nancy had noticed a change right away. Rain was not her usual self.

Nancy did not know how Danny was going to take this rejection, but his reaction actually surprised her. He replied with wide eyes and an understanding nod.

"That's all right," he said quickly. "I was just leaving. I understand. I'll see you tomorrow."

"Yeah," replied Rain. "See you tomorrow."

They watched Danny turn and go, but Nancy had the sudden realization that the young man was not as socially clueless as she had first thought him to be. He did not take Rain's rejection personally, and he was quick to empathize with the young woman's situation.

Danny rounded the back fence of Rain's yard and disappeared from sight. Nancy shook her head as she watched him vanish.

"He's really surprised me today," she said thoughtfully. "He really opened up…although I don't think he realized he was doing it…"

Her voice faded out as she heard a low whimper from behind her. Nancy turned to view her best friend's devastated expression, and there were visible tears rolling over the thick grey fur on Rain's face. Rain started sobbing a moment later, and this stunned Nancy. She had never, *ever* seen Rain cry…not once.

The sight of it made her own eyes moisten; it was just stunning and heartbreaking to see that expression upon her best friend's face, and for a moment, she did not know what to do.

"Oh, Rain…" she said gently.

"*Heeee's gooone!*" cried Rain, and that was about the only thing she could say before she started sobbing again.

Nancy hugged her as Rain completely broke down.

Chapter 9...The Ninth Shift

Nancy awoke in a dark place. There was no light at first, only an ebon wall of *nothing*, and this terrified her. She whimpered once before a light picked up, and it was so bright, she had to cover her eyes with her right hand.

It took her a moment to realize she was wearing her outfit from the Breckenridge explosion, her spotless white shirt with the matching red shorts with the white stripes down the sides of them, and this bothered her almost as much as the bright light shining directly in her face. She did not want to be reminded of that terrible incident, and now that she was wearing those clothes again, this only exacerbated the fact that something very weird was going on in general.

"Nancy," came a voice in the distance.

The voice was familiar; she had heard it once before, but the description of "voice" was inadequate. It was more like *voices*, all speaking her name at the same time, male and female mashed together in one perfect collage of strange synchrony, and this frightened her even more.

"Who are you!" she screeched.

"Nancy," came the collection of voices.

The light shone brighter in the distance, and though it illuminated her surroundings, what Nancy saw did not lessen her fear. There was *nothing* around her, and even the ground beneath her was nothing more than hard black stone. Peering into that void was like peering into madness itself, and this panicked Nancy, made her want to run and hide and cower in a corner, but there was no corner to go to...It was all just darkness.

The light in the distance moved forward, but this intrusion only made Nancy cower more.

"Nancy Clark," came the collection of voices.

That was enough for her; she did *not* want to be here any longer.

"Leave me alone!" she screeched. "LEAVE ME ALONE!"

She sat up in bed as the word "alone" escaped her lips. It was Sunday morning, the dawn light streamed through her bedroom window as it always did, and though this familiarity should have made her feel safe, her heart was still pumping in a furious thunder of adrenaline-fueled fear.

"Got to get it together," she thought in an attempt to calm herself. *"Get it together, Nance."*

She took in a deep breath to calm herself down. The first thing she noticed while she was doing so was that she looked human again…mostly. Her arms and hands were human, though they were a little paler than normal. She held up her right hand and inspected it, but it looked like her old human hand as far as she could tell.

She squinted in the sunlight streaming through her window, but the light itself hurt her eyes a little.

"Things are getting better," she thought in sudden hopefulness. *"Getting a little better…Just keep it together, Nance. Keep it together."*

She hopped out of bed and walked toward the bathroom, but the light from the sun continued to mess with her vision. She pushed open the bathroom door and flipped on the light, but the light of her fluorescent bulb was much dimmer and much softer than what she was used to.

Nancy did a once-over of her reflection in the mirror and sighed.

"So close, yet so far away," she said unhappily.

Her voice was normal, and she looked human for the most part, but there were other differences that stood out in immediate attention. For one thing, her hair was jet black, and she was not used to that color, but that was nothing compared to her other "features." Her skin was pale, as if she did not get enough sun, but her eyes…her eyes were the most striking. They were not the pleasant hazel she was used to, but red, all crimson with black pupils, and the whole picture of it together made her look like a monster, like some kind of demon, or perhaps a ghost from a horror film.

"Oh, come on," she sighed. "Ugh…Just look on the bright side, Nance. You don't have a bald streak running down the middle of your head, or hair on your back, or…you know…the whole *spider* thing."

She took her shower, toweled off, got dressed, this time in a plain sky-blue T-shirt with matching stonewashed jean-shorts, and left her room with a sense of urgency, that urgency caused by the need to see her best friend…and more importantly, to help her. She did not know how Rain was holding up after the death of Weirdo, so Nancy hustled to get ready and get gone.

*****

Nancy biked up to Rain's but nearly crashed due to the savage yipping and chasing of her tires by a tiny ball of white fur that she determined was a dog. The little thing was not even bigger than a foot in size, and she could just make out a little black nose and beady little black eyes upon its rather flat face.

"Buster!" called Rain in the distance.

Nancy's best friend came running up from the vicinity of the backyard and into the street to grab the little nuisance, but Nancy herself was too busy protecting her pale ankles from its tiny little teeth.

Rain scooped up the little dog into her pale arms and gave Nancy a sheepish smile.

"He's not used to strangers," she said quietly.

Today the eccentric girl was dressed in her "Remember the Irish" shirt and a pair of normal blue jeans, but large, green, four-leaf-clover earrings dangled from her ears, and this was yet another difference that Nancy marked down for later inspection within her own mind. Aside from that, Rain looked almost exactly like Nancy in overall appearance; she had rich black hair and red eyes to accent her pale skin.

Nancy gave a cursory nod toward the new dog.

"Is this little guy yours?" she asked.

"Yeah," said Rain. "My mom went out and got him last night after…after what happened yesterday. He's a little handful. He's not like Weirdo at all."

The little dog struggled in Rain's arms as it gave a few more tiny growls and yips at Nancy as she got off her bike and pushed it toward Rain's backyard. They walked around to the back patio where Rain unceremoniously dumped the little munchkin into the kitchen of the house and closed the back door.

"I'm glad you came over," said Rain. "I know that yesterday wasn't a great day. I mean, we took a picture yesterday, but I didn't get a chance to show you the notebook."

"That's okay," replied Nancy. "I'm really surprised you took the picture in spite of…"

"Oh, yeah," shrugged Rain, "but you should know me by now."

And Nancy did know her. If Rain's parents had suddenly died in a horrible fiery accident, Rain would have still taken the picture simply for science's sake. That was Rain to a T.

"It's fine," shrugged Nancy. "It's all right. It doesn't really matter right now."

"Of course, it matters," scoffed Rain.

She walked over to her dad's grill, opened the big red lid, and pulled out the precious green notebook.

"Take a look," said Rain.

Nancy studied her best friend for a moment. If there was something funny going on with the notebook, Rain was not giving her any clue as to what it was.

"*Okaaaay...*" said Nancy in slight hesitation.

Rain opened up the notebook and...Nancy gave herself a triumphant smile.

"I *knew* it!" said Nancy in exultation.

The notebook pictures had stayed the same in spite of the fact that Rain had kept the green notebook and had even hidden it. Even the incredibly depressing picture of their fur-covered selves from yesterday had kept, though Rain looked thoroughly depressed within it and Nancy looked thoroughly worried in an attempt to match Rain's thorough look of depression. Nevertheless, this was the evidence Rain had been looking for, and that gave Nancy a smile.

"I told you," she grinned.

"I know," breathed Rain.

She sidled in close to Nancy, but her voice lowered to a near whisper.

"Do you know what this means?" asked the eccentric genius.

"Yeah," said Nancy in slight confusion. "It means I was right."

"I know," whispered Rain. "That means we have to keep this to ourselves for the time being...probably for quite some time, in fact."

"I thought that's what we were doing, Rain," replied Nancy. "And why are you whispering?"

"Because this is...It's serious," whispered Rain. "If anybody found out about this, then they would...they might take us away. They'd *definitely* take you away."

Nancy considered this logic to be stupid, but she did not want to upset her best friend. Yesterday had been upsetting enough for the poor girl.

"I don't think that's going to happen," she said firmly.

"Of course, it will, if we're not careful!" whispered Rain.

"No, I don't think so," chuckled Nancy. "No one would ever believe us in a million-billion years. They'd think we were just two stupid kids cosplaying. In fact, it's not a big deal unless we make it one. I'm pretty sure that whispering and acting suspicious will draw more attention than just acting normally."

Rain chewed on her lower lip as she raised her head to stare off into the distance. Nancy could tell that the young genius was mulling over this information, but it didn't take the girl long to think about it.

"You're right," shrugged Rain, only this time she spoke at a normal decibel. "I don't know what I was thinking…Still, do you know what this means? Do you have any idea *at all* what this means?"

"That I'm not a liar looking for attention?" asked Nancy.

"No!" said Rain a little too excitedly. "I mean…yes, but no, that's not what I was referring to. It means we really *are* the first people in the entire history of the human race to study this! Don't you find that exciting?"

Nancy shrugged. Her feelings about shifting had not changed one bit, and for that matter, it had only been a week since she'd started doing it, anyway.

"I guess?" she asked.

Rain's face fell at her lackluster reply.

"I'm sorry, Rain," said Nancy in quick apology. "It's just…you know I want this to stop."

"I know," replied her friend. "I get that, but…now that I know with a million-percent certainty that it *is* real, it's the most exciting thing that's ever happened in my life. Can't you understand how I feel?"

"In all fairness, Rain," sighed Nancy, "the explosion of the Breckenridge Institute of Discovery was the most exciting thing that's ever happened in my life…and not in a good way."

Rain shook a little as her face contorted in an odd way, and Nancy honestly did not know what to make of it, but then the young genius closed her blood-red eyes and took in a deep breath. She opened them a second later and slowly released her held breath.

"Okay," said Rain calmly. "Okay. Let's just back up a bit. I just want to ask you a few questions."

"Okay," said Nancy in nervous reply. "Fire away."

She was not really sure what Rain was going to ask, but the eccentric young woman's strange behavior, coupled with her current appearance, made her look…creepy.

"What was it like yesterday?" asked Rain. "What was it like being…whatever it was we were?"

"I don't know," shrugged Nancy. "It wasn't *that* different except for all of the fur…Wait…We had a *super* sense of smell. That was new."

"Really?" asked Rain in an eager tone. "What was it like? How do you know it was super?…Wait…Wait a moment…"

The eccentric young woman produced a mechanical pencil from her back pocket and flipped open the notebook to the page documenting their fur-covered selves.

"Okay…" she said in barely contained excitement. "What was it like?"

Nancy gave herself an inward smile over this.

"This is exactly what Rain needs," she thought in strange happiness. *"The way she broke down after losing Weirdo…I was really worried about her."*

It occurred to her that for once she was not concerned with her own predicament, and this made her feel…*happy*. It gave her a little push in the right direction, and that was strange, because she had forgotten that other people had problems, too. They weren't like *her* problems, but they still existed and persisted regardless of what universe she shifted into. She felt better for some reason over this, but it was not a selfish reason…She genuinely wanted to help Rain, so she answered the young woman as best she could.

"I could smell *everything*," replied Nancy.

"Everything?" asked Rain.

"*Yes*," said Nancy emphatically. "You have *no* idea…and even worse was the fact that I could actually tell when different scents were mixed together."

"Okay, okay," said Rain as she jotted down the information. "How do you know it wasn't just limited to you?"

"Oh, that's easy," said Nancy. "Danny picked out what I smelled like just as easily as I could with him."

"You were *smelling* each other?" smirked Rain.

"Not like *that*," frowned Nancy. "It was automatic, and I could smell him, from like, thirty feet away. He smelled like a musty attic mixed with bacon."

Rain's face wrinkled up as she visibly tried to picture this within her mind's eye.

"What did he say you smelled like?" she asked.

"Like pancakes and old lady perfume," replied Nancy.

Rain cracked up at this remark, and Nancy followed suit. The descriptions of their scents sounded pretty stupid when she said them out loud.

"What else?" chuckled Rain.

It took the young genius a moment to settle down before motioning Nancy onward.

"Continue," she waved.

"I don't know," shrugged Nancy. "Oh wait…Our clothes were *super* thin, like *see-through* thin. It was weird."

"Really?" asked Rain in surprise. "How thin are we talking?"

"Like 'we'd get arrested if we wore that in public' thin," said Nancy. "I figured out why they were that way, though. We had so much fur that I imagine regular clothes would have been too—"

"Hot," finished Rain. "I getchya. Wow…This is…It's fascinating beyond imagination, Nance! Thank you, thank you for letting me keep the notebook. Now that I know it's all real, I'm practically shaking in my skin."

"That's okay," said Nancy. "I just want to help."

"Tell me, tell me…" said Rain excitedly, "what's different about today?"

"A *lot*," said Nancy.

"How so?" asked Rain.

"For starters, we've gone back to looking human, for the most part," said Nancy.

"So we're closer to your original universe?" asked Rain.

"Yeah, but 'closer' is a relative term," frowned Nancy. "My hair is black here instead of brown, my skin is super pale and not my normal peach slash tan color it normally is, and…the biggest difference is that my eyes are red and not hazel."

"You had hazel eyes?" asked Rain in amazement. "Brown hair?…Peachy-tan skin?"

"Yeah," shrugged Nancy.

"That is *so* weird," breathed Rain. "Crazy, crazy methinks, methinks…What else did you notice? Anything else?"

"Not really," said Nancy. "No…No, wait. Mom served us *steak* for breakfast. Can you believe it?"

Rain looked confused for a moment.

"Steak?" she asked. "How is that different?"

Nancy looked at her in surprise. It was clear by the look on the girl's face that she had no idea that this was unusual.

"It was *steak* for *breakfast*," repeated Nancy. "Steak is a dinner meal. We normally have pancakes, eggs, and bacon for breakfast...sometimes hash browns."

"Really?" asked Rain in strange wonder. "How do you get your iron and protein, then? I suppose eggs and bacon will do...but pancakes are a special treat. You'd get really sick if you ate them every day."

This, of course, made no sense at all.

"Rain, what are you talking about?" asked Nancy in growing confusion.

"We...We need iron and protein to keep healthy," said Rain. "I mean, your family are preparers, so I figured that you'd have to really watch what you eat."

"Preparers?" asked Nancy. "What is a preparer? What on earth are you talking about?"

"Pre...Preparer," stammered Rain. "You know...People who cook their food."

Nancy was not quite sure she had heard that correctly. For some strange reason, this comment angered her a little, but she did not know why. It was a growing seed of discord born of frustration, and it was tugging at her in a mercilessly annoying way.

"*Cook* their food?" asked Nancy in growing anger. "What do you mean *cook* their food?"

"Y...yeah," said Rain nervously. "Those people who cook their food."

None of this made any sense, and for some reason, it flipped a switch in Nancy's mood. She went from cold to hot in a second, and she let it happen, but she had no clue as to why she was so mad. It confounded her, and this only angered her more.

"Everybody cooks their food!" she exploded. "Are you stupid! What is wrong with you!"

Rain backed away at her sudden outburst, a look of slight fear upon her own pale face.

"Calm down," she said quickly.

"I am calm!" said Nancy, but she was not calm, not in the slightest.

She was terribly angry for some reason, and the strange thing about it was that she hadn't the faintest clue why. She realized by the look on Rain's face that she was scaring the poor girl, and that was unacceptable behavior in her own mind, but she was too heated to do anything about it.

"Close your eyes and take a deep breath," said Rain nervously. "Don't argue with me, Nance, just do it. Close your eyes and take a deep breath and then slowly release it."

Nancy suddenly wanted to punch Rain's face in, but she knew this was wrong, and what her best friend had said actually made sense, so she closed her eyes and took in a deep breath. She held that breath for a moment and then slowly released it. This helped a lot, and when she opened her eyes, she suddenly felt much better.

"Are you okay?" asked Rain hesitantly.

"Yeah," said Nancy in surprise. "That was weird…What the heck was that? For some strange reason, I felt like taking your head off…Does this have anything to do with this…"

"Universe?" finished Rain. "Y…yeah. You don't know?"

"No," said Nancy in confusion.

"That's the rage, Nance," explained Rain. "It's something we learn to control from, like…age three on up. I forgot that since you're a visitor here today, you wouldn't know that. Plus, your family are preparers, and I know it's for a good cause and all…the whole animal cruelty thing…but…but the thing is, though…without iron and protein, you…you can't really control it. The rage, that is.

The human body needs iron and protein, or we start breaking down. Without that, you get…you know…*murderous*."

"*Really?*" asked Nancy in surprise. "I had no idea."

"That's okay," said Rain softly. "Your family kind of takes things a step further than everyone else, so I understand. You're probably just a little on edge."

"Takes things a step further?" asked Nancy in confusion. "How so?"

"You cook your food," explained the young genius. "Most of us just eat it raw. Of course, I understand why your family does it. You want to bring attention to all of the countries out there that eat their food while it's still alive…"

This stopped Nancy cold.

"Say what now?" she asked in stark disbelief.

She couldn't imagine eating anything that was raw, and she certainly couldn't imagine eating anything that was still *alive*.

"Yeah, yeah," said Rain. "If we don't get our necessary nutrients, then we go nuts and develop all kinds of harmful symptoms."

"*Really?*" asked Nancy.

She had said this word just a few seconds ago, but the surprising strangeness of this universe merited such a repetition.

"Yeah," replied the young genius. "I mean, the rage is the worst one, but you can also get photo eczema…That's where you break out in a rash when exposed to light…and you can get light blindness, where you're sensitive to light, and in the worst-case scenario, anaphylactic shock from light that can kill you. Some people have just spontaneously combusted because they couldn't get enough nutrients."

Nancy thought about this and realized that Rain's brief description described Nancy's very own experience with sensitivity to light the moment she had woken up. And though she knew every universe had its challenges (she'd had a steep learning curve with that little eye-opening truth), she had mistakenly thought that this particular universe would be "safe" due to the fact that she looked mostly human, yet this was far from the case.

This was yet another crazy fact she stowed away for later inspection.

"Good grief," she said after a moment. "That is crazy…That *is* crazy. This universe is actually stranger than the time we were all spiders."

"Oh, the spider drawing!" said Rain in surprise. "You mean that was *real*?"

"Yeah," frowned Nancy. "But that was before we figured out that we could take photos with your dad's instant."

"Oh, man," frowned Rain as she snapped her fingers in obvious frustration. "I mean, the snake people picture is good, but a spider picture would have been…"

"Awesome," frowned Nancy. "I know. Hey, but look on the bright side…I might shift back to that universe again. You never know."

"You really think so?" asked Rain with wide eyes. "I would *so* love to get that picture…I don't think I'd want to *stay* looking like a spider, but…"

"I know!" laughed Nancy. "That day was also crazy! And what's really funny is it was only my *second* real shift."

"That must have been an eye-opener," laughed Rain.

"It opened all *eight* eyes, let me tell you," replied Nancy.

"*Ooooh*!" gasped Rain. "Multiple eyes!...Err…More than two, I meant. You know what I meant…Anyway, what was that like? What was it like having more than two eyes?"

Nancy shrugged. Having that many eyes wasn't that different, because only her two original ones saw color and detail anyway.

"It really wasn't that different," she replied. "I saw color and fine details for these two eyes, our normal ones, but my other eyes only gave me a sense that something was moving toward me or away from me, and they could pick up light and shadow fairly easily. I guess it was like having really good peripheral vision…Yeah, I think that's the best explanation I can come up with."

Rain's scarlet eyes moved from right to left as she visibly pondered this.

"Fascinating," she breathed out. "Absolutely fascinating."

"I guess," shrugged Nancy.

The truth was and always had been that Nancy did not want to shift anymore; she wanted to go back to her original universe and stay there, and that was all there was to it. She humored Rain, however, because the poor girl had suffered enough with the loss of her beloved dog, so giving her this little concession really wasn't that big of a deal. If giving detailed explanations of the worlds she had been to helped Rain cope, then Nancy was all for it, even if that meant pretending to be a little excited about her own unwanted shifting.

*****

Nancy shut the door to her bedroom, walked to her bed, and laid down for a moment. "A moment" was a relative term, as her phone rang a few seconds later.

She took her phone off the nightstand and looked at the number, but she did not recognize it. It was highly possible it was just a scam call; everyone was getting a lot of those lately, but the number was local, so she took a chance and answered it.

"Hello?" she asked.

"Nancy?" came a dimly-familiar male voice.

"Yeah?" she replied in a wary fashion.

"This is Danny," said the voice.

She was relieved that her caller was not another scam job, but she was also confused as to why Danny would be calling her at all.

"Danny?" asked Nancy.

"I got your number from Rain," he explained.

"Oh," blinked Nancy.

"Well, that explains how he knows my number," she thought warily, *"but not why he called."*

"What is this about, Danny?" she asked cautiously.

"I thought about what you said yesterday," he replied. "I want to…to open up more. I want to try meeting someone. Rain…can't really give me any advice. It would be great if she could, but…you know what she's like. I need the advice of someone who…who understands what normal girls want."

"Ooooooh," she thought in sudden comprehension. *"Of course. I should have known."*

"What do you want to know?" she asked.

There was a pause for a moment before he spoke again.

"I…I want to know what girls want," he said.

"Seriously?" thought Nancy in disbelief.

"Hoo boy," she said with a shake of her head. "That's a tall order. Ummm…I…don't even know where to begin on that…Let's see…Ummm…First, let me ask you a question."

"Okay," he said.

She knew what she wanted to ask, but the last thing Nancy wanted to do was offend him. Still, she needed to know if he was…*dangerous*, dangerous in the "showing up on school grounds with a shotgun" dangerous, but the problem with that was that if he *was* dangerous, then she might be first on his hit list. Of course, it occurred to her that she had already treated him in an unjust manner for quite some time, and if he hadn't done anything to her by now, then he probably wasn't going to anyway.

"At least, I hope so," she thought.

"I need to know some things about you," she said nervously. "Do you…Do you, like…ever have…uhhh…suicidal thoughts?"

"What?" asked Danny in a thoroughly-confused tone.

There was a pause over the phone, but Nancy could swear she could hear him mumbling to himself.

"Why would you ask that?" he asked.

"It's just…well…I…" stammered Nancy. "It's just that…"

"Just spit it out, Nance!" she mentally screamed.

"It's just that you come off as…you know…" she said slowly. "You come off as that 'quiet' type that might be…I don't know…*dangerous*."

"What is *that* supposed to mean?" he asked, but this time he did sound offended.

"Danny…" sighed Nancy. "I'm not trying to be mean. One of the reasons I've had a hard time talking to you is because you're so…*grim*…You're always reticent and by yourself, and you tend to talk to yourself sometimes. It's off-putting."

"Oh…" replied Danny. "I…I don't…It's just…You think I'm dangerous?"

"Well," said Nancy, "if I can judge by the sound of your voice…I would say no. It's your *actions* that speak for you. The dark look you have, being off by yourself all the time, and talking to yourself…Those things weigh heavily against you."

"But that's who I am," said Danny in audible confusion. "I don't understand."

"You talk to yourself, right?" she asked.

"Yeah…I guess," he said after a short pause.

"There's no 'guess,'" replied Nancy. "I've seen you do it."

"That's because…It's because I like to voice my thoughts," he said.

"I understand that," said Nancy. "I do that too…but what I *don't* do is do it in public. It comes off as creepy and weird. Coupled with your dark clothes and your morose attitude…it's a red flag for any girl."

"Oh…" said Danny, but this time he sounded surprised.

"One of the first things you need to do in order to open up…" continued Nancy. "One of the very first things you need to do is to come out of your shell. Wear some different colored clothes for starters…

"Stop talking to yourself and talk to *other* people instead. You don't have to walk up to someone and start a conversation out of the blue, mind you, but you can start in little ways…Ask what time it is, for instance. You can pretend you've misplaced your phone or something. Ask for help on a question in class…Anything like that will break the ice.

"It's really a matter of fitting in. Everybody wants to be unique in their own way, and I get that, but they also need *some* conformity whether they like it or not. You need to find the balance between the two."

"Oh…" said Danny once more.

"You can always talk about something interesting you and your family did together," said Nancy. "You can talk about a movie you just watched…anything like that. You would be *amazed* at how many things you have in common with other people if you would just *talk* to them…Do you understand?"

"I…I'll try," replied Danny.

"Hmmm…" thought Nancy. *"I might actually be getting through to him."*

"That's good," she said. "That's a start…Now…as for what girls want…all I can say is that every girl is different. I mean, look at the guys around you. They're all different, aren't they?"

"Y…yeah," said Danny in meek reply.

"Some guys like sports, for instance," continued Nancy. "Some like cars, and others like intellectual pursuits, right?"

"Yeah…" replied Danny hesitantly.

"You like science fiction and fantasy," explained Nancy, "but obviously, not every guy does. It's the same with girls. When you open up and talk to the girls around you, then you can find out pretty quickly what they like and what they don't like. You'll eventually find one that has the same interests as you. That's just how it works."

"I…I see," said Danny. "I think I see what you're saying."

"Think of yourself as a private investigator," said Nancy. "Look for information in subtle and clever ways. You'll find someone who likes the things you like, you'll see. Now don't get me wrong, I don't mean *stalk* them or anything—that's crossing the line—but that doesn't mean you can't learn if someone has your likes or dislikes.

"But even if they share your interests, they may not be interested in *you*. That can happen, too. If that happens, there's no reason why you still can't be friends with them. You don't want to talk to a girl to find out about her and then be a cold jerk afterwards if she's not interested…That's not cool at all. I guess what I'm saying is that…that girls are people too, and you don't want to treat them like tools to be used. None of us, guy or girl, wants to be treated that way."

There was a pause on the phone as he took in a deep breath. Nancy was afraid she was losing him, so she anted up to keep his interest.

"Let me ask you another question," she said quickly. "What do you imagine when you imagine courting a girl? Do you have, like, a pick-up line or anything? What do you imagine doing when you really like a girl? How would you get her to date you?"

"Oh…" replied Danny. "I…I imagine I'd…bring her flowers, and…and write poetry for her."

"What now?" asked Nancy.

She wasn't sure if she had heard him correctly.

"I'd treat her the way she deserves to be treated," said Danny. "I'd want her to see that I care. I…I don't think a pick-up line would do that for me."

This stunned Nancy. She'd had no idea that he was an actual romantic.

"Wow," she thought in complete surprise. *"That's actually kind of sweet…Naïve…but sweet."*

"Well," she continued, "that's a good way to start…It's a little old-fashioned, though. Some girls might find that a turn off, but…there's no way to tell unless you try. Even so, and I don't think you'd do this, but…don't come on too strong. That can *really* drive girls away."

"Oh…yeah," replied Danny. "I don't think I'd do that."

"Well," replied Nancy, "I'm going to test you a bit on that. Let me ask you a hypothetical question…Let's say you were on a date, and…you felt like the time was right to put in your first kiss. How would you go about doing that?"

"Uhhh…" came Danny's voice.

"Take your time," said Nancy. "You wanted my advice, so I'm giving it. I'm just asking how you'd do it. Would you put your arm around her while you're watching a movie, or…maybe lean in a little closer as a hint…?"

"I'd ask," said Danny quickly.

"Excuse me?" asked Nancy.

She wasn't sure if she had heard him this time, either.

"Seriously?" was all she could think.

"I'd ask," repeated Danny. "It…It seems rude of me not to. I mean…if *she* wants to kiss me, I wouldn't object, but I…I just don't want to look like a…one of those guys that…that does that kind of thing."

"Uh, huh," replied Nancy. *"Oooookay*…I'll go with that. It's a little weird, in my opinion, but at least it's courteous. That's more than I can say about…oh…ninety percent of the guys I know, but whatever."

"I don't think it's weird," said Danny uncertainly. "Is it?"

"It's not a usual thing, no," replied Nancy, "but it's about as nice as you can get. You can't go wrong with being nice, Danny. If a girl doesn't like you because you're too nice…she's not worth your time, trust me. Just move on."

"Oh," said Danny. "But…But what if I really like her?"

Nancy sighed. She knew this was going to come up at some point…It was human nature.

"There are gonna be girls you 'really like,'" she said, "but just remember that those girls may not 'like' you. You don't want to put yourself in a toxic situation, and imposing upon a girl that isn't compatible is toxic…Well, imposing at all is toxic, but I think you get my drift…

"Oh, and that doesn't just apply to you; it applies to her, as well. If a girl wants you to change the best parts about yourself…don't let her. If she's manipulating you into changing who you are, then *she's* the toxic one, not you.

"And that goes double for you. If you really want to look like an honest and good guy, then don't try to force your ways on somebody else. There's an old saying that goes: 'Every man hopes his woman will never change, and every woman hopes to change her man.' If you pick that statement apart, you can see how wrong it is. The man is wrong because he's imposing his 'ideal' of a perfect girl upon the woman, and the woman is wrong because she's doing the exact same thing, only on the opposite end.

"Personally, I think those old sayings are pure nonsense, but the logic in what I said is sound. The man in that scenario is forcing his ideal upon the woman so much that she feels she has to pretend to be something she's not, while the woman is planning to manipulate the man into being something he's not. Like I said before, though, I think that particular saying is garbage, simply because it runs on old stereotypes…You know what I'm talking about…seeing men as aggressive jerks while women are manipulative backstabbers…but you get what I'm saying."

"But…" said Danny slowly, "But you just told me I had to change. You told me I needed to open up."

This gave Nancy a slight smile. It was clear Danny was no fool.

"That's because you asked me for advice," she replied, "and I agreed to give it to you with no strings attached. I don't expect to get anything *from* you, Danny, so…I'm just being honest. What I was saying before was about trying to undermine someone's identity because you *want* something…Me, though…I'm just trying to help you because you asked."

"I see," said Danny quietly. "It's about motivations."

"Exactly," said Nancy. "Try and see it through other people's eyes, or try and understand what someone else may be thinking about how you 'come off' toward them. If you really want to be honest and sweet with a girl, then try and understand how she feels. Do you understand?"

"Yeah," replied Danny. "Yeah, I think so…but this…this all sounds really complicated."

Nancy burst out laughing at that remark. Danny had honestly hit that nail *way* too accurately upon its head.

"I know," she chuckled. "Trust me, I know, but…but I'm just telling the truth…Actually, now that I think about it, I have some really high standards. No wonder I don't have a boyfriend…Never mind. Just think about what I said. You asked me for advice, so I gave it. Are we cool?"

"Yeah," breathed Danny. "Thanks, Nancy…I'll…I'll try and follow your advice."

"Good," said Nancy.

They said their goodbyes, and Danny hung up. Nancy set her phone back upon her nightstand and pondered the strange conversation she had just had with someone she had hated not that long ago.

"I didn't realize he was such a gentleman," she thought in mild amusement. *"I guess it's just how he comes off that blinded me…so negative and weird…How odd. I never would have guessed in a million years…He really is naïve, though. If he's not careful, he'll end up with someone who will chew him up and spit him out. I…actually don't want that to happen to him…Weird…Never thought I'd care about what happens to Danny Princeton."*

She dropped that train of thought as she yawned and rubbed her eyes. School was tomorrow, and she really was tired.

Chapter 10…The Tenth Shift

Nancy woke up and stretched in the morning light. She yawned, smacked her lips, blinked a couple of times, and then inspected her hands…They were normal.

"No way!" she breathed as she hopped out of bed.

She reached up and touched her ears, but they were round, inspected her arms, but they were fine, and her heart raced in excitement at the ramifications of this inspection.

It was too good to be true; it had to be. She dashed to the bathroom and flipped on the light, and…it was indeed too good to be true.

She was back to normal, completely and utterly, except for one small difference…There was a third eye smack in the middle of her forehead.

"Oh, come on!" she said angrily.

Nancy had said this before, just yesterday, in fact, but the disappointment was too bitter for her to just up and swallow. She wanted to be normal, needed to be, and being this close to it was like taunting her, making her feel like a fool.

"So close," she frowned. "So, *soooooo* close."

She undressed and inspected herself, but there was nothing strange about anything else upon her, so she took her shower and got ready for school. She picked out a simple outfit of a dark-blue shirt and blue jeans, put on her socks and shoes, picked up her backpack, and made her way down the stairs.

She got about halfway down when the dizziness struck. She clutched the rail as she realized it was her new vision that was causing the problem. Her field of vision had dramatically expanded thanks to her new third eye, and it was giving her vertigo.

"Oh…no…" she said as she caught herself.

It took her a bit to go down the stairs, and she could not help but wonder if she was going to be all right for the rest of the day.

"What's wrong with you?" asked Jason.

Nancy looked up to see her younger brother giving her a strange look. Jason stood near the living room couch with backpack in hand, but his expression was not one of compassion but rather strange curiosity. He raised one eyebrow as she bent over in a fit of nausea.

"I…I need help," she said unhappily.

Normally, it was beneath her to ask the young man for help; he was an annoying little jerk most of the time, but her current circumstance had killed that reluctance rather quickly.

"What the heck?" he asked. "Are you drunk? You practically staggered down the stairs."

"I'm dizzy," she choked out. "Oh…I need to sit down…"

"You can't," said Jason. "The bus will be here any minute."

Nancy had no wish to argue with him. The third eye on her forehead was messing with her sense of awareness and therefore messing with her balance, and this was the most definite cause of her vertigo. She could not afford to argue with him.

"I don't want to fight!" she said in urgent reply. "I need help walking! I need to sit down!"

"The bus is going to be here soon," said Jason. "You can sit down there."

"I need your help to get to it!" whined Nancy. "It feels like I'm going to throw up!"

"All right, all right," frowned Jason. "Just hang on a second. Come sit on the couch."

He helped her move to the couch, but she nearly vomited on the way there.

"Are you even going to make it to school?" asked Jason.

Nancy thought about this.

"I have to go," she mentally winced. *"I can't keep missing all the time because of shifting related events. I...I don't have a choice. I'm behind as it is."*

"Yeah," she breathed. "I just need to get my bearings."

"Well, you don't smell drunk," said Jason. "Are you pregnant or something?"

Nancy looked up at him in pure umbrage. Jason looked exactly the same as he always had, save for the third eye in the middle of his forehead, but that one small difference changed everything for her, and she found herself holding her tongue. For some strange reason, he looked wiser than he normally did, creepier, for sure, but wiser, nonetheless.

"No," she frowned. "You should know me better than that. I...I've just been sick lately."

"Yeah," shrugged Jason. "I figured that out...Wait a minute...You're not going to die on me, are you?"

"No," breathed Nancy. "No, no. I've just had a hard time lately. Wait...Why do you care?"

But her question struck a nerve, and now it was Jason's turn to sound upset.

"What do you mean *why do I care*?" he frowned. "I don't want you to die. You're my only sister...Heck, you're my only sibling, period."

"Yeah," chuckled Nancy. "I think Mom and Dad gave up after putting up with us."

Jason returned her laugh, and this made Nancy feel a little better. It was a rare instance when she got along with her brother, so she marked it in her memory as a special occasion.

"Well, try not to fall down the stairs," said Jason. "Then I'd have to call 911, and it would totally ruin my day."

"I think my day would be a little more ruined than yours if that happened," frowned Nancy. "I think I'll feel better once I get to school. I just need a minute to feel well enough to get going…You…You'll help me to the bus…won't you?"

"I guess," shrugged Jason. "Neither one of us has called the other a name yet, so what the heck, right?"

Nancy smiled at this little development. The truth was something she hadn't realized until this moment, and that was that she would rather get along with her little brother than not. It caused her no end of wondering, but that was par for the course as of late.

"I guess I never really delved too deeply into things before the accident," she pondered. *"I've had to think about things a lot more since I started shifting, but I think that's a good thing. I've never really gotten along with Jason in the past, but he's helping me now, so maybe things aren't as bad as I thought they were. This might turn out to be a good day after all."*

She thought about this as the bus pulled into their little cul-de-sac.

✳✳✳✳✳

Nancy walked down the hall to her locker. The hallway was packed with high school kids between hours, all heading in different directions, all gabbing as social creatures did and do. She made her way through that menagerie to her locker, and though she may have shifted universes every day for a week now, her locker location had never changed, so that was good.

It had taken her a good two hours for her brain to adjust to having a third eye. She figured that this adjustment was actually exceptionally quick by formal scientific standards, and though that thought was not normal for her, Rain had rubbed off on her, so Nancy was thinking like the eccentric genius that was her best friend, and not because she wanted to, but rather because she had to.

The only thing she could surmise was that *this* universe's Nancy had a brain that was already adjusted to the third eye from birth on up, and considering that it was her *consciousness* that was travelling from one universe to the next and not her physical brain, it made sense that she, the original Nancy, simply had to let that brain function as it normally would *here*, in Third Eye World.

"I guess I wouldn't mind living in Third Eye Nancy's world," she thought in quiet retrospect. *"It's not so bad once you get used to it. It is weird being able to see what's up above a little farther than I normally see in my field of vision, but that expanded view gets to be 'normal' after a while, and I can't even remember it as 'expanded'...So, so odd. Still...if I get stuck here...I won't cry about it. It's better than Bald Streak Nancy, that's for sure."*

She put in the combination to her locker, opened it up, and exchanged books for her next class. It was then that she saw Danny walk by, oblivious to her presence. Nancy gave a mental groan as she realized he was wearing his collared red shirt and his tan slacks, a style that had died many, many moons ago.

"At least he's trying to wear something other than black," she thought. *"He wore that same combo last week when we were all birds...Hmmm...I doubt he has much in the way of other clothes BUT black...That's...kind of sad...I'd better say something. He clearly needs help with this."*

"Danny," she called out.

He turned at the sound of his name but then recognized her and walked forward.

"Hey," she said as he walked up to her.

"Hey," he said in return.

It was strange to look upon him with that third eye in the middle of his forehead, but this did not detract from his sheer social awkwardness. His features were the same as she remembered them, dorky and gawky, and the clothes he was wearing did not help at all.

It occurred to her that the only things he was missing were the horn-rimmed glasses and a pocket protector; those were all that were needed to seal his look as a gigantic nerd for all eternity. She knew she had to address this sooner or later, or he was never going to get anywhere with *any* girl.

"Let's meet up for lunch," said Nancy quickly. "You can eat with me and Rain."

"Oh," said Danny. "Okay. I'll see you there."

"Good," started Nancy. "We can talk about…"

She was rudely interrupted by the passing presence of two freshmen, girls she did not know or care to know, but the looks they gave Danny were like the disgusted looks passersby give when seeing vomit.

One of them had short dark hair and tanned skin, and the other was a squat blonde with a pug nose, and both had extremely rude looks upon their young faces…and Nancy did not like this at all.

"The eighties called," said the one with dark hair. "They want their clothes back."

"What?" asked Danny in confusion.

The two girls laughed as they walked on, and Nancy distinctly heard the squat blonde say, "What a loser."

This immediately sparked a fire within her.

"Hey!" she barked without thinking.

She was in their faces before she realized what she was doing, but her anger was stoked to the point of an inferno, so reason was out the window.

The two girls jumped a little as Nancy appeared before them like an enraged ghost.

"Keep walking, you little zygotes!" she yelled out.

The various teens around her stopped talking as all eyes turned on them.

"You don't *get* to act that way to my friend or anyone else!" hissed Nancy. "We don't do that here, and if I catch you two doing that again, I'm going to shove your smug little faces in the boys' bathroom toilets!...Got it!"

"Get away, y…you psycho!" sputtered the dark-haired one.

Nancy took a step forward, but the two girls beat a hasty retreat. She watched them take off through the crowd as high schoolers all around her went back to walking and talking.

Nancy took in a deep breath in order to calm down, but it was difficult. It occurred to her that she still had a short temper at times and that all of the stress that had built up over the last week had only exacerbated that flaw.

She turned back toward Danny, but the look on his face was one of surprise mixed with alarm. Nancy really did not know what he was going to say now that she had blown up right in front of him. In fact, he actually didn't say anything at first.

"What!" she asked in irritation.

That irritation was a leftover from that very brief altercation with those two little punks, but she had not intended to aim it at Danny, as he was the victim in this situation.

"I…am…your friend?" asked Danny in a very slow, drawn out, and confused manner.

"Oh, Danny, I'm sorry," breathed Nancy. "I…I didn't…I didn't mean to snap at you. I couldn't stand by and let those two girls insult you. Nasty little…"

"I…I can see that," stammered Danny. "Are…you okay?"

Nancy held her head and sighed.

"Yeah," she said with a weak nod. "Yeah, I'm just…I'm just worked up. It's…It's *stress*. Those girls caused me to snap, but…I should have just turned them in. We could have hauled them up to the office or something…by their ears or…*other* parts."

Danny's eyes went wide for a moment, all three of them, and this gave Nancy a chuckle, as his current look combined with the immediate situation was magnanimously stupid in her opinion.

Danny gave her a weak smile and nodded.

"I don't think they'll cause any more problems," he said. "I think you put a stop to that really fast…but that's not…I don't know…It doesn't matter…What matters is…I just…You…You called me your friend."

"Yeah," shrugged Nancy. "Of course. Why wouldn't I?"

Danny looked thoroughly confused, even more so than he normally did.

"But you hated me just last week," he said quietly.

Nancy winced at this. It annoyed her that he would keep bringing up that mistake, but then it occurred to her that she had hated him for quite some time before the truth had come out, so for her to suddenly do a one-eighty on the matter had to be confusing for him. There was no way he *couldn't* be confused over the matter.

"I know," she sighed. "I made a mistake. I'm just trying to get past it. It's more than just making up for it…I also think you're a pretty good guy, so I'd just like us to be friends from now on…Okay?"

She watched as all three of Danny's eyes moved back and forth as he worked this out in his own mind.

"Okay," he said, but he didn't sound very convinced.

"Do you need time to think about it?" she asked.

"No," said Danny with a shake of his head. "No, I'm good. Let's just meet up for lunch like we were going to. We're gonna be late for class if we don't get moving."

"Too true," smiled Nancy.

She said her goodbyes and made her way to class, but she felt better now, empowered, and this really boosted her confidence in the belief that today was going to be a good day.

*****

Nancy sat down in her usual spot for lunch. Rain was already there, as was Danny, and that was good, at least for the moment.

"Finally!" said Rain. "What took you so long?"

"What are you talking about?" asked Nancy in a slight huff. "I'm right on time. For one thing, there's normal food today."

Today's choice of fresh eats was Salisbury steak, mashed potatoes, green beans, and an apple fritter, and though this wasn't her favorite meal, at the very least it didn't consist of earthworms, raw meat, or God forbid, a living animal, so everything was good.

"What do you mean 'normal'?" asked Danny. "It's been normal every day."

Rain shot Nancy a "careful what you say" look and smiled over at Danny.

"Something she likes, Danny," explained Rain. "Don't worry about it."

Nancy took to eating and had maybe two bites before she looked up and once more noticed Danny's outdated clothing. It caused her to shed a mental wince at the sight of it, so she decided to address the matter before she forgot to and moved on to something else.

"I wanted to talk to you about your clothes, Danny," she blurted out. "We need to get you a better wardrobe."

She had not intended to sound so pushy, but for some reason, it came out sounding exactly that.

Danny eyed downward at his red shirt and then back up at her, a look of frowning confusion upon his dorky, three-eyed face.

"What's wrong with my clothes?" he asked in a defensive tone. "You told me that I needed to wear something other than black."

"I…I know," sighed Nancy. "I just…well…I didn't realize that all you really had *was* black."

"I could have told you that," said Rain.

Nancy gave her a swift frown at that remark.

"Thanks, Rain," she said unhappily.

All three of Nancy's eccentric friend's eyes widened as she went back to eating her meal. Nancy sighed and turned her attention back upon Danny.

"Look, Danny," she said after a moment. "Those girls were wrong to insult you, but your clothes are…kind of…well…"

"Outdated," finished Rain.

"What?" asked Danny. "They look fine to me."

"They're way outdated," blurted Nancy. "You just need some more current fashion. Something that will help you blend in but won't be too garish."

She was really sounding pushy now, but she couldn't help it. She genuinely wanted to help Danny fit in, and a large part of her wondered if that was because she was feeling guilty over the way she had treated him.

Rain, however, did not seem to hold such reservations. She moved the conversation along without even the slightest hitch.

"How often do you buy clothes?" asked Rain.

"I don't know," shrugged Danny. "Not that often. It's not like I can't shop for clothes. I have money in the bank I've saved for six years now. I just don't like spending it."

"Would you be opposed to spending some on some new clothes?" asked Rain.

"No," shrugged Danny. "I guess not."

"Well…" continued Rain, "we can always go with you when you decide to go shopping for some."

Nancy thought about this and realized that Rain was indeed on the ball over the situation. All Danny needed was a little help with picking out some new clothes.

"That would be a major boost to his confidence," she thought. *"He can get some decent clothes…nothing too fancy…and he'll be one step closer to getting a girl. Who better to help him with that than a couple of girls?"*

"That's a good idea," said Nancy. "We can go with you and help you pick out something current. I mean, I prefer simple clothing and Rain likes edgier stuff, but it's not outdated or just solid black. Just let us know when you're free, and—"

"I guess I could do it tonight," shrugged Danny. "I mean, I'm not doing anything later…"

"What?" asked Nancy in confusion. "Wait…how? Can your parents just take you into town…?"

"What?" asked Danny in equal confusion. "I don't need them to take me into town. I'll just drive."

"You have a license?" asked Nancy in disbelief.

It had never occurred to her that he had a license.

"Yeah," snorted Rain. "Some people still get them when they turn sixteen, Fance…I mean, I don't have one because I feel I don't need one yet."

"Yeah," said Nancy in surprise. "I didn't think I needed one, either."

Danny looked at both of them as if they had suddenly turned into pillars of salt.

"Neither one of you has a license?" he asked in surprise.

"No," shrugged Nancy. "I figured I'd get one later on. It's just not high on my list of priorities right now."

All three of Danny's eyes blinked as he visibly tried to process this.

"Okay," he said. "I guess if…I guess we can meet at Rain's and drive into town, then."

Rain looked upon Nancy and gave her a wicked smile.

"Sounds good to me," said the eccentric young woman. "Doesn't it?"

Nancy did not know what that look was for, but she went with it.

"Yeah, I guess," she said in slight confusion. "I'll have to tell my mom I'm going out, but as long as we get back before eight, then we're good."

"Okay," said Danny. "I guess I'll have to clean out my car…"

"You have your own car!" blurted out Nancy.

She had not meant to sound so incredulous about that simple statement, but this was definitely not something she had expected of Danny, or from many of her other peers, for that matter. Owning a car was a big responsibility, as was paying for it. There were tag fees, insurance, maintenance and parts, the actual cost of the car…

"Yeah…" said Danny cautiously. "Why? What's weird about that?"

"I just…It's, well…" sputtered Nancy. "How in the heck can you afford one?"

"My parents gave it to me after they got a hybrid," shrugged Danny. "It may not be a hybrid, but it still gets good gas mileage."

Nancy had to do a doubletake in her brain over this. It was one thing to judge a person based upon their appearance and mannerisms, and she had thought she had Danny figured out, but she was still learning some very surprising things about him. Her thought process, however, was interrupted by a timely statement from him, so she did not get to fully process what he was saying.

"I thought girls liked guys with cars," said Danny.

"Twenty years ago, maybe," said Rain. "It's not a big deal for us anymore. There are a lot of people that don't have cars and don't have licenses. I guess it's just not a priority anymore. Still, it is nice to have your own set of wheels…or know someone who has them, as it were."

"Wait…" said Danny cautiously. "You guys aren't going to pester me to take you places, are you?"

His somewhat insulting statement pulled Nancy out of her stunned amazement.

"What?" asked Nancy. "No, no…I wouldn't do that. I don't use people for what they have…I don't use people at all. That's just wrong."

Rain elbowed her and gave her another wicked grin.

"Why did you go and say that?" she chuckled. "We almost had him!"

Nancy rolled her eyes at that one.

"Danny is definitely more interesting than I first thought he was," she thought. *"Still, I'm not going to use him to go places, and I know Rain won't. She must have known that he already had a car and a license…They are neighbors, after all…*

"Wait…Why didn't she tell me that in the first place? What's her deal?…No…No, this is Rain we're talking about. If the subject isn't about particle physics or divergent evolution, she doesn't care…Still, you'd think that would be something important to mention."

She thought about this as she went back to eating her lunch. She would have time to dwell on it later, but the whole of it was confusing to her for some reason, and at this point, it should have seemed trivial in light of her own situation. Even so, it bothered her, nonetheless.

*****

The three of them walked inside Percy's and made a beeline for the men's wear. Nancy was a little afraid at first of getting into a car where Danny was driving; he was still little more than a stranger, but he drove like a little old man, so her fears proved unfounded.

"You are the slowest driver in the world, Danny," said Rain as they walked through the department store. "Where did you learn to drive?"

"What?" asked Danny in notable offense. "I'm a good driver. I just don't like speeding."

"Yeah," snorted Rain, "but you can go faster than two miles under the limit."

"And risk hitting someone?" asked Danny. "I don't want to do that. I'd rather be slow than do something stupid. What if some little kid starts chasing a ball out into the street?"

Nancy pondered this. Whatever she may have thought about Danny in the past was completely false, and she realized that. He thought more about the feelings and safety of others than she had wanted to admit, but he had plenty of flaws to make up for this, so there was that.

"He still has a lot to learn if he wants to get a girl," she pondered. *"He's still a gawky-looking dork, but he does have his positives. I can't believe I thought he spread that rumor. Now that I know more about him, there's no WAY he could have spread it. It's not like him at all…I put the hate on him all because of Brinn…Brinn Clevenger…You are going to pay one of these days, Brinn. I will see to that, personally."*

Her thoughts were interrupted yet again by her companions.

"Yeah, yeah," said Rain. "Whatever, old man."

"Very funny," replied Danny.

Nancy ignored them as she followed them toward the men's wear. She was not a frequent visitor of Percy's; it was a department store like any other, but it just wasn't one of her favorite places.

She wasn't a "shopper" like some people were, and buying things just didn't do anything for her. She'd rather save her money for a rainy day. It occurred to her that perhaps this was the way Danny was, that he had no other clothes but black because he had bought into that identity and did not need other clothes, and he would not spend more money than he had to. It also occurred to her that she was inadvertently forcing him to spend money, and that had not been her intention. She was just trying to help him.

She had the looming problem of her shifting over her, *always* over her, so sometimes it did not occur to her that she might be screwing up someone else's life without even thinking about it. This bothered her more than her actual shifting.

"Listen, I'm sorry, Danny, if you're spending money that you don't want to spend," she said as an afterthought.

He turned to give her a puzzled look.

"It's a little late for that now, isn't it?" he asked. "We're already here."

Nancy felt her cheeks blush in embarrassment as she realized how correct he was.

"Uhhh…I know," she said uncertainly. "It just occurred to me that…we may be forcing you to spend your money, and that was not my intention."

"It's not a big deal," shrugged Danny. "I would have told you no if I didn't want to spend it. If you two can figure out some decent clothes for me to wear…I'm cool with it."

"What about me?" frowned Rain.

Nancy gave her a curious stare. She had no idea why Rain was irritated.

"What about you?" asked Nancy. "You're not spending money."

Rain gave her a "seriously?" stare and frowned.

"You said '*we* may be forcing Danny to spend money,'" grimaced Rain, "but then you said 'that was not *my* intention.' What about me? That wasn't *my* intention, either."

Nancy realized her mistake and immediately corrected it.

"I'm sorry, Rain," she apologized. "I wasn't thinking. You know my mind is a million miles away right now…and you know why."

"No kidding," snorted Rain. "Your plate is full, that's for sure."

"What are you two talking about?" asked Danny.

"Don't worry about it," sighed Nancy. "I just…Things have been a little more normal today…but then I realize that things will probably never be normal, and I get confused."

"You're confusing me right now," said Danny.

"It's a private matter, Danny," said Rain. "Don't worry about it. You two just focus on picking out some decent threads. I'll be back in a bit."

This was not something Nancy wanted to hear. She had thought that if they were going to help Danny pick out clothes, then Rain would be right there with her. It was that "we" part that mattered the most in her eyes.

"Hey, wait a minute!" protested Nancy. "Where are you going?"

"I have to go to the restroom," frowned Rain.

"Oh," said Nancy.

"You two aren't going together?" asked Danny.

Both Nancy and Rain had to give him a quizzical look. It was an incredibly strange question, and Nancy could not help herself about being smart with it.

"No," scoffed Nancy. "Why would we? Rain is a big girl. She can go potty by herself."

Rain let out a short and rather obnoxious guffaw as Danny turned red.

"I thought girls went to the restroom together," he said meekly.

Nancy could not help but burst out laughing as Rain followed suit. This, of course, only made Danny fold in on himself.

Rain swatted him on the shoulder and shook her head in amusement.

"Don't believe everything you hear," she chuckled. "I'll be back in a bit. You two start looking…We're on borrowed time here."

"Do tell," smiled Nancy. "We'll start looking."

They watched Rain go, and Nancy gave Danny a sympathetic look.

"Oh, cheer up," she said earnestly. "You made us laugh. That's actually a plus for you. You want to be more open, right? You're saying what's on your mind…regardless of how inaccurate it is…and that's good."

"I guess," said Danny in sheepish reply.

"Look," said Nancy. "The way I see it, we just need to get you dressed in something that most people wear. It's good that you want your individuality; I get that, but you also have to make some sacrifices for the things you really want in life…Now…I'm going to ask you a question, and I want an honest answer."

All three of Danny's eyebrows furrowed as he looked her over.

"Okay…" he said hesitantly.

"Do you really want a girlfriend?" asked Nancy.

It was a legitimate question. It was only natural for someone to *not* want to be alone; humans were social creatures, after all, but there was still the question of whether Danny really wanted to be with someone or whether he just *thought* he did because he thought it was what he was *supposed* to want. Nancy had plenty of experience with dilemmas like this; she had plenty of time to think while biking.

"Yeah," replied Danny. "I really want to be with someone. Is that so wrong?"

"No, no," said Nancy with a shake of her head. "It's just that…being in a relationship…it's a lot of work, Danny. It's fun at first until you get to know someone, really *know* them, and then the relationship either works or it dies out. It sounds cynical, but it's just a fact. The odds of staying with someone in a relationship when you're as young as we are…they're not good."

"I don't know," shrugged Danny. "I don't know at all. How can I make that judgement without ever having been in one?"

"That's just it, Danny," sighed Nancy. "A single bad relationship, especially if it's your first, can kill your ability to start another one. I'm not Dr. Deena from TV, but I know enough about this stuff to give you some advice."

"But you're only…what? Seventeen?" asked Danny.

"*Yeeeeah*," said Nancy cautiously, "but I have experience in the teen romance genre."

"But those are just stories for the masses," frowned Danny. "That's not real."

"No, it's not," shrugged Nancy, "but so what? I know what's fake and what's not. The reason I'm telling you this is because I can tell you're a romantic…You want to be in a lasting relationship, right?"

"Yeah," said Danny. "What other kind is there? I don't want to use anybody, and I certainly don't want to be used. That's just wrong."

All three of Nancy's eyes widened as she processed this.

"Danny's a better guy than ninety percent of what's out there," she thought in surprise. *"It's too bad he's such a dork. I think he really deserves someone."*

"That's sweet," she said, "but it might end up getting you hurt. Not all girls are nice inside. They'll use you just to get whatever they can get."

"I don't want someone like that," said Danny. "I think I can tell when someone is trying to use me. I'm not stupid."

"You say that now," said Nancy, "but you never really know until you're in an abusive relationship. It can sneak up on you."

"I'm not an abuser," said Danny in unhappy reply.

"Of course not," explained Nancy. "I meant *you* could find *yourself* in a relationship where *you're* being abused. Abuse isn't limited to violence, you know. It can also be verbal and emotional abuse, or what I just mentioned…being used. I'd call being used abuse, wouldn't you?"

"Yeah, I guess," said Danny. "I think I'd know if someone was that shallow, though."

"Really?" asked Nancy. "We don't have robot brains, you know. You can't just automatically identify someone that's a user. That can really sneak up on you. It's little things at first, and then all of the sudden, most of what you own is gone. That's usually how that works."

Danny shook his head no a couple of times.

"I get that," he said firmly. "I understand that, but…robot brain? Why would a robot brain give you the ability to tell if someone's a user or not?"

Nancy chuckled at his remark. It occurred to her that he would naturally go there, but that was something she liked about him.

"I don't know," she said in her own defense. "Because it's analytical? How would I know how a robot brain works? I don't even know how our own brains work. I can't imagine having a chunk of mine taken out and replaced with a computer."

"I guess if it's not related to personality and it's just memory, then I wouldn't mind," shrugged Danny. "You could process stuff a lot faster, for one thing. Maybe speed-read and stuff with a near perfect memory. That would be awesome."

"I suppose that's useful," said Nancy. "It would be handy when it comes to homewo…Wait, wait, wait. How did I get on this tangent?...Never mind. The point I was making was…was to be careful when it comes to girls. They're not always nice and kind and beneficent. I think it's a fallacy that we tend to believe that women are just automatically nicer than men. Brinn Clevenger should be an example of that."

"Yeah," chuckled Danny. "I see that…but…anyway…are we gonna pick out clothes or what?"

Nancy gave herself a smack to the forehead and then immediately winced as her palm impacted her extra eye. She shook her head for a moment before replying. She'd actually forgotten she had an extra eye, but more importantly, she'd forgotten the purpose of herself, Danny, and Rain being at Percy's in the first place, and that smack to the head may have hurt, but her own thoughtlessness was worth a smack to the head.

"Right," she said in stupid reply. "I temporarily forgot why we're here."

She looked toward him, but he only shrugged.

"*Soooo*…what should I get?" he asked.

Nancy smiled as she thought about this.

"Whatever you want, Danny," she said earnestly.

"What?" he asked in confusion. "But I thought—"

"The problem you're having is that your clothes aren't up to date," explained Nancy, "or that they're all just solid black. Just get some clothes here that have some color in them. I'm not going to pick stuff out for you, because you still need to put in your own individuality of choice."

"Oh," said Danny in slight confusion.

"Look," said Nancy.

She waved her hands over the simple ensemble she was currently wearing.

"My clothes identify me," she said. "I like simple color combinations that sometimes have sports logos…but that's me. Do you understand? If I pick out clothes for you, then they'll be simple color combinations that sometimes have sports logos. If that's what you want to wear, then fine, but I figure you had something else in mind. Do you really want to wear my style?"

"No, not really," said Danny.

Nancy noticed his fixed stare upon her chest. She was not sure of what he was looking at, but considering she had drawn his attention there, it was somewhat her fault. Still, she did not exactly like the implications behind his gaze.

"Ahem," she said in a fake cough. "You can stop staring at my chest now."

He turned red as all three of his eyes widened, and then he quickly stared off in the direction to his immediate right. His reaction was so funny that Nancy burst out laughing; she couldn't help it.

"Your face!" she laughed. "You should see your expression!"

Danny did not say a word. He stared down at the floor and stroked the back of his neck with his right hand.

"Look," chuckled Nancy, "we all have a tendency to have wandering eyes. I've been caught staring at a guy's butt before. You just can't be so obvious about it. The last thing you want is to be labeled as a pervert. That'll chase off girls like nothing else."

"Got it," said Danny meekly. "Maybe we all should have robot brains. Then I could just download all of this relationship stuff."

Nancy laid her right hand on his left shoulder and gave him a slight push.

"Oh, come on," she smiled. "You don't need a robot brain for that. That's just common sense…but don't crawl inside yourself over it. It happens to everyone. We sometimes get caught staring at others, or we have that embarrassing moment when we walk in on somebody…Heck, my brother walked in on me the other day when I was naked. You should have seen his face…I think I gave him a complex."

Danny's eyes widened as he stared at her. His gaze went from her shoes all the way up to the third eye on her forehead. Nancy rolled all three of her eyes and shook her head. She was the one who had said it, but she was also the one who had forgotten who she was talking to.

"Don't imagine that, please," she said, "…or at least don't be obvious about it."

Danny's face burned an even brighter red as he stared down at the white tiles beneath his shoes.

"Right," he said sheepishly, but his reply only made her laugh.

Chapter 11…The Eleventh Shift

Nancy awoke at the crack of dawn as usual. The first thing she noticed was her right hand and arm. Her hand was made of white metal with black, rubbery joints in the fingers and thumb, and this white metal extended all the way up to her elbow. The second thing she noticed was the digital time in the upper right corner of her vision, its placement quickly followed by a list of things to do for the day, including her class schedule.

"What!" she said as she hopped from her bed. "No!"

She dashed to the bathroom to look in the mirror and was stunned at what she saw. She realized it was strange that she would be stunned after a week of such transformations, but she was stunned, nonetheless.

The whole left side of her face had been replaced with sleek white metal, a perfect symmetry of technology that split her face in twain. The left side of her head was a bald and gleaming white, while her right side still sported her fine brown hair. Half her nose was made of ivory metal, while half her lips were made of the same rubbery black material in her right-hand fingers, but this was not as disturbing as her eyes. Both of her eyes were now yellow, or rather they glowed yellow from some internal light, and upon closer inspection, her pupils were shuttered, much like the lens of a professional camera.

"Who would do this to themselves!" she spat in disbelief. "Why would anyone do this!"

She was afraid to take off her nightgown, but she did so just so she could get into the shower as she did every morning. Her entire left leg along with her left foot was made of the same white metal, and turning around in the mirror revealed a long, white, metal stripe right along her spine, all the way down to her tailbone.

"Half of my body is gone!" she whined.

She realized that she was whining, and for that matter, whining to no one in particular. It was an insult to her as such, a base feeling of childishness that she did not like, so she took in a deep breath and tried to calm herself.

"Think, think, think!" she mentally shouted. *"What is this called? It was...was uhhh...cybernetics. This world must be into heavy technology. We don't have anything this advanced on my world...or maybe...maybe this Nancy was in some kind of terrible accident. Maybe it's just particular to me. I don't know...I won't know until I see Jason and Mom and Dad...*

"Wait...Wait a minute. Can I even take a shower? Will I short out or something if I get wet?...No...No, that can't be right. This schedule thingy in my vision is telling me it's time to take a shower, so it must be okay. I guess I'd better follow this schedule...just to be safe. I'm only going to be here for one day anyway, right? So I'll just follow the schedule."

She quickly took her shower, but what was most disturbing was that she could not feel the droplets of water upon the metal parts of her body, at least not in the normal way. There was a kind of tingling sensation, almost like a notification at the back of her mind that she was being hit by water, and how that worked, she had no idea.

"This day is already starting out weird," she said to herself as she toweled off. "Hopefully, it doesn't have any more surprises. I can't handle any more surprises."

"Nancy," came her mother's voice.

Her mother's voice sparked up in her left ear so suddenly that she gave a slight shriek and a jump.

"Wh...What?" she asked as she looked around in confusion.

Her mother was nowhere to be seen. The older woman's voice had come through like a ghost, and this freaked her out even more.

"I just got a call from a Perry Gillam's mother," came her mother's disembodied voice. "Did you hear me? I got a call from Perry Gillam's mother, and she was not happy."

It took Nancy a couple of seconds to realize she was only hearing her mother's voice in her left ear…her cybernetic one. She answered the older woman, even though she had no idea how they were actually talking to each other.

"I don't know anyone named Perry Gillam," she replied.

"She said you threatened her yesterday at school," said her mother. "Is that true?"

"I didn't threaten any…" began Nancy, but then she trailed off as she realized what this was about. "Wait…Is that one of those two nasty little freshmen girls who were insulting Danny?"

"Danny?" asked her mother. "Who is Danny?"

"Danny Princeton," replied Nancy. "He's Rain's friend…uhhh…I guess he's my friend, too."

"Did you threaten this girl or not?" asked her mother.

"I didn't…I just…" stammered Nancy.

She honestly did not know what to say. She had the feeling she was in trouble regardless of what she said, so she simply decided to tell the truth.

"They…They were insulting Danny!" she sputtered out. "All I did was get onto them about it!"

"Nancy…" said her mother slowly. "Did you threaten her?"

"I just…It's not like…" stammered Nancy.

She took in a deep breath to calm herself down yet again. Today was already turning out to be a bad day, and by the looks of it, it was only going to get worse.

"Look…" she said calmly. "I was talking to Danny in the hallway when these two freshmen girls insulted Danny's clothes and then called him a loser. We'd never seen them before that, I swear. Danny wasn't going to do anything, so I told them they were not to do it again, or I'd…"

"Or you'd what?" asked her mother.

"Or I'd shove their heads in the boys' bathroom toilets," finished Nancy.

That honest statement was met with a slight chuckle in her left ear.

"Is that the truth?" asked her mother a moment later.

"Yes," said Nancy firmly. "I just…I couldn't stand there and let those two nasty little chipmunks bully Danny. It wasn't right. It's not like I just walked up to them and started bullying them myself. You…You should know me better than that."

There was a long sigh in her left ear.

"Fine," said her mother after a moment. "I'll take care of this. Get down here and get ready for the bus."

It suddenly occurred to Nancy that she had no idea where her mother was at the moment.

"Wait…Where are you, Mom?" asked Nancy.

"In the kitchen getting ready for work," said her mother. "Where did you think I was? Get down here and get something to eat before you go."

"I have to get dressed!" frowned Nancy. "You caught me as I was getting out of the shower."

"Nancy…" warned her mother. "Tone…"

"Yes, Mom," sighed Nancy.

She shook her head as she once again realized that some things…no matter what universe she was in…some things never changed.

"Then again, she did say she would take care of it," she thought warily. *"Maybe things really are getting better between her and I…I don't know. I just hope they are."*

Nancy went to her dresser and picked out a pair of denims and a solid red shirt with a white #1 emblazoned across the front. She quickly dressed and then picked up her socks and shoes, but it was this step that confounded her a bit.

"So do I wear a sock over my fake foot here or what?" she thought in mild confusion. *"I realize that every day is something new and different, but it's the little things that really confuse me. I don't know if we're supposed to walk around barefoot or what…You know what? To heck with it. I'm just slipping a sock over it and wearing my shoes as normal. I don't care what anybody thinks. I can't afford to."*

She put on her socks and shoes, grabbed her backpack, and hurried downstairs. Her mother was indeed still in the kitchen, and Jason was waiting in the living room as he did every morning.

One quick inspection was all Nancy needed in order to gauge her "world" situation. Jason and her mother looked exactly like she did, right down to their weird-looking yellow "camera" eyes, so her fears about being unique were unfounded.

"So this is what this world's like, huh?" she asked herself. *"I guess everyone here really dove into the whole cybernetics thing…*

"I wonder why? There's probably a major reason why, something very different from my world must have happened in order for everyone to be like this, but I really don't have time to look that up. I could ask, but that would just make me look stupid, because this Nancy would

*already know the answer to that, so…not gonna happen.
I'll just have to wing it…*

"At least it beats Spider Nancy or…ugh…Bald
Streak Nancy…You know, it's sad that I would prefer
looking like a spider to having a bald streak,
but…whatever."

"Nancy, come get some toast," said her mother.
"You've taken long enough as it is."

Nancy wisely decided not to bite down upon that
bait. She was infinitely tired of arguing with her mother,
and she was stressed out enough as it was, so she simply
frowned and took the plate her mother offered her.

The plate was a simple, white, ceramic disc with a
plain brown piece of wheat toast laid upon it, but at least
there was strawberry jam smeared across that crispy piece
of bread, and that was the way Nancy preferred it.

"Thank you," she said begrudgingly.

That, in itself, was enough of an olive branch for the
rest of Nancy's day, but her mother sabotaged any
semblance of calm Nancy may have collected from it. That
calm was shattered by the sheer force of what the older
woman said next.

"I just found out yesterday that you have a Friends
and More Space page," said her mother, "but I only took a
glance at it. I guess I'll have to read it later today. You
should have told me you finally had one."

Nancy had turned around and had her toast halfway
to her mouth when her brain finally put together all of the
words her mother had just spoken. She immediately
panicked, a loud gasp left her, and she dropped her plate.

The plain white disc shattered into small ceramic
shards as it impacted with the kitchen tiles below.

"Nancy!" barked her mother.

Nancy turned and shook her head no before any
protest left her mouth.

"Y…You can't!" she sputtered.

"Wow," said Jason from his seat at the kitchen table. "It must be really good. I'll have to look at it, too."

"N…No!" stammered Nancy.

"Nancy Amelia Clark!" scolded her mother. "What is wrong with you!"

It occurred to Nancy that there was no getting out of this one. The truth was and the truth had always been that she should have contacted the F and M site and gotten that page taken down a long time ago, but for some reason or another, her own stubborn pride had made a solid refusal to even *look* at the page, much less interact with it.

Now she was in the hot seat, and there was no getting out of this one, because her family was going to look at that page whether she liked it or not.

It took her less than a second to come up with a plan, and that plan was an unhappy one…She had to tell the truth.

"You can't look at it!" she cried.

"What!" exclaimed her mother in growing anger. "You don't tell me…"

"N…No!" sputtered Nancy.

She was so upset and so out of sorts that she accidently crushed the piece of toast that was currently in her cybernetic hand. The red jam smeared all over the white of her fingers as the bread ground into powder between the tips of her cybernetic digits.

"It's bad!" she exclaimed, though she did not mean to sound so panicked. "It's really bad!"

"What are you talking about?" asked Jason in audible confusion.

"What do you mean, '*it's bad*'?" asked her mother, and her tone was not friendly.

"It's…It's not…It's not mine!" stammered Nancy. "It's not mine! I didn't write it!"

The visible anger on her mother's "robotic" face changed to noticeable confusion.

"What?" was all the older woman could say.

"I didn't write it," said Nancy, but this time her voice was shaky with rising emotion.

She felt like crying, and she didn't want to, but her tear ducts worked against her on this one.

"It's not mine," she choked out. "A girl at school wrote it to say bad things about me…"

"What!" exclaimed her mother once more, but her confusion was gone, and her anger was back in force.

"There's a girl at school who h…hates me," choked out Nancy, "and she made up some nasty thi…things about me on F and M."

"Who did that!" asked Jason, and even he was starting to sound angry.

"Was it one of those freshman girls?" asked her mother.

Nancy wiped her "eyes" and shook her head no. Apparently, having cybernetic eyes did *not* mean having no tear ducts, which of course, she just learned the hard way. She really did not like crying in front of her mother or Jason; it was an embarrassment that was hard to swallow. She forced herself to calm down just for the sake of her own pride.

"No," she said after a moment of composing herself. "It wasn't one of them…This happened last year."

"What!" cried her mother.

The older woman shouted with enough force to startle both of her children at the same time.

"Nancy!" exclaimed her mother. "Why didn't you say something about this *last* year!"

Nancy did not have a good explanation for this particular failure on her part. It was partly pride and partly shame that had prevented her from even *looking* at the webpage, even though she had done nothing wrong.

"I don't know!" she whined. "I just…I…I don't know…"

"You stay put," huffed her mother. "I'll drive you two into school today. Right now, I have an F and M page to read."

"Mom, no!" protested Nancy.

Her mother didn't say a word but instead marched right past her and into the living room.

"Mom, please!" cried Nancy.

Her mother just shook her head and walked straight into the study.

Nancy felt like melting into a puddle of angst-ridden goo. She turned to look at her younger brother, but the look on his face, that wide-eyed look of frightened surprise, stopped her from saying anything more.

*****

Nancy lingered outside her locker even though she already had her books. The halls were still packed between classes, so there was time to stand around and do nothing. She usually did this to kill time if she didn't feel like going to class, and today she most certainly did not feel like doing anything, much less sitting through another class.

Her mother had been good on her word and had driven her to school, but the older woman was furious over that slanderous F and M page, so Nancy was currently eaten up with anxiety over the matter. She did not know what her mother was going to do, and that uncertainty spiked her blood pressure and kept it at dangerous levels.

Something else bothered her, though. She had seen Danny walking around with another girl, talking to the young lady as if they had known each other forever, and this new face, a tall and pretty girl with straw-blonde hair, was not someone Nancy recognized.

It bothered her for some reason, and that was unfathomable, because Danny was finally being sociable, and that was something he had needed in his life for a very long time now, and she had wanted to help him with that. She should have been excited for him, proud of the small accomplishment he had made of coming out of his shell, but she felt something else instead, a strange anger at the sight, and this made no sense to her.

She would have stewed more upon the events of the day, but a familiar voice broke her downward spiral of thought.

"Hey," said Rain from behind her. "Are you all right?"

"What?" asked Nancy.

She turned and gave a brief study of this universe's Rain. Rain looked as she normally did, but the young woman had the right side of her face replaced with sleek black metal, half of her lips were a rubbery grey, and her eyes were a bright silver color, shuttered like Nancy's own.

The young genius wore a white T-shirt with a black panda in the center, only the panda's face was a skull, and big black letters spelling "Panda Parkour" ran in a line beneath that disturbing image. Other than that, she had on her black cargo pants and black hiking boots, a combination she often wore and rarely changed for any reason.

Her quick study of Rain's appearance, however, was interrupted by Rain herself.

"Are you okay?" asked Rain.

Even with half of the eccentric genius's face replaced with cybernetics, Nancy could make out the look of concern upon her best friend. It was clear that Rain could see the dark cloud hanging over Nancy's own head, and that was a nuisance in and of itself. She did not really feel like talking to Rain, or at least not giving her a straight answer, mainly because she did not have one to give.

"Oh," sighed Nancy. "I don't know."

Actually, she did know, but she was not going to admit her depression to Rain. It wasn't that she didn't want to talk about it, it was that she didn't care enough to.

"You look like someone whose parents just died," said Rain, "so I know something's going on…What's up?"

And that was Rain in a nutshell. As different as they were, the young genius was still a real friend, but this realization only made Nancy unhappier, because she, herself, did not feel that she was as good a friend in return.

"Today has been terrible," sighed Nancy, "and it's not even lunch. Mom found out about '*my*' F and M page, so now she's off on a crusade to take it down, and there's no telling what damage *that* will do. Even Jason was mad about it, and he usually doesn't care about what happens to me."

"He's still family," shrugged Rain. "Family sticks together."

"I guess," replied Nancy, but her tone was as listless as she felt.

"At least they're on your side," said Rain with an optimistic smile. "It would be a lot worse if they weren't."

"Yeah," sighed Nancy. "My mom drove us both in this morning, and that was nice, but there's something else that's been bothering me, not just the F and M page…It's…It's uhhh…It's just…Ugh…Never mind."

"What is it?" asked Rain.

She wanted to say something about Danny and the new girl, but she also didn't, and this confused her, but only for a moment. After dithering over this mental stalling, she bit down and decided to just spill it. Rain was the only one she could talk to about it anyway.

"It's nothing," frowned Nancy. "It's just that…I was going to go over some things with Danny this morning, but he's hanging around with some girl I've never seen before. I don't know who she is."

"Ah, the new girl," said Rain. "The principal picks a student to show transfers around. This was Danny's turn. I think her name is Sarah."

This news made Nancy feel a little better, but even that was odd, because she shouldn't have been down about the situation in the first place. It was good that Danny was given the chance to talk to a girl other than Rain and herself…wasn't it?

"Oh," she said in reply. "I didn't realize…I thought…Never mind what I thought."

It was then that Nancy noticed something strange in Rain's behavior. There was a sly glimmer in the young woman's silver camera eyes, a strange spark there, like she had let slip a glance at a deep secret she held close to her chest.

Nancy did not know what to make of that very brief look, a change in demeanor that had occurred for less than a second, and she may not have caught it at all if she still had a "normal" pair of eyes, but whatever the case, Rain eased back into her normal self as if no change had occurred, so Nancy banked this information for later scrutiny.

"I don't know what Danny thinks about her," shrugged Rain. "I guess I'll ask him at lunch. You never know, she might end up liking him."

"I hope not," frowned Nancy, but then her brain realized what had just come out of her mouth, and she was stunned for a second.

It took her a few extra seconds to realize how this might sound, so she tried to recant as quickly as possible.

"I mean, Danny just met her, right?" she asked. "It's not like he can just automatically get attached to the first girl he talks to, right? He wouldn't be *that* pathetic…"

Nancy could swear there was that sly glimmer in Rain's eyes once more, but it was so brief she chalked it up to her own imagination.

"I don't know," said Rain with a slight smile. "He might. He's kind of desperate, you know."

"No kidding," snorted Nancy. "I've really tried to help him with that, but I think I may just be confusing him. I mean, I want him to find that special someone, but…"

"But what?" asked Rain. "He's following your advice, and the best part is…is that it just fell into his lap. Isn't that good?"

Nancy thought about this, but the conclusion ate at her. She just couldn't bring herself to agree, but that in itself was confusing on a deep level, so she searched hard for a reason why this was not a good idea.

"He just met her," she replied after a moment of intense thought. "Plus, she's a transfer. We don't know anything about her. I mean, I could look her up on F and M, but we both know how accurate *that* can be.

"I just…I mean…I don't want him chasing windmills. This girl may have been popular at her last school…I mean…she kind of looks like she hung out with that crowd…In fact, she probably doesn't have any interest in Danny at all. She *probably* thinks he's a giant dork that she has to put up with for a day…That's what *really* bothers me. I don't want Danny getting his hopes up over *that* kind of girl. That kind of rejection will set him back forever."

"Oh, you think?" asked Rain. "How would he know if he doesn't try?"

This offended Nancy for some reason. She wasn't sure why, but it made her a little angry that her friend would be pushing her reasoning on this. It stuck in her like a splinter in her finger.

"He'll be devastated, you wingnut!" she said a little angrier than she had intended to. "How am I supposed to help him if he goes inside his shell and never comes out again?"

"How are *we* supposed to help him," corrected Rain.

"What?" asked Nancy.

"How are *we* supposed to help him," repeated Rain. "You said 'I.' Both of us are helping him, not just you."

"That's what I meant," scoffed Nancy.

She waved off her friend as she shook her head.

"Never mind," she huffed. "I'll talk to him about it at lunch. Just don't interfere."

"I'm not," said Rain. "I was just stating the obvious."

"Whatever," frowned Nancy. "I have to get to class."

"Okay," shrugged Rain. "See you."

And that was that. Rain walked off without another word, but Nancy could swear she saw that sly glimmer in her best friend's eyes; it was there again for half a second, and this bothered Nancy.

It was as if Rain knew something that she didn't, and though she knew Rain had a huge collection of knowledge that Nancy did not know nor wish to know, this was something else, something unrelated to scientific knowledge. Whatever was going on inside Rain's mind was something the young genius was deliberately keeping from Nancy; she was sure of it.

*****

Rain smiled at her as Nancy parked her bike next to the side of Rain's house.

Buster, Rain's new little friend, ran in circles within the grass as he chased a butterfly, but the tiny ball of fur did little but exhaust himself in a futile attempt to catch the winged insect.

Nancy smiled in spite of herself at this little foray against butterfly kind; she was still feeling down because of the day's events, but Buster was unintentionally helping to lift her spirits.

She took a moment to consider what had gone on during school. Nothing noteworthy had happened during lunch because Danny had not sat with them, so Nancy could not grill the young man about the young woman he had taken on a tour of the school. It was frustrating, really, annoying at best, but even this sensation was new and confusing, because Nancy could not think of one good reason why such a thing would bother her at all.

Aside from that, she was drawn out of her temporary funk by the sight of Rain's obnoxious little dog, and Rain immediately picked up on this.

"You look a little less down," smiled Rain. "Are you feeling better?"

"I guess," shrugged Nancy. "I'm still wondering why Danny didn't show for lunch."

"Why don't you ask him?" asked Rain.

Nancy turned her attention from her best friend to the young man that came walking up to them. She had not noticed him enter Rain's yard, but now that he was approaching them, she studied Danny in earnest, if only to spot the day's differences.

Danny was dressed in some of his new clothes, of course, a plain blue and white striped button up accented by fine black slacks, and normally this would have helped his appearance somewhat, but with the changing of universes each day, Nancy could not accurately assess any improvements the young man could make in his appearance, and this frustrated her.

As it stood, the entire left side of Danny's face was made of sleek silver metal, and his eyes were a shuttered green, like emeralds set on a silver and peach platter. The right side of his face was still the same gawky dork-face that Nancy cringed at on a daily basis, and she wondered if she was a bad person for suddenly wishing that all of Danny's face had been silvered.

He walked up and nodded to both of them before speaking.

"Why wasn't I at lunch today?" he replied. "I was showing someone around."

"The new girl," frowned Nancy.

"Yeah," replied Danny, but his eyebrows furrowed as if in concern. "Her name is Sarah. She just transferred in from Carlton, but she's only been there for a year. Before that, she lived in San Diego."

"San Diego?" asked Rain. "What in the heck is she doing all the way out here?"

"Her parents decided to take jobs out here?" he shrugged. "Don't ask me. She didn't talk much about that. She didn't really talk much at all."

"No shocker there," thought Nancy.

She had suspected as much. This girl must have been top dog where she had come from, and Danny was nothing more than a momentary nuisance. Nancy wanted to give Danny the benefit of the doubt on this one, but she did not like this new girl, and that was that.

"What was she like?" she asked.

"She was nice," shrugged Danny. "I thought maybe we could be friends."

And there it was. Nancy did not like that statement at all, because she knew deep down what this girl was like, another Brinn Clevenger, and she would not have it.

"Danny, I don't think that's a good idea," she frowned.

"Huh?" asked Danny.

His face was lined with genuine surprise, as if Nancy had just shot him in the foot.

"Why not?" he asked.

"It's…She's…" stammered Nancy.

She discovered quite by accident that she was having a more difficult time with this than she had first thought she would.

"That girl looks like the…the popular type," finished Nancy.

"So?" asked Danny.

"He is making this very difficult," thought Nancy with a mental sigh.

"So she'll be hanging out with people like Brinn Clevenger," she finished.

Danny frowned and shook his head. It was clear he was not going to let go of this so easily.

"I don't think so," he said unhappily. "She wasn't mean or anything."

Nancy looked over to Rain for help, and the eccentric young genius raised one eyebrow at her. It was a motion of understanding made in silence, a chord of quick thought in agreement with the situation at hand, so Nancy was grateful when Rain turned her attention back upon Danny a moment later.

"I think you should trust Nancy on this one," said Rain. "I'm getting the same vibe from this girl. Maybe you should wait a couple of days on it, and if she actively talks to you during that time, then do what you want. If she ignores you, though…you don't need to waste any time on her."

Danny frowned and stared down at his black shoes. He looked back up at Rain after a moment and gave a quick nod.

"Fine," he said. "I'll wait…but I don't really see it. I don't think she's that bad."

"No one said she was 'bad,' Danny," said Nancy. "It's just…I don't think she's the right kind of person for you."

"Yeah," agreed Rain. "I think you should definitely wait. Let's just get a sense of where she's at first, okay?"

"Yeah, I guess," frowned Danny.

"It'll be fine," said Rain. "It's not like we're asking you to punch her in the face. It's just…let *her* talk to *you*."

Danny looked somewhat confused for a moment, but what he said next certainly made sense.

"But I thought you guys told me to open up," he said. "That's what I was doing."

"I…I know that," stammered Nancy. "It's good that you're opening up. That's excellent…It's just…Now is the time for…uhhh…step two. Now it's time to see if this girl is worth your time. I want you to be…I mean…both of us want you to be happy, Danny. What we *don't* want is for you to get hurt by some insensitive girl."

"I can take care of myself," frowned Danny.

"Of course," said Rain matter-of-factly. "We know that. We're just trying to be good friends, is all."

Danny looked down at his shoes, scrunched up his lips after a moment, and then nodded a couple of times as if agreeing with himself.

"Okay," he said, and this time he sounded definitive. "I understand."

"Good," smiled Nancy.

She genuinely felt better now that he was listening, but that general feeling of improved welfare still confused her, because she shouldn't have been down in the dumps over Danny's situation anyway.

Whatever the case, Danny must have picked up on her improvement of mood, because he flashed a quick smile and nodded one more time. Nancy was surprised once more, and that surprise was due to the fact that Danny's mood was affected by her own, and she could not fathom a reason why that would be.

"Anyway…" said Danny after a moment, "I've been thinking about the sort of romantic things I would like to try out. I've come up with some things."

"Oh, really?" asked Rain. "Like what?"

Nancy gave an internal groan at this. Whatever Danny had come up with…it was bound to be awkward and thoroughly mashed all over the dork page of life, but at least the conversation had gone somewhere other than that new girl, Sarah.

"I wrote a poem," continued Danny. "I saved it last night."

"Really?" asked Rain in open curiosity. "Let's hear it, then."

Danny's emerald camera eyes widened as he realized he was on the spot, or at least that's what Nancy got out of the awkward expression upon his cybernetic face.

"Come on," urged Rain. "Out with it, then."

"Uhhh…okay," agreed Danny, but he didn't sound certain.

Danny stopped and stared off into the distance for a second, and then he started reciting his poem. Nancy wasn't sure if he'd memorized the piece of original verse, or if he was reading it in his "vision" like she had read her class schedule right after she had woken up in the morning. Whatever the case, she put aside all her thoughts just to listen to his poem…For some strange reason, she really wanted to hear it.

"The title of this poem is 'A Cosmic Truth,'" he said. "'A Cosmic Truth,' by Danny Princeton. Okay…here goes:

How do I love you?
In the beginning, there was an explosion,
It was of immense proportions,
Immeasurable to our mortal minds,
And from it formed our universe.
It formed out of nothing,
Not darkness,
Because even darkness is something.
It was there that quarks and electrons formed,

The building blocks of everything,
And it was there
That the quarks assembled
Like ministers at council
To form protons and neutrons,
And these in turn became nuclei,
The very first seeds of the void.
Much time passed before these seeds
Trapped the rogue electrons
Into a binding orbit,
And from that orbit
Came the first atoms.
Helium and hydrogen grew
Like husbands and wives,
Coalesced into families,
And became the first stars.
In these stars were impregnated
The heavier atoms,
Carbon and oxygen and iron,
And they were birthed by supernovae,
And the rest of the universe was born.
And that, my love…
That is how I love you."

He finished speaking and stopped staring off into the distance, turning his attention back upon them.

Nancy was stunned for two reasons. The first reason was educational, and that was the fact that she actually understood the finer scientific points of his poem, which was odd, because she would have probably thought it gibberish before she had started shifting.

The second was the powerful feeling of warmth she felt glowing inside her over that strange piece of verse, as if the piece had been written directly for her and no one else. It was a truly weird feeling, because she had never felt that way about anything before, and it would have never occurred to her in a million years that Danny Princeton would be the one to invoke it. She was truly speechless for once.

"What do you think?" he asked. "Is it good?"

"I like it," smiled Rain. "Actually, that's not true. I *love* it. It's too bad more poetry isn't written that way."

Danny turned his attention upon Nancy and gave her an earnest look.

"Did you like it?" he asked.

Nancy felt the human side of her face grow hot from embarrassment. She nodded without saying anything, mainly because she couldn't think of anything to say.

"Good grief, Nance," said Rain as she cocked her own head to one side. "You're as red as a rose. If you were a plant, you'd be in full bloom."

Nancy hid her face in her cybernetic hand and shook her head once. It was no good lying about this one; she had to say something that made sense, so she decided to tell the truth.

"It was good," she said in a muffled voice.

She removed her hand from her face and looked up at Danny. She tried to calm herself as she spoke, but it was difficult.

"It got to me," she said in sheepish reply. "You have a real gift, Danny."

"Really?" smiled Danny. "I…I wasn't sure about it."

"Are you kidding?" smiled Rain. "It was super good…You should get that published. The beginning of it kind of reminded me of Elizabeth Barrett Browning's Sonnet 43."

"Yeah," shrugged Danny. "That's what I looked up first for ideas. I like that piece."

"Makes sense," said Rain. "It's a good reference point."

Actually, none of this made sense to Nancy. The day had started out awful and had steadily progressed toward its end destination of weird, and considering that she was shifting along dimensional lines every day, "weird" was a relative term anymore, so describing the "normal" events of a day as "weird" was actually saying something.

Chapter 12…The Twelfth Shift

Nancy awoke to the dawn's light, but she laid still for a moment just to feel its warmth. There was nothing particularly special about the morning rays shining through her bedroom window, but for some reason, it felt good on her skin, and she soaked in that feeling for a minute.

It took her a bit to sit up and inspect her bare arms and hands. They looked normal except for one notable difference…They were green. It was a lighter green than grass, but still a color she had not expected to see upon her skin.

Her nails were as brown as bark, a comment she made within the back of her mind, but upon further inspection, she realized the protective coverings at the tips of her fingers had the same texture and look as bark, and rubbing them upon her skin felt *exactly* like rubbing against bark.

"Interesting," she said quietly, but her voice sounded perfectly normal.

She felt quiet today, relaxed, though she knew a new day of school was looming ahead of her. It did not bother her so much today, this shifting, though she did not know why. She would have been freaked out at this in the beginning, but today, her twelfth day of shifting, felt a little different, a little less panicked.

"This could be a good day," she smiled.

She hopped out of bed and made her way to the bathroom, flipped on the light, and closed the door.

Her image in the mirror did not repulse her today, though it was still odd. Her face, her eyes, her ears and nose…all normal, but her hair certainly wasn't. In fact, she had no hair, but rather a thick coat of dark-green leaves, all narrow and heart-shaped and attractive in their own way.

Between the leaves were large bulbs similar to asparagus bulbs, and she reached up and tweaked them between her fingers. She could feel them just as if they were skin, the leaves as well, and this was a new sensation, considering that actual humans did not have nerve cells within their own hair.

"Weird," she said to herself. "I guess we don't get haircuts in this world. We'd be amputating something."

She undressed and took her shower, but there was nothing unusual about the rest of her, save that her skin was green and her toenails were also made of "bark." The only unusual thing about her shower was that she had the distinct feeling of "drinking" as the water hit her skin, and that was extremely odd, but she figured it to be part of the physiology of being a plant-like being, another oddity to add to the notebook once she met up with and discussed her changes with Rain.

She toweled off, went to her dresser, and dressed in a plain brown T-shirt and regular blue jeans for the day. She had normal undergarments and socks, and her shoes were still the plain white sneakers she always wore, so that was good.

"This world is a lot like mine," she thought with an inner smile. *"It wouldn't be so bad to be stuck in this one. If I do get stuck in it, I won't mind. I'm still pretty in my own way...At least, I think I am. I kind of like the way the leaves look on my head...It's weird being green, though...But that makes me wonder...If I really am like a plant, I wonder what I eat? Hmmm...That's a good question. I should go down to the kitchen and find out."*

She grabbed her backpack and hurried downstairs.

Jason was there in the kitchen rummaging through the fridge without a mind to her presence. He looked exactly the same as she did, light-green skin and leaves and bulbs for hair, and his face was the same Jason face as always, so there wasn't some big difference between them, but Nancy could not help but notice that their mother was nowhere to be seen.

"Where's Mom?" she asked.

Jason looked up from the fridge and gave her a disinterested look.

"She left early," he said matter-of-factly. "She said something about making up for lost time. Probably has to do with all of those work hours she missed because of you."

That particular comment was not appreciated. Nancy sighed and shook her head. She did not want to argue with Jason, so she wisely decided to keep her mouth shut in regards to retaliation. She decided to ask something more practical instead.

"What's there to eat?" she asked.

Jason pulled out a small plastic container filled with what looked like dense chocolate fudge.

"Mom left some peat or silt," he said without looking. "Take your pick."

Nancy wasn't sure if she'd heard him correctly.

"Say what now?" she asked.

Jason gave her an irritated look and shook his head as he pushed past her toward the kitchen drawers next to the sink. He opened up a drawer and pulled out a rather large, shovel-shaped spoon.

"The bus is going to be here in ten minutes," he said as he made his way to the kitchen table and sat down. "I'm getting breakfast before I go, but if you want to be a diva and think you're getting loam again, you're going to starve."

Her eyes widened as she thought about this for a moment.

"We…We eat *dirt*?" she asked in a slight daze.

He shot her an "are you stupid?" look.

"Nancy, are you brain damaged?" he asked in a strange, slightly-frustrated tone. "What in the heck do you think we eat? Concrete?"

Nancy did not really know how to process this, so she stared down at her shoes for a moment in confusion.

"I…I just…" she stammered.

She thought about this for a few seconds and simply resigned herself to the situation.

"Never mind," she sighed. "I guess I'll have silt."

"Good," said Jason quickly, "because I'm eating the last of the peat."

He popped open the lid of his container and shoveled out a large portion of "peat" with his weird trowel-shaped spoon. This action offended Nancy somewhat, because he was always doing stuff like this, being selfish and deliberately taking things without asking her first, and in spite of her better judgement, her anger got the best of her, and she said something about it anyway.

"Typical Jason," she said unhappily. "You give me a choice and then take it away."

"Hey!" he said rather forcefully, a look of borderline rage etched upon his green face.

His tone and look startled Nancy. He was actually upset this time, and this frightened her a little, because he wasn't usually this angry. They argued a lot, but he never looked like he was going to *hit* her. It wasn't like him.

"I spent all yesterday trying to figure out who put up that F and M page!" he said angrily. "Mom's at work making up for lost time, because she wasted a lot of time taking *you* to the doctor and taking down that F and M page…So *don't* give me an attitude."

This made Nancy feel strange inside. She had not realized Jason and their mother would take that F and M page so seriously, though in retrospect, she probably should have.

His words hurt, and though she knew that none of this was her fault, that was the only thing that ran through her mind over it.

She went to the fridge, took out a small plastic container of "silt," went to the kitchen drawer, removed a small "trowel," and sat down at the kitchen table across from her brother. She popped the lid off of the container in front of her, scooped up a mini-trowel's worth of dirt, and stared at it. Her tears came a second later, and the small drops splattered down into the dirt she was staring at. She did not even bother wiping them away.

She looked up at Jason, but he was staring at her, his mouth open and his trowel/spoon hovering just near his open mouth. The look on his face was no longer anger but surprise, followed by something else, probably pity, but Nancy couldn't tell.

He set his trowel down in his container of peat and frowned.

"Don't…Don't cry," he said unhappily. "I…I'm sorry if I…Never mind."

She nodded her head in a weak motion of recognition and absentmindedly popped her trowel/spoon into her mouth. It did not occur to her what she was doing until she was already chewing her chunk of dirt. All in all, the taste reminded her of cornflakes, so it occurred to her that her taste buds probably changed along with the world she was in. If Rain's theory was correct, she was borrowing this body anyway.

"Mom's gotten that page down," said Jason in a defeated voice. "The only thing I could find out about that page was that Danny Princeton put it—"

"No," said Nancy in a wavering voice.

She was still upset, but she was slowly and steadily shoving that feeling down.

"It wasn't Danny," she said quickly.

"What?" asked Jason.

"It wasn't Danny," repeated Nancy. "That's a lie. It was Brinn Clevenger. She wanted to date Bobby Schmidt, and she knew I was interested in him, so she put up that page and blamed it on Danny."

Jason's face worked into a mini-storm of rage as his eyes moved back and forth in what could only be furious thought.

"That lying, backstabbing, little…" he hissed. "Never mind. Mom needs to know about…"

Nancy shook her head no as she scooped up another chunk of dirt.

"I don't have any proof," said Nancy.

She took a moment to wipe her eyes free of tears.

"But it was her," she sniffed. "She blamed it on Danny because nobody likes him, so I just stupidly believed he did it."

"Why didn't you tell anybody when you found out?" asked Jason.

She studied him for a moment, but the only look on his face was one of frustration mixed with anger. She did not know what to say about that, so she just told the truth.

"I don't know," replied Nancy. "I have no idea. I just…I was angry and afraid and…I should have done something about it last year, but I thought that…once something was online, it just floated around there forever, so…"

Jason shook his head and frowned.

"We could have taken it down immediately," he said a little forcefully.

"I know that now," said Nancy. "I should have said something."

"It doesn't matter," frowned Jason. "None of my friends ever said anything about it, but I don't know if they knew or not. I don't think many people knew anyway. I think people hear something like that and pitch it in the trashcan in the backs of their minds. Those types of pages are pretty common on F and M anyway. Still…it ticked me off. Nobody talks about my sister that way. Nobody."

Nancy wiped the remaining tears from her eyes and looked at her brother in open surprise. She had not expected him to ever say anything like that.

"I didn't think you cared that much," she sniffed.

She was immediately shot with a look of indignation.

"Of course, I do!" he said unhappily. "Didn't I tell you you were my only sister?"

"Yeah," she said. "You did. And for what it's worth…I'd be mad if that happened to you."

He snorted out a short laugh and shook his head.

"That kind of page would have actually scored me some street cred," he chuckled.

Nancy gave a mental sigh and rolled her eyes.

"Typical Jason," she said quietly.

✶✶✶✶✶

Nancy sat down for Biology class. Rain smiled over at her, and Nancy gave her a quick once-over. Today, the eccentric genius had slightly darker-green skin than Nancy, and the leaves on her head were a very dark green, though the bulbs in-between them were the same color as her skin.

Rain wore a black shirt with white stripes running horizontally across it, but she wore the same black cargo pants and black boots she always wore. Her earrings were the large stars she wore in Nancy's own home universe, and that was a pleasant surprise for once. Nancy had not expected to see them again.

"You're wearing your stars again!" said Nancy with a little more excitement than she had intended.

Rain reached up and touched her right earring with her right-hand fingers. The look on her face was one of slight confusion, but that was to be expected.

"These?" she asked. "Nance, I've worn these for as long…"

"As we've been friends," finished Nancy. "I know. You say that about everything you wear."

"I do?" asked Rain.

"Yep," said Nancy. "It doesn't surprise me anymore, though…Well, that's not entirely true. It surprised me today because I didn't expect to see you with those stars again. It's usually something different every day."

"Really?" asked Rain. "Like what?"

The young genius shook her head and rolled her eyes.

"I don't know why I said that," she said. "You tell me every single day what's changed."

"Yeah," smiled Nancy. "It's just that those star earrings are what *my* Rain wears. The original Rain."

"I *am* the original Rain," frowned Rain.

"I meant where I'm originally from," corrected Nancy. "Even so, you're still Rain no matter what universe I'm in."

"I'd hope so," said Rain. "I hope I'm not a jerk in some other universe. That would be awful. I don't want to be that person who sets fire to puppies and kicks bags of poo."

Nancy let out a short guffaw and then shushed herself.

"I think you meant 'kicks puppies' and 'sets fire to bags of poo,'" she said.

"That's what I said…didn't I?" asked Rain.

Nancy gave another chuckle and shook her head no. Rain merely smiled and waved her off.

"You know what I meant," she said.

Nancy looked around for a moment and realized that everyone in class was talking with everyone else. This was mainly due to the fact that Mr. Wagner had not yet arrived.

"What's going on?" she asked. "Where is Mr. Wagner? Class should have started by now."

"You didn't hear?" asked Rain.

"Hear what?" asked Nancy.

"He's probably at the principal's office," replied Rain. "He had to break up a fight before class."

"Oh, really?" asked Nancy. "Somebody was fighting? Who?"

"I thought you knew," said Rain, a slight tone of confusion evident in her voice. "Danny and Bobby Schmidt got into it."

"What!" asked Nancy in alarm.

This was definitely news.

"No, I did not know that, Rain," she said unhappily.

She honestly could not imagine Danny in a fight.

"Which is funny," she thought in grim retrospect, *"because I could definitely imagine him coming to school with a shotgun before I really knew him. I'm so glad I was wrong about Danny. He's definitely not like that…Still…fighting?…with Bobby Schmidt?"*

"Why in the heck was Danny fighting?" she asked a second later.

Rain gave her the strangest look in the world before giving her a very simple yet stunning reply.

"It was over you," she said.

"Say what now?" asked Nancy.

That statement hit her like a punch to the chest. She had never, *ever* had anyone fight over her before. It evoked a feeling she could not begin to describe.

"They got into it over something Bobby must have said," continued Rain. "I only caught the tail end of it. I think Bobby's the only one that got in trouble, though, because Danny was pretty much a punching bag from the start. Whatever happened must have really made Danny mad to take on Bobby. That was pretty stupid."

Nancy stared down at her thoroughly green hands for a moment. They rested upon the blacktop of their lab table, and staring at them made everything come together in one weird cosmic explosion. It was that surreal quality of everything colliding, all of the strange occurrences within her life over the last twelve days colliding at that moment, that got to her in the strangest way.

She felt a strange heat in her chest, a building of warmth that was followed by a fluttering in her stomach; it raised her blood pressure and caused a slight tremor in her hands. She felt that heat move to her cheeks and then to her scalp. She could feel her cheeks burning with embarrassment, or perhaps something else, but what that something else was could not be defined, at least not by her. Her scalp, however, felt like it was on fire, and she detected the distinct but pleasant aroma of flowers a second later.

Rain grabbed her by the left wrist and pulled her attention within that direction. The young genius's face was a mix of surprise and alarm, and this reaction snapped Nancy from her strange, surreal daze.

"Nancy, you're blooming!" she hissed.

"What?" asked Nancy in honest confusion.

Rain quickly pulled out a small, pink, compact mirror from her backpack and flipped it up toward Nancy's face. Nancy grabbed the small object a second later and stared at her own reflection within the small reflective oval.

All of the buds on her head, the small bulbs in-between the leaves that made up her hair…they had all blossomed into small pink and delicate-looking flowers. It looked as if she was wearing a bouquet of pink roses upon her green head.

"To the restroom, now!" hissed Rain.

Rain stood, pulled Nancy up from her chair, and pulled her along toward the door.

Nancy had no choice but to follow, but that was not what got her attention. The entire class picked up in a loud and embarrassing "Ahhhhhh!" all at the same time, like a convention of hecklers all gathered in one spot. This only further embarrassed Nancy, but she had no idea why she should even be embarrassed, so she simply and stupidly allowed Rain to pull her out of the classroom and down the hall to the restroom.

Nancy was pulled into the restroom without so much as a word of why, and Rain spun her around to give her a look in the mirror. Nancy got a full view of the flowers blooming upon her leafy head, but inspecting them as such, she thought them rather pretty, although her scalp still felt as if it were sunburned.

"What are you doing!" said Rain in clear exasperation. "Are you *trying* to ostracize yourself?"

"I don't..." stammered Nancy. "What?...I don't understand!"

Rain gave her an openmouthed "are you stupid?" look. She threw out both hands palms up in an act of supreme frustration...At least, that's what Nancy took from the action.

"You're blooming!" exclaimed Rain. "In the middle of class!"

"I don't even know what that means!" hissed Nancy. "I'm not even from this world! Haven't you figured that out by now?"

Rain smacked her own green face with her own green right hand and groaned into her open palm. She lowered her hand and shot Nancy a rather unhappy frown.

"Seriously?" she asked. "Why didn't you say anything? Most of the time you seem normal, but are you saying that today..."

"Yes," frowned Nancy. "This is the first time I've been here. This isn't like the other times, Rain. This is my first real visit here."

Rain closed her eyes for a moment, scrunched up her lips, and nodded once, but Nancy was not sure what that meant. The eccentric young lady opened her eyes a moment later and shot Nancy a serious stare.

"Okay, okay," said Rain. "So the Nancy I've been talking to for the last twelve days is the…the 'remnant' Nancy, the one left behind…Good grief…This makes even less sense than before, even when I explain it to myself."

"I have no idea what you're…" began Nancy, but then she realized that she did in fact know. "Yeah…Yes. I *do* understand. The other Nancy you saw is the…the 'remnant.' I'm the *real* Nancy…uhhh…the Nancy whose mind is shifting across dimensional lines."

"Okay, okay," nodded Rain in understanding. "We need a system for figuring out when you're actually all together in there. You need to tell me every day if you're the 'real' one or not."

"I don't think that's feasible," replied Nancy. "My guess is that I'd simply say I was the real one every single day."

Rain frowned, put her hands on her hips, and shook her head. She held up her left hand palm out and shook it for emphasis.

"Doesn't matter," she said quickly. "I'll just ask you something that you would only know if you were native to this world, and if you're clueless, then I'll know you're the one."

Nancy thought about this and realized it made perfect sense.

"Okay," she said after a moment. "Yeah, we'll do that."

"Still…" said Rain after a moment.

She made a motion with both hands toward Nancy's reflection in the mirror.

"This..." she said. "*This!*"

"What about it?" asked Nancy. "In the world I'm from, we all have hair. We certainly don't have leaves on our head."

"Hair?" asked Rain in open curiosity. "You mean like on a Venus flytrap?"

"Something like that," said Nancy.

Rain closed her eyes and shook her head as if to get her mind back on track.

"Never mind that," she said quickly. "Look, blooming is...is what a person does when...when they're...*in love*...with someone."

It made a certain sort of sense to Nancy why that would be taboo, but there was one giant hole in Rain's explanation...Nancy was not in love with anyone.

"I'm not in love with anybody, Rain," she replied.

"Then why are you blooming?" asked the eccentric young genius.

"I don't know," shrugged Nancy. "I just...I couldn't believe that two guys were fighting over me, and I thought...I just...I felt really weird about it..."

Rain gave her a wicked grin that slowly spread across her green face.

"Oh, *really*?" she asked, but her voice held a note of teasing to it.

Nancy did not really like the implication behind that answer.

"Don't give me 'oh really,'" she frowned. "I'm not in love with Bobby. If that jerk really said something nasty about me, then he'll never get a second look from me. Not to mention that he's dating Brinn Clevenger, so how smart could he be?"

Rain's smile died on her face as her shoulders slumped in what looked like supreme disappointment.

"You clearly have strong feelings for someone, Nance," she said in an unhappy tone.

And Rain was clearly working hard on frustrating her. It was irritation at its finest, and she didn't feel like putting up with it.

"I just told you I don't!" hissed Nancy. "Aren't you listening? I don't like Bobby anymore!"

"I wasn't talking about Bobby," frowned Rain.

"What?" asked Nancy. "Who are you talking about, then?"

Rain simply stood there, hands on her hips, frowning at her. It took Nancy a moment to make the connection in her brain as to whom Rain was speaking of, but the idea of that was so ridiculous it nearly caused an overload in Nancy's active neurons.

"D…Danny!" she choked out. "Are you kidding me! Are you out of your mind!"

Her best friend simply stood there and scrunched up her own lips in what was a facial expression that Nancy had not seen before.

"What do you think?" asked Rain.

"I think you're delusional," snorted Nancy. "I think this blooming thing was just a…a reaction to the fact that two boys were fighting over me. That's it…That's all. There's nothing else to it."

Rain studied her for a moment and then shrugged.

"Okay," she said in a laissez-faire voice. "You know what you feel better than I do…Still…you're probably going to have to hang here in a stall and wait for the blooming to stop."

"How long is that going to take?" asked Nancy.

"A few minutes," replied Rain. "Shouldn't take too long…that is, as long as you don't think about your *lover boy*."

"Rain, please," said Nancy in her warning tone.

Rain gave her a rather short but obnoxious chuckle, but Nancy was not particularly amused.

*****

Nancy parked her bike next to Rain's house while the eccentric young genius threw a tennis ball to the little ball of fur that was her dog. Actually, Rain's dog, Buster, was now a little ball of *leaves*, dark-green leaves that were nearly black, but other than that, he still had the same beady little eyes and the same annoying high-pitched yelp that Nancy had already witnessed days before.

"Buster's not like Weirdo," said Rain as she struggled to tear the tennis ball from the little dog's mouth. "He's so hyper…but he has helped me with the loss of Weirdo. I sometimes think about Weirdo, and I start to cry, but seeing Buster helps keep my spirits up."

"That's good," replied Nancy. "I miss Weirdo too, even if he wasn't my dog."

"That's okay," said Rain. "He was kind of your dog, too…Anyway, let's talk about yesterday. I took a look in the notebook, and…it's really weird…even for you."

"I already know," said Nancy. "I was there, remember?"

"Oh, really?" asked Rain. "Then what did we look like?"

"Cyborgs," replied Nancy. "And we had hair, not leaves."

"So *that's* what that was!" breathed Rain. "When you said 'hair,' I thought you were talking about stiff bristles, like spiky…bristly…stuff."

Nancy rolled her eyes at that one, but Rain only laughed at her reaction.

"I could have described that better," smirked Rain.

"You think?" grinned Nancy.

She was feeling better after being out of school; the day had been really weird as far as she was concerned. She had indeed stopped "blooming" after a few minutes, but the feeling of displacement in her soul over the whole boys fighting thing wore on her, and her classmates bringing it up had not helped, either. She had been teased the entire day about it, but at least it was good natured and not done out of malice…At least, she hoped it was.

Rain diverted her attention from her recollections with an issue that was far more pressing.

"Let me get the notebook," said the young genius. "I'll get my dad's camera, too."

Something occurred to Nancy that had not occurred to her before. It came to her in a flashfire of epiphany, and she was surprised she hadn't thought of it sooner. In fact, it was so obvious to her now that she felt like a fool for not seeing it to begin with.

"Wait," she said quickly. "Wait a minute…Rain…where was your dad's camera when you heard that broadcast?…You know…the broadcast that occurred around the same time that I said the Institute exploded?"

"Oh," said Rain as she blinked her eyes in thought. "Oh…uhhh…my dad keeps it in a box beneath…his…radio…"

Rain's eyes widened as she figured out what Nancy already knew.

"Bingo!" smiled Nancy. "That's what I thought. His camera was affected just like the notebook. That means we don't need to use it. We can just use my phone's camera."

"Your phone?" asked Rain.

"Think about it," said Nancy. "My phone was with me during the explosion, which means it's 'tuned in' to whatever's going on with me. Remember how my phone got destroyed, and then it suddenly started working again? That's evidence that it's tuned in."

"Okay," said Rain. "That makes sense…however…we should take a picture on my dad's camera and yours as well…just in case."

"Works for me," said Nancy.

Rain's logic made sense; it was a backup issue anyway. If the phone idea didn't work, they already knew the old instant camera would, so it was a solid go on covering both bases.

"I'll be right back," said Rain. "Let me go get the…"

She stopped speaking as Danny rounded the fence at the end of Rain's backyard.

"On second thought," said the eccentric genius, "why don't you take Buster for a walk while I get the camera? I forgot that my dad is in the study today, so I'll have to find a way to get it while he's in there. It may take a bit."

Nancy wasn't sure about this. She didn't really know Buster, and more importantly, he didn't really know her.

"I don't know, Rain," she said unhappily. "Buster doesn't really know me…"

Her best friend gave her a confident grin and waved her off.

"It'll be fine," she said.

Danny walked up to them, and Rain quickly addressed his presence.

"Hey, Danny," she smiled. "You can help with Buster, too."

"What?" asked Danny.

"Yeah," smiled Rain. "I have to run an errand, so why don't you help Nancy walk Buster? I usually walk him to the end of the street and sit on the bench next to the small park down there. He likes to run around there and chase the birds."

"Uhhh…" began Danny.

"It's fine," said Rain with another wave of her hand. "I'll be back in a little bit. I'll just meet you two down there."

"Okay…" said Danny.

Rain ducked out through her backdoor before Nancy even had a chance to protest. She sighed at the behavior of the young genius, but that was Rain, and this didn't surprise her at all. She was always like that.

"Hey, Danny," said Nancy as she picked up Buster's leash.

"Hey," said Danny quietly.

Nancy caught the little ball of leaves that ran around her feet and attached the leash to his collar. She looked up and used this moment to study Danny, give him a once-over, because she was curious as to what changes were made with him due to this new world.

Danny's skin was a slightly darker green than her own, but the leaves on his head were a lighter green than the ones on her head.

He wore one of his new outfits, a plain blue T-shirt with matching tan slacks, and he had on a pair of blue canvas sneakers instead of his normal dark boots/shoes.

What stood out the most on him, however, was the nasty grey bruising around his right eye and the slight cut across his lower lip. Seeing his injuries gave her a strange feeling inside, a twisting like her guts were being tied in a knot, and she could not help but think that these injuries were somehow her fault.

She didn't say anything as she stood and led Buster along by his leash. The little ball of leaves ran out ahead of her and toward the front of Rain's house, and Nancy merely followed, Danny in tow. It took her a moment to get up some nerve to say something, anything at all to him.

"So…" she said carefully, "what's been going on?"

They walked side by side as the dog trotted out in front of them.

"Nothing really," shrugged Danny. "Other than the…Never mind. It doesn't matter."

"I think it does," said Nancy. "You got into a fight, didn't you?"

Danny shrugged again but said nothing.

"I hope you hit him at least once," frowned Nancy.

"Yeah," said Danny quietly.

They walked farther down the walk toward the small residential park in the distance. Nancy could hardly call it a park; it was more of a grassy lot with a swing set, a jungle gym dome, and a couple of wooden benches.

"I don't condone fighting," said Nancy, "but I suspect he deserved it."

If Bobby had said something nasty about her, then he most certainly did deserve it.

"He said some things about somebody that…" said Danny. "Doesn't matter. He said something that wasn't true, and I couldn't…I couldn't let it slide."

"He insulted someone you knew?" asked Nancy. "…or did he insult you?"

"Both," frowned Danny. "I don't care about me, though. He shouldn't have talked trash about somebody…someone he doesn't know."

"Really?" asked Nancy.

She was curious about what Danny thought of her. This word dodging was an interesting way to get inside Danny's head, plus it was clear he did not want to admit that he had been fighting over her.

"Why did you stick up for this person?" she asked.

They reached the first bench and sat down on it. Nancy unwound the loop of leash in her right hand and let Buster dash into the park, the little ball of leave's only intent to chase the various small birds hopping along the edges of the jungle gym dome.

"It doesn't matter," shrugged Danny. "He was being a jerk. I told him off, and he thought he was just going to bowl me over. It didn't work out that way for him."

"Yeah," replied Nancy. "Did you get in trouble?"

"Not really," said Danny. "Mr. Wagner saw him hit me, so he got in-school suspension…My parents weren't happy, though. They got onto me even though it wasn't my fault."

Nancy was all too familiar with the injustices of parents, her mother in particular.

"Ah," she frowned. "I know all about that. My mom can't keep her nose out of my business."

"Yeah," said Danny. "My parents…they don't get me. They still think things work like they did when they were young."

"Ha!" snorted Nancy. "I know, right? Nothing is the same. Not a thing. My mom always barges into my room without asking and never listens to a word I say."

"Yeah," shrugged Danny. "My dad's a real handyman. He can do repairs and work on cars and stuff, but I'm no good at that. He can't understand why I don't want to do those things."

"The world doesn't work that way anymore," shrugged Nancy. "My grandparents are the same way. There wasn't all of this technology when they were young, so they learned other skills. Shoot, they wouldn't even know how to work my phone. I think they still have a landline."

Danny laughed at her remark, and Nancy joined him in a short chuckle. It was funny when put in perspective, but her laughter died down as she realized she had gotten off topic.

"Anyway," she said after a moment, "back to my original question…What made you think it was a good idea to go after Bobby?"

"What?" asked Danny.

The look on his face was one of confusion mixed with surprise.

"How did you…" he began to ask.

"Everybody knows, Danny," said Nancy. "At least, everyone that I know had a story about it."

"Oh," said Danny quietly.

He stared off into the distance, and Nancy wasn't sure if he was looking out toward Buster or just staring off into space. She decided to push him on it; she wanted to know what was going on in his head.

"Why would you get into a fight over something Bobby said?" she asked. "Especially if it was about…me. You don't owe me anything. Heck, I've been mean to you for a long time. We just started talking in a civil manner last week."

He stared off into the distance for a moment, and Nancy wasn't sure if he was going to answer at all, but he answered her anyway after that quiet length of time.

"I just…I wanted to be a friend, you know?" he said. "A real friend. I don't have many friends…not ones I can talk to anyway. He said some pretty nasty things about you, and I wasn't going to…I couldn't let him get away with it. A real friend wouldn't let it slide."

Nancy felt strange inside over this. The only "real friend" she had was Rain; everyone else she knew were more like acquaintances than "friends." Nevertheless, she felt a strange longing inside, like a pull in a direction that she did not understand, but she ignored it in spite of herself.

"I don't know what to say about that," she thought in strange wonder. *"I guess that's good that he wants to be friends…It's just…I don't know. I feel sorry for him more than anything else. I know he has friends…He must have."*

"Isn't Allen your real friend?" she asked after a moment of careful thought.

"He's a friend, sure," shrugged Danny, "but he's not someone I would confide in. You do that with

Rain…At least, I think you do…Doesn't matter…That's what I want. I want to have *real* friends. I was thinking that…maybe you and Rain could be like that. I was thinking that you could be my friends."

Nancy did not know what to think about this, but there was not one good reason she could come up with as to why she could not be friends with Danny. He wasn't exactly smothering or insulting or mooching…He was just a dork.

She made the decision to just go with it. There really wasn't any reason not to.

"I don't mind, Danny," she breathed. "I'm not really a 'people' person, though. I prefer to be by myself or with Rain, and that's about it."

"Yeah," said Danny quietly. "I'm that way, too. A lot of the time I just like to do my own thing. I don't really like big crowds."

"Yeah," sighed Nancy. "I guess that rules out customer service for either one of us."

Danny gave a short laugh, and Nancy joined him in it. He gave her a strange look a moment later, but she did not know what to make of it.

"My family is having a cookout on Friday," he said. "Rain's coming over. I was wondering if you'd like to…to show up."

"Your family?" asked Nancy. "Wouldn't they mind if some stranger showed up?"

Danny shook his head and waved her off.

"Nah," he said. "They've seen you over at Rain's. They don't care. I mean, my aunt and cousin are coming over, and my cousin is bringing one of her friends, so I don't see the problem."

"Okay," shrugged Nancy. "I guess, if that's okay with them."

"Yeah," said Danny. "They're having a cookout on Friday night. We usually do this every year…Yeah, I'm going to have a busy weekend. I have the cookout on Friday, and then I'm going to the Autumn Fair on Saturday with Allen."

Nancy had plain forgotten that the Fair was this weekend.

"The Autumn Fair's on Saturday?" she asked in surprise.

"Yeah," he replied. "Didn't you see the stuff they're setting up downtown? I think they already have a carousel set up."

"I don't really get downtown that often," said Nancy.

She had honestly forgotten about the Fair, but then she had been struggling with major problems of her own, her shifting being number one on that list. Still, she had never missed the Fair, not once since she was little, and it bothered her that she could have missed out on it. She was suddenly glad that Danny had informed her of it.

"I'll have to catch it," she said in honest reply. "Thanks for letting me know. I really am clueless sometimes. I just can't seem to see what's right in front of my face."

"Well, you can always meet up with us," he said thoughtfully. "I mean, I thought you and Rain would be going…"

"We will…We *are*," corrected Nancy. "Rain and I have gone every single year since I can remember. Yeah, we'll definitely be there…Yeah, sure. We'll meet up with you."

"Cool," said Danny, and that was that.

Chapter 13…Stasis

Nancy awoke to the morning light but did not wish to move. She enjoyed the light on her skin; it felt good for some reason, and it occurred to her that she had felt exactly the same way when she had awakened the day before. She raised her right hand up in front of her face to inspect it, and her heart jumped a little as she recognized the light-green color of her skin, the same color as yesterday.

She sat up, got out of bed, and trotted into the bathroom. One look in the mirror confirmed what she had already suspected…She had not shifted this time. She still had the same green skin, the same leaves and bulbs on her head, and this made her stop and catch her breath for a moment.

"It stopped," she whispered to no one in particular.

"It finally stopped," she pondered. *"I'm not shifting anymore. That means…That means I'll be Plant Nancy from now on…I guess that's not too bad…Yeah…This isn't bad at all. I mean, I'll be eating dirt for the rest of my life…literally, but it's not that bad. I can get used to this…At least it's not Spider Nancy or…shudder…Bald Streak Nancy. This is good. This is really good. I'll have to tell Rain. She'll certainly want to hear about this."*

She took her shower, dressed herself in a plain purple T-shirt with yellow stripes along the shoulders to accent her stonewashed jeans, grabbed her backpack, and practically skipped downstairs. Today was going to be a good day.

✳✳✳✳✳

Nancy sat down for lunch right next to Rain. The young genius looked exactly the same as yesterday, though she had worn her "Remember the Irish" shirt again, along with her black cargo pants and black boots. She was consistent in clothing, just not accessories.

Nancy was glad that this Rain, Plant Rain, had gone back to wearing the star earrings. At least that was the same and held some sense of normalcy for her.

Nancy's stomach growled from prolonged hunger, and she stared down at the plate before her. Today's meal was a mound of sandy soil mixed with clay, along with a side of some kind of potted soil that was, as Rain described, "mystery peat." Apparently, flavor was dependent upon whether a particular soil was acidic or alkaline, though Nancy had no idea what that meant. On the bright side, there was a big mound of live earthworms on her plate, and this was considered a delicacy, kind of like a dessert but a lot wrigglier.

"Great," she said with a forced smile. "Earthworms again. Wonderful."

"I know," smiled Rain. "And it's only Thursday. It's because we have an early out tomorrow."

"What?" asked Nancy. "We do?"

Rain gave her a strange look. It consisted of one leafy eyebrow raised with a sort of half frown, but Nancy did not know what that particular look meant.

"Are you all right?" asked the young genius. "Do you actually *want* to go to school all day long tomorrow?"

Nancy gave her a facetious frown and shook her head no.

"Clearly," she said in her best sarcastic voice, but Rain only laughed at her.

The young genius shrugged and dipped her spoon/trowel into her own mound of clay.

"I know you've been confused because of all the shifting," she said thoughtfully, "but I'm glad that some things haven't changed. You still have the fair. *We* still have the fair."

"Yeah," said Nancy. "It's weird, though. Everything physical changes with the shifting, but a lot of things don't change at all. It's like events unfolded throughout history in a universal way. Don't you find that weird?"

"Unusual, yes," shrugged Rain, "but this is uncharted territory, so everything is weird right now. I'm more concerned about the fact that you didn't shift today. Maybe it's slowing down or something."

"Maybe it's stopped, you mean," corrected Nancy. "I actually kind of like this particular universe, and I'm hoping that my shifting is done, because I don't want to end up in another world like Bald Streak Nancy."

Rain guffawed and then quickly shushed herself. She shot Nancy a truly amused look and shook her head.

"You just can't get over that, can you?" she asked. "Out of all the weird things we've apparently been, *that's* the one you hate the most."

"Can you blame me?" asked Nancy. "You may not understand what it's like to have hair, but I can tell you that the feeling of having a bald streak on your head and a big mane of hair on your back is…it's not something you like…or forget."

Rain chuckled and then popped her spoon/trowel in her mouth.

Danny took that moment to walk up and sit down across from them. Today the young man was wearing a burgundy T-shirt with matching black slacks. It occurred to Nancy that dressing differently didn't mean Danny couldn't ever wear black again, he just needed a little more color to prevent his previously morose appearance. Even a little color helped; it made him look more personable, though even as a plant, he was still a giant dork.

"Hey, Danny," said Nancy.

"Hey," smiled Danny.

He sounded a little different today, almost…hopeful.

"You look happy," noted Nancy.

"You know Sarah?" he asked. "That new girl? She's coming to my family's cookout."

Rain swallowed her dirt and then gave him a confused look.

"Really?" she asked. "You asked her to come?"

"No," smiled Danny. "She's the friend that my cousin is bringing. She went to school in Carlton with my cousin, and they were friends there. Her parents were there for a year after they moved from San Diego, but then they moved here…I had no idea that Erin knew her. It's just weird how she would be the friend that my cousin, Erin, is bringing, don't you think?"

Nancy felt a strange disappointment inside, a tugging at the back of her mind that upset her, but she was not sure why. She chalked it up to being concerned for Danny's wellbeing, as this girl "Sarah" did not look like the type that would be friends with him or even give him the time of day unless forced to.

"Danny, I don't know…" she said uncertainly.

"Don't know what?" he asked.

"I just…" she stammered. "Are you sure this girl is all right?"

"Yeah," he said quickly. "Why?"

Nancy gave Rain a look for some help, but the eccentric genius was of no help this time.

"It'll be fine, Nance," said Rain. "Danny will see *exactly* what kind of girl Sarah is at the cookout. It's a good thing she's coming, you'll see."

Nancy frowned at this. She was more certain than ever that this was a disaster in the making.

"Well, I don't think it's a good idea," she said, a clear note of unhappiness in her voice.

She did not mean to sound so bitter about it, but it was impossible to perceive it any other way, and this was not lost on Danny. He shot her a confused frown a second later.

"Why not?" he asked. "There's nothing wrong with her. She's been nothing but nice to me."

"Because she was forced to," thought Nancy in a mental frown.

"I'm sorry, but I don't trust her," she said, but she had not thought about how this would sound to Danny, and she regretted saying it as soon as it had left her mouth.

"Why not?" asked Danny, but there was a clear note of anger in his voice this time.

This conversation was going nowhere fast, and Nancy did not really wish to argue with him over this girl, so she backpedaled a bit.

"It…It doesn't matter," she stammered. "I just…I just don't want this girl to make a fool out of you, that's all."

"What?" asked Danny in open confusion.

And confusion was right. Nancy had no idea why she had just said that. She did not owe Danny anything, and he did not owe her, so the idea of being *concerned* for him did not make sense, not in retrospect of her very recent hatred of him.

"I…am…just a little worried about you, is all," said Nancy.

Danny blinked a couple of times before shaking his head while muttering something under his breath. He stared down at the utensil in his right hand as if it had just suddenly popped into existence. He held his spoon/trowel between the fingers of his right hand, and it hovered just above the mound of earthworms on his plate. It was clear he wanted to dip it in and take a bite, but he looked up at her and gave her a confused frown a moment later.

"I'll be fine," he said. "Don't worry about me…Actually, I don't even know why you'd worry about me at all. You hated me just last week."

Nancy sighed and shook her head.

"It's clear he's not going to let that go," she thought in unhappy silence.

"I know that," she said. "I get that. I said I was sorry. That wasn't your fault; it was mine. I just…I think you should be careful, is all."

"Why?" he asked, clear frustration in his voice. "I can take care of myself. I don't need you to watch over me."

Now this frustrated Nancy. Danny got into a fight because of her, and now he was telling her she couldn't do something similar in return, not fight, per se, but watch his back, as it were. It seemed like a double standard, and it probably was, now that she was thinking about it.

"You wanted a friend, Danny," she replied. "That's what friends do. They look out for each other."

Danny stared at her for a moment as his eyes moved back and forth in thought, and then he slowly nodded his head in agreement.

"I…I get that, too," he said slowly. "But I'll be all right. If I really need help, I'll come get you."

That was not exactly what she wanted to hear, but it was better than arguing.

"Okay," said Nancy. "I'll help you if you need it. I'll be at the cookout anyway."

"Good," said Danny. "But you'll see what I'm talking about. She's a really nice person."

Nancy just nodded in return. She did not have his enduring faith in the matter. Even though she knew it was not her business, she still felt conflicted over it, and for some reason, that conflict was even more stressful than the fact that she was the world's first "dimensionaut."

It occurred to her that her shifting had not bothered her as of late, mainly because it had stopped, at least for the time being, but even so, the fact that she was now a "plant hybrid" should have made any sane person suffering the same experience to lose their mind, but this was not the case with her. No, her mind was only on one thing, and that thing was Danny's impending fall from his current high. She was sure of that impending fall; she felt it deep in her bones, and that bothered her far more than anything else, even being stuck as a plant.

*****

Nancy tossed a tennis ball across Rain's backyard and watched as the little ball of leaves that was Buster chased after it.

"So, do you think your shifting has really stopped?" asked Rain.

Nancy turned toward her best friend and shrugged. The truth was and had always been that she had no idea what was happening to her. The fact for now was that she had not shifted today, the thirteenth day, and though thirteen was supposedly an unlucky number, she felt herself to be very lucky at her imposed dimensional stasis.

"I don't know," she said in honest reply. "I just hope it has. At this point, I'm not worried about getting back to 'my world'…I just wanted to stop shifting, and I finally have."

"For today," emphasized Rain. "We don't know if it's permanent."

"I know," sighed Nancy. "I'm just being hopeful."

"Don't get me wrong," shrugged Rain, "I'm really happy that you want to settle down in my universe, but…I also love documenting all of the changes we've made over the last twelve days. Did we really eat plants and animals where you came from?"

"Yeah," replied Nancy. "We do in most universes. Back where I'm from, the term 'eating dirt' is not a pleasant one. It usually implies that you're mangled or dead."

"Oh," said Rain in obvious surprise. "I don't think I'd want to live there. No offense, Fance, but I like this universe just fine."

"It's not bad," said Nancy. "I do find it odd that we can drink through our skin. That took a little getting used to."

"And not the eating dirt part?" asked Rain.

Nancy chuckled and waved her off.

"I just pretend it's fudge," she said.

"I don't know what that is," replied Rain, "but you do know that you can drink through your mouth, right? That's how most people do it. In fact, if you relied on just your skin, you'd dehydrate. That function is for drawing moisture out of the air so that our cells…"

Nancy cut her off before the young genius could go into a full-on "sciencey" explanation. Those tended to kill any interest in their conversations for her.

"Yeah, yeah," she said. "I get it. That's how I've been doing it all day long and all day yesterday."

"Oh…" said Rain after a short pause. "I…just wasn't sure if you knew."

Nancy sighed as she bent down to tear the tennis ball away from Buster's little mouth.

"It's fine," she said. "I'm sorry if I sound frustrated. I've been shifting universes for the last twelve days, and now that I've finally settled on one, I've realized that I still have to learn about the one I'm in. I don't think of myself as being 'stuck' in it, mind you. Almost everything about our lives is the same…which is really weird, now that I think about it. Why in the heck *are* our lives almost exactly the same?"

"Beats me," shrugged Rain. "In a scientific sense, it makes *no* sense. Even a slight change in evolution for humans would cause massive changes in our brains, which would alter how we think, which would in turn alter our actions. Absolutely *nothing* should be the same, but you say it is, so I have to go with that. I can only work with the information I have."

"Well…you're still smart," said Nancy, "Brinn Clevenger's still a backstabbing little liar, my mother's still a control freak, and Danny's still a social outcast slash dork, so there you go."

"Hey, now," frowned Rain. "You shouldn't talk about Danny that way. He stood up for you, you know."

Nancy knew it had been a mistake to say that as soon as it had left her mouth, but the damage had already been done. It was the offended look on Rain's face that made her cringe, but she had no good response as to how to deal with it.

"I know, Rain," she sighed. "I know he stood up for me. I was just stating the obvious."

"Don't you want to be his friend?" asked the young genius. "You said you did."

"I…I do," stammered Nancy. "I wasn't trying to be mean or anything. I just…He's…He's a giant dork. I don't know how else to say it."

Rain frowned and shook her head in obvious disapproval.

"And here I thought you were actually worried about his wellbeing with that Sarah girl," she said.

This incensed Nancy. She did not want to be vilified like this, especially by her best friend.

"That's not fair!" she exclaimed. "I wasn't being mean, so don't treat me like a criminal!"

Rain raised her hands palms out and moved them downward in a slow "shushing" motion.

"Inside voices, Nance," she said calmly. "I know we're outside, but let's keep the volume down."

That was Rain. She could be calm under the worst pressure, and she could use that ability to make Nancy feel like a royal fool too, which was exactly what she was doing right now.

It incensed Nancy even further, or it would have had not Danny decided to make an appearance right then. He rounded the back fence of Rain's backyard and ambled toward them in a more relaxed manner than Nancy had ever seen him do before. It was a little odd to witness this change in him, so her anger was put on hiatus for the time being.

"Hey, Danny," said Rain confidently. "We were just talking about you."

Nancy shot her best friend a "what are you doing?" look, as she did not want Rain saying anything about what Nancy herself thought of Danny. It was her own fault that she had said anything at all; she should have kept her mouth shut about Danny, but now it was too late to do anything about it. She was anxious about what Rain was going to say about the situation, because she truly did not know what the eccentric genius was up to.

Danny looked at them in open curiosity.

"Oh?" asked Danny. "Why's that?"

"Oh, I wanted to know who you thought was prettier," said Rain with a wicked smile. "Do you think Nancy is prettier…or that new girl, Sarah? I was wondering if Nancy was a little jealous of her."

Nancy could not believe this. What had just come out of Rain's mouth was not characteristic of her. Yes, she was a bit mischievous at times, but nothing so brash as to throw it in Nancy's face.

The only thing Nancy could do at that moment was stare at her best friend with the most obvious "you have betrayed me" look she could muster, a slightly frowning, open-mouthed stare with partially wide eyes, something that even Rain could not fail to register. However, Rain deliberately ignored her; she stared directly at Danny while waiting for an answer from her socially-oblivious neighbor.

Danny, on the other hand, looked like he had just been caught in a thunderstorm without any protection. He looked flustered as his eyes switched between the two girls before him, and it took him a moment to say anything at all.

"I…don't…know if…" he stammered, "I should tell the truth."

"Oh, *really?*" asked Rain. "It's fine. No one's going to get mad at you."

"It's not that," replied Danny in an obvious fluster. "I just…I thought the answer was obvious."

"No," replied Rain. "No, not so much."

Nancy simply stared at Rain in open-mouthed horror, then at Danny, then back at Rain. She was honestly at a loss for words or action at this point.

"O…*kay*," said Danny uncertainly and with a shrug. "I thought it was actually…uhhh…*really* obvious. First of all, Nancy has an athletic form, slender with muscle, really fit and in shape, while Sarah is the average weight for a girl that engages in moderate exercise…

"Don't get me wrong, Sarah's attractive and all, and she's definitely not *ugly* by any means…She *is* a natural forest jade, after all, and I don't see too many of those, but if this is a hands-down case of natural beauty here, then I'd have to say that Nancy is better looking…from my point of view anyway. She has a narrower chin with a rounder face and slightly larger eyes, and coupled with her shade of summer grass, she has a natural, classic beauty that Sarah simply doesn't possess…in my opinion anyway."

Nancy did not know what to think of that answer. Danny's inspection of their looks stopped her thought process cold, but the confused look on Rain's face actually added to that ceasing of neurons firing within Nancy's brain. Rain looked truly out of sorts over Danny's reply, and that was not normal.

"How in the heck did you make *that* critique?" asked the eccentric young genius in obvious surprise. "I was just expecting a name drop, not an in-depth case study."

Danny looked truly embarrassed as he threw up his hands and shrugged.

"I spend a lot of time critiquing my friends' art," he said quickly. "I sometimes even critique Nancy's brother, Jason's, art. I can't really draw myself, not as good as you anyway, but I do like sci-fi and fantasy art, and you wouldn't believe how many female characters people like to draw…"

"I'm pretty sure I do," snorted Rain, "but that's neither here nor there. The point is…is that you are the expert here, for lack of a better term, and you proved my point, which is that Nancy has nothing to be jealous of."

Danny turned his attention upon Nancy and gave her a quizzical look.

"Why would you be jealous of Sarah?" he asked. "I didn't think you'd be jealous of anyone. You can pretty much get any guy you want…except Bobby…but he's a jerk anyway."

All of this stacked to make Nancy feel like a fool. Rain had done it to her *again*, made her feel the fool, but the young genius had done it in such a way that Nancy could not even be angry with her. It was infuriating, and there was absolutely nothing she could do about it.

"I am *not* jealous of Sarah," she denied. "I'm not. I was just saying that…that I didn't trust her, but we already went over that during lunch, so there's no reason to go over it again."

Rain gave her a coy smirk and then shrugged.

"Okay, whatever," she said in an innocent tone.

But she was far from innocent. Nancy did not know what her best friend was playing at, but she was clearly up to something.

"There's no 'whatever,'" frowned Nancy. "Let's just drop it."

"Okay," said Rain. "But…I was wondering…"

"But what?" asked Nancy in irritation.

Now she was getting annoyed. It was quickly becoming clear to her that Rain would not let this go.

Rain looked Danny over and then rested her gaze back upon Nancy. She gave Nancy that same coy smirk that was so infuriating, but Nancy waited to hear what the girl had to say. If she needed to verbally tear into the eccentric genius, however, she would…That was a guarantee. She would not be humiliated this way, or in any way, for that matter.

"We've gone over Danny's social failings," said Rain matter-of-factly. "You know all of the things we've worked on with him about that, but I was wondering what you thought about his good points. I mean, *I* know all of his strengths, but what about you? *You're* the one with all the social grace, Fance, so why don't you shine your expertise on this? What is it about Danny that's good for a girl to know, hmmm?"

Danny looked at Nancy with furrowed eyebrows, those eyebrows consisting of slightly darker and smaller leaves than the ones on his head. Nancy did not know what to make of that expression, but one thing was for sure…She was on the spot now.

"Danny is…" she stalled out.

Both Rain and Danny stared at her, waiting for her to finish that statement, but she was at a loss for a moment, but only for a moment. It occurred to her that there were a lot of good things she had noticed about Danny recently, and this was due to the fact that he had asked for her help…and that she didn't hate him anymore.

"Danny is very intelligent," said Nancy with an upturned hand toward him. "That's obvious…but there's more to him than just that. He's socially oblivious, I'll give you that, but he wants to learn, and he's followed our advice…mostly…but we're working on that.

"He has an artist's eye and the soul of a romantic, and once he has a friend, he's loyal to the point of endangering himself for them…uhhh…and I really think he cares about what happens to other people, which is more than I can say for most people. He thinks about what he wants to be to the woman who falls in love with him…and I don't think most guys do that…"

"Practically zero," finished Rain.

"Yeah," breathed Nancy. "He's really a gentleman, which you don't see anymore…"

"Like ever," finished Rain.

"Rain," frowned Nancy.

"What?" shrugged Rain. "I was just agreeing with you."

"I…" started Nancy.

She closed her eyes, took in a deep breath, and shook her head no. Whatever Rain was up to, she was very good at hiding it, and Nancy did not want to put up with it. She raised up her hands, frowned, and gave Rain her best "stop it" stare.

"Just let me finish, please," she replied in open frustration.

"Okay, whatever," shrugged Rain.

But it was too late. Rain had already ruined it.

"Never mind," huffed Nancy.

Rain rolled her eyes and shook her head.

"Look," she said quickly. "It's clear Danny needs a little help in the social department."

"I don't think I need *that* much help," frowned Danny.

Rain ignored him and centered her unwanted attention upon Nancy. Nancy was not sure what was going on with her best friend, but it was getting annoying.

"*We* are going to help him with that, right?" asked Rain.

Nancy wasn't sure what *that* insinuation meant, but she wasn't going to have it.

"Enough!" she said in a little angrier tone than she had intended. "I said I would help him, didn't I? Why are you acting like this?"

"Uhhh, I don't know what's going on, but…" began Danny.

Rain simply smiled at him and gave him a quick shake of her head.

"Don't worry about it," she said quickly. "I just wanted to make sure that Nancy and I were on the same page, and we are."

"Exactly," huffed Nancy. "Finally, you're making sense."

Rain looked at her and tilted her head to one side while raising one eyebrow.

"I was always making sense, Nance," she said in a serious voice.

Nancy really had no idea what was going on in her best friend's head. Somehow, she must have triggered something in Rain's brain, because the eccentric genius had *never* acted this way in the past…At least, not at any time that Nancy could remember.

"We're both helping Danny," continued Rain, "so we're on the same page."

"That's what I've been saying," replied Nancy.

"Good," smiled Rain. "Well then, I think we should take this to the next step."

"Next step?" asked Danny.

Nancy was curious about this as well. She did not have a clue as to what this "next step" was or how they were going to help Danny with it.

Rain smiled at Danny and nodded slowly a couple of times. The motion was curious to Nancy, because it almost looked condescending.

"You like this Sarah girl, right?" asked Rain.

Danny looked uncomfortable for a moment, but he gave a short and honest reply anyway.

"Yeah," he shrugged. "She's nice. She was nice to me, anyway."

Nancy gave herself an internal groan at this. She really should have expected such a reply, but in the world of "reallys," the cold hard truth was that she *really* did not trust that girl, especially with someone as vulnerable as Danny.

"Well, then we'll move on to some light affection," replied Rain.

"Light affection?" asked Danny.

"Yeah," smiled Rain. "Let's see how comfortable you are with some light affection…uhhh…holding hands, for instance."

"Holding hands?" asked Danny. "How is that light…"

Rain cut him off before he could argue.

"Of course, it is," she said as she waved him off. "Holding hands is as old as time…Okay, maybe not as old as time…Actually, I have no idea how long that particular symbol of affection has been around…"

"Rain…" frowned Nancy. "Topic, please."

Rain was still Rain, even if she was up to something that Nancy could not determine as of yet. She suspected Rain was playing her over something, but what that was, she did not know.

Nevertheless, Rain could be a little scatterbrained when it came to tangents in general, and sometimes Nancy found herself automatically leading her best friend back to the original point, hence the "topic, please" instead of "stay on topic, please," because it had become more convenient to shorten the phrase after such heavy use in the past.

Rain closed her eyes, shook her head, and then frowned.

"Oh, yeah," she said after a moment. "Where was I? Oh…uhhh…we can practice holding hands."

"What?" asked Danny.

"Yeah," shrugged Rain. "You need to know the proper way to hold hands with a girl."

"There's a proper way to hold hands?" asked Danny.

Nancy was with Danny on this one. This was the first time she'd heard of this.

"What are you talking about, Rain?" she asked.

Rain turned to her and gave her a strange look, that look consisting of a half-frown with furrowed eyebrows.

"It comes naturally to you, Nance," she said with slight unhappiness. "Danny's inexperienced when it comes to things like this."

"It's just holding hands," frowned Danny. "How hard can it…"

"Pshaw," said Rain as she waved him off. "Let the expert handle this."

She turned up one hand toward Nancy and gave her a mischievous smirk.

"You've got *way* more experience with guys than me, Fance," she smiled. "Why don't you take Danny to the end of the street and back. Just show him how to walk naturally while holding hands."

"Say what now?" asked Nancy.

This was completely unexpected.

"Yeah," smiled Rain. "Just walk up to the park and back. I'm not saying that things will work out with Sarah, but if they do, Danny will need to know some of these things."

That was logical, and logic was Rain's forte, but the whole idea of it made Nancy uncomfortable. She was uncomfortable with the idea of things "working out" with this Sarah girl when it came to Danny, and she was uncomfortable with the idea of holding hands with him in the first place.

It was a dichotomy of strange, because on the one hand, Danny was a complete and utter dork that she had hated not more than two weeks ago, but on the other hand, she just didn't like the idea of him hooking up with this "Sarah," even though the idea of *that* was ridiculous in itself. He had just met her, and his chances with girls in general were next to nil anyway. Still, it ate at her, and she hadn't the faintest clue as to why.

"I guess…" said Danny, but his voice was rife with confusion.

Rain focused her attention back upon Danny.

"Just walk to the park and back," said Rain confidently. "Nancy is an expert at this, trust me. She'll show you how to act naturally and not be nervous."

"O…kay," said Danny hesitantly.

Nancy was still lost in her own surprise as Danny walked over and took her left hand into his right. It stunned her for a second, but she really didn't have the chance to think about how she even felt about it before she found herself walking next to him and away from Rain.

"If there's anything you need to know about this," said Rain with a smile, "then just ask Nancy. She's an expert at these things."

Nancy did not exactly like this; it had been decided without her consent, but now that she was doing it, it was fine for the moment. Rain had thrown her a curve ball, led her down a strange road, but she was also confused about the eccentric young genius's odd behavior. Rain was being very pushy over this, and that in itself was suspicious. Still, the more she thought about it, the more it made sense.

"Rain has always gotten along with Danny," she mused, *"and they are friends…I think…No, they're definitely friends; she's just never talked about him…for obvious reasons. She just wants Danny to be happy…and SHE doesn't want to date him…but that's not his fault.*

"Rain doesn't want to date anybody. She's in love with science. If science were a person, she'd club him over the head and drag him up to the alter to tie the

knot…Ha!…Still, she could have ASKED me to help him. She's so pushy…"

Nancy concentrated upon her surroundings and realized that they had left the safety and comfort of Rain's backyard. They were now headed down the sidewalk toward the small park at the end of Rain's street, and that wasn't so bad in itself…It was the fact that she was holding Danny's hand along with an uncomfortable silence between them that made her somewhat nervous.

She felt her palms get sweaty, and a strange feeling gripped her. It was like butterflies desperately trying to escape her stomach, and she suddenly felt light-headed. She felt an itching sensation begin to bud on her scalp, and then she remembered what had happened yesterday, and this sent her into a mental panic.

"Calm down, calm down, CALM DOWN!" she mentally screamed. *"Don't go 'blooming' again! That was embarrassing…Not to mention that I still don't know what the ramifications are for doing that in class…Ugh…That will come back to bite me in the…Ugh…Never mind…Still, this silence is awkward. I should really say something…"*

She felt herself calming down as she thought about looking at this situation in a logical manner. Danny couldn't learn how to behave around girls if she didn't actually *teach* him anything, and saying nothing wasn't the way to learn…not in this particular situation, anyway. The slight itching on her scalp had faded, so that was one danger passed, but she still needed to say *something* to break the ice.

She opened her mouth to say something, anything, but to her surprise, Danny beat her to it.

"Gee, this isn't awkward," breathed Danny.

He had said it quietly and under his breath, but considering the total lack of conversation between them, his statement had been well heard. It struck a humorous chord in Nancy, and she gave a short guffaw over it.

"Not awkward at all," she chuckled.

Danny smiled and looked down at the sidewalk for a moment. Nancy took that as a sign of slight embarrassment, as the green in his cheeks made it difficult to tell if he were blushing. She intervened anyway for his sake and for hers.

"That was good," she smiled. "You made me laugh. That doesn't work on every girl, but it's better than an awkward silence."

Danny gave her a weak nod.

"Rain was right," he said after a second. "I really have no idea what I'm doing. I thought just holding hands with a girl would come naturally, but…now that I'm doing it, I feel lost."

They walked up to the park benches and stopped for a second. It surprised Nancy to find out that Danny was so honest about himself, that he was really willing to point out a fault in his own character, because she did not know many guys who would do that, or many *people* who would do that. It was endearing, and she liked this new fact about him.

"That's good that you say that," said Nancy. "You're being honest about yourself, and if a girl is annoyed with your own honesty, if she has a problem with that, then she's not worth having around."

"I guess," shrugged Danny. "I don't really understand girls, so I'll take your word for it."

Nancy gripped his hand and gave him an encouraging smile.

"You're doing fine," she said. "You're not rude or pushy or manipulative. What you say is what you mean…I like that."

They turned and started back down the walk toward Rain's house. Danny gave her a confused look after a moment of strange silence, but when he spoke, his question was in response to her previous statement, though somewhat delayed.

"You do?" he asked.

"Yeah," shrugged Nancy. "You're doing so much better than a lot of guys out there. I think you need to work a little on your people skills…talk a little more often…but that's something I think you'll ease into after some practice."

"I never know what to talk about," sighed Danny. "I can't think of anything a girl would *like* to talk about."

Nancy rolled her eyes at that one. It was clear that Danny saw guys and girls as two different species, when in reality, they were two halves of the same coin.

"We all like different things, Danny," she said. "You just have to figure out what a girl likes in her life, and then you can see if you have anything in common with her. Small talk can help with that. Just bring up a topic that caught your eye recently…See if she bites. It's like casting out a line to catch a fish. You've got to throw it out there before you can catch anything…Hrmm…Try it now. Just bring up something that caught your interest recently."

Danny stopped walking, and this stall in his movement caused Nancy to pause as well.

"Uhhh…Let me think," said Danny after a moment. "Oh…uhhh…yeah. Something interesting happened at school yesterday."

"Really?" asked Nancy. "Like what?"

She gave him her "I'm listening face"; it consisted of a slight nod of her head to the right coupled with a slight smile, and she hoped that this would embolden him further in his conversational practice.

"Oh, it's kind of funny," he replied. "I heard some girl in our grade started blooming in the middle of class. Can you believe that?"

The world tunneled into a very narrow and embarrassing view for Nancy at that moment. She hid her face in her right hand and tried unsuccessfully to get her heart beating again.

Apparently, her social faux pas did indeed have ramifications, and that was not good. Her embarrassment shot up to well over a thousand on her humiliation scale, and she shook her head no for a moment, her face still well-hidden behind her right hand.

"What?" asked Danny. "What is it? Did I say something wrong?"

Nancy lowered her hand and shook her head no. There was no point in hiding the truth, considering that someone somewhere had told Danny about it. Knowing that, she decided to just spill it.

"No, that's not it," she sighed. "That girl was *me*, Danny."

Danny's eyes widened as comprehension set in, but his surprised expression was actually somewhat humorous, and this caused Nancy to smile in spite of herself.

"Of *all* the things to bring up," she said with a slight laugh.

Danny smiled as he lowered his head and stared down at his shoes.

"I'm sorry," he said with a nervous laugh. "I'm really not very good at this."

This gave Nancy an internal smile. Danny had far more potential than anyone had ever realized, but this revelation was also a little disheartening. Danny deserved better than the girls that went to their school, and she still wasn't convinced that this "Sarah" girl was anything good for him, even in passing conversation.

She did not trust the new stranger, but that was something that would have to pan out for itself. She obviously could not convince Danny that this girl was no good for him until she had proof…but she wasn't sure how that would play out, either. Danny was no fool, but he wasn't really observant when it came to the opposite sex.

"I hope this girl doesn't hurt him," she thought in slight worry. *"I don't even think this Sarah girl would be interested in Danny if they were trapped on a deserted island together, but getting Danny to see that is…difficult…I was so wrong about him. He's not creepy…He's just…awkward. He definitely deserves someone special in his life…I just don't know how he's going to find her."*

She thought about this as they walked hand in hand back to Rain, but even these thoughts were odd, because she had hated his guts not that long ago.

Chapter 14…The Mystery Girl

Nancy awoke to complete and total darkness. She did not know what was happening or where she was, but she knew that she was standing and that she was wearing regular clothes and not her nightgown. It confused her, frightened her, but a soft glow picked up in the distance, and this gave her enough light to see around herself.

A quick look at her hands told her that she had human skin again; it was the color she had grown up with, and a brush of her fingertips against her long brown hair confirmed that she had changed back to her original self.

She was dressed in her spotless white tee with her matching red shorts with the white stripes running down the sides of them, and upon her feet were her white socks and white sneakers. It was the outfit she had been wearing when she had ridden down Bitter Creek Road as the Breckenridge Institute of Discovery had exploded, and this revelation immediately set her on edge.

Beneath her feet was what looked and felt like black marble, and all around her was darkness except for the soft glow in the ebon distance. The void before her lit up as a great ball of light appeared, though she could not tell how far away it was.

"Nancy," came a voice in the distance.

She realized the voice was coming from the light, but this did not calm her fear, no. It only intensified it.

"Nancy!" came the voice again, only more urgent.

The voice did not sound male or female but both, and it was more of a soft chorus, a mix of many voices all at once, all male and female, but neither at the same time.

"NANCY CLARK!" boomed the mixed voices in a thunderous echo.

The ball of light grew brighter as it grew larger, and Nancy knew with one-million-percent certainty that it was headed straight toward her like a freight train on a track. She screeched in complete terror and ran into the darkness behind her, her mind only intent on fleeing.

"NANCY AMELIA CLARK!" boomed the voices. *"STOP!"*

"Stay away from me!" she screamed.

She panicked as she ran at top speed, tears welling up in her eyes, unable to form a cohesive thought. At the very back of her consciousness, she was grateful she was so athletic, because she was terrified out of her mind, and her natural running speed was a Godsend at the moment.

"NANCY AMELIA CLARK!" boomed the voices. *"YOU MUST LISTEN!"*

Nancy ran with tears spilling down her cheeks. She could feel the heat of intense light upon her back, and she turned out of instinct, but she immediately regretted it.

The ball of light was huge…It was a giant face, a glowing bald head that was androgynous, neither male nor female, and it was so close she nearly wet herself out of fear.

"GET AWAY FROM ME!" she shrieked "LEAVE ME ALONE! LEAVE ME AL…"

She stumbled and fell. The palms of her hands impacted against the cold black marble beneath her, and she felt that impact vibrate up through her wrists. It hurt like mad, and that pain was only compounded by even more pain as her right knee bounced off of that same hard marble.

She held up her hands in front of her face in a defensive reaction as the giant face closed in on her. She screamed as it came upon her; she felt its light all around her, and then she woke up.

*****

Nancy's heart was beating a mile a minute. She felt the warmth of the morning sun upon her skin, felt that same "drinking" feeling of taking in the light, and then she held up her green hands in front of her face to confirm what she already suspected…She had not shifted again.

She closed her eyes and gulped down a wad of her own saliva. She reached up and wiped tears from her cheeks, but it hurt to move her wrists when she did. Her wrists hurt for some reason, and as she sat up and tried to get out of bed, she nearly fell. Her right knee hurt like mad; she cried out in slight pain, and she pulled up her knee to see a nasty grey bruising forming upon it.

"I somehow hurt myself while I was asleep," she thought in anxious tremor. *"That must be why I had that nightmare…again…That's the second time that's happened, but those voices…I've heard them before…that day I was a snake. Rain said my eyes were moving back and forth like I was in REM sleep…It must have been a…a waking nightmare. If I can have those, then…it doesn't surprise me that I hurt myself somehow."*

She stood on shaky legs and tried unsuccessfully to calm herself down. She had never been so terrified before, and she wondered if this nightmare was going to be a recurring one…She did not relish that thought.

She went to her bathroom and looked herself over in the mirror. Yet again, she had not changed, and she had been a "plant" now for three days straight, so she resigned herself to learn all she could about this world, because this was probably where she was going to stay for the rest of her life.

"It's not that bad, Nance," she said to herself. "You're apparently very pretty in this world…at least according to Danny."

The thought of him gave her a strange feeling inside. She had hated him not that long ago, yet she had been holding hands with him just yesterday, and this confused her.

"That was all Rain, though," she thought. *"That was just practice for Danny...Tfff...I know that...Durrr....Danny knows that, too...I just...I really want him to find that one true love out there...*

"But he's SUCH a dork. I don't see how that's possible. Maybe a makeover would help...something other than just clothes...No, that's not going to work. He's been a giant dork in every universe; a makeover's not going to do him any good...

"He's just so...so...ugh...I don't know how to describe it...No, no, no. I can't be mean anymore. I can't. I wronged him, and I know that, but...No, I can't be mean anymore. I have to help him. He's a good guy. In fact, he's a much better guy than any guy I've ever met...He stood up for me even though I treated him like trash..."

The thought of what he'd done in defense of her honor brought upon that strange and uncomfortable feeling inside her. Her palms felt sweaty, and she had butterflies in her stomach, but that was nothing compared to the burning and itching sensation upon her scalp.

"Oh, don't start this, Nance..." she said, but her own scalp cut her sentence short.

She watched in complete fascination as the buds on her head opened up in all their pink glory, and the soft and subtle scent of roses filled the air. She reached up and touched one of the soft pink petals, and she could actually feel her petal as if it were living skin.

She squeezed it a little harder, dug into it with her nails, but this was a mistake, and she cried out from the sudden and sharp pain it caused. It was clear to her these petals were not like hair but were part of her body, and actually pulling one out would be like cutting off a finger.

"Ooh," she winced. *"That* was a mistake. Good grief, I'd better not play 'he loves me, he loves me not.'

It'd be like getting scalped…Wait? Haven't I thought this before?…Great…I'm repeating myself."

"Ugh," she thought unhappily. *"I've really got to control this. Hopefully, this will go away by the time I go downstairs. It took about ten minutes last time, but my showers aren't that long, so…ugh…whatever.*

"And to think I'm going to be stuck here for the rest of my life…Nah, it's not that bad. There are worse fates methinks, methinks…Eh heh?…Now I'm sounding like Rain. That nightmare must have rattled me more than I thought."

She took her shower, toweled off, and went to her dresser to get her clothes for the day. She put on her underclothes, but pulling open the top drawer to grab a shirt stopped her cold.

Her spotless white tee was there at the top of her folded shirts, and pulling it forth revealed that it was indeed spotless. A cold fear took her; the shirt brought back the horror of the nightmare she had just experienced, and she actually felt the petals on her head fold back up into their buds.

"This was shredded and permanently stained with blood," she thought in sudden anxiety. *"Now it's like brand-new. It must be like my phone and…and me. It just 'repaired' over time…like my phone and me…*

"Weird. I'm not going to freak out about this. This is nothing to panic over. I healed like I'd never been hurt in the first place, and my phone repaired itself, so it makes sense that the clothes I was wearing during the explosion got all ship-shape as well.

"That nightmare is messing with me, and that's not good. I've got too much to worry about right now, and some stupid dream is not going to interfere with me dealing with the problems I already have."

She folded the shirt and put it back. She chose a dark black shirt with a single white stripe across the chest and matched it with regular blue jeans and black socks. Just being in different clothes that were nothing like the colors of those old clothes put her in a better mood, and she smiled in spite of herself.

"See, Nance?" she breathed. "Problem solved."

She grabbed her backpack and headed downstairs. Nancy knew she was running short on time, but to her surprise, her mother was still downstairs and in the kitchen. The older woman was in a smartly-pressed grey business vest and skirt as usual, but it was the fact that she was still *here*, in the house, that confounded Nancy.

"Oh, good," said her mother. "You're finally ready. You need to hustle, young lady."

"Mom…" said Nancy in slight irritation.

"Nancy," frowned her mother, "don't give me an attitude. You were late getting up, and now there's no time for you to eat."

"I know that," frowned Nancy. "I had a terrible nightmare last night. It took me a while to get…to get myself together again…That's why I'm a little behind…Wait…That explains why *I'm* here, but…why are *you* still here?"

"I'm here because the office is sending me to manage their stall at the fair," replied the older woman.

"You have a stall?" asked Nancy in surprise.

And it was a surprise. She could not remember a time when her mother had ever run a stall at the fair.

"What is it?" she asked.

"Swirl paint," replied her mother.

"Swirl paint?" asked Nancy. "What the heck is swirl paint?"

"It's where you put a circle of paper on a spinning wheel and then drip paint on it," explained her mother. "It makes designs. It's mainly for kids, but there are teens that like to do it…and a few adults. At least, that's what I've been told."

Nancy thought about this, but she had a hard time picturing it.

"Huh," she said after a second. "Well, that explains what the stall is, but why are you running it? I can't remember a single year you've ever run a stall."

"Rodney is out with surgery for his diverticulitis," explained the older woman. "This is the first year he couldn't do it, so they chose me to represent the office in his place."

"Got it," nodded Nancy. "Well…I guess I'll come see you tomorrow. My friends and I are planning on going to the fair together…At least, I think we are."

"*Friends*?" asked her mother. "As in plural? I didn't know you had any other friends besides Rain."

Nancy was slightly offended at this at first, but then she realized that her mother's statement, as tactless as it was, was fairly accurate.

"I…I really don't," she replied. "Or I guess I didn't until recently. I made friends with Rain's neighbor, Danny. He's already friends with Rain…"

"Danny?" asked her mother. "That boy Jason was telling me about?"

This was troublesome. There was no telling what her brother had said about Danny. She sincerely hoped that Jason had *not* told their mother that Danny was the culprit behind that slanderous F and M page, because aside from the fact that it was untrue…it would simply pile more guilt upon Nancy than she already had when it came to her past treatment of Danny. He had not deserved her hatred, and he certainly did not deserve it from her mother. Nancy was well acquainted with her mother's anger, as it were.

"Y…yes," she said hesitantly.

"What was I telling you about?" asked Jason.

Her brother walked out of the downstairs bathroom and shut the door behind him. He was in a dark-green T with black jeans today, but his attitude was not as dreary as the colors of his clothes. He held an almost whimsical expression upon his green face, and Nancy did not know what to make of it. He walked into the kitchen with his backpack slung over his right shoulder to shine his full attention upon their mother.

"Danny," replied the older woman. "That boy you were telling me about. It's a terrible thing what that nasty young lady at school did to him…blaming him for her libel of Nancy."

Nancy breathed an internal sigh of relief upon hearing this. Apparently, Jason had already informed their mother of the real culprit, for whatever good that would do. Without proof, there was nothing the older woman could do, but that didn't matter to Nancy. She was just glad her mom was on the same page with her for once.

Jason raised both eyebrows and scrunched up his lips in open curiosity.

"Oh?" he asked. "What about him? I mean…did you find out something new?"

"No," replied their mother. "Nancy was just telling me she was going to the fair with him tomorrow."

Jason turned and gave Nancy the strangest look she had ever seen on his face. He had his left "eyebrow" raised like Rain would do, but unlike Rain, Nancy did not know what that expression meant on him. She could only guess that it meant confusion.

"*Danny*?" he asked, a note of disbelief in his voice. "Danny Princeton?"

Nancy did not like the connotation behind that question, and she voiced as much.

"With *Rain*," she said in irritation. "With Rain, thank you."

Her brother gave her an obnoxious smirk and a slow nod.

"*Riiiight*," he said, clear disbelief in his voice.

Nancy gave him a deep and very unhappy frown. She'd already had to put up with this kind of talk from Rain; she did not have to put up with it from Jason.

"Don't give me that look," smirked her brother. "I'm sure he'll like being out with a couple of girls. That will definitely help his street cred."

Nancy rolled her eyes and shook her head.

"Whatever," she breathed. "The bus will be here any second, so…"

"Oh, I know," shrugged Jason.

"So get going," warned their mother.

"Sure thing, but…" said Jason, "something funny happened at school the other day, Mom."

"Really?" asked their mother. "What happened?...Make it quick, because you're out of time."

Jason looked straight at Nancy and gave her the most evil grin. She already knew what he was going to say before he said it, it was clear he had been planning this and that's why he was in such a whimsical mood, and she should have steeled herself against it, but it made her cringe anyway.

"I heard a girl in Nancy's grade started *blooming* in the middle of class," he said, and Nancy mentally kicked herself for being right.

"Ugh," said their mother in obvious disgust. "Kids today. That young lady's parents need to do their job and discipline her. There's no cause for parading around like a tramp like that."

Nancy wilted inside. She had suspected that "blooming" in the middle of class was considered a trashy thing to do, and coupled with her fake F and M page, this only further damaged her once spotless reputation. Nevertheless, there was absolutely no reason for Jason to bring it up at all.

She resisted the urge to kick her younger brother in the groin. It was pointless, considering the bus was pulling up outside, but she would get onto him later…That was a guarantee.

*****

Nancy slowed her bike as she pulled up to Rain's house. The half-day at school had been uneventful, though Danny had expressed some unusual excitement over his family's cookout when she had run into him in the hall. She wanted to tell him that this whole thing was ridiculous, that there was no way in this world or any other that this Sarah girl would give him so much as the time of day…but she didn't. She had wanted to, but that was a dead horse, and she refused to beat it.

She thought about this as she walked her bike around to the back of Rain's house.

"This is stupid, it's stupid, and he's going to get hurt," she thought as she chewed on her lower lip. *"That girl doesn't hold an ounce of care for him, and she doesn't even want him around—I can tell—but Danny's not going to figure that out until she breaks his heart into little teeny-tiny, itty-bitty pieces…*

"But what do I care, right? I'm the girl who goes around 'blooming' in the middle of class, the tramp who says dirty things online, so I obviously don't know what I'm talking about…even though none of that was my fault, so what the heck, right?

"I was the one who fell for Brinn's—that backstabbing little liar—Brinn's rumor and treated Danny like dirt for the better part of a year, so he's not going to listen to me, even if I pressed it.

"Oh, and don't forget that we're all plants now. Oh, I've been other things too, but at least I didn't 'bloom' when I was them. Of course, there was that day I was 'flashing' like a neon light, but hey, that would have only gotten me arrested and/or shot in the street by police, so

you take the good with the bad. At the very least, I'm not Bald Streak Nancy, so there is SOME karma in the universe."

Rain was standing in her backyard tossing a tennis ball to the little ball of leaves that was Buster. Nancy pushed her bike up to the side of Rain's house, but one look at Nancy's expression caused the eccentric genius who was her best friend to stand stock still.

"What's up, Fance?" asked Rain. "You look like your leaves are ruffled. Something bad happen?"

Nancy gave her best friend a once-over. Today, Rain was wearing a dark-blue shirt with her trademark black cargo pants, but the young genius wore her star earrings again, and one look at those brought Nancy back up a little from her angry and frustrated funk. It was something familiar she could hold onto, and seeing them always made her a little happier.

She decided to be civil in her answer; Rain did not deserve to be chewed on just because Nancy was angry over something that had nothing to do with her genius friend.

"I'm just frustrated," replied Nancy.

"Oh?" asked Rain. "About what?"

"I don't like this whole cookout thing with Danny," frowned Nancy.

Rain's face fell in disappointment.

"I thought you were getting along with Danny," she said in a slightly morose tone.

"Of course, I am," frowned Nancy. "It's not about that. I don't like this 'Sarah' girl. I think Danny's making a huge mistake thinking he's ever going to hook up with her…thinking he even has a *chance* of hooking up with her."

Both of Rain's "eyebrows" raised in surprise, but that surprise quickly turned into a barely concealed smile. The young genius was trying to hide some sort of amusement, but Nancy was not sure why, and for that matter, the expression was not wanted. Nancy did not think the situation funny.

"I was being serious," frowned Nancy.

"I believe you," said Rain. "I personally don't see it working out, but…don't you think that's for Danny to discover?"

"No, I don't," replied Nancy. "If someone could have warned me about what a jerk Bobby Schmidt was and what a liar Brinn Clevenger was, I wouldn't have wasted my time on them."

"Hey, now," frowned Rain. "I told you many a time what a good guy Danny is, but you never listened to me."

Nancy thought about this. What Rain had said made sense, but she still didn't like it. Rain had often defended Danny, but Nancy had not listened then, and it took something drastic for her *to* listen, so it looked as if Danny was going to have to find out the hard way about what this "Sarah" girl was really like, and Nancy did not like this one bit.

"You're…right," sighed Nancy. "Ugh…He's not going to listen until he figures it out himself."

"Exactly," said Rain.

The young genius pried her tennis ball from Buster's mouth and tossed it back into the yard. The little ball of leaves took off after it at top speed, grabbed the ball in his mouth, laid down in the grass, and chewed on the fuzzy yellow orb. Normally, Rain would have called him over to give her the ball, but her attention was elsewhere. She took a long serious look at Nancy and cocked her head to the left as if deep in thought.

"So why do you care?" she asked after a silent moment.

"What?" asked Nancy.

She didn't quite understand the question.

"Why do you care?" repeated Rain. "You hated Danny because of something you *thought* he did, but before that, you avoided him like the plague. Why do you care now? What's different?"

This flustered Nancy. She wasn't sure why she cared, and that was blocking her as surely as any brick wall from giving a good explanation.

"I just…It's…He's a…a good guy," she stammered. "That's all. I was wrong about him. He's actually a really good guy."

"Really?" asked Rain.

The young genius cocked her head to the right and raised her left eyebrow.

"*I* know he's a good guy," she said in a serious tone, "but I've known him a lot longer than you have. You've only really gotten to know him since your shifting started, and that's been, like, what? A couple of weeks?...So how do *you* know he's a good guy?"

This irritated Nancy. Rain was grilling her like she was on trial or something. She wanted to *help* Danny, not tear into him. There was not one good reason why Rain would be upset over that.

"Because I like him!" she hissed. "I don't just like anybody and everybody, Rain! You're my only other friend, because…because I don't really like anybody!"

Rain's eyebrows raised as she took a step back.

"Really?" she asked. "You *like* him?"

"Yeah," shrugged Nancy. "Yes, I like him…as a friend. He's a good guy. He's worth hanging out with, and I don't feel that way about too many people. He's smart and he's sensitive and he really tries to treat other people with respect. He doesn't just do things to be a jerk and be…*selfish*."

"I thought you said he was a giant dork," said Rain. "A social outcast."

"He is," shrugged Nancy. "So?...It doesn't matter whether he is…I just…I know that's what's preventing him from getting his girl, so I wanted to help him with that."

"You want to help him with getting a girl?" asked Rain in surprise. "I thought you were against this Sarah girl…"

"Not *her*!" hissed Nancy. "She's not a suitable candidate."

"Then who is?" asked Rain.

"I don't know!" said Nancy in frustration.

She stopped for a moment and realized that she did indeed know, or at least she had an idea of the qualities in a girl that were right for Danny. He deserved someone special, someone above the normal rabble that was out there.

"Actually, I do know," she said a moment later. "I think…I think the right girl for Danny is going to be tough for him to find. First of all, she's going to have to overlook the fact that he's a giant dork, that's a given, but there's more to it than that.

"She has to be smart, and she…she has to say it like it is and not lie to him. She has to like him for who he is and not for what she can get out of him, and she should be able to take a step back and give him good advice once in a while, because I think he's going to need a lot of it…

"Yeah, I think she doesn't have to be interested in what he likes, but…she should support the things he does like."

"Shouldn't she be pretty?" asked Rain. "Athletic, maybe?"

The thought of that was somewhat funny to Nancy. She couldn't really imagine Danny hooking up with a model or anything.

"Pffffft," she said with a wave of her hand. "Like that's going to happen. I mean, don't get me wrong, that's what every guy wants, but Danny's going to have to settle for average, I think."

"So you don't think he deserves someone pretty and athletic?" asked Rain.

"Of course, he does," shrugged Nancy. "I was just saying it's not really a possibility…And why 'athletic'? What does that have to do with anything?"

Rain smiled, rolled her eyes, and shook her green head.

"To carry him over the threshold, of course," she chuckled.

Nancy released a short, loud, and rather obnoxious guffaw. She could just picture an attractive, yet muscular girl carrying Danny across the threshold of a brand-new house. Of course, that image put Danny in a wedding dress, and this made the image far more entertaining. She busted out into laughter, and Rain followed her lead a moment later. It took them both a moment to settle down in order to continue some semblance of a coherent conversation.

"Very funny," giggled Nancy. "Anyway…I think Danny *deserves* a pretty girl…who is athletic, I guess…but that's not really going to happen. I was thinking realistically."

"I see," said Rain with a nod. "So there are no pretty and athletic girls in the area, huh?"

"None that I can think of," shrugged Nancy. "I guess there's Sonya Derman, but I think she has a boyfriend. There are the girls on the cheerleading squad, but…blech. They have the mentality of a pack of mint gum…Wait…There are a couple of them that are pretty nice, but…the cheerleaders always have boyfriends, and they're always the guys on the team, so that's out."

"Uh, huh," said Rain. "Hmmm. I'm sure there's someone pretty and athletic that Danny could hook up with. Probably closer than we think."

"Why would you think that?" asked Nancy. "Why does that even matter, anyway? When you like someone, what does it matter if they're pretty or athletic? If you like someone, you like someone."

"Even if they're a giant dork?" asked Rain.

"Yeah," shrugged Nancy. "Exactly. Danny's a giant dork, but I'm positive he'll find someone. We shouldn't judge someone on how they appear on the outside anyway. I mean, I don't think you do, but I am curious as to what you think on the matter. What qualities in a girl do you see for Danny?...Wait, that sounded weird. I meant, what do you think are the qualities a girl should have for Danny to be happy with her?"

"Let's see," said Rain thoughtfully. "I still think Danny deserves a girl who is pretty and athletic, but…that's neither here nor there. I think she should be smart too, but not necessarily like a scientist. There are different types of intelligence, but this is a case in which this girl should have good common sense and really good social skills.

"She should be a really loyal friend who cares about what happens to other people, and…she should say what's on her mind and defend what she says…unless she's wrong, and then she should admit to being wrong. A girl that can admit she's made a huge mistake is a good catch, don't you think?"

"Oh, yeah," nodded Nancy. "But good luck with that. No one wants to admit that they're wrong."

"Yeah," smiled Rain with a roll of her eyes. "That *never* happens."

"It really doesn't," frowned Nancy. "I know my mother never admits when she's wrong…or Jason…He was *such* a jerk this morning…but that's beside the point. I want what's best for Danny, and the qualities you mentioned *are* good qualities, but we should be realistic. I think he deserves *all* that, but he's not going to get it."

"Oh?" asked Rain.

The eccentric young genius was smiling, but her smile was wayward, as if she were in on the biggest joke in the world.

"I think we can get him his ideal girl," said Rain with a smirk. "Maybe the girl he needs is just oblivious. My guess is that she needs him too, but she just hasn't realized it yet."

Nancy did not know what that meant, but then again, Rain was pretty out there to begin with. Still, Nancy did not like being patronized, and she suspected that Rain already knew about someone and wasn't sharing.

"What are you smiling at?" asked Nancy in frustration. "And who are you talking about anyway? I don't know of anybody like that, so how in the heck could you?...Well, I guess you do have a lot of social media stuff you do, but still...finding someone like that for Danny would be a miracle, don't you think?"

"No," shrugged Rain. "I mean, I have an *idea* of who he should hook up with, but...convincing her of that would be a bit of a pickle. The girl I have in mind is very pretty and very smart, but she's going through some things right now, and you know what it's like to have problems and then have some guy try and hit on you..."

"Hmmm, I never thought of that," replied Nancy.

Rain had touched on something that might actually help Danny, and this caused Nancy to stop and wonder about it.

"It does suck to have problems and then have other people lay their affections at your feet," she said. "I've had that happen before...not that often, but hey...

"Still...Danny's a good listener...at least, he's listened to my advice so far except for the whole 'Sarah' thing...so maybe his way in is to help this girl with her problems...but not in a selfish way. We have to...to 'trick' Danny into helping her. You know, like, have him understand right from the get go that she's not interested so that his help is altruistic."

"Danny only helps people for altruistic reasons, Nance," sighed Rain. "He's not a player, nor does he use other people like they're tools or something."

"Well, that's even better," said Nancy. "That's great, actually. He really is a good guy, so this girl…uhhh…should feel lucky to have his help. I mean, I'd still have to meet her to make sure she's shipworthy, but she's *got* to be better than this 'Sarah' girl. Of course, helping her might get him stuck in the friend zone…"

"I don't think so," said Rain. "This girl's been through a lot recently, but she's still the right person for Danny, and he's still the right person for her."

The idea of this struck Nancy in a strange way. She really wanted to help Danny find his girl, the right girl for *him*, but she was still worried about someone else hurting him, because *she* had unjustly hurt him over a rumor that she had never bothered to validate, so she knew firsthand how nastily people could treat him.

He was unjustly shunned and ridiculed at school; he just seemed to attract that negative attention upon himself, so it would not take much for this "mystery girl" to turn on him. If this mystery girl really had been through a lot recently, then that trauma could turn outward toward Danny and blow up in his face. In fact, the more she thought about it, the more Nancy disliked the idea.

"I don't know about that," she frowned. "A girl like that sounds great at first, and helping her with her problems sounds great, but she could turn her frustrations, anger, depression…whatever…against him. I don't want him to get hurt."

"I don't think she wants him to get hurt," said Rain. "In fact, I know she doesn't. She's said as much."

That statement was like the sound of an old record player scratching to a halt. Nancy sucked in an unhappy breath, as she felt at that moment she was going to have to get angry with her best friend over this lack of information.

"Say what now?" she asked. "You didn't tell me he already *knew* her."

Rain shrugged and gave her a sheepish smile.

"You never asked me how many girls he knows," she said matter-of-factly.

"No, no, no," said Nancy as she wagged her right index finger for emphasis. "No, no, no. This changes *everything*. You're telling me that Danny already *knows* a girl that's right for him, yet he's choosing to hang his hopes on a girl that doesn't even care if he's alive or dead? Not only that, but not *once* have you ever mentioned this to *me*, and *I'm* the one who's trying to help him get a girl here."

"I thought we were both helping him," frowned Rain.

"I thought we were, too," said Nancy. "That's why I want to know why you didn't tell me about this…this '*mystery girl.*'"

Just saying it out loud made her feel even angrier. This information was important, and Rain had just conveniently kept it to herself.

"Nancy…" sighed Rain, "don't be mad at me. This isn't about me…It's about Danny. I just think…he's a good guy…just like you said. I'm not right for him, or I'd have picked him up by now. Heck, I've known what he's really been like for years now. There was a time when he was very smitten with me, but…it took him a little while to figure out that I was not the one."

Nancy thought about this and realized that her best friend was right.

"Yeah, he mentioned that," she frowned. "I'm not…I'm not trying to be angry with you. It's just…Nnnng…It would have been nice if you had mentioned this earlier. I could have at least used this girl as an example when I was trying to dissuade him from going after that 'Sarah' girl."

"I know," said Rain in a slightly disappointed voice. "And I agree with you…I don't think Sarah is a good match for him."

"I don't think she even wants to give him the time of day," frowned Nancy. "She looks like another Brinn Clevenger to me, and I've never even met her."

"I know," frowned Rain. "But this 'mystery girl,' as you put it, has been through a lot lately, like I said, and she's not quite ready for Danny's affection. She's *almost* there…but not quite."

Nancy sighed and threw her hands up in frustration.

"Great!" she breathed. "If she's *almost* there but not *quite* there, then she doesn't really matter, does she? Why in the heck are you even bringing her up? If she's not there yet, then she's not a candidate, and if she's not a candidate, then why mention her at all, Rain? Are you *trying* to raise my blood pressure?"

Rain cocked her head to the right and gave her one of the most serious expressions Nancy had ever seen upon her young face, and that was in spite of the fact that Rain's face was green and that she had leaves and buds on her head.

"Because *she's the one*," said the young genius in a tight-lipped frown. "Look…don't worry about the 'mystery girl.' If you really want to help Danny, then I suggest you keep an eye on him at the cookout, because I really don't know what he's going to do when it comes to Sarah.

"*I* think…I think just like you do…I don't think Sarah has any interest *at all* in Danny, and for all I know, she may be rude and spiteful toward him, and that is the *last* thing he needs right now."

Nancy nodded in vehement agreement.

"Yes! Yes!" she said in excitement. "That's what I've been trying to tell you!...and him."

"Exactly," nodded Rain. "We'll worry about the 'mystery girl' after the cookout. I really don't think this Sarah thing is going to pan out in any way, shape, or form, so let's get back to the mystery girl once we're done tonight."

"Agreed," said Nancy. "But I need to know who this girl is, Rain. I can't help Danny with her if I don't know who in the heck I'm talking about."

"You've got your own problems to worry about," said Rain. "Don't worry about *that*."

"You mean my shifting?" asked Nancy. "It's stopped. It stopped in this world two days ago. I haven't shifted for two days now."

"I know," said Rain with a slow nod, "but that doesn't mean it's *permanently* stopped. This may only be temporary. We don't know. We really don't know anything about this shifting, although we have a pretty good idea of the cause.

"I admit that I didn't believe you when you first described it to me, but I absolutely believe you now. With my descriptions and photos in the notebook, I think that's enough evidence for me to believe that what you're saying is true. Those photos didn't just magically change by themselves, and what I wrote in the notebook didn't just magically change by itself...

"Plus, what I've written hasn't changed in the last two days, nor have the photos... You understand why I still use the instant camera, right? I love the idea of using your phone, but since you haven't shifted, I have no idea if your phone will even work with this."

"I understand," sighed Nancy, "but I really, *really* hope this has stopped, though. I just want to live a normal life, and if being part plant is the only thing I have to put up with, then I'm fine with it. I do have to eat dirt now, but I can live with that."

"I'm glad you feel that way," shrugged Rain. "For what it's worth, I believe you now, and…I will say that I think your theory about what happened to me has weight."

"Oh?" asked Nancy. "What theory?"

"That I was affected by the explosion, too," said Rain.

This was news to Nancy. She was pretty sure Rain had thought that idea ludicrous.

"Really?" she asked. "Why's that?"

"The notebook, the camera…" said Rain. "There are other things, too…Well, not things, but…*a* thing. I've had some really weird dreams lately. *A* dream, actually."

Nancy felt her heart skip a beat. Rain mentioning weird dreams made her think of her own nightmare, and she really didn't want to think about that.

"What dreams?" she asked.

Rain shrugged and looked off into the distance for a moment. The look on her face was…odd.

"I usually don't remember a lot of my dreams," she said slowly, quietly. "But last night…I…I don't even know how to describe it. I was at school and in my underwear…"

Nancy's fears disappeared in a puff of smoke and were replaced with her own giggling.

"Yeah, yeah," smiled Rain.

The eccentric young genius waved her off and nodded a couple of times. Nancy had to hold her right hand over her mouth to keep from laughing in the most obnoxious manner possible.

"Let me explain," smiled Rain. "*That* kind of dream is normal for me. Usually, I'm at school or speaking on a stage, and I'm in my underwear. One time I was dressed like I always do, but everyone *else* was in their underwear at school, even you."

"Uh, huh," snickered Nancy. "So if it happens all the time, then why was it weird this time?"

"That's just it," said Rain. "It was normal up to a point. I was at our desk in Biology, but you weren't there. I was dressed in my underwear like always…"

Nancy let out a giggle, but Rain patiently waited for her to stop before continuing with her story.

"I was sitting at the desk in my underwear as usual," said Rain, "but I kept wondering where you were, so I asked Mr. Wagner where you were, and that's when it got all weird.

"He just looked at me and said, 'Rain.' I said, 'Yes?,' and he said, 'Rain Fischer.' I said, 'That's *my* name, but what about Nancy? Where's Nancy?' He looked at me and said, 'Rain Dillon Fischer.'

"Now you know I *hate* my middle name…The only reason I have it is because my dad wanted a boy…but, but anyway…there's no *way* Mr. Wagner could have known my middle name…mainly because I never tell anyone…but that's not what was weird.

"It's like…It's like I got tunnel vision at that moment…like the walls all narrowed in and the lights dimmed down…and Mr. Wagner said, 'Rain Dillon Fischer…Nancy Amelia Clark must listen.'

"It was the way he said it, too. His voice went all weird…It was like a lot of different voices all mashed together, as if a bunch of people all spoke the same line at the same time…"

Nancy felt what passed for blood drain from her face. She knew enough about this world to know that her blood was green, not red, but apparently that made little difference to Rain, who immediately knew something was wrong.

"You okay, Fance?" asked the young genius in open concern. "You look like you're going to faint."

"I've had that same dream," breathed Nancy.

She felt like she was going to hyperventilate, so she leaned over and put her hands on her knees for a moment.

She stood up and forced herself to be calm enough to speak.

"I've had that same dream," she repeated. "Not the underwear bit, and I wasn't in school, but I've had that happen to me twice now. I've been in a dark place with no light, and then this light appears and starts calling my name, and it sounds like all of these different voices meshed together."

"That *is* weird," said Rain. "I was just going to say that I felt like it had something to do with what had happened to you…a…a *feeling* more than anything."

"I wasn't finished," breathed Nancy. "I had a nightmare last night. It was the same dream, but this time the light looked like a giant face, and it kept calling my name, and it chased me…and it said, 'Nancy Amelia Clark…you must listen.'…What…What does that mean, Rain?"

Rain's eyes went wide as she gave a clueless shrug.

"I have no idea," she said in honest confusion. "I really don't know. I have no theory on this one. It could be related to what's going on…or it could just be you. You could be reaching out in dreams now, for all I know. Since we're best friends, maybe I'm sharing some of your dreams…but I really have no idea."

"You're saying I'm psychic?" asked Nancy.

She had not thought of that possibility.

"It's a possibility," shrugged Rain. "Psychic ability is still kind of grouped in with the paranormal, but I still think it's a valid subject of scientific study. There's a lot we still don't know about the human brain and the mind itself, so…maybe you are psychic. I would have laughed at such a thing before, but considering you've been shifting from world to world recently, I'll believe almost anything now."

"But why would you think it was connected to the explosion?" asked Nancy. "You said you believed my theory about you being affected."

"It was just a feeling, Nance," said Rain. "It was a really *strong* feeling, but it was just a feeling…Heck, for all I know, I might start shifting, too…but you *stopped* shifting, so…I guess we'll see."

"Yeah," breathed Nancy. "I guess we will."

Chapter 15…The Cookout

"Look, I don't want to talk about this anymore," frowned Nancy. "We have more important things to worry about…For one thing, I need to know who this mystery girl is, Rain. Seriously, stop ducking the question."

Rain scrunched up her lips and then shook her head no.

"It's pointless to tell you that," she said. "She's not ready, so there's no point in interfering with her."

Nancy gave her best friend a hardline stare.

"She's not ready, but 'she's the one,' eh?" she replied. "Look, you don't get to be the only one to play cupid here…"

"No," frowned Rain. "I won't do this. Just drop it."

"What!" asked Nancy in barely contained umbrage. "Why not! I'm your best friend!"

"Yes, you *are*," said Rain matter-of-factly. "But if I interfere with this girl right now, it could hurt Danny's chances of being with her, and I've known him a lot longer than you have. It's risky to set up any friend with someone, because it can easily blow up in your face. If we're going to do this, then I need you to understand that Danny has been my friend for years now, much longer than you've known him, so if anything, it's *my* responsibility to make sure he doesn't get hurt, not yours…so just drop it."

This was infuriating to Nancy. She did not know anything about this "mystery girl," and without having any information to go on, she couldn't just trust that this girl was good for Danny. It was a mistake to leave her out of the loop; she knew this with all of her heart and soul.

"Fine!" she huffed as she crossed her arms. "Be that way! But if you can't tell me who she is, then I can't trust her…Ugh…You make her sound like a saint, anyway. She must have some bad points, you know. Nobody's entirely an angel."

Rain gave her a half-smile and then a slow nod.

"Yeah, she's not entirely an angel," breathed the eccentric young genius. "She's got a bit of a temper. When she gets mad, it can be kind of scary…She's kind of stubborn too, and if she doesn't get what she wants, then she can be *really* pushy. It's kind of annoying."

"There, see?" said Nancy with a wave of her hand. "I told you. Nobody's perfect. How can I help Danny if I don't know what I'm dealing with?...Ugh…I'm going to have to meet this girl."

Rain frowned and shook her head no.

"Trust me, you don't need to meet her," she said. "She's got a lot of problems right now, and this would only complicate things."

Nancy felt like pulling the leaves off of the young genius's head. She threw her hands up in anger and let out a frustrated cry.

"What is so special about this girl!" she exclaimed. "What 'problems' could she possibly have that prevent me from meeting her?...Is she a drug addict? Is that it? Are you hooking up Danny with a drug addict?"

"No," said Rain, and this time she looked offended.

Nancy realized that her own frustration was getting her nowhere with Rain. She decided to use a more tactful approach.

"How can I relate to her plight if you don't tell me anything about her?" she asked.

Rain looked thoughtful for a moment before she gave her reply. She stared off into the distance while cupping her chin within the green fingers of her right hand.

"Well, she has problems with other girls at school," said the eccentric young woman, "and she doesn't get along with her mother. They argue quite a bit."

Nancy nodded in appreciation of what little information Rain had given her. It was helpful, because this "mystery girl's" problems were actually something Nancy could relate to.

She motioned with her right hand palm up for emphasis as she made her case.

"You see?" she breathed. "*That* was helpful. Those are problems I can relate to. I have the same problems, you know. I could talk to her about them, break the ice...In fact, there's no reason why I can't meet this gi—"

Nancy was cut short as Danny rounded the fence within Rain's backyard. He had a big smile on his face and a wistful look in his eyes, and this unusual happiness about him set Nancy on edge. She was sure it was because of the impending cookout and the arrival of this "Sarah" girl.

Today, he was wearing a beige button-up with short-sleeves, a shirt Nancy had personally helped him pick out, and it was matched with a pair of black slacks, another article of clothing Nancy had helped him pick out.

Seeing him wearing these clothes twisted something inside her, knotting her up inside, as she knew without a shadow of a doubt that this "Sarah" girl was not going to appreciate the sentiment he was putting forth over her. It made her angry on more than one level, but it also gave her a strange feeling inside, a longing of sorts, and this confused her. Seeing him dressed in his new clothes, clothes she had helped him decide upon, hurt her for some reason.

"Why am I so out of sorts about this?" she thought unhappily. *"It's because that 'Sarah' girl is going to treat Danny like crap. I know it, and that's why."*

"Hey, Danny," said Rain. "You wanna hang out with us for a while?"

"Oh, no, that's okay," he said. "I came over to tell you that you can come over any time now. My parents are setting up. My aunt and cousin are already here anyway."

"Ah," said Rain. "Well, we'll be right over."

"Cool," said Danny. "I'll see you in a bit."

He walked back around the edge of Rain's backyard fence and disappeared from sight.

Rain looked over at Nancy and gave her a half-frown.

"Be cool," she warned as she held up both hands palms out. "Just observe. There's no reason to get upset…"

"I'm not upset!" hissed Nancy, but her own forcefulness in that statement made her balk.

Rain raised both eyebrows and took a step back. She kept her hands up as if to ward off Nancy's sudden explosion.

"Uh, huh," she said after a second. "If that's your calm pose, then I'd hate to see you angry."

Nancy held her face in her right hand and took in a deep breath. She slowly released it and felt her anxiety ease up a little.

"I'm sorry," she said as she lowered her hand. "This just…It irks me."

"I know," said Rain with a half-smile. "I can see that. Everything will work out, Nance. We already have an idea of what's going to happen, so let's just take a step back and watch, okay?"

"Yeah, yeah," breathed Nancy.

Rain looked toward the fence that blocked their view of Danny's backyard.

"Still…" said the young genius, "Danny was looking pretty good in those new clothes, huh?"

"Yeah," sighed Nancy. "He was almost handsome."

Rain turned and gave her a semi-offended look. This look consisted of lowering her head while raising her left eyebrow, all while giving her a tight-lipped frown.

"*Almost*?" she asked.

"He's still a dork," shrugged Nancy, "but he looks good for a dork."

Rain gave a wistful smirk and then shook her head.

"You *are* a stubborn one," she said.

"What's *that* supposed to mean?" asked Nancy.

She did not really like the sound of that.

"It means Danny's waiting for us," said Rain matter-of-factly. "And I don't know about you, but I don't want to leave him at the mercy of his cousin and her friend. His cousin's been over before, and she is *not* a nice person. I call her 'the Wicked Witch of the Suburbs,' if that gives you any indication of her personality…so we'd better go."

"I agree," replied Nancy. "Let's just go and get this over with."

They walked around Rain's fence and into Danny's backyard. Nancy felt strange walking into some other family's yard, but she chalked this up to just being nervous about the situation. She did not know what to expect, but she had a bad feeling, an omen of sorts that something was going to go very wrong.

Danny's family had a stone-tiled patio that covered half of their backyard, along with a huge stone grill near the back half of the patio. There were four, round, white, metal outdoor tables with red, white, and blue parasols affixed within their centers, and each table had four, white, metal mesh chairs pushed in to encircle them.

The back porch, itself, was a wooden structure complete with a wooden bench swing and a large wooden shelf which held an old-fashioned boom box, something Nancy had heard of but had never seen before.

Upon each corner of the yard were planted large wooden tiki torches, and standing side by side them were citronella candles fixed upon slender poles of black wrought iron.

The whole thing was impressive to take in for Nancy, and she stood back a moment to appreciate the view of it.

"Wow," she breathed. "Danny's parents must really like to cookout."

"Oh, yeah," said Rain. "I think it's because they couldn't afford a pool, but I think this is better."

"I like it," said Nancy.

The backdoor of the house opened, and Danny stepped out. He had a slight smile on his green and gawky face, and he appeared to be really happy for once, at least, that's how he appeared to Nancy. She was genuinely glad he was happy, but something told her he would not be happy for very long.

"Everybody's inside," said Danny. "I guess we can hang out here until they get everything ready."

"Sounds good," said Rain.

She gave Nancy a strange look; there was a slight sparkle in her eye and a smirk on her lips, but Nancy did not know what to make of it.

The young genius turned to Danny and gave him a mild grin.

"Aww, you look so happy today!" she said. "You look really good in those clothes, Danny."

He stared down at his shoes for a moment and then shrugged.

"Thanks," he said, but he sounded embarrassed.

"You know what?" said Rain. "We could use some music to set the mood."

"Mood?" asked Nancy. "What mood?"

She really had no idea what Rain was up to, but she suspected the eccentric young woman was up to something. Rain, however, ignored her question altogether.

"Do you still have that song your mom likes?" asked Rain. "That one from that movie from the '90s?"

"Yeah, I guess," said Danny. "I think the CD is still in the player."

"Good," said Rain. "While everyone's inside, we can give you some more training."

"Training?" asked Danny and Nancy at the same time.

"Yeah," smiled Rain. "Danny, come stand over here between the tables in this open area."

"Err…okay," said Danny in a meek voice.

He walked over to stand next to them. Rain held her chin between the green fingers of her right hand and cocked her head to the right as she inspected him.

"Mmm, hmm," she said after a moment. "Yep. I think it's time we took this to the next level."

"Uhhh…sure," said Danny.

Nancy had no idea what was going on inside Rain's head. Whatever this was, it had not been shared between them beforehand.

"Yep, yep," said Rain. "I think it's high time you learned how to dance with a girl. I'll turn on the music, and you can dance with Nancy."

"Say what now?" asked Nancy.

This was not what she had expected.

"Yes, yes," said Rain. "Danny, you just take her right hand in yours like this…"

Rain coaxed him forward as he was forced into Nancy's personal space. Nancy was so taken aback that she simply stood there in a mute daze as he took her hand; she did not even have any thoughts running through her head.

"Now, you put your left arm around her waist while she does the same…" said Rain.

He put his arm around her waist, and Nancy put her arm around his waist out of instinct. They were about the same height, so she had to turn her head down and to the side to keep from staring directly into his face. She did not find him intrusive, no, but this came as such a surprise that she did not really know how to feel about it. She felt her cheeks grow hot without meaning to.

"That's perfect, methinks, methinks," smiled Rain. "Now just a second! I'll turn on the music, and you follow Nancy's lead, okay?"

"O…Okay," stammered Danny.

Rain trotted over to the boom box and messed with a bunch of buttons on it. The music started playing a moment later; it was soft and slow at first, and then it picked up to a quicker beat. Though Nancy had not heard this particular song before, it was sweet and memorable.

"Okay, let Nancy show you what to do," urged Rain.

Nancy had danced like this before, several times, in fact, but those times had been with various boys at school dances, and though those boys weren't the best in the world, they already knew how to dance, and she could tell that Danny had no such experience.

It was painfully clear now that Rain had hung her out to dry, and she had been forced into doing this, so she decided to just go through with it. Danny needed all of the help he could get anyway.

"Uhhh…" she said in a nervous temper. "Uhhh…just…We just step in a circle…not too fast…and don't step on my feet…"

She stepped backwards to her right to allow Danny to lead in a simple box step, and though he had no experience with the action, it did not take him more than a couple of steps to ease into the motion.

They slow danced to the music, but Danny's proximity, coupled with the very action they were performing, made Nancy feel strange inside. She felt a warm glow inside; it was not something she had felt before, and she found herself smiling in spite of herself.

She lowered her head as she felt her cheeks grow hot, and there was a tingling sensation upon her scalp, but she was used to that danger sign, so she mentally kept the buds on her head in check.

She felt her heart beat faster, and time slowed as the music played on. It felt like they were dancing for half-an-hour before the music ended, and Nancy felt a twinge of disappointment as they stepped away from each other, which was odd, because Danny was a complete and utter dork, and she had hated him with a passion not that long ago.

She was pulled away from her internal oddness by the sound of Danny's voice.

"Was that okay?" asked Danny.

Nancy could not say anything at first. She simply nodded her head for a moment before she could find any words *to* say.

"That was really good," she breathed. "You must be a natural, Danny."

"That *was* really good," smiled Rain.

The eccentric young woman stood a few feet away from them, and though Nancy wanted to be angry with Rain for the stunt her best friend had just pulled, she found that she could not.

"Don't get mad," thought Nancy. *"Rain said she was the one who needed to help Danny, and she trusts me with the things she's not good at, all of the social stuff, so this shouldn't surprise me. She just wants to help Danny."*

If there was anything to say to Rain over it, it was postponed as the backdoor to Danny's house opened and his parents walked out, along with Danny's aunt, his cousin, and the girl who Nancy only knew as "Sarah."

She did not know what was going to happen, but that bad feeling she'd had earlier came back in force, and this killed any warm glow inside she may have thought she'd experienced.

*****

Nancy left the downstairs bathroom and walked toward the kitchen to get some more ice for her drink. So far, things had gone okay, though it was clear to her and Rain that this "Sarah" girl was not interested in Danny at all. The new girl had been polite as of yet, but she had made it a point to avoid Danny altogether, and she had not been talkative toward Nancy or Rain.

They had all eaten, and Nancy had talked with Danny's parents, but she felt like leaving…She did not feel like she fit in.

Danny was still clueless over the whole affair; he could not tell what was going on with the very peers around him. His cousin and Sarah wanted nothing to do with him…obviously…but he couldn't even seem to tell that Nancy herself was unhappy with the situation, and this bothered her even more.

She did, of course, realize that she was not the important person at this cookout…*That* was Danny, but…for some reason, it irked her that he did not notice how she felt. It offended her on some level, and that was odd.

She walked into the kitchen to grab her glass she had left upon the kitchen sink, but she was sidetracked by the presence of Rain.

Nancy still wasn't used to the "plant" version of Rain, with her olive-colored skin and her dark, dark-green leaves for hair, but even in this form and even viewing the young genius from behind, Nancy could tell something was wrong.

Rain was leaning over the sink while staring down into it, and though this pose was not entirely unusual, it was the aura of unhappiness that radiated out from the eccentric young woman that caught Nancy's attention.

"Rain?" asked Nancy carefully. "Are you all right?"

Rain turned and wiped her dark eyes free of fresh tears.

It stunned Nancy to see her best friend this way; this was not the norm for the happy-go-lucky young woman, and her first thought was that Rain was still in grief over the death of her beloved dog, Weirdo.

"Why are you crying?" asked Nancy. "Do you still miss Weirdo?"

"I'll always miss Weirdo," sniffed Rain, "…but no, it's not about that."

"What's it about, then?" asked Nancy.

Rain wiped some more tears from her eyes and sniffed once more.

"It's just…I…" she stammered.

"Take your time," said Nancy.

Rain choked in a short breath before continuing.

"It's just that…" she said slowly. "It's about…It's about you."

This was a surprise to Nancy. She had absolutely *no* idea why Rain would be crying over her.

"What about me?" she asked.

"I know it's selfish…" sniffed Rain as she shook her head. "I know it is, but…you stopped shifting."

Nancy had not thought of this. Rain loved science, and Nancy's shifting was probably the most important scientific discovery of their time, so it only made sense that Rain was upset about not being able to study it anymore.

"You're upset because I stopped shifting?" asked Nancy. "You do realize that this is a good thing, right? I needed to stop shifting, Rain."

"I know," sniffed Rain as she nodded her head in vigorous agreement. "I know that. It's just…you stopped shifting, and…I don't know if you'll ever start again.

"I thought, maybe…when you told me how I was affected by the Breckenridge explosion…I didn't want to believe it at first…but now that's all I can think about. I thought maybe…maybe *I'd* start shifting, too…

"Once I started thinking about it...I couldn't stop thinking about it. You don't even want to shift...You never wanted it. It should have been me who started shifting. I'm the one who wants it. It's not fair."

Nancy had not thought of this, either. It had never occurred to her that Rain would be jealous of her shifting. She had said so once before, but Nancy had never taken much stock in that. She had just thought Rain was simply trying to make her feel better by pretending to be jealous of her.

"Rain..." breathed Nancy, "if I could give you this shifting...I would. You're right...I don't want it, and...I think you should have had it instead. I consider it a curse, but you don't, so...if I could give it to you, then I would."

Rain nodded and wiped away the remainder of her tears.

"Well," she said with a weak smile, "if you ever get the chance, then by all means, hand it over."

"Will do," smiled Nancy. "You know I would, so...don't be jealous of me, okay? I've got enough problems as it is. I thought once my shifting stopped, my life would go back to normal, but that's not how it worked out. Now I'm worried about Danny...I'm afraid that girl's going to humiliate him, and that bothers me a lot."

"Danny's a big boy," sniffed Rain. "He can take care of himself."

"I know that," replied Nancy. "I just think he's vulnerable when it comes to girls, and I don't like what's happening here with this...'you know who.' I don't like it at all."

"Yeah," said Rain. "We both know that outcome."

"Exactly," said Nancy. "Come on. We'd better get back to Danny. I only came inside to use the bathroom and get some ice for my drink, so..."

"Yeah," agreed Rain.

They walked out the backdoor and onto the large patio where Danny was being chatty with the other two girls.

Nancy took a moment to study Danny's cousin and this "Sarah" girl, but she did not like what she saw.

Danny's cousin, Erin, was a short, snub-nosed little brat with a round face, dark-brown eyes, leaf-green skin, and very light-colored leaves upon her head.

Rain did not like her at all, and with good reason…She was just mean.

Erin wore what looked like an expensive black short-sleeve with intricate silver-looped designs around the sleeves, neckline, and hem, and this was matched by an immaculately clean pair of tan slacks with black dress shoes.

Sarah, on the other hand, was taller than even Danny. She had a pleasant face with forest-green skin and leaves upon her head that were the exact same color, but there was something within her blue eyes Nancy did not like, a haughtiness matched with a disgust over Danny's presence, but this was something Danny was apparently oblivious to.

The young woman wore a sweet summer dress that was a white-cotton floral print; it gave her a more attractive quality than she would have normally had, and for some reason, this irked Nancy even more.

"I'm almost done with my book," said Danny with a slow and bobbing nod. "I mean, I've already given away a lot of the plot, but I haven't decided on the ending yet. I've narrowed it down to two possible choices."

"Fascinating," frowned his cousin. "*Truly* riveting."

The unpleasant young woman shook her head and rolled her eyes, but Danny missed the action, mainly because his attention was focused upon Sarah. He leaned against the wooden railing of the patio with a confidence unbecoming of him, but this new girl, Sarah, had nothing more than an amused smirk on her face over the action.

Nancy felt a burning ember stoke to a flame inside her over these two young women… She did not like them at all.

"I was thinking that maybe Bruin would either steal the Cat's Eye from the temple and make the final wish," continued Danny, "or that he'd shatter the Cat's Eye while the high priest was holding it…Either way would give me a cool ending."

"Oh, look, your friends are here," said Erin. "You can talk to them for a bit. We're going to go get more ice."

She motioned toward Nancy and Rain before stepping away from Danny and walking straight toward the backdoor. Sarah followed her lead as Nancy and Rain stepped out of the way to let them pass.

Nancy's anger flamed even higher at this, and she looked toward Rain for confirmation, but the young genius's eyes only widened in surprise and worry.

"Nance…" warned Rain. "Don't…"

Nancy gently pushed her away as she followed the two incorrigible brats through the backdoor and into the kitchen, and she was immediately met with the tail end of an undeniable beratement.

"Oh my God, he is such a dweeb!" breathed Sarah.

"I told you," said Erin. "This is why I hate coming over here."

"He's like a squid that just attaches to you and won't let…" began Sarah.

She stopped speaking as the backdoor shut on its own. Nancy stood there before the both of them; she was burning with rage, and only a fool would not have noticed the pure animosity etched upon her green face at that moment.

"Can I help you?" frowned Erin.

Her tone was derogatory in its meaning, a snarky and superior sound that really made Nancy mad.

"Are you done being a nasty little rodent?" hissed Nancy.

"Excuse me?" asked Erin in a hostile tone.

There was no denying the offended sound of her tone. Her dark-green lips opened slightly as she frowned, and her eyebrow-leaves came together for a second in wrinkled disbelief.

"*What* did you say to me?" asked the noxious young woman.

"You heard me!" hissed Nancy. "You can't talk about Danny that way!"

The terrible young woman gave her a nasty smirk and moved her head back a bit.

"He's *my* cousin, not yours," she replied. "He's a waste of breathable air, not that it's any of your business."

"It is my business when you two little vermin start trashing on him behind his back!" barked Nancy.

She was really mad now, and she wasn't going to hold back anymore. Rain had warned her to be cool, but that advice had flown south for the winter and wasn't returning anytime soon.

Sarah's mouth dropped open as her eyes widened a little.

"Are you talking about *me*?" she asked in disbelief.

"She's the one I told you about," said Erin. "She's friends with that nasty little scab neighbor of Danny's."

Sarah looked Nancy over and then gave her a deep and angry frown.

"I've heard of you," she said. "You're that tramp who started blooming in class."

She looked over and nodded once toward her equally vile friend.

"*She's* the one who's been putting herself out online," she said.

"That was *her*?" smirked Erin. "How funny. No wonder Danny likes her. He'll attach to anything that looks in his direction."

"I am not a tramp!" said Nancy, her voice rising to an unacceptable level. "You two will not talk about me, or Danny, or Rain that way…or anybody else like that! Danny's been nothing but nice to the both of you, and you've been nothing but nasty little witches!"

"Did that little scab, Rain, talk trash about me?" sneered Erin. "Ugh…She's so nasty, even Danny won't touch her. It doesn't surprise me she's friends with a harlot."

That cut it. Nancy felt her anger boil over as she stepped forward with a raised fist. Sarah backed away toward the round kitchen table behind her, her eyes wide with surprise, but Erin simply gave her a nasty smirk and shook her head no.

"What are you going to do?" asked the nasty young woman. "Are you going to hit us?...Go ahead. You'll go to jail, and that'll just speed up the next step in your life. You should get used to wearing orange anyway, considering all of the time you'll be spending out on a street corner."

Nancy felt hot, and she had the distinct sensation of tears reaching her eyes. She refused to cry, however, at least not in front of these two. Her voice wavered as she verbally tore into them.

"You can say what you want about me," said Nancy, "but you *do not* insult Danny. He's a better person than you'll *ever* be, and unlike you, he has a heart, and not a shriveled little raisin like you."

"Is that supposed to hurt me?" scoffed Erin. "He's a giant zit that needs to be popped. I only put up with him for my mom's sake, but if I were running from a bear, I'd throw him down as bait in a heartbeat."

Sarah gave a slight chuckle at that remark.

"What a loser," said the tall young woman. "I can't believe they stuck me with him on my first day."

"I know," smirked Erin. "Losers tend to swarm together like flies, and Danny's the cow patty they've landed on."

"Stop it!" screeched Nancy. "Stop treating him like that! You can't treat anyone like that!"

She couldn't control her tears anymore. She began to cry without volition, and that really twisted her inside. She did not want to give these two little vermin the satisfaction of seeing herself break down in real time.

"Or what?" asked Erin. "I was only stating the facts…Ha…Look at her now, Sare. She's actually crying over him…You know, if I didn't know better, I'd think she's in love with him."

"I…I am not!" choked out Nancy. "He's…You can't…You can't talk that way about people!"

Sarah gave her a truly offended look.

"You insulted us first," she frowned.

"Don't bother reasoning with her," said Erin. "She's in love with a loser."

"Shut up!" screeched Nancy. "Just shut up! I am not!"

Her face was as hot as an oven, and she really wanted to lay into the both of them with her fists, beat them both down to the floor, but she was afraid of being arrested, and she knew she was being baited into doing just that. She forced herself to talk instead of yell, but it was difficult.

"You'd better leave him alone," choked Nancy. "I mean it!"

"Sure, you do," scoffed Erin. "I'm *soooooo* scared. I've met your kind before, you know. You think you can intimidate anyone who tells you like it is, but then you fall apart when you realize there's nothing you can do about it. Danny's a loser, but at least he's not a little baby. I've seen people insult him to his face, but he's never cried like a little girl."

Nancy closed her eyes out of emotional pain more than anything else. She wanted to rip the young woman's leaves off her head and shove them down her throat, but she was interrupted by the opening of the backdoor. Danny and Rain walked in a moment later, but that was the last thing Nancy needed right now.

"What's going on in here?" asked Danny.

The awkward expression upon his face, coupled with his wide eyes, made him look like even more of a dork than usual, and this pushed Nancy over her limit. She resented everything at that moment…her shifting, Brinn Clevenger, the cookout, these two girls…*and* Danny. She was supposed to defend him, keep these two girls from humiliating him, but it was just too difficult.

They were right in some respect; he was too much of a social outcast to actually defend. He was a dweeb, a dork, and a loser, and the act of defending him for even a second was squarely in the ranks of the impossible. It could not be done, and that hopelessness broke her in that instant, so she fled.

She pushed past both Rain and Danny as she hid her face; she did not want them to see her crying. She left via the backdoor, walked past the tables where Danny's parents and his aunt were chatting, and went back into Rain's backyard. She walked over to Rain's tiny patio (tiny in comparison to her neighbor's, anyway) and wept.

She was truly out of sorts now, truly lost, and she could not cope with it anymore. That bad feeling had come true exactly like she'd thought it would, but the painful truth was that it had been a self-fulfilling prophecy; she had brought that misery down upon herself, and now she was paying for it.

She held her green face in her right hand and wept into it, but the sound of approaching footsteps made her look up to see who was intruding upon her misery. It was Rain, of course; Nancy *was* standing in her backyard, after all.

"Hey," said Rain quietly.

Nancy wiped at her eyes as she nodded toward her best friend in recognition.

"Today's going just great," said Rain with a sad smile. "First I was crying in the kitchen, and then you decided to imitate me."

Nancy shook her head in a silent no. She knew Rain was only trying to cheer her up, but it wasn't working.

"I…I'm going home," she choked out after a moment.

"Eh," shrugged Rain. "We'll just explain things to Danny tomorrow. He'll understand."

Nancy nodded in agreement. She wasn't really sure if Danny would be unhappy with her sudden departure, but she decided to be an optimist about it and look on the bright side. It couldn't get any worse anyway.

"Are you going to tell me what happened?" asked Rain.

Nancy shook her head no. She did not want to relive that experience. She had never had to deal with anyone like Erin before…Danny's cousin was truly vile.

Rain gave her a worried look and then shrugged.

"I told you not to go in there," said the young genius. "Well, I didn't use those *exact* words…I said, 'Don't,' but I thought that was clear enough."

Nancy nodded and wiped away more tears. She was starting to calm down now, and this made it easier for her to talk.

"I just wanted to defend Danny," she said in a wavering voice. "You wouldn't believe what they said about him…about us."

Rain turned up her mouth in a curly-q and rolled her eyes to her right.

"Oh, I'd believe it," she said in amusement. "I know all too well what Danny's cousin is like."

"I was right, too," sniffed Nancy. "Sarah is almost as bad as Brinn Clevenger. I knew she was a nasty little witch…I knew she didn't want Danny around…much less be *interested* in him."

"He did his best," said Rain. "He was following your advice…*our* advice."

"I know," nodded Nancy. "I get that. It was my fault for going in there. I should have just waited for the cookout to be over, but…I just couldn't stand by and let…*those* two happen."

"Well, nothing's going to happen," said Rain in a confident tone. "It's obvious that it's not going to work out with Sarah."

"Yeah," said Nancy with a nod. "I figured that out."

"Then you should be happy," said Rain with a sad smile. "Now we don't have to waste any more time worrying about *her*. Now we can move on to the mystery girl."

Nancy shook her head no. She did not even want to think about this "mystery girl" at the moment.

"I don't want to," she said in defiance.

Rain gave her a disappointed look as her own face fell.

"Why not?" she asked.

"Because…" choked Nancy.

She felt like crying again, even though she didn't want to. The fact was that those two girls had ruined it all for her…She really didn't want to help Danny anymore.

"He's…He's too much of a…a dork," said Nancy in a wavering voice. "I tried my best…I can't help him. I just can't."

Rain frowned and cocked her head to the left.

"Is that how you really feel?" she asked. "Do you really feel that way just because those two said some nasty things?...That doesn't sound like the Nancy I know."

Nancy thought about this. What Rain had said was true, but Nancy was still in anguish over it. She didn't know what to think about Danny or why it even mattered so much to her. In all truth, it shouldn't have mattered at all what those two girls had said, because Nancy was only doing Danny a favor, and that was because she had wronged him, and she'd felt she had needed to make it right between them.

"I don't...I don't know," she stammered. "I want to help him...I think...I don't know..."

"What's really wrong, Nance?" asked Rain. "Something's wrong, or you wouldn't be so upset. Just because a couple of nasty people said some nasty things about you doesn't make you anyone but what you are right now...a good person. I assume they said some nasty things about you? You said about 'us,' so..."

Nancy nodded in agreement as she wiped her eyes clear of fresh tears.

"They called me a tramp and called Danny all kinds of things," she said, "and they called you a...a 'nasty little scab.'"

Rain let out a guffaw and shook her head no as she gave a short stint of laughter, but Nancy could not believe her best friend's reaction to that horrible insult.

"You think that's funny!" she asked.

"Of course," smiled Rain. "Those two are nasty *because* they said those things. That's what nasty people do. They say nasty things. It's in their job description."

Nancy looked down at her shoes as she wiped at her eyes and sniffed.

"Look, Nance, this is how it is," said Rain. "I know what I am. I am a...someone who loves science and punk metal. I know those two things don't seem to go together, but I think they do. I try and help people when they need help, and I don't ignore other people's problems. *That's* what I am, and…do you know what you are? You're not a tramp, for one thing, so that shouldn't get to you."

Nancy nodded in agreement with that statement. She didn't want Rain to try and make her feel better, but it was working in spite of her adamant refusal to be helped.

"I know *exactly* what you are," smiled Rain. "You're a great person, Nance. True, you're stubborn sometimes, you're really pushy when you want something, and you're totally oblivious when it comes to the important, but you're really sweet and loyal and smart and a great friend, and you stood up for Danny against Erin, the Wicked Witch of the Suburbs, and that takes some guts.

"You say what's on your mind, and you admit when you're wrong…That's more than I can say for ninety percent of the population out there. How can two nasty little witches say that you are anything different…or that I'm anything different…or Danny? That doesn't just make them wrong…It makes them liars."

Nancy nodded in agreement. She was really appreciative of Rain at that moment, and she said as much.

"Thanks, Rain," she breathed. "I am so glad you're my friend and not…not my friend."

Rain let out another guffaw, rolled her eyes, and shook her head.

"Ditto, mi compadre," she smiled. "Now…I know you still want to help Danny, I can tell, so…we need to start working on setting him up with the mystery girl. She's the one, I know this, and I've never been so sure of anything in my life, so don't argue with me about it."

Nancy frowned at the thought of this. She did not know why, but she did not like the idea of this "mystery girl" either, even if Rain vouched for her.

She gave Rain a hard stare and frowned.

"I still have to meet her," she said in an unhappy tone.

"You will," said Rain with a knowing smile. "I take it that this means you're still going to help?"

"I guess," sighed Nancy.

She did not want to go through this again, getting Danny's hopes up and then dashing them to the ground, but she also didn't want to leave him hanging out on a wire, and for the life of her, she had no idea why that even mattered anymore.

She had given it her best shot; she didn't owe Danny anything anymore, and there was no reason for her to get involved in his affairs at all…but there was still a part of her that wanted more when it came to Danny, but she did not know what that "more" was, and that was the *real* problem.

Chapter 16...Entropy

Nancy woke up and drank in the morning light. She stretched and knew before she had even looked that she had not shifted again, and that was good. She wasn't unhappy with being a plant; there were worse fates, so she was fine with it.

She looked over at the clock and realized it read, "9:00 A.M." She rubbed the crust from her eyes and shook the grogginess from her green head. Apparently, the upsetting day that was yesterday had taken its toll, and she had slept in…That, and no one had bothered to wake her up. She didn't mind, though. Yesterday *had* been upsetting, and she had needed all of the sleep she could get just to forget it.

She had not had any nightmares; she had not dreamed at all, and that was also a boon for her. She did not need any more nightmares, especially considering all of the other problems she was dealing with, Danny being number one on that list.

She walked into the bathroom and looked in the mirror. She looked exactly the same as she had yesterday, so there was no change there, but what *had* changed were her priorities. Danny was now her number one problem, *not* her shifting, and that was new.

"I never thought I'd see that day," she mumbled to herself. "Not in a million years."

She took her shower and toweled off, went to her dresser, put on her undergarments, and opened her top drawer. She pulled out her spotless white tee, the one she had been afraid to even look at, but now she just thought it a normal shirt like any other.

"I don't know why I was afraid to wear this," she said in mild amusement. "You know what? I miss my old biking outfit. I think I might wear it anyway…To heck with it; I'm going to wear it anyway. Just because an entire building complex full of scientists blew up in my face while I was wearing it doesn't mean it's going to happen again…Heh…"

She was a little nervous putting on her white tee and matching red shorts with the white stripes down the sides of them, but she did it anyway.

Satisfied that lightning was not going to strike her from above, she put on her white socks and matching white sneakers and grabbed her phone from off the top of her dresser.

The phone rang the moment she picked it up, and…it was Rain.

"Hello?" she said.

"Nance?" asked Rain.

"Yeah?" she replied.

"Are you up?" asked Rain.

Nancy rolled her eyes at that one.

"Obviously," she snorted.

"Good," said Rain. "I need you to get down here right away."

"Down where?" asked Nancy.

She could hear the sounds of various people-made noises in the background, and it did not sound like a TV.

"Wait, are you at the fair?" asked Nancy.

"Yeah," replied Rain. "I'm at your mother's stall. It's right across from Jones' Tires. Do you know where that is?"

"Of course," said Nancy. "I know where my mother's office is, Rain…Not to mention that I know Schiffman like the back of my hand."

"Good, because I need you here *now*," said Rain, and she sounded urgent.

"Rain, what is this about?" sighed Nancy.

"I'm down here with your mother and Danny…and Jason and…and Allen Smith," said Rain. "You need to get down here *now*. It's…It's bad."

"Bad?" asked Nancy. "What in the heck are you talking about?"

"Just get down here," said Rain. "I can't stall Danny for much longer."

"Okay, okay," said Nancy. "I'm on my way. It's a good thing I'm already dressed."

"Yeah," said Rain. "I'll see you soon."

Nancy hung up and then gave herself a mental frown. Whatever this was…it wasn't good, and she was not in the mood to deal with anything bad right now, but Rain had specifically used the word "bad," and that word did not sit well with her.

*****

It took Nancy about fifteen minutes to bike from her house to the beginning of Main Street. She locked her bike in the bike receptacle outside the library and hurried down the walk toward her mother's office and the stall her mother's firm sponsored. That particular stall would be right outside of her mother's office as it was every year…only this time her mother would be running it.

Nancy had no idea why Jason and Allen Smith would be waiting there for her. She was expecting Danny and Rain to be waiting, but the other two? That made her nervous. Something was definitely up. Danny had said he was going to the fair with Allen, but…it still made her nervous.

The streets were crowded with fairgoers, especially Main, and there were various stalls and other things lining the walks, along with a large wooden stage in the distance where some country band was crooning out a cover of some hit single.

Nancy could spot small rides in the town distance, the largest being a Ferris Wheel, but that was neither here nor there. She had to get to her mother's stall and find out what was going on.

She made her way through the crowded walk, pushed past a number of parents with small children, and walked up to the small, red, wooden stall where her friends were waiting for her.

Her mother stood behind the stall while the others were ringed around it, including Rain, but something was off. There was a cloud of angst hanging over them, and this made Nancy nervous. She did not like the implications of this already.

"What's going on here?" she asked nervously.

"Nancy," frowned her mother, "you have some explaining to do."

"What?" asked Nancy.

She looked between the faces of all of them, and this made her balk.

Jason stood next to Allen Smith, and they both had a look of strange concern on their faces, Rain had a look of anxiety that was unusual for her, but Danny…Danny looked like he was on the verge of tears. His green lips were pulled down so far that Nancy feared they would melt off his face. Furthermore, he was not wearing his new clothes but his black ones, the ones he wore before Nancy and Rain had helped him pick out something more sociable to wear, and that wasn't a good sign, either.

"What's…going…on?" asked Nancy in a slow and staggered question.

"You know what!" exclaimed Danny, but his voice was strained, agonized.

"I don't know," replied Nancy in wide-eyed confusion.

"Don't lie to me!" hissed Danny. "You said those things about me on purpose! You told Sarah all kinds of terrible things about me! You told her I called her a 'little rodent' and a 'piece of tramp trash'! Then you tried to hit Erin!"

The world closed in around Nancy as the whole street seemed to cave in at once. Out of all the outcomes she had expected while she had been traveling to her mother's stall, this was definitely not the one she had expected, nor had it even been on the list. It had never occurred to her in a million years that those two little witches would lie about her in this way, set her up to take a terrible fall, to drive Danny away from her on purpose. It simply had not occurred to her.

"I...I didn't say anything like that!" stammered Nancy. "I didn't do that!"

"Don't lie to me!" said Danny angrily.

And he truly was angry. Yes, his face was green, and he had leaves on his head, but his tears were real, and that was something Nancy could not ignore.

"They called me all kinds of names because of you!" he said, his voice barely below a screech. "Why would you do that! Why! I never did anything to you!"

"Danny, I didn't..." said Nancy desperately, but he cut her off.

"You've always hated me!" he choked out. "Always! You only pretended to be my friend so you could screw me over when it counted the most! I thought you cared, but you're a liar! I would have never done this to you! Not ever!"

This time Nancy felt tears come to her dark eyes as well. This was so much worse than she had expected, and she was not prepared to deal with it in any way possible.

"I didn't say those things!" she choked out.

He waved both hands down at her as if to say, "I'm done," though he said nothing at that moment, but Nancy clearly understood what the motion meant. He walked away, stormed off into the milling crowd, head down, nothing more to say.

Nancy was in shock. She was stunned at all of this, and she turned to the others to see their reaction, and it was…not good. Her mother scowled at her from across the stall, Jason frowned and looked down at his shoes, but Allen…he was the only one who said anything.

Allen Smith stood next to Jason—he still looked like Allen anyway—though he had grass-green skin and dark-green leaves on his head, but his face was not approving at all. He shook his head and gave her a deep frown.

"Not cool, man," he said grimly.

"I didn't say those things!" choked Nancy. "I didn't! They were lying!"

There were tears rolling down her face now, but it was not her tears that swayed them, but Rain. Her best friend stepped forward and put an end to their chastising before it could truly begin.

"She didn't say anything like that," said Rain in quick reply. "I know Danny's cousin, Erin, and she is as nasty a human being as they come. They were insulting Danny last night while he wasn't around, and Nancy overheard them. She *defended* him…and knowing Erin…this sounds *exactly* like something she would have told Danny…just to get back at Nancy."

"Is that true, Nancy?" asked her mother.

Nancy wept as she nodded out a yes. This was twice now she was crying in front of other people, but what was done was done, and she had to defend herself.

"They were talking…about…about what a 'loser' Danny was," choked Nancy. "I got onto them for it…You wouldn't believe the things they…they said about us…me and Danny and Rain…They called me a tramp and a harlot and Rain a nasty little scab…and they wouldn't stop insulting Danny."

"It's true," said Rain. "Nancy would have never said those things about any of us, including Danny."

"But Danny doesn't know that," said Jason. "You need to go find him and tell him."

But it wasn't that simple. This time she was really hurt, Danny was really hurt, and Nancy simply didn't want to deal with it or him anymore. She felt broken inside; Danny had genuinely hurt her, and she could not for the life of her understand why she felt hurt over anything he said anyway. Hearing those things come out of his mouth hurt her to the core, made her feel like less than nothing, and she just couldn't cope with it.

She threw her hands up, palms out, and backed away a bit.

"I don't...I don't want to do this anymore!" she stammered.

"Danny really liked that girl, Sarah," said Allen. "I've seen him upset before...but not like this. It's never been this bad."

"You have to go talk to him, Nancy," said her mother. "You can't leave that poor boy thinking that you ruined this for him."

"Just leave me alone!" choked Nancy. "I tried to help him! I tried to tell him that girl wasn't right for him...He didn't listen..."

"You still have to explain it to him," said Jason. "You can't leave him hanging like this. I'd go, but..."

"You need to be the one to do it, Nance," said her mother. "You know that."

Nancy shook her head no. She didn't want to be a part of this anymore.

"I don't want to screw up his life anymore," she said as she wiped her tears away. "Besides, Rain...Rain said there was another girl interested in him."

Jason gave her a look of pure confusion.

"Wait, what?" asked Jason. "I think you meant *Danny's* interested in another girl, right?"

Nancy shook her head no as she tried unsuccessfully to stop crying.

"No," she said in a wavering voice. "No, I meant what I said. Rain said there's a girl who's interested in him. I don't know who this 'mystery girl' is, though."

All eyes turned toward Rain, and the eccentric young genius seemed to shrink in on herself.

"Is that true?" asked Allen. "There's a girl who's actually interested in *Danny*?"

"Uhhh…" stalled Rain.

"Rain Fischer," said Nancy's mother, "I think you'd better explain yourself right now. Did you lie to Nancy?"

"No, ma'am," said Rain with a shake of her head. "No, there really is someone who likes Danny. She really likes him a lot."

"Who?" asked Jason.

Nancy wiped at her tears and swallowed hard as everyone waited for Rain to answer. The eccentric young genius simply turned her left hand palm up toward Nancy. All eyes swiveled from Rain to land upon Nancy, and she felt the heat of their stares upon her green skin once more.

Jason smacked himself in the forehead as if to punish himself.

"Oh, my God, it all makes sense now!" he said after a moment. "No wonder!"

Nancy had no idea what he was talking about.

"What?" she asked. "Why is everyone staring at me? Rain never said who the…mystery girl…was…"

They were in fact all staring at *her*, and that's when she figured it out. Rain had said she was truly oblivious when it came to the important, and apparently, this was about as important as you could get.

"I'd better go stall Danny," said Rain quickly. "You're right; Nancy has to talk to him, but I can't let him get away. See if you can talk some sense into her."

"Rain, you can't just…" said Nancy's mother, but Rain was already pushing past people on the walk in the direction Danny had gone.

"Talk some sense into her!" called Rain, and then she was gone.

"And there she goes," frowned Nancy's mother.

Nancy looked between the remaining faces.

"What?" she asked as she wiped the rest of her tears from her eyes. "What are you looking at?…It's not me…Rain's wrong. It's not…"

"Yeah, I'm gonna have to agree with Rain on this one," said Allen. "I realize what Danny said was upsetting, but…"

"I know," agreed Jason. "I think Rain's right. Nobody breaks down into tears over someone else like that. I mean, they might get angry or out of sorts, but…"

"What?" asked Nancy. "No…No, that's not right."

"Nancy," said her mother, "it doesn't take a degree to see what's right in front of my face. It's obvious that you care about that poor young man, and I normally don't say things like that to you."

Even her mother was against her on this one. Nancy looked between them, watched the crowd pass them by for a moment as if there was a bubble of doom around them, and then she shook her head no. There was no possible way she liked Danny in that way. He was too much of a…a dork for that.

"No," she said in adamant defiance. "No, that can't be right. Danny's a total dork. He's…We don't have anything in common. He's a…a social outcast…I…I hated his guts not that long ago. There's no way I could like him like that."

"Nancy Amelia Clark!" barked her mother.

Nancy looked up into the older woman's face, and…her mother was not happy with what she had just said.

"I know we don't get along like I'd like us to," frowned her mother, "but even I know better than that!"

This angered Nancy. Barging into her room was one thing, but interfering with her "relationship" with Danny was entirely another. It was absolutely unacceptable.

"No!" she hissed. "I don't care what you say! You don't know anything about it, so butt out!"

Nancy cringed and waited for the inevitable explosion, but it never occurred, and this caused her to listen in stunned silence to her mother's unusual response. The older woman merely shook her head and frowned.

"Nancy," she said in a stern voice, "your father and I taught you better than that. Love…real love…is when you love someone for *who* they are…not *what* they are. If that weren't true, your father and I would have never gotten together, and then you would have never been born."

Nancy did not feel like arguing with her, but she did it anyway. It was an old and tired habit, and doing it here instead of at home was nothing more than a change in location.

"You are actually telling *me* that you married *Dad* even though he was a dork?" she asked. "Dad isn't a loser! He's not a dork! In fact, he was never a…"

Her mother cut her off with a shake of her green head.

"No," she said firmly. "*He* put up with *me*. I wasn't the nicest person in the world when I was your age, believe it or not."

This stunned Nancy. She had never in a million years believed that her mother would admit to being hard to get along with. It stopped her from arguing due to sheer and stunning surprise.

"Hey, I may just be an observer here," said Allen, "but your mom's right."

"Thank you, Allen," said Nancy's mother.

"No one says 'I don't want to screw up his life anymore' unless they care about that person," said Allen. "Nobody cries over someone like that for no reason."

"Yeah," agreed Jason. "I can see it, Mom can see it, and it only took Allen twenty seconds to see it. You care about him, Nance. That's about as obvious as it gets."

This was going very badly for her. Nancy did not want to believe what they were saying, but she suspected they were right, and *that* drove her to a point of panic she had not felt before. She put her hands up to her temples and shook her head no.

"This wasn't supposed to happen!" she exclaimed. "This shouldn't have happened at all!...It was those scientists' fault!"

"Scientists?" asked Jason. "What scientists?"

Nancy felt herself hyperventilating. Her universe was crashing down around her, and there was nothing she could do about it.

"If I hadn't started shifting, then none of this would have happened!" she choked out. "He wouldn't have been a spider, and then I wouldn't have talked to him at all!"

"Spider?" asked her mother. "Nancy, are you all right? You're not making any sense."

"No, it's those scientists!" cried Nancy. "This is all their fault! It's all their fault! I shouldn't be here as a plant...I shouldn't...I wish I could just tell them what kind of monsters they are! It's their fault! I wouldn't be here at all like this! Not like this! I didn't want any of this, I didn't...Danny was never supposed to...He was not in the...I would have never...Those scientists...It's their...It's...their...It's..."

She could no longer breathe. Her vision went crazy as her eyes began to vibrate rapidly within her head. They moved back and forth and up and down and diagonally, and everything around her looked like a blurry haze as she dropped to her knees.

"Whoa!" exclaimed Jason.

"Oh, my God!" cried her mother.

Nancy felt her mother's hands upon her shoulders a moment later, but it was too late. Everything was going dark, the world around her was dissolving from view, and she could see the hue of her skin change from green to peach and back again in rapid succession.

"Somebody help us!" screeched her mother, and that was the last thing Nancy heard at that particular moment.

*****

Nancy stood up in total darkness, but that darkness did not last long. A bright light appeared in the distance, but this time she was not confused as she had been in her nightmares. This time she knew wherever she was…was *real*.

The light shining in the distance gave her enough illumination to know she was back to being human, the human she had been for seventeen years before the shifting had ever started, but that revelation was cut short by the light in the distance.

"*NANCY AMELIA CLARK*!" came a booming voice.

The voice was actually a cacophony of different voices, an orchestra of male and female voices, all taking at once, all saying her name at the same time. The great and terrible face of light that had haunted her dreams now appeared in the distance and zoomed toward her at blinding speed.

Nancy did not even have the mental wherewithal to scream. She held up her arms and hands in front of her face in an instinct of defense and shouted the first word that came to her mind.

"STOP!" she shrieked.

And it worked. The giant head slowed down until it was a mere ten feet from her. It looked neither male nor female, but a combination of both, and when it had spoken, it had spoken with that strange mix of voices, that strange amalgamation of both sexes.

"It's real, I'm not dreaming, not this time…" ran her thoughts. *"It stopped when I told it to, like it's waiting for me to say something, but…what is it? The last thing I remember was hearing Mom call for help…but before that…the scientists…I was thinking about the scientists…This is all their fault…This is…The scientists?…The scientists!"*

"I know who you are!" cried Nancy.

"NANCY AMELIA CLARK!" boomed the giant head.

Nancy flinched at the sheer magnitude of its voice, but she did not waver in her resolve, not this time.

"I know who you are," repeated Nancy. "You're the scientists from the Breckenridge Institute of Discovery…aren't you?"

The face broke apart in a burst of bright light, and then the figures of many people, all glowing in a pure white light, all beings *made* of light, began to walk past her, surrounding her, and this set her at an ease she had never felt once within her dreams. She could inherently sense they meant her no harm, and though that was strange, it still set her at ease.

One of the figures of light stepped before her and addressed her as a single entity.

"Nancy Amelia Clark," said the voice, but this time it was male and only male.

No other voice was merged with the being, something that had once been a man, though Nancy did not recognize him, who he may have been. He had no features to speak of; he was only a shape of light, and that was it.

"Yes?" asked Nancy. "What…What do you want? What is it you want from me?"

"We have been waiting for you," said the "man" in front of her. "You must listen."

Nancy had already thought as much. It was clear now that these "scientists" had been trying to contact her this whole time, the whole time she had been shifting. She decided to ask the obvious, though she was scared and confused…It was better than shaking and quivering in place.

"Wh…Where is this?" asked Nancy in a quavering voice.

The being of light before her waved one hand out toward the other figures and toward the infinite darkness beyond them.

"We exist outside of time and space," said the being.

His voice rang as if it were in a vast auditorium, even though hers did not.

"We are everywhere and nowhere," said the being.

Nancy gasped as visions of her life appeared all around her; they floated like giant movie screens above her head, above all their heads, and she could see various activities and conversations and interactions with others from various points in time, even ones when she was a little girl. Her fear was momentarily replaced with awe, and she forgot herself for that brief span of time.

"What is this?" she asked in breathless wonder.

"The explosion you witnessed was part of a grand experiment," said the being of light. "We attempted to open a door to another reality…but we failed…but we did not."

It explained so much. Nancy was never much into science fiction; it was not her strong suit, but she had seen a movie or two on the subject, so it made sense that this was what had happened.

"I knew it," she breathed. "I knew something like that must have happened."

"You thought we were erased from existence," said the man made of light, "but we were not. We transcended our limited forms and became this…beings of pure thought. We cannot exist in reality as you see it, so we exist here."

"Out….Outside of time and space?" asked Nancy.

She did not know exactly what that meant, but it was the only possible explanation, the only one they had given her.

"Yes," said the being. "We exist here because of the experiment, and because we exist here, we exist in all time, all space, and all realities at once."

"How is that possible?" breathed Nancy. "I can't exist outside of time and space…can I? How can I even breathe here? There wouldn't be any air, or…or gravity, or air pressure, or anything like that."

"What you see here…" said the man of light, "your body here…it is an extension of your mind. You are a being of pure thought here. It is the only way you can exist here. You were part of the experiment as well, though you did not intend to be. We needed to tell you this, because it was our fault this has happened to you."

"But I wasn't in the explosion," said Nancy. "I haven't 'ascended' or anything."

"No," replied the being, "but you were close enough to be affected. That is why you have 'shifted' every day since the experiment."

Nancy had already known as much. Rain had figured this out early on. The only thing left was to ask them how to stop it, the shifting, or rather how to get back to her original world. She did not mind being in the plant world, but she had not grown up that way, and she just wanted to be like she was now, her original self.

"So what do I do?" asked Nancy. "I don't want to shift like this! I want to go back to *my* reality. I want to be like this again in my world!"

"There is a way," said the being of light. "The experiment caused a breach in realities, all realities, but the order of all realities cannot be undone, existence cannot be undone, because we exist…We exist in all of time, all of space, and all realities, so that breach was naturally contained, though we had no hand in its containment."

"If there's a breach, then that means…" thought Nancy in excitement. *"That means I might be able to get back to my reality! All I need is to find it! I need to ask them…"*

"Contained?" asked Nancy. "Contained how? I need to find it, so I can go back! I need to go back to my reality!"

"It was contained within you," replied the man of light.

"Me?" asked Nancy in surprise. "How can it be contained within me? I don't even know what that means…What does that mean? I…You're not making sense. If the breach is in me, how do I know it won't close! I need to get back! I can't shift anymore; can't you see that? I stopped shifting three days ago! Does that mean the breach is closed?"

"It means the breach will remain until your body ceases to function," said the being.

Nancy thought about this for a second.

"Ceases to function?" she asked. "You mean…You mean when I die? The breach will only close if I die?"

"No," came another voice. "The breach will move once your body ceases to function."

Another figure stepped up from Nancy's left and addressed her, but the voice was distinctly female this time.

"You contain the breach," said this new being of light, the "woman." "You shift because you exist in all realities at once."

"I don't understand," said Nancy.

And she really didn't. Nothing really made sense now, but at least they were answering her questions with all honesty, though she did not really understand them.

"Every sentient being is thought," said the "woman" of light. "You and every other being in existence exist in every reality at once. Your minds are too limited in scope to comprehend such an existence, so your minds only focus on one existence at a time. You exist in every reality because you are connected with yourself in all other realities. Only your bodies are different. Your mind is the same and is thus connected."

"Is that why I kept shifting when I went to sleep?" asked Nancy. "My…My mind was wandering?"

"Yes," said the "man" of light. "Yes and no. You are unique. You can focus your attention on any reality you choose."

"But I didn't choose any reality to focus on!" said Nancy. "I always just woke up in a new one!"

"But you did," said the woman of light. "Every time you felt strong emotion or concentrated thought on something, you chose your destination. It stayed with you when you slept, your unconscious mind focused upon it, and you shifted."

"Observe," said the man of light.

He directed Nancy's attention toward one of the memories above her by pointing toward it with the brightly shining index finger of his right hand. Nancy stared in fascination as she watched the memory of Rain explaining the importance of the filmy dome spider to her.

"In this memory, you thought of the spider as you lay down for sleep," said the man of light, "and you chose your destination."

The memory upon the screen of light changed to one of her sitting outside the nurse's office with Danny while they were both spiders. It was surreal to see her memory as such, but it was also an enormous smack to her brain to realize that she had been the one choosing each of her "destinations," even the one with Bald Streak Nancy. Still, it did not answer why she had stopped shifting over the last three days.

"But why haven't I shifted over the last three days?" asked Nancy. "Why haven't I shifted if I contain the breach and it hasn't closed…or moved, or whatever?"

"Because your thoughts have only been on one thing over that time," said the woman of light. "These thoughts invoked feelings so strong that they annulled all other thoughts and feelings…They have only been on one thing, a sentient being…Daniel Linus Princeton. He is a sentient being that exists in all realities as all sentient beings do, so you did not shift."

This uncomfortable truth hit Nancy like a freight train. It was becoming more and more obvious that her feelings toward Danny were more than just "friend I want to help," but realizing this also meant accepting these feelings as truth, and she wasn't sure she could do that.

"That…That can't be right!" she winced. "I…I can't...That's not true! I can't have feelings for Danny!…Not after two weeks! I hated him just two weeks ago!…Not Danny…He's a social pariah!...That…That's stupid!...I…This can't be right!"

"You cannot lie to us, though you lie to yourself," said the man of light. "We can see your past, your present, and your future, and we see you in all realities at once."

Nancy's shoulders slumped as she stared down at her spotless white sneakers. The gravity of everything was sinking into her all at once, but her mind simply could not handle it. She questioned everything now, everything she believed in, and she could not help but do so; it was automatic.

"I don't feel that way about him...do I?" she thought in a strange daze. *"He's a dork and a social outcast and a dweeb and a loser...and...and I hated him so much...It was so easy to hate him...It was much easier to hate him...than to...than to...Why is it so hard for me to...to..."*

She looked up and watched as all of her memories of Danny played out on the screens of light around her. She listened again as Danny read off his poem, she watched as they walked down Rain's street hand in hand, and she gazed in confusion at how her own face blushed as she danced with him, but seeing all of this hurt her inside.

It tore something open, a gateway to her true self, and it tore off that gate like a scab over a wound. She bled inside, but that bleeding was like nothing she had ever felt before.

She felt a warmth build up inside her as she looked upon those damning images, a glow of light like nothing she had ever felt before; it was a longing to be with him, painful to be without him, and she so desperately wanted to help Danny, to tell him that she hadn't said those terrible things about him, that everything would be all right, and this confused her even more.

"Why are you showing me this!" she demanded. "Why!"

"We are not," said the woman of light. "You are seeing what is in your own consciousness."

This was unexpected. It was a difficulty of believing that assaulted her, and yet she knew it to be true, and that knowing was even worse.

"I...I'm doing this?" asked Nancy. "I...I don't understand!"

"This person is the most important thing in your life at this time," said the woman of light. "This person is where your thoughts are. You exist in the reality you are in because you exist with him. He is where your thoughts are. He is where your feelings are."

"What does that mean?" asked Nancy. "I don't understand!"

"It means you have a way to go back to your 'original' reality," said the man of light. "All realities are 'original' to us, but we understand that the scope of your mind cannot see this. Nevertheless, Daniel Linus Princeton is how you will go back to your 'original' reality."

"What?" asked Nancy. "What does Danny have to do with that?"

"He is your focus," said the woman of light. "If you concentrate on him in his original form, the form you think of as 'original,' you will return to the reality you believe you came from. He is where your thoughts are. He is where your feelings are."

Nancy closed her eyes as a wave of strong emotion overtook her. She did not want to believe it, she did not want to believe that she was…*in love*…with Danny, but she could no longer deny it.

She felt a couple of tears spill from her hazel eyes as she finally realized that she was indeed in love with Danny Princeton, and there was nothing she could do about it. It had only taken a group of near godlike beings to make her see it, to overcome an age of bias against him, and that was all there was to that.

She opened her eyes and took in a deep breath.

"Fine," she said after a moment. "That explains how I can get back, but…how do I close the breach without dying?"

"You cannot," said the woman of light. "The breach cannot be closed. It has always existed, though it has not always existed within you."

This was not the news Nancy wanted to hear.

"But I'll just keep shifting!" she whined. "There has to be a way to close it!"

"There is not," said the man of light, "…but it can be moved."

"Moved?" asked Nancy. "Moved where?"

"There is another who was affected by the experiment," said the woman of light, "though she is only indirectly connected to the breach. She was not near the explosion, though she detected it through radio waves, and thus was affected."

"Oh, my God," said Nancy as her eyes widened in realization. "Rain!"

"Rain Dillon Fischer may contain the breach," said the man of light. "She was also affected by the experiment, though she is like a small funnel compared to the opening of a cave. She cannot shift, but she can sense ripples in the realities."

Nancy did not need a detailed explanation of what that meant…Rain could contain the breach. Furthermore, there was no moral quandary about moving the breach to her best friend…Rain wanted this more than anything.

When she had promised Rain if she could give Rain her shifting, she would…she had not thought that scenario was ever an actual possibility.

"How can I move it?" asked Nancy. "Rain wants this. She actually wants to shift."

"We know," said the man of light. "That is why you must go back now. You must focus your mind upon the one you have your strongest feelings for, the one where your thoughts are, and we will attach our will to yours until the breach is moved. We cannot leave this place, but we can attach our will to yours for a short time, and we shall move the breach as you shift."

"That's all I have to do?" asked Nancy.

She could not believe it. It all seemed so simple now that it was ridiculous she had not seen any of it before.

Of course, it was ridiculous to think she could have actually seen this coming in the first place, but that was beside the point. She now had a chance to make everything right again, and she was going to take it.

"Yes," said the woman of light. "We will send you back to the reality you were in, but *you* must return to your 'original' reality, only you can do that, and once you start, we will move the breach to Rain Dillon Fischer as you shift."

Nancy took in a deep breath and closed her eyes.

"I'm in love with Danny Princeton," she thought in mental surprise. *"I would have never guessed...You could have knocked me over with a feather..."*

She opened her eyes as she exhaled and nodded twice.

"I'm ready," she said nervously. "Send me back."

"Then prepare yourself, Nancy Amelia Clark," said the man of light.

Nancy watched as every being of light coalesced back into the giant, floating, androgynous head. The face moved toward her, Nancy felt a strange but not unpleasant heat as its light surrounded her, she felt like she was floating for a second, and then everything was so bright she could no longer see.

Chapter 17...D-Shift

Nancy felt her mother's hands helping her to her feet.

"I'm all right, I'm all right!" she gasped as she stood up.

Her mother turned her around to stare directly into her face. It was a little odd seeing the plant version of her mother after being where Nancy had just been, but then again, it was a *lot* odd being where she had just been, outside of time and space, so this was not so bad.

"Nancy!" asked her mother. "Are you all right!"

"Yes, yes," breathed Nancy. "I'm fine."

"Dude," said Jason. "You scared us. Your eyes were like…"

"Crazy," said Allen. "You even freaked me out."

"Yeah, they were moving all over the place," said Jason. "They were moving at, like…jet speed. That was nuts, Nance."

"I'm fine," breathed Nancy. "Actually, no I'm not."

"What!" cried her mother in a panic. "What's wrong!"

The older woman shook her a little bit, and Nancy realized that her mother not only cared about her, but cared about her to the point of hysteria. She gently pried the older woman away from her and took a step back.

"I was wrong," frowned Nancy.

She reached up and wiped some old tears from her cheeks.

"What do you mean?" asked her mother in a nervous tone.

"Everyone was right, and I was wrong," breathed Nancy. "I see that now."

"*Okaaay*," said Jason in obvious confusion.

"You were right," said Nancy. "You were all right. I *do* care about Danny. I have to…I have to talk to him. I need to tell him!"

"Whoa," said Jason. "What?"

"Nancy?" asked her mother.

"I think…" said Nancy very slowly.

It was actually somewhat painful this time to admit that she was wrong, mainly because it was she who had been her biggest denier. Rain had clearly known the whole time, and the eccentric young genius had deliberately thrown Nancy into situations where Nancy had been forced to get close to Danny, but there would be time to chastise her best friend about that later. Right now, Rain had hopefully found Danny and was trying to talk some sense into him, and more importantly, Nancy needed to talk some sense into herself.

She looked her mother in the eye and nodded once.

"I think I'm in love with him," she breathed.

"Nancy Amelia Clark…" breathed her mother, "normally I'd cringe if my daughter told me that…but that poor young man needs to hear it straight from your lips."

Nancy turned to look at Jason and Allen, but the both of them simply stared at her in wide-eyed amazement.

"Hoo boy," said Allen a second later. "That would make Danny's day…No, no…That would make his *year*."

"Yeah," said Jason. "I would normally agree with Mom and want to knock you on the head for saying something like that, but you couldn't be any righter if you tried. You need to go tell him."

"Wait just a minute now," said her mother.

She grabbed Nancy by the shoulders and looked her over.

"Are you sure you're all right?" asked the older woman.

"Yes," nodded Nancy. "I'm fine now. I think I just got worked up over everything and had an anxiety attack. I'm fine. I…I really need to go find Danny."

"That was one heck of an anxiety attack," said Allen.

"Too right," said Jason.

Nancy looked toward them to address their observations of her, but her mother reached up and turned her head back toward her with her left hand.

"Look at me," ordered the older woman. "Look me in the eye. Are you sure you're okay?"

"Yes," breathed Nancy.

"And are you sure about this?" asked her mother.

Nancy did not need an explanation for the meaning behind that question.

"Yes," she said confidently. "I've never been more sure of anything in my entire life."

Her mother looked her over again, a tear formed in the corner of the older woman's right eye, she cocked her green head slightly to the right, and then she gave Nancy a proud smile.

"Then why are you still here?" she asked. "Go get him."

"Right," smiled Nancy.

She did not need any more encouragement, but she did need to contact Rain. She could not let Danny get away.

"Do you have your phone?" she asked her mother. "I need to call Rain. I need to know if she found him!"

The older woman walked back around the stand and dug her phone out of her purse. She handed it to Nancy without saying a word.

Nancy dialed Rain's number and waited for the eccentric young woman to pick up.

"Hello?" asked Rain.

"Where are you?" asked Nancy.

"Nance?" asked Rain.

Nancy didn't even bother to answer that question; she simply repeated herself, only this time with more force.

"Where are you!" she asked.

"We're down by the Ferris Wheel," said Rain.

"Stay there," said Nancy. "I'm on my way."

"Uhhh…" was all Rain got to say before Nancy hung up.

She handed her mother back her phone and took off running without another word.

"Go get him, Nance!" yelled Jason.

She had not expected her brother to say anything like that. She stopped momentarily, turned, and gave him a smile. The look on his face was priceless; it was the "What are you doing looking at me when you should be running!" face, and she took that in for a second, absorbed it into memory, and then took to running once more.

Nancy pushed past people as she ran along the sidewalk down Main. She felt that glow inside again, that burning heat that gave her a strange euphoria, something she had never felt before the strange events as of late, and this empowered her to move even faster.

She thought about the way Danny looked in her original reality, her original universe, and though the memory of him was the same dorky, gawky dweeb she had always seen walking the halls in a lonely slump, she found she no longer cared about such a shallow notion.

A burst of light radiated out from her in a wide ring as she focused on this image, and she watched in amazement as the people around her transformed.

*****

Rain hung up her phone and gave Danny a worried frown. He was still crying, but he was hiding it well; she was positive he did not want any passerby to see him in such a weak state.

"Just give her a chance to explain," she said. "She didn't say those things, Danny. You *have* to believe us."

Danny shook his head and wiped at the tears on his cheeks.

"Don't lie for her!" he choked out. "She's always hated me; you know that! She's just been waiting for the chance to do something like this…She blamed me for that F and M page when I had nothing to do with it, and she didn't even come and ask me about it! She hates me, so don't lie for her!"

It was clear he was not listening. It was going to take something drastic for him to change his mind, or maybe Nancy could finally…Well, the possibility of that was pretty much null now. Rain had spilled the beans on her little setup, so that was spoiled. She wasn't sure what Nancy was going to say when she got here, but for Danny's sake, she hoped it wasn't going to be anything mean. She didn't think Nancy would say anything bad, but she was worried, nonetheless.

"Danny, you have to give her a chance to explain," said Rain. "I've known Nancy almost my entire life. She *is* a good person…just like you. She cares about what happens to other people…She would have *never* said those things about—"

Her sentence was cut short as she watched a ring of pure white light pass through her and everyone else. Her scalp sizzled with a weird heat as she felt her skin crawl all over her body. Her eyes widened as she watched her right arm turn from green to peach, but it was her left arm that really caught her eye.

She looked past the black sleeve of her skull pony T-shirt to watch her left arm turn to black metal. A list of things to do popped up in her vision upon her upper left, a schedule of sorts, and her vision suddenly became clearer than she had ever known in her entire life.

Her mouth dropped open in sudden shock, and her eyes felt like they were going to pop out of her head at this development. She looked to Danny for help, but he only looked upon her with strange curiosity.

"Are you all right?" he asked.

His face had changed as well. The whole left side of Danny's face was made of a sleek silver metal, and the right side of his face was no longer green but peach in color. His eyes were a bright green, but they looked like little shuttered cameras. It was even stranger seeing him this way than it was seeing herself as…whatever this was.

Of course, the revelation of what had just happened struck her all at once.

"Oh, my God!" said Rain in open shock. "Are you seeing this!"

She looked around and realized that everyone else looked as they did, only she seemed to be the only one that even noticed.

"Seeing what?" asked Danny.

He cocked his head to the left and looked at her as if she were crazy.

"What am I supposed to see?" he asked.

"I…I shifted!" said Rain in excitement. "I'm shifting! Can't you see it?"

"Shifting?" asked Danny.

He reached up and wiped a tear from the silver side of his face.

"What are you talking about?" he asked in obvious confusion.

✸✸✸✸✸

Nancy pushed past the crowd gathered around the temporary stage. The band on the stage was still playing as if nothing had happened a moment ago, as if the entire universe had not just changed, and they had not even skipped a beat in-between the shift from "plant world" to "cyborg world."

"It's working!" thought Nancy in unbridled excitement. *"This is really happening!"*

She thought about Danny's face again, and coupled with her realization that she was actually going back to her original reality, her spirits soared higher than she had ever known in her entire life. She felt nothing but elation as she weaved through the crowd; that warm glow inside was like nothing she had ever felt before, and she realized this all too well.

"This is what love feels like!" she thought in a strange joy. *"I really am in love with him! I'm in love with Danny Princeton, and I don't care!"*

Another burst of light radiated out from her, and she felt so much as saw herself shift again. This time her vision changed so radically that she had to slow down and catch herself before she fell over from vertigo.

"Stupid third eye," she breathed as she bent over.

*****

Rain both watched and felt another blast of light travel through her and everything around her. She felt that sizzling sensation again, only this time the schedule disappeared in her vision and was replaced with…more vision.

"What the heck!" she said as she looked around in a panic.

Her skin had not changed in color again; she was still stuck as a peach, but one look upon Danny told her what had changed. He was no longer half-metal, no, but he did have a third eye right in the middle of his forehead.

"Rain, are you on drugs?" asked Danny.

There was a supreme look of confusion upon his face, and with his third eye smack in the middle of his brow, he looked even stranger than he should have, with his peach skin and weird…stuff…on his head.

It took Rain a moment to notice that he did not have leaves on his head but bristles, the stuff that Nancy had called "hair," and then it hit her...She figured out what was going on in a brainstorm of epiphany.

She reached up and touched her own third eye and then ran the peach fingers of her right hand through her new "hair."

"Oh, my God!" she said yet again. "I'm not just shifting…I'm shifting backwards through all of Nancy's shifts! Everything that was in the notebook…"

"Notebook?" asked Danny. "Rain, you are really…You're freaking me out. I don't know what's going on, but you're not making any sense."

"I'm not making any sense because you can't see it!" said Rain excitedly. "Oh, if you could see this, you'd…you'd probably pass out!"

"Right," frowned Danny. "I see what's going on now. You're trying to make a fool out of me like Nancy did!"

This brought Rain's excitement to a screeching halt. She had momentarily forgotten all about Danny's predicament.

"No, no!" she said in urgent reply. "No, I'm not! I'm sorry, Danny, I just got a little excited, is all…I know you can't…Whoa…"

Another ring of light passed through her and sizzled through everyone. This time she stopped checking herself and just watched as a line of light ran down Danny and transformed him yet again. This time he was a very pale peach and his eyes were a deep red. It was somewhat frightening but also fascinating to witness it happening right in front of her.

"If you're not making fun of me," frowned Danny, "then there's something wrong with you. Do I need to call someone to come get you?"

"No, no," said Rain. "No, you don't understand. You can't see what I'm seeing…and no, I'm not on drugs, so drop that thought right…"

Another wave of light passed through her, and she watched as Danny transformed, but this time his transformation was even more radical than the previous transformations. This time he had light brown "stuff" all over his body, that weird "hair," only it was much thicker than before, and he had a thick, thick dark-brown shock of it running in a line upon his head.

The second thing she noticed was the absolute plethora of smells that assaulted her nose all at once, a cornucopia of weird scents; there were smells from everyone and everywhere, and it was almost too much for her brain to handle.

"Oh, my God!" said Rain for a third time. "I can smell everything!...This is incredi…No, no wait. I wanted to shift, but this is too fast! How do I slow it down? I can't even study anything!"

*****

Nancy ignored the various smells and scents around her as she tried to get through the throng of people gathered around the wooden stage in the middle of Main Street. It had taken her a moment to get over her vertigo, two shifts worth, in fact, but she was feeling better now, and she was ready to move on.

Her mind was only on Danny, and thinking of him made her heart twinge with both elation and regret.

"I've treated him so horribly," she thought unhappily, *"even after I apologized to him. He's a giant dork—I know that—but I just couldn't let that fact go. Why*

couldn't I see it before?...Mom was right...Real love is when you love someone for who they are...not what they are.

"Danny is a better man than any of those fakes at school...He's better than all of them put together, and I was such a fool for ignoring that fact...and it is a fact...I...I love him, and...Oh, my God...I actually love him...That is so weird, and yet...I know it's true..."

She could not get his face out of her mind, his original face, and she did not want to.

Another burst of bright light ringed out from her, and she felt that sizzling sensation on her skin, but that was nothing compared to the feeling of her own heart awakening to the truth she had been denying for so long.

The simple truth was that she had a real and honest love for someone who was not part of her family, was not her best friend, someone who probably deserved love more than she did, and someone who was worth giving that love to.

"Danny, I'm coming..." she thought in slight worry. *"Just hold on a little longer...Please, don't leave..."*

She watched the ring of light blast out from her again.

The mass of fairgoers around her were all see-through now; they had transparent skin and rubbery, tentacle-like hair. It was *that* universe she had crossed into, but that mass parted somewhat as she, herself, began to glow, and though it was dim at first, she suddenly lit up in a bright and vibrant pink that shone like a beacon even though it was the middle of the day, and she did not need a detailed explanation as to what that color meant.

* * * * *

Danny gave Rain an even deeper frown than before and shook his head in obvious disapproval.

"You're on drugs," he said grimly.

"No, I'm no—" frowned Rain, but she was cut short again.

This time a blast of light sizzled through them as before, but the result was far more striking than the previous transformations, even the one she had just been in. Rain's skin went transparent, she could actually *see* through it, she could see the bones in her arms, and Danny was…kind of horrifying to look at. She could see through the skin on his face, his skull, his eye orbs, everything…Even the "hair" on his head looked different, like tentacles, and it freaked her out.

Her skin started to glow a dark blue, and that strange light picked up, brightened in magnitude, and Danny took a step back from her as she began to shine like a ghostly lantern.

"This is *craaaaaazzzzy*!" she exclaimed.

"You're crazy!" hissed Danny.

A blast of light struck them again, searing straight through them, but this time Rain was glad for it. Her arms coated over with sandy-colored scales with streaks of a brown, diamond-like pattern across them, and one look at Danny told her that she had now entered "the snake universe," as Nancy had called it.

Danny's scales were a slightly darker red than royal red, and he had pretty white and black lines looping around the red at regular intervals. He reminded Rain of a common milk snake, or perhaps its deadlier clone, the coral snake, but for all that, he still looked like Danny in recognizable features, the way his face was shaped, his eyes, etc.

"That's so weird!" said Rain in uncontained excitement. "You still kind of look the same no matter what universe you're in…I mean, we look different and whatnot with the scales and stuff, but you still look like 'Danny.'"

"And you look psychotic," frowned Danny. "If you're going to keep making fun of me, then you can leave now!"

"Danny," protested Rain, "I'm not making fun of you! I'm just…I'm having a problem right now discerning what reality I'm in and why I keep shift—"

The ring of light went through them yet again. This time Danny looked all peachy in his skin, and he had a full head of that strange stuff called "hair," but there weren't any particular features on him that stood out, no third eye, no weird tentacles or fangs or anything.

"I wonder if this is…the original one…" said Rain slowly.

She looked around at the various fairgoers and realized something was off. The women…and *only* the women…had large bald streaks running down the middles of their heads where their "hair" was supposed to be.

Rain reached up and touched the bald part of her head, felt around the streak where bare skin met air, and winced at the alien feel of it.

"*Ewwww!*" she said in protest. "No wonder Nancy hates that!"

"Nancy hates everything!" said Danny in bitter reply. "She hates me, and you're being weird to make fun of me! I know she told you to do this!"

"Danny, for the love of—" she began.

She was interrupted yet again by another shift. This time, beautiful grey feathers speckled with black spots sprouted all over her arms. Danny sported dull red feathers upon his face with long black and sweeping feathers upon the top of his head. The sight of it brought Rain back to the memory of the photos in her notebook.

"This must be the 'cockatiel' world!" she said in excitement. "Danny, you look really good! You really do! You remind me of a cardinal."

"Stop making fun of me, Rain!" said Danny.

This time he was on the verge of tears again. He had stopped crying some time ago, but now it looked as if he were going to start all over again.

"I thought you were my friend!" he choked out.

He began to cry again, and the sight of this caused Rain's spirit to fall from a great height. She had nothing but wired excitement in her because of the shifting she was now experiencing, but to Danny…nothing had changed.

"I am *so* sorry if you thought that was an insult," she said in a sad tone. "I really am. And for that matter, I really *am* your friend. I really am. You have to believe me, Danny. We…Nancy and I…We just want to help you—"

The ring of light arced through them again, but this time it caught Rain by as much surprise as the see-through skin from three shifts ago. This time she held up her six arms in front of her face and inspected all six of her hands, each with two large finger digits and a large thumb, each black and leathery and weird-looking. She didn't even bother to look at Danny; her own form freaked her out too much to see it upon someone else.

"What in Einstein's ghost!" she exclaimed.

Her lips split in four directions; she could actually *feel* them split, and her voice sounded all garbled and hissy. She felt a weight attached to her back and turned to gawp at the large arrowhead abdomen covered by her black cargo pants as if this new part of her had always been there.

She looked up and was hit in the face with another beam of light.

"Oh, Haley's Comet!" she exclaimed as she temporarily went blind.

Rain was indeed blinded for a second. She reached up to rub her eyes, but they felt *huge*, twice the size they normally were. She turned to look upon Danny as her vision cleared, and that vision cleared to reveal Danny's enormous eyes as well, and fresh tears spilling from those eyes, and this brought her back to reality, and the reality was that no matter what reality *she* shifted to, Danny was still angry and miserable and obviously feeling cheated, and this bothered her a lot.

$$*****$$

Nancy pushed past person after person as she made her way to the Ferris Wheel. She had already blown past every shift she'd been through, and now she was at the "elf" stage, the very first crazy reality she'd stepped into.

She was pretty sure that her first shift had occurred during the actual Breckenridge explosion, the shift where they'd all looked the same but Rain was slightly different and nobody remembered the Breckenridge Institute of Discovery, but at this point, she didn't care. *That* particular reality was pretty much home, and she was more than happy to settle in it. Nevertheless, the "elven" reality wasn't that bad in comparison to some of the others, so she wouldn't exactly mind it, either.

She saw them standing on the walk near the Ferris Wheel as she made her way around the last of the crowd barring her path.

"Danny!" she called out. "Danny, wait!"

He turned at the sound of her voice, but he did not look happy. His long and slender face held a deep scowl, and it was obvious that he had still been crying just a short time ago.

Rain, on the other hand, looked…Nancy could not really describe how her best friend looked. Rain's face was a mix of shock, happiness, and alarm, and Nancy did not know what to make of it.

She ran up to Danny and stopped just in front of him, but he took in a broken breath and turned away from her, intent on walking off.

"Danny, wait!" she said with an intensity she had not known she possessed. "Please!"

He turned and looked at her again, but this time he reached up to wipe away a fresh tear from his huge right eye.

"No!" he hissed. "Just leave me alone!"

"No, I won't leave you alone!" she replied. "I can't…I swear to you with all my heart and soul that I *did not say* those things! I would never do that to you!"

He turned, walked up to her, and for a moment, she honestly thought he was going to hit her, but he didn't. He clenched and unclenched the fingers of both hands, and Nancy could tell he was moving on from shattered to furious.

"This is a trick!" he hissed. "This is all a trick! You and Rain are trying to make a fool out of me!"

"No, we're not!" argued Nancy. "It's not like that at all!"

He turned in a circle while clenching and unclenching his fists before settling two very large and very hurt, teary eyes upon her once more.

"First you, and now Rain!" said Danny. "Stop lying to me!"

Nancy turned toward Rain for help, but the eccentric young woman only stood there with her mouth dropped wide open. The young genius looked as if she had just stepped on a live power line, and she shook a little bit, had a tremor in her as if she were scared or excited to the point of speechlessness.

"Rain…" said Nancy desperately, "say something…"

"I've been shifting!" said Rain in a near whisper. "It's been happening really fast!"

"See!" said Danny as he turned up the palm of his left hand toward her. "This is what I'm talking about!"

Nancy gave herself an inner smile at this news. Rain had obviously noticed each and every shift that had just occurred. That meant she was shifting too, and that was good news, but for the moment, it was out of place. Nancy knew she would have to explain it to Rain after she took care of the more immediate situation with Danny.

Nancy turned toward him and shook her head.

"Ignore her," she said quickly. "She was just trying to stall you until I got here."

"Well, it worked," scowled Danny. "Now go away!"

"No," said Nancy with a shake of her head. "No, I will not go away. I can't go away."

"Why not!" asked Danny. "Why can't you just leave me alone!"

"Because, Danny, I…" she started.

She closed her eyes and took in a deep breath. Now that she was here…now that she wanted to confess how she really felt about him…it was *much* more difficult than she had first imagined.

"I didn't say those things," she said. "I didn't. I overheard those two…I overheard them trashing on you, and it ticked me off."

"No," said Danny with a shake of his head. "No, Sarah was nice to me…"

"No, she wasn't," said Nancy in a sad tone. "Rain and I had her figured out from the moment we saw her…and your cousin…I *really* hate to say nasty things about your family, but…"

Rain stepped up to stand on her right and cut in on their conversation. Whatever shock the eccentric young genius had been in was gone, or at least, temporarily put on hold.

"At *what* point has Erin *ever* been nice to you?" asked the young genius in a deadly-serious tone. "You know *exactly* what she's like, Danny. *You* were the one that came up with the 'Wicked Witch of the Suburbs' reference, remember? Why would you believe *anything* she said? *Why* on Einstein's grave would you take *her* word over Nancy's?"

Danny lowered his head and reached up to brush the long slender fingertips of his right hand against the pointed tip of his right ear.

"No," he said, but this time he sounded defeated. "No, that can't…that can't be right…"

"You know it is, Danny," said Rain. "They said those nasty things to you, and then they blamed Nancy, because they knew you'd believe it."

"And that's exactly what I did to you," said Nancy. "Remember? Brinn Clevenger started that rumor and put up that horrible F and M page, and I believed her when she said that you were the one who did it. I…I didn't even think about it. I didn't come and talk to you about it…I just stupidly believed it… So *why* in this reality or any other would I say terrible things about you when I *know* you weren't the one who did all that? Why would I do that?"

Danny turned in a circle as he clutched his head with both hands. It was clear he was anguishing over this in his own mind, but there was nothing Nancy could do about that. He had to work it out for himself, and more importantly, he had to convince himself of the truth.

He threw his hands down a moment later and shook his head no.

"No, no, NO!" he said angrily. "That can't be right…No, she was nice to me…"

"She was only pretending to be nice," said Rain. "She was pretending to be nice, because she was forced…in *her* mind, anyway…she was forced to hang out with you…She's a stuck up little…Ugh…Girls like her are a dime a dozen. Trust me, you *don't* want someone like that."

"That's right," said Nancy. "You really don't…Besides, I *know* you're going to find someone very special very soon."

Danny shook his head no.

"No," he said in adamant denial. "No, I won't. Don't lie to me anymore! If what you're saying is true, then I never…there was never…It doesn't matter anymore! Just leave me alone!"

"No," said Nancy in a flat-out refusal.

Her tone was one of no nonsense this time. Rain apparently sensed the change of attitude within her and looked up at her in surprise.

"Nance...?" she asked in a worried tone.

Danny looked at her in a disbelief fit to match anything Rain could show.

"No, Danny, I will *not* leave you alone," said Nancy.

"What!" hissed Danny.

"I know…for a *fact*…that there is someone out there for you," said Nancy slowly and confidently.

"No there isn't!" hissed Danny.

He threw up his hands in frustration and shook his head once before looking around at various passerby.

"Where is she, huh?" he asked. "Where, huh? Nobody cares about me! They always call me a loser and treat me like trash! Nobody cares! Your…Your stupid advice and your stupid clothes don't work! There's no one out there for me! So you tell me right now where she is, or you can just leave me alone!"

Nancy knew he had said that out of frustration and anger, but it irked her that he would think that, so she threw what little was left of her caution to the wind and acted. She stepped forward and grabbed both of his slender hands, held them in her own and looked him straight in the eye. He was stunned for a second at this action, so she capitalized on it.

"She's standing right in front of you," said Nancy.

The look on Danny's face was unreadable. Either his brain had shut off or he had forgotten how to speak, because it took him a full ten seconds to say anything at all.

"What?" was all he could say when he finally did speak.

"I…I am…I'm in love with you," breathed Nancy.

This time it was Rain's turn to give her a look of absolute shock.

"What?" was all the eccentric young genius could say.

"N…no…" stammered Danny as he shook his head in disbelief. "This is…This is another trick…"

"No, it isn't," smiled Nancy. "It isn't, and I can prove it, and I'm not even going to ask first. I'm just going to do it."

She let go of his slender right hand, grabbed the back of his head with her own left, and brought her lips to his. He was too stunned to do anything at first, but then he relaxed as the kiss lingered for more than four seconds.

Nancy's heart soared with elation; she felt that familiar blast of energy surge from her, that sizzling feeling of changing, transforming, and then Rain's commentary upon the shift reached her ears a moment later.

"Oh, my God!" exclaimed the eccentric young woman. "It was *you* the whole time! *That's* what's been going on!"

Nancy pulled her lips away from his, stepped back, and smiled. She looked upon Danny's human face, his original face, and smiled. She really did love him, even though he was still an incredible dork.

Danny was dumbstruck. His mouth dropped open as he let out a short little gasp of quickly dying disbelief.

"Y…you…" he stammered out. "You…*love* me?"

She stepped back and held his left hand with her own right and then took his right in her left.

"Yes, Danny," she said with a smile. "I was trying so hard to help you get a girl that I…I realized what a great guy you are, and I somehow fell in love with you, but I was too stubborn to see it. That's why when you accused me of doing something so horrible to you, it really, *really* hurt me. That's when I finally accepted the truth.

"I really *do* love you, and you have to believe me when I say that. You have to, because it's true. I know I hated you all that time, and I know I told you not to just fall in love with the first girl who looks your way, and now it sounds really hypocritical of me to say that I love you after two weeks since I stopped hating you, but…I would rather be a hypocrite than a fool, and only a fool would pass up on a guy as sweet and as caring and as…as great as you…I…I *love* you, Danny Princeton, and I don't care if I'm a hypocrite for saying it."

Danny looked down for a moment as his eyes widened in comprehension. He slowly looked up toward her face as a sad smile crept across his lips.

"Really?" he asked.

His voice was so meek, so pathetic, that it was actually funny, and Nancy burst out laughing. She pulled him in for a close hug, but he did not resist.

"I…I'm sorry I said those things," breathed Danny. "I thought…I didn't know…"

She released Danny and took his left hand into her right again.

"That's okay," smiled Nancy. "You can make it up to me by realizing that you're my boyfriend now, okay?"

Danny's cheeks flushed red as he slowly nodded yes.

"O…Okay," he said in a quiet voice. "I guess I have no choice."

"No, you don't," chuckled Nancy. "You really don't."

She turned to gauge Rain's reaction, but the eccentric young woman had nothing to say for once. The young genius was struck speechless, wide-eyed and silent, and it was so odd to see her this way that it gave Nancy a short chuckle.

"Well, Rain, you got what you wanted," she smiled. "You hooked up your 'mystery girl' with Danny. Aren't you happy?"

"Are you kidding?" asked Rain. "I'm ecstatic!...I thought it was going to take *at least* six months to get you two to come around."

"Wait, what?" asked Danny.

He gave Rain a hardline stare and raised his left eyebrow.

"You knew about this?" he asked.

Rain rolled her eyes and gave him a wide grin.

"Duhhh," she chastised. "Of course, I knew! Why do you think I kept leaving you two alone together?"

"Even I didn't know, Danny," said Nancy. "Rain was a tricky fish on this one. Leaving us alone together and having us hold hands and even having us dance together? Very clever."

"Pffft," said Rain with a wave of her hand. "That was nothing."

"Uh, huh," smiled Nancy with a roll of her eyes. "Right…but enough of that. We have to get back to my mom's stall. They're waiting there to find out what happened."

"You told them?" asked Rain.

"Of course," said Nancy. "You should have seen their faces when I said I was in love with Danny."

Danny chuckled and shook his head.

"I wish I could have seen that," he said.

"I wish you could have seen the look on your face when Nancy told *you*," snickered Rain.

"It doesn't matter," smiled Nancy. "We should probably go back."

She clutched Danny's left hand as all three of them started forward.

"What did your mom say when you told her that?" asked Danny in a worried voice. "She's not going to be mad at me…is she?"

Both Nancy and Rain let out a short guffaw at that question.

"No, Danny," chuckled Nancy. "No, she will not. In fact, she was mad at *me* for the way she *thought* I treated you, but once I told her the truth, she told me to come tell you at once. She was pretty forceful about it."

"Oh," said Danny, and he said nothing more on that note.

They walked along the sidewalk and through the crowd toward the wooden stage in the distance. They were quiet for a moment, but that awkward silence was broken by a very excited and rather insistent Rain.

"Nance, Nance!" breathed Rain. "Nance, I…I have to tell you something!"

Both Nancy and Danny turned their full attention upon the young genius, but none of them stopped walking toward their end destination.

"What is it?" asked Nancy. "Wait…Let me guess…It's about that story we were working on, right?"

"Story?" asked Rain. "What stor…*Oooooh*…right. Yeah, it is. I…err…I had an *idea* of what happens next in it. Let's say the girl from….uhhh…Let's say that the girl from the 'plant' universe suddenly started shifting along dimensional lines like the main character, and now she was, like…in the 'original' universe of the main character…Now she has peachy-tan skin and that 'hair' and stuff…I'm pretty sure she'd be confused as to *why* that happened, and she'd want an explanation."

"Uh, huh," nodded Nancy. "Well…I'd say the main character managed to travel to a place outside of time and space, a place where the scientists from the explosion now exist because of the accident they caused…"

Rain's dark eyes nearly popped out of her head.

"Really!" she breathed. "Oh, my God! Tell me what happened…I mean, tell me what happens next!"

Nancy chuckled under her breath and nodded once.

"They told her how to get back to her 'original' universe," said Nancy, "and they explained—here's where it gets really weird—that she contained a 'breach' in all realities within herself, and…and that she actually had the power to cross dimensional lines to wherever she chose to go. She had that power all along."

"That sounds like an interesting story," said Danny.

Rain ignored his comment and looked at Nancy with nothing short of fascinated amazement.

"So she could *choose* where to go?" asked Rain. "How did you…*she* manage to do that?"

"She just had to focus on something really important," said Nancy, "and her mind would take her there."

"What did you…*she* focus on?" asked Rain.

"The man she was in love with, of course," smiled Nancy.

"*Oooooh*," breathed Rain. "Oh, wow…but wait…She can still cross to other worlds, right?"

"Nope," smiled Nancy. "But that doesn't matter, because here's the best part. Apparently, the breach in realities couldn't be closed. The scientists had to move it, so they did."

"Really?" asked Rain. "Where did they move it to?"

"To her best friend," grinned Nancy.

"To her best friend?" asked Rain in slight confusion. "What do you mean, 'to her best…'"

Nancy watched as comprehension dawned upon the young genius's face, and an ecstatic Rain gave such a wide grin that Nancy feared her face might split in two.

"That ending is *perfect*!" spouted Rain.

"I thought so," grinned Nancy.

Epilogue

Rain awoke due to her own snoring. She was lying face down on her bed with her arm slung over the side, so she rolled over to her right to lay fully on her bed and bask in the morning light.

She smiled as her skin drank in the light, and she held up her hands to reveal that they were green once more. She sat up and looked past her nightie to see the green on her skin all over the rest of her body, and she was satisfied with that observation.

She hopped out of bed, threw on her Brat Cat Confessions black tee, coupled that with a pair of old and torn jeans, and picked out her black boots for the day. There was no reason to take a shower...She did not take her showers in the morning but at night, and then only every other day…She was not Nancy.

She went to the upstairs bathroom and checked herself in the mirror. She had her olive-green skin again, along with her dark leaves and buds on her head, and that brought her a smile.

"Ah, mah good ol' face," she said to herself.

Rain enjoyed shifting to somewhere different from one day to the next, to shift along dimensional lines to wherever she wished to go, and she had done this for a week now, but she was homesick for the time being, so she had come back to "her" world, the universe she had been born in.

She walked downstairs, grabbed Buster's leash, attached the leash to the little ball of leaves' collar, and ushered him outside. She was supremely surprised to see Nancy walking her red bike up to the side of her house as she always did, and though that was normal, it was barely after eight in the morning, and that was unusual.

"Early, early?" asked Rain. "I thought you'd be biking down Bitter Creek this morning."

Her best friend gave her a warm smile.

"I thought I'd come see you this time," said Nancy. "Danny will probably walk over here after noon, but…I wanted to hang out with you for a little bit."

"I getchya," smiled Rain. "I was just going to take Buster for a walk."

"Sounds good," said Nancy.

They left the comfort of Rain's backyard and headed down the sidewalk toward the small park at the end of Rain's street. The little ball of leaves that was Buster ran out ahead of them to sniff and hop and do the normal Buster things that Buster did.

Rain felt Nancy's elbow nudge her in the right arm a moment later.

"So?" asked Nancy. "It's been one week. What do you think?"

"It's been awesome!" breathed Rain.

And it certainly had been. She was happier now than she had ever been in her entire young life…but Nancy gave her a half-frown and looked her over, and this killed her buzz a bit.

"How can I tell which Rain I'm talking to?" asked Nancy. "Is this my Rain?...or a remnant?"

"Well," said Rain thoughtfully, "if I were a remnant, I probably wouldn't think I was a remnant, now would I?"

"No, I suppose not," frowned Nancy.

"Actually, it doesn't matter," shrugged Rain.

And it didn't. She knew the truth behind this one.

"Why not?" asked Nancy.

"Because the first place I went to was…uhhh…the 'Outside,'" said Rain.

"You went *there* first?" asked Nancy in surprise. "That place terrified me."

"I didn't have much of a choice," shrugged Rain. "I woke up there after going to sleep that last Saturday night…Ugh…I know we both promised not to talk about it each day so that we'd have something to talk about on the weekends, but…I *soooooo* wanted to tell you about *that* one."

"I'll bet," said Nancy. "What happened? Did the scientists tell you anything new?"

"Oh, yeah," nodded Rain. "They told me a number of things, but…only having to do with how the shifting *works*…not about the individual places I could go."

"So how does it work?" asked Nancy.

Rain gave her a wide grin and nodded.

"It's like they said," she replied. "All of our different selves…each and every version of us in every universe…are connected. We're all the same person with a mind stretched out in an infinite expanse…That's why people's personalities never change when I shift from place to place, or when you shifted from place to place."

"That's interesting," said Nancy thoughtfully. "I suspected as much."

"Yep, yep," said Rain happily. "If you really want to know, though, today I came back to this world so that I could see you…So to answer your previous question…err…Yes, it's the 'original' me."

"Good," smiled Nancy. "I'm glad you came back, but to be honest…I really can't tell if you've been shifting or not."

"I know," smiled Rain. "That was the problem I had with you. You would say you were shifting, and the notebook and the pictures would change, but that was the only evidence I had. You see how frustrating that was now?"

Nancy nodded in slow thoughtfulness.

"Yes," she said, "but I still prefer not to shift. I prefer it this way."

"I know," smiled Rain.

Nancy elbowed her and gave her an amused grin.

"You smile all the time now," she said. "You're so happy, it's kind of disgusting. You're just like Danny."

Rain nodded vigorously in adamant agreement.

"I know," she replied. "I'm just…This is my dream, and I'm living it. As for Danny…that boy *better* be happy considering all the work I did setting you two up. He owes me, you know."

"That he does," chuckled Nancy. "I suppose I owed you too, but I take it that granting you my shifting paid that debt in full?"

"That it did, methinks, methinks," said Rain with a nod and a smile. "That it did."

About the Author

Mr. Marlott has a background in psychology and classic literature, and he enjoys literature of all types and genres. Mr. Marlott lives somewhere within the United States, has two Gen-Z children, and enjoys telling stories to anyone who will listen.

D-Shift